Catalyntje Trico
A Life in New Amsterdam

Lana Waite Holden

To all who have gone before us,
whose names we may not even know.

Jacket design by Jonathan Polido

LIBRARY OF CONGRESS CATALOGING-IN-PUBLICATION DATA
Name: Holden, Lana Waite, author
Title: Catalyntje Trico: A Life in New Amsterdam

ISBN 979-8-9909815-0-8 (hardcover)
ISBN 979-8-9909815-1-5 (paperback)
ISBN 979-8-9909815-2-2 (eBook)

Subjects: Trico, Catalyntje, (1605-1689) – Historical Fiction. |
Biographical Fiction – Historical Fiction. | Colonial America – Historical
Fiction | Women, New Netherland – Historical Fiction. |
Women's History – Historical Fiction. | New World life and trials –
Historical Fiction.

Preface

Catalyntje Trico (1605-1689) holds a unique spot in the history of the Dutch Colony of New Netherland. She is the only European who lived in this settlement from the first day colonists stepped off the ship until the English took over forty years later. Others were on the ship with Catalyntje but died in the New World or returned to Europe before New Netherland became New York. She is the only witness of each day of the colony.

Catalyntje's name is pronounced Ca-ta-LAHN-cha. Records show numerous ways of spelling her name, but I have chosen to use Catalyntje in this book. Additionally, I use older versions to spell the names of her children and acquaintances.

This book contains some inconsistencies regarding the dates of events in Catalyntje's life. In the records I researched, different years are mentioned for some events, making it difficult to line them up precisely. Some of these discrepancies may be due to changes in the Gregorian and Julian calendars. Additionally, literacy rates were low where Catalyntje grew up, so not everyone kept records.

Until she was seventeen years old, Catalyntje lived in the town of Hainaut in the southern Netherlands with her widowed mother, Michele Sauvagie. Michele's first husband, Claus Flamen, died after their child, Marie, was born. After his death, Michele married Jeronimus Jan Trico, the father of Catalyntje and her younger sister Margriet. Jeronimus died before the two girls were old enough to remember him. The family was Walloon, a

French-speaking ethnic group in the southern Netherlands, now part of Belgium.

Walloons were generally Catholic, but Catalyntje's family was Protestant. By the time she was seventeen, the Eighty-Years' War (1568-1648), waged by the Low Countries for independence from Spain, had been going for nearly 55 years. This rebellion against Spanish rule had multiple causes, mainly King Philip II's religious persecution and heavy taxation of those who would not follow him. His viceroy harshly punished those who voiced dissent for any reason.

Once the war resumed, repressive Spanish rule extended to the southern Netherlands, where Catalyntje lived. So, Catalyntje and her sister, Margriet, took a chance to escape to the more liberal and prosperous north. Their destination was Amsterdam, where their half-sister Marie lived. They hoped to find freedom to worship and enjoy a prosperous future there.

When I began writing this account, it started as a history book about Catalyntje and her role in New Netherland, but this original plan changed when I visited New York. While there, I made a pilgrimage to each place Catalyntje lived in New Netherland. One of my favorite memories of this trip was sitting with my husband on the steps of a towering skyscraper on Pearl Street, where Catalyntje's home once stood. As the sun began to fade, I shared stories and described what it must have looked like there nearly four hundred years ago. At that moment, I realized I needed to share more than facts about Catalyntje; I must put flesh on her bones and make her story real and relatable. At this point, I changed directions and rewrote Catalyntje's story as historical fiction.

I purposefully wrote this book from a woman's perspective, so the woman's name always appears before her husband's. I have also omitted some prominent members of the colony to keep the focus on Catalyntje and the other women of New Netherland.

When she died on September 11, 1689, Catalyntje had eleven children and over 150 descendants. With so many family members, the births and marriages in her family would inundate this story. So, I mention all Catalyntje's children and their families but only follow the details of the life of her oldest child, Sarah.

Most of the people on the pages of this book lived in New Netherland and were associated with Catalyntje. Because she was illiterate for the first part of her life, there were no diaries or journals. However, there are several court records documents, depositions, and one journal entry written by Jasper Danckaerts, a Labadist missionary who described Catalyntje in her seventies. To most accurately place her in New Netherland, I have read hundreds of books about the colony, then carefully and creatively put Catalyntje in this setting. I have used imagination, facts, and creative license to shape a detailed and engaging picture of Catalyntje's life.

During my trip to New York, I visited the cemetery where Catalyntje is most likely buried. There is no marker for her among the sunken and weathered headstones, and a covering of oak trees protects the graveyard from the bustling streets surrounding it. As I looked across the headstones speckled in shadow, I spotted some acorns on the ground, and my husband helped me gather a few. I put them in my pocket and hoped they would allow me to take the spirit of that place with me across the continent to my home.

I still have those acorns on my desk to remind me that over four hundred years ago, an incredibly strong-willed and kind woman worked, loved, and lived in the Dutch Colony of New Netherland. Catalyntje's life happened at a different time and place from mine, but I still feel connected to her as a woman, striving to help those around me and positively impact the people I meet each day.

Prologue

Catalyntje Trico had only ever known the familiar hills surrounding her home, where animals grazed peacefully on grass-covered hummocks. There had always been aprons filled with apples and a garden full of turnips, onions, and carrots. But things had changed over the past few years for young Catalyntje and her family. Spanish rule in the Southern Netherlands brought heavy taxes, leaving them impoverished. Additionally, they were Protestants, so they were persecuted by those who ruled. Because of this, life in Hainaut, where she and her sister Margriet had spent their childhood, was no longer a peaceful place. To help keep them safe, their mama sent them to live in Amsterdam with their half-sister Marie.

With this hope, Catalyntje and Margriet said a tearful goodbye to their mama and set out one night to avoid undue attention. Their mama planned to stay in Hainaut, working the land and hoping the ruling body and the Catholic church wouldn't notice her alone until her two daughters were far enough north to be safe.

Part 1: Escape
Spring 1623 - Spring 1624

Traveling North

Spring of 1623: 17 years old

The sun had set, and fear flooded Catalyntje's mind as she crept through the tall grass. The light of the near-full moon might allow others to see them, so they avoided the road.

"Are you certain we can find our way?" her sister, Margriet, asked.

"I do not know," Catalyntje answered. Margriet reached for her sister's hand, grabbing it tightly as the two silently crept past a stand of trees.

They traveled noiselessly long enough for the moon to slip behind a hill, making it more difficult to find their way through the unfamiliar landscape. Eventually, they found a small group of trees and rested beside their strong trunks. Though she was exhausted, Catalyntje had difficulty falling asleep. Margriet did not, as she wedged between her sister and the rough tree trunk. Catalyntje stared into the darkness, her eyes darting quickly to catch any movement that might threaten their resting place. After Margriet's breath steadied with sleep, Catalyntje's heart stopped racing; she took a deep breath and looked up through the tree branches where a few stars danced between the leaves. *These trees have been here for years*, she thought to herself. *They will surely keep us hidden for one night.* As these thoughts settled in her mind, Catalyntje's eyes slowly closed as the cool breeze played in the leaves above her. She and Margriet would be alright, at least for tonight. They would face tomorrow when it came.

*****

Rustling leaves woke Catalyntje up. Opening her eyes, she noticed the sun had risen, shyly hiding behind the low mist. Margriet stirred beside her and quickly looked around.

"It's alright, Margriet," she responded to her sister's wakefulness in a tone to convince herself and her sister.

"When are we leaving? Have you seen anyone yet today? Can we have some bread to eat before we go?" Margriet asked.

"I do not know any more than you do!" Catalyntje snapped back, which she immediately regretted. "I am sorry, Margriet. I have just as many questions as you do. We must figure all of this out," she replied. "I know Mama sent us an entire loaf of bread and some cheese. We can have a little to start the day. Does that sound alright with you?"

"Yes. I will try to think about things before blurting them out. I know you are also trying to figure this out," Margriet replied with a weak smile.

The two sisters quietly ate a small piece of bread and some cheese, believing that eating only a little at a time would make it last the entire journey.

"Since it is light, we can travel on the road, looking like we are on an errand," Catalyntje suggested as they stood up and straightened their clothes. It had been so dark when they arrived the night before that they were unsure where the nearby road was. Margriet noticed a break in the trees and headed in that direction, hoping it was the road.

As they approached the opening, they realized Margriet had been right. Even though the road wasn't wide, they could tell it was well-traveled and hoped it led to Brussels, where their mama had told them to go first. They walked silently for a while, not daring to speak. But after some time, they realized that quietness didn't show the confidence they'd hoped to portray, so they began talking to each other about unimportant things. As the sun set that evening, the two were satisfied with their day's journey and grateful they still had some bread and cheese for an evening meal.

*****

After nearly a week of walking, Catalyntje and Margriet's confidence grew weary. They were out of food and exhausted from traveling. But soon, they realized that the people passing them were dressed more fashionably than anyone who lived in Hainaut. Then, as they crested a slight hill, they could see Brussels in the distance, with its large buildings and long orchards.

Eventually, the two sisters made their way to the Brussels marketplace, and it was then that they realized how hungry they were. Their eyes widened at the loaves of bread, the bowls of berries, and the piles of yellow and red carrots. Catalyntje didn't know how long they stood there staring until suddenly, a deep voice echoed through the crowd. A strong man with a scowl shouted at them, "Well, look at these two young girls. It seems they aren't from these parts; they look near starved," he bellowed with a low laugh. "Where are you girls from?" he asked threateningly.

"We are here at the market for our mama," Catalyntje answered in a shaky voice as she grabbed Margriet by the arm.

"Why are you running away then? What will your mama say when you come home without the goods, she sent you to buy? I think you two are on the run. Am I right?" his voice boomed behind them, adding to the darkness of the heavily clouded sky.

"Run, Margriet!" Catalyntje yelled, tears falling down her cheeks. As they ran, the sky continued to darken, and the clouds couldn't hold back any longer. Soon, rain mixed with their tears as the city fell behind them, and dust turned to mud. They finally reached an apple orchard, and Catalyntje slowed to glance behind them to see if anyone had followed them. Her tired legs wanted to stop, but the rain didn't, so she and Margriet found a large apple tree to sit under, waiting for the rain to stop.

"I cannot get warm," she groaned as she hugged herself and tried to stop shaking.

"I can't either; what will we do?" Margriet asked in a quaking voice.

"We cannot stay here. We must find some sort of shelter. Let's keep going down the road," Catalyntje suggested as she reached down to help Margriet get up. They crept along in the rain for some time, continually glancing behind them to be sure the man with the loud voice wouldn't suddenly appear.

"I see a building up ahead," Margriet exclaimed. "We can get out of the rain and maybe get dry."

"I do not think that is a good idea. We cannot just go into someone's barn. You saw what happened in Brussels. When they discover us, they will know we are running," Catalyntje replied firmly. But as she spoke, a flash lit up the sky, and a low rumble sounded overhead, which meant the thunderstorm would soon overtake them. She remembered storms like this at home. Mama would let the animals come inside to escape the rain during those times, and if animals couldn't be outside in this weather, neither could Catalyntje and Margriet.

"I think it's our only choice," Margriet implored.

"You are right," Catalyntje whispered with fear as they walked quickly to the barn and slowly opened the door. With the bit of light that shone through the clouds, they found a pile of hay and posts covered with roosting chickens. The sisters sat down, careful not to disturb the birds, while the rain danced steadily on the roof. They had found a sturdy shelter, but the wind still slipped into every crack. They huddled close together as they burrowed in the hay, hoping it would keep them warm enough to make it through the night.

"I put some food in our basket if you'd like something to eat," offered Margriet.

"Where did you get it?" asked Catalyntje.

"I picked up some apples while we hid under the trees in the orchard. They were all over the ground, so I grabbed the ones within reach," Margriet smiled.

"Thank you! I am starving," Catalyntje said, standing up to get the basket. Then, suddenly, she froze when she saw a faint glow outside. The barn door opened, and a figure carrying the lantern entered. Catalyntje was caught in the lantern glow, her eyes wide with fear.

"It's so cold, please," she said, closing her eyes to prevent tears from running down her cheeks.

"I . . . I didn't mean to frighten you. But, yes, dear, it is freezing. Please let me help you," the woman implored as she quickly set down her lantern and wrapped her shawl around Catalyntje's wet shoulders. The woman was about the same age as her mama and had a kind smile.

"Thank you," Catalyntje responded as she welcomed the embrace of this woman she'd never met. Then Catalyntje turned to look for her sister; the woman followed her gaze and gasped when she saw Margriet hiding beneath the hay.

"Oh, my dear girl, come here," the woman called out, motioning for Margriet to join them. "My name is Griet. What are you doing out here alone on such a cold and wet night?" she asked in an anxious tone. The girls needed her help, and although Catalyntje didn't know her, she felt they were safe, so she answered Griet's question. Then, after only a few moments, Catalyntje realized her instincts had been right. Griet understood why they were hiding since she was also a Protestant.

"Let's go inside. You may certainly stay as long as you need," Griet offered.

"Thank you, we would appreciate getting warm," Catalyntje replied.

"We are happy to help. I will bring you in to meet my family," Griet assured. She grabbed the lantern, and the three ran toward the dimly lit house in the pouring rain. When they reached the door, it flew open, and a young boy ran out, excited that his mama was back. But then, he noticed the two strangers standing in the doorway and hid his face in her wet skirt. Next, a young woman about the same age as Catalyntje came around the corner from inside the house and stopped short.

"Mama, I didn't know we had visitors," the young woman remarked with concern.

"They need our help, dear. These girls are friends. Go! Fetch some dry blankets," Griet directed.

"Yes, Mama," the young girl answered and quickly disappeared.

Before too long, Catalyntje and Margriet had met the entire family, and soon, they were all talking around a warm fire with hot tea, rye bread, and cheese. Overcome by the warmth and food, Catalyntje couldn't keep her eyes open any longer. She remembered Griet helping her and Margriet make a place by the fire to sleep. They needed to make travel decisions, but her mind was exhausted, and for the first time in several days, she could relax.

The night passed quickly, and after no time, Catalyntje realized there were sounds around her. She could hear Griet talking about food; her voice mixed with the clanging of dishes.

"I think she is awake, Mama!" one of the children whispered loudly.

"Shhhh, Dear. Let them rest for as long as they can. These girls have had a difficult journey and still have far to go," Griet replied. Catalyntje lay with her eyes closed, pretending to be asleep, giving herself time to think. These folks had been so generous to her and Margriet, but they couldn't spend too much time here.

Soon, Margriet began to stir, so Catalyntje pretended to wake up, too. After they enjoyed a warm breakfast, Griet could tell the two sisters wanted to continue their journey without delay. But she wasn't about to let them go without some supplies. Margriet helped bake bread while Catalyntje worked outside. She always enjoyed breathing fresh air and seemed to have a talent for charming seeds out of the ground. Mama had always said she was the best at it.

After the evening meal, Griet gathered plums, carrots, and bread. Then she gave them each a wool scarf she had made. Catalyntje knew these were not extra items, and Griet would have to make more to replace them before winter.

"I have one more thing for you to take along with you. Our friend, Daniel, moved to Antwerp a few years ago with his family. They have dealt with much hardship but will give you a place to rest," Griet explained.

"Give Daniel these," she instructed, handing Catalyntje a carefully folded green cloth.

"What is inside?" Margriet asked excitedly.

"Tell Daniel they are from Griet's garden," the kind woman answered with a smile.

"And these are for you, Catalyntje," Griet added. "I noticed your work in my garden and thought you would appreciate them," she said, taking another small cloth from her apron pocket. Catalyntje pulled back the edges and saw two pinches of turnip seeds.

"For me?" she smiled, taking the cloth from Griet. "I have never had my own seed," Catalyntje bowed her head as she spoke, "Thank you."

"You are very welcome, my dear. I expect to hear of you growing turnips along the dikes of Amsterdam," she responded.

*****

As Catalyntje awoke the following day, apprehension and hope filled her heart. They ate a simple breakfast and gathered their meager supplies. Then, they said their goodbyes and headed down the road. It looked like a good day to travel; the morning air was fresh, and soft clouds littered the sky.

After a few days of walking, the sisters knew they were nearing Antwerp when they began to pass more travelers on the road, just as they had when they had been close to Brussels.

Once they entered the city, Margriet was the first to notice a river filled with large ships. The deep, flowing water was a new sight for both of them, and they were excited to get a closer look. When they reached the dock, they paused, uncertain if stepping onto the boards that hovered over the river would be safe. Then Margriet grabbed Catalyntje's hand and shouted, "Let's just go! We may never see water like this again."

As they reached the edge of the dock, they could feel the boards sway underneath them; the gentle splash of waves on the bottom of the pier was unfamiliar. They stood, not daring to move or speak, and watched a large ship leave a nearby dock, swaying back and forth as it sailed into the river. They had lost track of time and suddenly realized the sun had dropped lower in the sky, so they needed to find Daniel's house. But, before they turned to leave, Catalyntje took one last look at the rows of houses lining the river. *Living here and watching ships coming in and out of the docks all day must be interesting. What an incredible life these people must have,* she thought to herself.

Once the sisters found the narrow road Griet had described, they walked along until they saw what they hoped was Daniel's house. They approached the door, and Catalyntje raised her fist and knocked. She took a deep breath as she heard heavy footsteps approaching. Once the creaky door opened, a tall, stern-faced man stood at the entrance.

"Can I help you?" he asked coldly.

"Ah, yes. I am Catalyntje, and this is my sister Margriet. We stayed with Griet in Brussels. These are from her garden," she sputtered, fumbling in her pocket for the seeds. "They are for you," Catalyntje said, timidly reaching out her hand.

"Thank you for this. Griet was always one to raise a good garden. But why did you come all this way to deliver me seeds?" Daniel questioned gruffly.

"Well, Griet convinced us that we might be able to stay here for a night. We have traveled from Hainaut and are on our way to Amsterdam. We are Protestants and must be careful where we lay our heads at night," Catalyntje answered.

"Yes, if you don't mind the floor. We're preparing our meal now and would accept your help," Daniel replied.

"Oh, of course. We do not require much food and do not want to be any trouble," Catalyntje answered.

"You won't be any trouble at all. Come and meet my children," Daniel announced. As they entered his house, Daniel introduced the sisters to his three children, who were all chattering as they cut vegetables near the hearth for the evening meal. Catalyntje and Margriet jumped in and helped where they could. They had forgotten that it had been a few days since they had eaten a meal.

After enjoying the warm soup and bread, Daniel invited Catalyntje and Margriet to join the family by the fire before bed. Catalyntje shared their experiences traveling.

"Difficult times seem to find all of us," Daniel said. "My dear wife, Mia, passed away from illness a year ago, and it has been difficult to go on; my children have been a great help, though," Daniel admitted with sadness.

"I am sorry about your wife," Catalyntje replied, and a sense of sadness filled the room. After a brief conversation, Daniel somberly showed the sisters a place on the floor where they could sleep for the night. A gloom hovered over Daniel's house, which felt very different from Griet's cheerful home.

*****

Early the following morning, Catalyntje and Margriet quickly folded their blankets, thanked Daniel and his family, and said their goodbyes. Unfortunately, Daniel didn't give them any traveling food when they left, and they worried about not having enough to eat before they reached Utrecht, about fifty miles away.

With several days of travel still ahead, Catalyntje and Margriet would need more food. It was still early in the spring, a challenging time to find food because the sun hadn't yet warmed the soil enough to yield its plenty. As they continued to walk each day, the two sisters foraged some food to satisfy their stomachs, but they were usually hungry when they fell asleep at night. Their hunger made them less alert, so sometimes, they wandered along the dirt road without saying a word.

One afternoon, after three days of finding only berries to eat, the sisters trudged silently along the road until a voice startled them.

"Hallo, where are you going?" The voice cut through the quiet. Catalyntje spun around to see who was speaking.

"Hallo!" they heard a second time.

"Hello, what are you doing here?" Catalyntje asked with a quivering voice as a smiling boy with a brown goat stood up from the tall grass.

He laughed and waved at the two sisters, "I am Klaas, and this is my goat, Pieter. I usually only see people I know walking on this road," he said with a huge smile.

"My name is Catalyntje, and this is my sister Margriet. We are on our way to Utrecht. Are we close?" she asked.

"You probably have about four days of travel left. My family and I live on some land outside the city," Klaas offered.

"We are far from our home," Margriet admitted as Catalyntje gave her a warning look, fearing she had offered too much information.

"It was pleasant to see you. We will be going now," Catalyntje stammered as she grabbed Margriet's arm.

"You don't need to hurry off!" Klaas replied excitedly. "You haven't even talked with Pieter. Are you hungry? My pa baked bread for the market today." Catalyntje and Margriet looked at each other with wide eyes at the mention of bread.

"Umm, well, I suppose we could stop for a little while and talk to your goat," Catalyntje agreed, noticing an entire loaf of bread lying on a cloth. Soon, they were laughing at Pieter and eating bread with Klaas. While they ate, Pieter put on a show by galloping across the grass, kicking his hooves, and throwing his head at an unknown target.

Soon, the three became more serious as the sisters anxiously sought word about Utrecht. As the conversation lagged, Pieter decided to liven things up by leaping towards the group and trying to bite Klaas' shirt.

"No, you silly goat! You know that Ma will be upset if you do that again," Klaas warned, grabbing the goat's floppy ears and rubbing them.

"Klaas, thank you for spending the afternoon with us," Catalyntje smiled, reaching to scratch the goat's chin.

"It will be dark before you know it. Come to my house. I am certain Ma and Pa would be happy to let you stay," Klaas suggested.

"They do not even know who we are, but that is kind of you. Thank you for the bread," Catalyntje replied, looking over at Margriet, who frowned.

"I think we should go with Klaas," Margriet said. "We have stayed with other people along the way, and they have all been kind. We could even sleep outside with Pieter," Margriet suggested with a determined smile.

"She is right," Klaas began with a nod. "Come on, let's get on our way," he said, marching towards the road with Pieter close behind him.

"Catalyntje, we could use a rest. Please," Margriet pleaded, wrinkling her mouth.

"All right. We are close to Utrecht and have found someone to help," Catalyntje admitted.

"Hey, Klaas, wait for us! We are coming with you!" Margriet shouted as she ran to catch up to him and Pieter. Catalyntje followed a bit behind. She was tired of relying on the kindness of strangers but also realized she would have done the same thing if she'd been in Klaas' place. She felt some hope as she silently followed the trio dancing before her.

Klaas' home was busy, and the unannounced arrival of Catalyntje and Margriet didn't slow the pace. There were outside chores, vegetables to prepare, floors to sweep, and laundry to be brought in and folded. The smell of fresh bread and roasted chicken filled the room, and the sight of fresh vegetables and cheese beckoned to Catalyntje. Soon, the room was quiet, and every head bowed as Pa said grace. A chorus of amens was followed by swift hands grabbing food from the center of the table.

Catalyntje and Margriet waited until the others had their food, then gratefully took a portion.

"You are on your way to Amsterdam, I hear?" Klaas' ma asked, breaking pieces of bread onto a young child's plate beside her.

"Yes," Catalyntje said, "We are meeting our sister there. Our town is no longer safe."

"Oh yes, my dear. I know of the torment brought to the Low Countries. It makes life worrisome," Ma replied, shaking her head.

"We thank you for your kindness. We have not had a meal like this for some time. We will not stay long and plan . . ." Catalyntje was interrupted.

"Oh, now don't you worry. You are both welcome at our table. We want to help you get to your sister safely," Ma proclaimed.

The two sisters felt at ease as they enjoyed the food and conversation around the crowded table. Being inside four walls was a comfort Catalyntje hadn't realized she had missed.

"Tomorrow is the Lord's Day, and I don't often recommend it for traveling, but I'm guessing it would be a safer day since most folks will be at church, and I don't think the good Lord will count you two as sinners for trying to get to your sister," Ma assured them.

After everyone helped clean up the meal, Klaas and his ma helped Catalyntje and Margriet gather supplies for their journey the following day. While they talked about how to get to Utrecht and how far away it was, Klaas' ma added more food to the sister's basket. After Catalyntje and Margriet convinced her, they had everything they needed, Ma gathered a few blankets and placed them on a straw mattress near the fireplace where the two sisters could rest for the night. It wasn't long before the soft crackle of the fire eased Catalyntje into a peaceful sleep.

*****

After a light breakfast and goodbyes, Catalyntje and Margriet left for Utrecht. It was mid-morning, and most people were dressed in their finest, heading to the Church of Our Beloved Lady that Klaas' ma had told them about the night before. She insisted they walk by to hear the organ's beautiful sound. "It will be unlike anything you've ever heard!" she had promised.

The two sisters stood in awe as they approached the church, whose steeple reached the clouds. Then, the sound of the organ filled the air.

"Can we go in and look?" Margriet asked excitedly.

"We are not dressed for the Sabbath, but I do not think God would mind us seeing the inside of the church," Catalyntje answered, taking Margriet's hand. They reverently slipped through the tall front doors.

Once they entered, they stood silently in the back of the large room as families bustled in to find their pews. But the sisters didn't pay much attention to the people; instead, they stared at the giant pipe organ, which filled the entire front wall and covered with paintings of angels and trumpets on a vivid blue background with gold trim. The two stood speechless until the music stopped, and a man stood up to begin the church service.

"We should be going," Catalyntje whispered to Margriet as they quietly tiptoed out of the church, still clutching hands.

*****

It took Catalyntje and Margriet four days to reach Utrecht, but they didn't want to stay there because their next stop was Amsterdam. Catalyntje had saved a few coins from home for any problems they might have. Being in Utrecht wasn't a problem, but it should be celebrated since they were nearing the end of their journey.

So, as Catalyntje and Margriet wandered through the market, they chose the food they wanted. They only used half of their coins but came away with aprons full of bread, cheese, dried fish, and turnips. After leaving the city, they emptied their aprons onto the grass and enjoyed a meal with the sun warming their backs.

*****

More people were on the road now than the two sisters had seen during their entire journey. As Catalyntje watched the loaded wagons passing by, she noticed that many had people riding in the back of them. *We could get a ride to Amsterdam,* she thought, glancing back, to find a wagon that might have room. Finally, after a few wagons passed, Catalyntje saw one with enough room for her and Margriet. She started running towards it until she caught up with the driver.

"Could my sister and I get a ride in your cart? We are traveling to Amsterdam. We can pay you for your service," she offered, holding out her hand with the remaining coins.

"You look like you've been on the road for a long time. Keep your coins, Miss, and hop on the back of the wagon. I'm heading to Amsterdam, so carrying you two won't cost me a thing," the driver replied, smiling down at Catalyntje and motioning to the back of the wagon.

"Give me a holler when you're aboard," he replied.

"Thank you! We are grateful to get a ride. It has been such . . ." Catalyntje started.

"You're welcome, Miss, now hop aboard; time is wasting," the driver bellowed with a smile. Catalyntje nodded and ran back to Margriet, who looked confused.

"Jump on the wagon, Margriet. We are riding to Amsterdam!" she cheered.

"We are ready!" Catalyntje called out to the driver. The wagon's jolt nearly knocked them both over, and the uneven road bounced them around but gave their weary feet some rest.

Amsterdam

Summer of 1623: 17 years old

As they rode in the back of the cart, Catalyntje noticed more wagons and walkers; they must be getting closer to Amsterdam. Finally, she and Margriet saw the city for the first time. The two sisters talked excitedly until their wagon found its way to the streets of Amsterdam, where it stopped at a market.

"Well, Miss, this is where I stop. I wish you two the best of luck," the driver cheered.

"Thank you again," Catalyntje called to the driver as she and Margriet leaped from the back of the cart. They walked to the horse at the front, rubbed the nose of the tall animal, and thanked the driver one more time.

As they stood staring, Catalyntje remembered that their mama had said Marie lived near the main docks of Amsterdam, so the two headed where they thought they might find them. Catalyntje took a deep breath. "This is our home now, Margriet," her voice cracked slightly, trying to hold back her emotions.

They had seen a few cities along the way but had never seen a place like this. People, wagons, and animals filled the streets, traveling in all directions but never getting in each other way. The smell of burning peat filled the air, and sloops and canal boats floated between rows of houses. As they wandered through the southern part of the city, they stopped and watched three men unload supplies from a small boat into a tall building near the docks along the canal.

Many of the items were unique and beautiful. One painting caught Catalyntje's attention. It was of a horse covered with black and white stripes. A man unloading goods near them saw the curious look on her face,

"They call it a zebra," he shouted to her. Catalyntje and Margriet looked at each other and laughed. It was a curious word, as most were since they didn't know many Dutch words.

As they wandered, their attention shifted to the houses along the canals. They were all connected and continued endlessly along both sides of the water. Many of their roofs, shaped like steps, had rounded tops with windows lined up in delightful patterns. The front stoops were clean and inviting, with benches in front of most houses.

Soon, they adjusted their attention to finding Marie. Their mama had described the part of town where she lived, and they asked several strangers if they knew where Marie and Phillip lived. After unhelpful but lively conversations, they asked a young man selling cheese if he knew Marie.

"She comes here often. I am not certain which house is hers, but she always comes from that direction," he replied, pointing to the right.

"Has she come today?" Margriet asked eagerly.

"No, I've not seen her today and most likely won't sell her more cheese for at least a few more days. She was here yesterday morning," the young boy answered.

"Thank you for your help," Catalyntje responded politely.

"Ah, don't you want a bit of cheese?" the young salesman asked without shame.

"I am sorry if we misled you," Catalyntje answered, her eyes to the ground. "We have no money."

"That's all right," he responded with a nod as they walked in the direction he had suggested Marie lived.

Many of the houses had three or four stories, with windows filling the front of each one. As they continued wandering, they noticed two houses with French words written on signs near their front doors.

"Catalyntje, do you think one of those houses is where Marie lives? She learned French from Mama; maybe we should try one of them," Margriet suggested.

"I think that is a good idea. Which one should we choose first?" Catalyntje asked with a sly smile.

"Let's go to the first stoop," Margriet said, and they both walked timidly to the first house.

Margriet boldly knocked on the door as the two heard voices inside. The door opened, and a well-dressed, confident-looking man stood there.

"May I help you two young ladies?" he asked. Although Catalyntje knew Marie was married, she hadn't expected a man to answer the door and was unsure what to say.

"Ummm, I am.. . ," she said, but she couldn't finish her sentence as Margriet pushed her aside and ran past the man at the door toward Marie.

"Marie! Marie! We made it!" Margriet couldn't contain her excitement. Catalyntje watched as her two sisters hugged one another while she stood alone on the stoop, overwhelmed to finally see her sister.

"I must apologize; I had no idea who was on my front stoop. Let me introduce myself. I am Phillip. Please come in!" he replied enthusiastically, pulling Catalyntje into the room with his handshake.

"Catalyntje, my sister! You have made it safely. How wonderful it is to see you again," Marie ran forward and hugged her tightly. Tears streamed down both of their faces. Everything would be alright now.

*****

Excitement filled the room as the three sisters continued interrupting each other's sentences. They didn't stop talking, even after they left the house and went to the market.

When they reached the market, the smell of fresh fish filled the air, along with carts filled with cheese. The two sisters had never seen so much cheese in one place. Each seller held platters filled with samples, pressing them into Catalyntje's face, inviting her to take a piece. She didn't resist because it had been a long time since she had enjoyed abundant food.

"Choose some food for our dinner this evening," Marie encouraged, sweeping her hand toward the baskets of apples, beets, and parsnips. Catalyntje chose four red apples and a handful of orange carrots, which were unfamiliar to her. She wondered how their taste would compare to the purple and yellow ones she had grown at home.

*****

It didn't take long for Catalyntje and Margriet to feel at home with Marie and her family. Life had changed drastically for the two sisters. They enjoyed being with Margriet, Marie, her husband Phillip, and Phillip's younger brother Jan, who often spent time in lively conversations with Margriet. It was apparent that Margriet wasn't as well off as the La Fontaine dit Wicart brothers, Philip and Jan, but the tales of her recent journey to Amsterdam captured Jan's attention.

*****

A few weeks after they arrived in Amsterdam, Catalyntje felt that Marie's home was too crowded for her and Margriet to live there and thought she might be happier to find work and a place of her own. Her sisters didn't oppose this idea as long as she promised to be within walking distance. The next day, Catalyntje wandered through the bustling streets of Amsterdam, looking for a way to earn a living wage.

She strolled through the city streets until she reached its edge, where her eyes caught a motion that held her gaze—the slow spinning of a windmill. Catalyntje studied the structure for a moment, then walked to stand close to it, where she stopped and watched its blades spin around and around and around. They were steady, predictable, and captivating. Catalyntje's thoughts calmed as her eyes followed their slow turn; she felt hope.

*****

Catalyntje continued to explore Amsterdam each day. As she observed the city, she recognized that many people there focused their efforts on trade with other parts of the world. She heard about the Dutch West India Company, which had just expanded its trade to nearly every corner of the world. It had only been organized for two years but had overseen all Dutch voyages to the Western Hemisphere.

Since Catalyntje enjoyed being at the docks near the water, it was the first place she stopped each day. One morning, she watched a man in worn clothes approaching a wealthier-looking man. She paid attention as they talked and strutted onto the ship. Next, they disappeared into one of the warehouses along the dock and came out in a heated discussion. Finally, their conversation ended with signing a paper, exchanging coins, and hearty handshakes.

After watching several of these interchanges, Catalyntje realized that the men were paying funds to the wealthier men on the docks in hopes of getting a return on their invested money. She questioned why the poor could even participate in such grand ventures.

After leaving the docks each day, Catalyntje went to the marketplace at Dam Square. There was no end to the people, market carts, or conversations she observed there. After a week, Catalyntje understood the market's rhythm, making her feel more comfortable and confident. These daily trips also helped her learn Dutch more quickly, and she practiced speaking with those she met.

One sunny afternoon, when Catalyntje was at Marie's house, a relative she hadn't met stopped by. It was her Uncle De la Grange, a wealthy and generous soul. Once he realized he had nieces he'd never met, he invited the entire family for dinner.

Catalyntje was impressed with Marie and Phillip's home, but it was a simple cottage compared to her uncle's. He had delicate vases filled with flowers and cupboards with breads, meats, and spices. Catalyntje visited politely but was distracted by the lovely paintings and decorative plates covering the walls of his house; each was intricate and intriguing. She tried to recreate their beautiful patterns as she fell asleep that night.

*****

Catalyntje's two favorite areas in the market were the fresh food from nearby gardens and the carts filled with bright fabrics. She talked to the merchants and realized many of them had also left their homes and moved to Amsterdam because of religious persecutions in their homelands.

One afternoon, Marie asked Catalyntje to go to the market and get some apples and turnips for their evening meal. As Catalyntje approached a nearby cart filled with colorful vegetables and a large basket of apples, she stopped to examine each one. The fresh crops reminded her of helping her mama since they had spent so much time together gathering vegetables from the garden. As Catalyntje was comparing two types of turnips, a woman beside her interrupted her thinking.

"What do you think of these turnips without any purple rings? " she asked no one in particular.

"They are quite mild but still have a wonderful flavor. I often gather more seeds from the white ones because I enjoy the mildness," Catalyntje answered knowledgeably.

"Why, you don't look old enough to know so much about turnips, my girl," the woman responded with a laugh.

"My mama taught me, and I am the one who usually saved seeds for the next year," Catalyntje responded proudly.

"Do you still save seeds?" the woman asked, "And where is your garden?"

"Well, I have just come here and live with my sister. I do not have a garden in Amsterdam, but I have brought seeds with me," Catalyntje answered.

"My name is Agnes, Agnes van Hoebeek," she exclaimed. "I am looking for help at our home. My husband, four children, and I have lived here for some time but now need extra help with house errands, entertaining the children, and working a garden. Would this interest you?" she asked as if she was worried Catalyntje would get away.

"It is good to meet you. I am Catalyntje Trico, and I come from Hainaut. I am looking for work in Amsterdam. Can I talk to my sisters and meet with you again? Please do not think me rude. I am glad for the offer," she replied in a shaky voice.

"Of course! Can we meet here tomorrow afternoon?" Agnes asked.

"Yes, I will be here," Catalyntje answered.

She felt excited when she left the market that day. As she burst through Marie's front door, Catalyntje talked about her conversation with Agnes and didn't stop until she realized she'd forgotten to purchase the food she'd gone for. Marie smiled at Catalyntje's excitement, and the three made supper with what they had.

*****

When Catalyntje met with Agnes the next day at Dam Square, she was surprised to see Agnes's husband and four children along with her. After introducing themselves, they all sat on a nearby bench to discuss Catalyntje's employment arrangements.

"Situations have improved for us," Agnes's husband assured Catalyntje as he straightened with pride. "I invested in three shiploads of goods that have been more profitable than expected. My dear Agnes could use the extra help with the children. We can pay you a weekly sum, and if it is agreeable, part of your wage could be a modest room to stay in along the Nes."

"I would be most grateful. I have been with my sister in her small home, but I feel I am taking too much advantage of her kindness," Catalyntje replied.

22

"Well, this place is no palace, mind you," Agnes's husband replied. "We will visit it, and then you could spend the rest of the day with us learning your duties."

"I would be most happy to get started," Catalyntje answered, nervously rubbing her hands on her apron.

"Then let's be off!" ordered Agnes's husband as he raised his hands, bidding everyone to stand.

As they strolled the short distance to Catalyntje's new home, the children ran excitedly beside her, taking turns asking questions and grasping her hand when they could. When they reached Nes Street, Catalyntje withdrew from the conversation, absorbed in the new sights around her. The street wasn't as wide as the houses were tall. They crowded along the curved road and stood four stories from the cobblestone. Many had tall windows, and most had shutters to keep the cold out in the winter. She also noticed that the tops of each house were all different shapes, and many had a post sticking out from the top above the street below. One of the houses had a rope attached to its post with a crate at one end, and a man pulled at the other. She watched as the crate was lifted upward with each rope tug until it reached the top window.

People filled the cobblestone streets of the Nes. Some carried baskets and pulled carts, while others swept their stoops as their children played nearby. In addition to the people, horses pulled wagons, and dogs roamed the streets, hoping for more food.

After passing several tall buildings, Agnes announced they had arrived where the room was. Catalyntje's eyes moved slowly upward to inspect the building. Tall rectangular windows filled the bottom, and its top was slanted upward and capped in a rounded shape. The top two floors only had one window each.

"That one is yours," Agnes exclaimed as she pointed to the single window second from the top. They all filed into the building, and Catalyntje followed Agnes and her husband up the steep, narrow staircase. When they reached the third floor, Agnes paused at the door near the stairs and reached into her apron pocket, taking out a large metal key.

"Open the door and see what you think," she encouraged, handing the key to Catalyntje. She placed it in the keyhole and turned it slowly. As she opened the door, she took a quick breath, and her eyes widened. Taking a few steps into the simple room, Catalyntje stopped, unable to say anything. The wall with the window had light streaming through it, leaving a stretched-out version of the window lying quietly on the floor. A small peg shelf hung near the top right of the window, and the slanted sides of the wall went nearly halfway to the floor. The back wall contained a meager dresser with a round mirror behind it and an empty chamber pot at its side. The only other furniture in the room was a tiny table and one three-legged stool.

"I like this," Catalyntje replied softly.

"We are delighted to give you a place to live while you help us. You would be close to Dam Square and could do our daily shopping," Agnes replied.

"I am glad for the chance to work," Catalyntje said, bowing her head slightly.

"Then it is an agreement," Agnes's husband smiled and reached out his hand to Catalyntje.

"Take a look around for a moment, and then we will go to our home," Agnes suggested. "Keep the key safe; this place belongs to you while you are with us."

After a few moments, they descended the narrow staircase and went to Agnes's house so Catalyntje could begin her work. First, she helped make a meal and played outside with the children; then, after dinner, Agnes took her to where she wanted the garden. It had been a busy day, and the sun was just beginning to set. There was still some light in the sky when Catalyntje hurried along the road to get to Marie's home before dark.

Once she arrived, Catalyntje talked for most of the evening, promising to bring her sisters to see her new home the next day. Marie helped her gather a few candles, some flint and steel, one cup, one bowl, and a spoon to bring to her new home. Next, she added two small washcloths and a basin for water. Catalyntje placed these items into the basket she had brought from Hainaut. Then Marie sat a stuffed mattress and folded blanket beside the basket. Finally, Catalyntje added the few belongings she had brought to Amsterdam: an extra apron, a pan, Jannetje's mortar and pestle, a thin coat, and her wrapped seeds. She was too excited to sleep that night.

Catalyntje's first full day at Agnes's house was a whirlwind of activities. By the end of the day, she had cooked, done laundry, played with the children, shopped, cleaned, and had another brief look at the soon-to-be garden. Late that afternoon, she went with Agnes to the market.

"Do you sew?" she asked Catalyntje.

"I do; my mama always said I was the best at making small, even stitches," Catalyntje answered proudly.

"Why don't we stop and get some cloth then? You and I could use a new apron, and the children all need new hats. I have been stitching them mittens for the winter, but if you could help with the other items, it would greatly help me," Agnes said.

"I have missed doing handiwork since traveling for the past few months. I could even take some of it home to fill my evenings," Catalyntje offered as they approached a textile booth. After some discussion and indecision, they finally left the market with enough material for their projects.

After their evening meal, Catalyntje helped clean up and then left to spend the evening at her new home. As she walked, she realized she would be entirely alone for the first time in a long time. As she neared the building, she took the key from her apron pocket, clutching it tightly as she walked up the stairs. Reaching her door, she unlocked it and went inside, quickly locking it behind her.

Catalyntje hung the key on one of the pegs near the window. Then, she lit a candle and fluffed her mattress before realizing she'd forgotten to get water to freshen her face. That would have to wait until the morning; she was too tired. Sitting on the bench by the table, she opened the window, and a gentle breeze replaced the stale air.

As she peered out, she noticed evening workers lighting the lamps on a nearby bridge. There were also lights shining through windows from across the street. Amsterdam grew quiet; a few dogs barked, some people laughed, and a wagon filled with cabbages rumbled by; soon, the silence was the loudest sound.

*****

After a few weeks, Catalyntje had settled into her new routine in Amsterdam. Each morning, she arrived at Agnes's house early to help light the fire, bring in wood for the day, and prepare breakfast. The children were always excited to see her and enjoyed helping with the chores.

She did the laundry once a week and was able to wash her own clothes then. The people of Amsterdam took pride in having clean homes. So, Catalyntje spent time shining the ironwork on the shutters and washing the windows. The floors also needed constant scrubbing, and the front stoop was always spotless.

And then there was the garden, which seemed too enjoyable to be work. Catalyntje spent two afternoons digging the soil to make it smooth enough to plant seeds. The children thought that was fun, but Agnes made them remove their outer clothing to avoid getting too dirty. Catalyntje enjoyed their company as they played in the garden beside her.

After a few weeks, the children were amazed as the first tiny lettuce, turnips, and parsley peeked their heads through the soil. Then, as the garden grew, Agnes's children swept Catalyntje away each day, and as soon as she arrived, they gave her detailed accounts of how each plant was doing. She could tell they'd spent time in the garden from the small footprints that had flattened the soil around each plant. Agnes gave Catalyntje a few coins to buy seeds at the market. But Catalyntje was excited to use some of her own seeds, ones she had brought from Hainaut and those that Griet had given her.

*****

As the end of summer neared, Agnes suggested the children needed new clothes to prepare for the cold weather. So, one afternoon, Agnes sent Catalyntje to Dam Square to look at what the textile workers had to offer. She found three carts selling fabric and saved the cart at the far end of the market for last because she had seen its brightly colored cloth and thought it would be a delightful way to end the day.

"Good afternoon," Catalyntje said as she approached the cart on the end. "I am here on an errand to find some cloth for children's clothes. I have looked around the market; yours is my last stop."

"I am glad," the clothmaker responded.

"Your cloth is beautifully made and has so much color," Catalyntje complimented.

"We came from Valenciennes and were textile workers by trade; we made some of the finest cloth in the area," the worker said, pointing to the other craftsmen working at the cart. But those who led our city began to charge higher taxes because of our religious choices. Because of this, many of us decided to come to Amsterdam. We have found the Dutch kind enough to allow us to sell our fabrics here."

"This is not my home either," Catalyntje offered, "and I have also found kindness here among the Dutch. My sister and I arrived earlier in the season from Hainaut."

"Well, it looks like we are both the beneficiaries of the Dutch's welcoming ways," he admitted with a smile. "My name is Joris," he announced, proudly putting his hand on his chest.

"My name is Catalyntje," she responded.

"It is a pleasure to meet you," Joris said confidently. They briefly discussed cloth, but soon, their conversation drifted to their journeys to Amsterdam. They continued to talk until a movement beside them caught Catalyntje's attention, and she realized the market was closing.

"Oh, I have taken too much of your time but have enjoyed talking to you," she replied with a slight smile.

"It has been a pleasure for me as well. I hope you will return to get some fabric for the children you speak of. Soon," Joris added.

"I most certainly will be back," Catalyntje assured him.

As she strolled back to her house, Catalyntje was happier than she'd ever remembered being.

Joris

Fall of 1623: 17 years old

Since they'd met, Catalyntje and Joris hadn't gone a day without seeing one another. Catalyntje regularly offered to go to Dam Square for any item Agnes needed. And, of course, she stopped to look at the fabric of a particular merchant from Valenciennes while she was there. After a few weeks, she told her sisters about Joris. Marie wasted no time inviting him to their home for a meal to get acquainted.

They all enjoyed the evening together, talking and sharing stories. Much of the conversation centered around the difficulties of life outside of Amsterdam. Joris's tales were rougher than those told by Phillip and Jan, probably because he had struggled more in life, which put him in more dire situations.

Joris was an illegitimate child and had been an orphan for a few years. But, he had still done well on his own, as he'd struggled to learn a trade and find his way alone. Phillip and Jan had no such stories to tell. They had always been well taken care of and had the necessities of life. Catalyntje could see this as the conversations fill the evening. Joris didn't have everything figured out yet, but he was always willing to work hard and learn.

One evening after work, Catalyntje made her usual stop to see Joris, and to her surprise, Marie was there. She had been on errands at the market and knew she would find Catalyntje there. After a brief conversation, Joris began putting away his folded pieces of cloth. Since Marie was there, he excused himself from walking Catalyntje home that evening.

"I'm glad I found you here," Marie replied happily. "It has been a while since you and I have been able to talk—just the two of us."

"I have missed that too," Catalyntje responded.

"I just invited Joris over again so Philip and I can get to know him better and see what future he has here in Amsterdam. You know we want what is best for you, Catalyntje," Marie replied, sounding more serious. "Margriet is content in Amsterdam and has found a young man she seems interested in - Phillips's younger brother Jan."

"I that the last time I was there. I am happy for Margriet; Jan seems like a fine man," Catalyntje said.

"He is, and he also has wealth attached to his name, like my Phillip. Of course, I love my dear Phillip with or without his prosperity, but I admit that having money makes life less worrisome," Marie cautiously suggested, looking at Catalyntje.

"What are you trying to say, Marie?" her voice turned tight. "Are you suggesting I need to find someone with wealth to have a good life?" Catalyntje asked with anger.

"Oh no, my sister, Joris is a wonderful man, and we can all see he loves you. But, you should consider where life might take the two of you if you struggle for necessities. Love is a wonderful and noble thing, but so is reality. The two of you would have children to provide for, and it would be heartbreaking not to be able to give them the comforts of Amsterdam," Marie said.

"Why does this concern you?" Catalyntje snapped back. "I need to get back home," she said, walking away from her sister without saying another word.

When she reached her house, Catalyntje rushed up the stairs. Then, angrily, she slammed her door, turning the key to lock it. *How could her sister doubt the feelings she and Joris shared? Marie had never been judgmental of her, so why now? Why, at this time, when she was happier than she'd ever been?* Catalyntje stared out the window for a long time without lighting the candle. The sun faded from the sky, the bridge lanterns glowed, and the sounds on the streets grew still.

*****

As Catalyntje worked in the garden that afternoon, one of the children didn't come out to help. When she asked the others, they told her their little brother wasn't feeling well, so he stayed inside with his mama. After planting more beets, Catalyntje took an early break to see if she could do anything to help with the sick child. She tiptoed into the house towards the sound of Agnes's voice but stopped short as she heard singing. She listened closely to the song Agnes sang:

Slaap, kindje, slaap
Daar buiten loopt een schaap
Een schaap met witte voetjes
Die drinkt zijn melk zo zoetjes
Melkje van de bonte koe
Kindje, doe je oogjes toe.

Catalyntje didn't move as she listened to the song's beautiful melody and simple words. Agnes sang it three more times, and each time, Catalyntje listened intently, trying not to miss a word. The song somehow brought her peace, and she wanted to remember it.

After work that day, Catalyntje went straight to Joris' market cart, but she didn't say anything about her conversation with Marie. She helped place the unsold fabrics into baskets, and she overheard some men talking.

"I hear the Company is expanding its trade soon. They certainly have done well for themselves. Sailing all over the world and bringin' back treasures from places I've never heard of," one man started.

"I like to wander about the docks just to see what they've found," a second man said, folding his cloth and putting it in the bottom of his hand wagon.

"I hear that they're even gonna send folks to the New World because I think they want to get there before the English. I also hear talk of beaver trade with the Indians. I think that place is too far away for me," the first man added.

"I agree. The Company would have to do somethin' mighty grand to get me to sail across the ocean. Some folks leave on them ships and is never heard of again," the second man ranted.

"How would you know what to do to trade with an Indian?" Joris chimed in.

"I don't know," answered the second man, "I'd hope they'd help you out with that before you went."

"It would seem a mighty lonely place to be. I hear its wilderness as far as you can walk in one direction and the ocean on the other," the second man said. Catalyntje didn't comment but agreed with the two men. It didn't seem like a venture that interested her; she was just getting settled in Amsterdam.

*****

It had been a few weeks since Catalyntje had seen Marie. But Margriet stopped by one afternoon, so they enjoyed the day together at Agnes's house. Margriet mentioned Phillip's younger brother, Jan, many times. Catalyntje could see a fondness had grown between them. She was happy for Margriet but felt separated from her sisters since they'd both found a similar path, but she seemed to be on a different one.

Margriet went with Catalyntje to her home that night, where they shared a simple meal of bread and apples. Catalyntje showed her the bridge lanterns, and they spent the night talking and laughing until the candle burned out, and they fell asleep on the stuffed mattress.

*****

The next day, as Catalyntje arrived at Agnes's home, she could hear one of the children crying. "I am glad you're here, Catalyntje," Agnes said. "My youngest is sick and needs extra attention today. Can you go to the market and get a chicken? We can add vegetables from your garden and make some soup."

"Yes, I will hurry back," Catalyntje answered, grabbing the metal meat bucket on her way out. When she reached the market, she knew she couldn't see Joris this time. She could tell by the urgency in Agnes's voice that she needed help as soon as possible. So, she quickly selected a chicken, brought it home, and began preparing the soup.

The day flew by, with tasks done out of order and many left undone. In the late afternoon, the youngest finally rested, and Agnes went for a walk, leaving Catalyntje in charge of the children. The other children seemed exhausted from the lack of routine and weren't as lively as usual. Soon, she heard a whimper from the sick child and brought a wet cloth to cool his head.

"I need Mama to sing to me," he sobbed.

"Your mama went for a short walk and will be back soon, dear," Catalyntje answered soothingly.

"My head hurts, and I need a song to help it," the child insisted. Catalyntje remembered the words and melody that Agnes had sung; they remained fixed in her mind. So, she sat near the child's rope bed and began to sing. When she finished, the young boy looked up at her. "I knew it would help my head be better," he mumbled. She sang it once more, then softly hummed the melody until he fell back asleep. *That will be a song I will sing to my children one day,* Catalyntje thought to herself. She would teach her children to speak French like her mama and Dutch so they could get along in the fine city of Amsterdam.

*****

It had been a busy week, and when Catalyntje awoke and heard the church bells ringing, she was grateful it was the Sabbath. On Sunday, she got a rest from her usual routine and could spend most of the day with Joris. They often met at her home on the Nes, then walked to the Walloon Church to attend services there.

After church services were over, Catalyntje and Joris enjoyed strolling about the city. The weather was noticeably colder, signaling that autumn had come to Amsterdam.

As they walked past the Dutch West India Company building, they observed a half-dozen men mingling outside; they looked like they were involved in something important. Catalyntje and Joris paused to watch. One man had a map, another had rolled up papers, and the others spoke excitedly. As Catalyntje and Joris listened, they overheard the men discussing plans for the New World. It sounded like they wanted to establish a fur trade there and send ordinary people and company workers to live in the colony.

"That would be quite an adventure, wouldn't it?" Joris replied.

"Yes, it would. I wonder what the Company would give people to make them willing to make such a journey?" Catalyntje asked.

"I don't know. The New World seems like such a big place and so far away," Joris responded.

"It does seem further away than we could ever go," Catalyntje uttered. "But I would love to see the great ship take off when they leave. I still remember watching them in Antwerp," she remembered with a far-off look.

"We should pay attention to when the ship is leaving and go see it," Joris agreed as the two continued to stroll along the canal.

*****

The warm days of the summer market at Dam Square were gone. Those who worked at the carts kept tin cups of heated broth and often had a modest fire burning to stay warm. There was always a pile of rocks in or near the fires. When the stones got hot, they were wrapped in cloth and kept in the merchants' pockets to keep them warm on a cold day.

Catalyntje realized that the cold in Amsterdam was more severe than it had been at her home in Hainaut, probably because she was farther north and closer to the water. Soon, being too cold became one of her most significant problems since she had no fireplace in her room. Marie had brought her two heavy quilts, which helped, but the nights were still too cold.

Catalyntje's building had a fireplace on the main floor for the residents, so she kept two larger rocks in her room to carry to the fire each night, and while she ate her soup, they gathered heat. Once they were too hot to touch, she kicked them from the fire and wrapped them in a heavy cloth. Then she carried them upstairs and put them between the quilts and her mattress on the floor. They usually provided heat for nearly half of the night, and then she had to rely on her clothes to keep her warm. She usually slept fully clothed with a hat, scarf, and mittens but still awoke each morning curled up in a ball and snuggled deep under the quilts. Most mornings, thin ice covered the water dish on her dresser.

Catalyntje had saved some money from her job, and since the weather had turned cold, she used most of it to buy items to keep her warm. She needed more candles, food, yarn, and sewing supplies. She thought saving money would be much easier but hadn't realized how expensive simple necessities would be.

One evening, after seeing Joris and heating her rocks, Catalyntje walked home quickly. The wind blew more fiercely, and it started raining. When she arrived home, her hair, coat, and stockings were dripping with bone-chilling water. She raced upstairs to get her larger rocks and hoped to dry off by the fire on the ground floor before bed. She didn't even take time to make any broth for supper that night since her only focus was to get warm and dry.

Several people were gathered around the fire, but Catalyntje wasn't in the mood to converse. Instead, she found a place for her rocks and stood silently by the fire to dry her hair and clothes.

"The first ship is heading out sometime in January and will be loaded with folks to live in their new colony," one man with a tall hat announced.

34

"January? That seems an unlikely time to leave; it would be better to sail when the weather is nicer," a second man with shiny buckles on his shoes replied.

"Yes, but the current will take them in the right direction in January. They say it's a three-month journey," the first man answered.

"I would be wary of being left in a place so far from the fine things of Amsterdam. I also hear there are Indians to deal with. How would the Company protect the people once they get there anyway? I don't see how they will get folks to take such a risk," the buckle-shoed man fretted.

"I heard they'll pay their ship fare and give them land once they arrive. I also heard they'll give supplies and food for the first few years until they can get on their feet," the man with the hat replied.

"I still think it's a bad idea. The colonists could just be left there, faced with danger, and no one would know until another ship came," the second man shuttered. "The Company should trade in other places around the world to make their money. There is no need to risk people's lives to make a profit," he added.

Catalyntje was exhausted from the day. She kicked her rocks from the fire, wrapped them in thick cloth, and felt a sudden relief as their warmth began to flow through her body. Once she'd walked up the stairs, she settled on her straw mattress without eating supper. Her coat was still damp, so she hung it on the peg by the key, put on two more thin sweaters, and put on a dry pair of socks.

As Catalyntje fell asleep, the conversation of the men downstairs floated through her mind. She thought about how far away the New World was and how dangerous the ship's voyage would be. But her last thought was remembering someone saying there were so many trees there that they would never run out. She thought about how many fires you could have to warm your home with an endless supply of trees, and as she drifted off to sleep, her last thoughts were of how having so many trees to keep warm would be worth all the risks to get to the New World.

Decisions

Winter of 1623: 17 years old

Winter came, filled with rain, wind, and the constant worry of keeping warm. As the river thickened with ice, more people were on these frozen waterways. Besides the ice skaters, Catalyntje usually saw children riding miniature wooden sleds. There were no hills to glide down, but they used wooden sticks as paddles to drag themselves along the top of the ice.

As the end of November approached, Catalyntje prepared for St. Nicholas' Day. There were cookies to make, special bread to bake, poems to write, and plans of where to hide gifts. She enjoyed the excitement of this holiday and spent time thinking of ways to help Agnes's children have fun during the celebration.

After the winter holidays passed, the cold settled in more severely than ever. Catalyntje obtained another blanket from Marie, and Joris bought her yarn to make an extra pair of mittens. One evening, he and Catalyntje walked home from the market together. He had purchased a portion of soup in his tin bowl and two pancakes they brought to Catalyntje's small room.

"Today, the talk of the market was about the Company asking people to sail to the New World. It sounds like it will happen," Joris announced, lifting a spoonful of soup to his mouth.

"I even heard it mentioned last week before church started," Catalyntje added.

"It will be quite an undertaking," Joris said, "and the Company seems to have planned well. They will pay for the ship fare and even give seeds and land to those who go." He sipped the warm broth from his cup.

"It would be a lot of work," Catalyntje looked intently at Joris. "It really would," she repeated, "but have you thought about what that would be like? I mean, really thought about it?"

Joris put his cup down, "What do you mean, Catalyntje?" he asked, his lips pursed together tightly.

"I enjoy being here in Amsterdam. I enjoy Agnes and her family, and they treat me well. I love my sisters - but," Catalyntje paused and looked at Joris, "I do not feel like my future could change much here. I would always be working for someone and probably never be able to save enough to be on my own."

"I hope that you and I will end up together. We have talked about that. If we put our earnings together, maybe we could do better for ourselves," Joris added.

"Yes, maybe we could, but you and I know we are refugees here. We will always be at the bottom, but we both have much to offer," Catalyntje added.

"Are you suggesting we leave here? That we go to the New World with the Company?" Joris asked in surprise.

"They will give us everything we need to get started. We could begin as landowners there! Can you imagine Joris, us owning a piece of land?" she suggested excitedly.

"Catalyntje, you might have a great idea," Joris responded as a slight smile crept over his face. "You have many hidden talents, but I never imagined you as an adventurer," he laughed. The room was quiet for a few minutes, except for the sound of people on the street below.

"My only problem with your idea is that I will not sail to the New World with you unless we are married first," he announced with a big smile.

"Well, we can take care of that!" Catalyntje responded and kissed him.

*****

Catalyntje and Joris were busy the following week preparing to marry. They were delighted that the Dutch West India Company accepted them to sail on the first ship to the New World. But they also found that the ship's departure was only three weeks away. Neither of them had many possessions, so packing wouldn't be a problem, but getting married soon enough might be. As tradition dictated, a couple who wished to be married would make an official announcement at church three weeks before the Sunday they were to be married. Then, the following week, they would give

38

a Proclamation of Banns, which continued for three more weeks. Doing this showed the couples' serious intention to be married. But for Catalyntje and Joris, there would be just two weeks to post banns before the ship left. Catalyntje knew she would need Marie's help but still felt a wedge between them since their conversation about Joris' ability to provide for a family.

That afternoon after church, Catalyntje shortened her time with Joris and went to speak with Marie. As she approached the front stoop, she knocked, opened the door, and went inside. Everyone welcomed her and talked excitedly about her plans to marry. After dinner, she quietly asked Marie if they could visit outside.

"Is everything alright?" Marie asked, pulling her shawl around her shoulders.

"Yes, everything is fine, but I wanted to talk with you before Joris and I are married and gone," Catalyntje answered. "I still feel badly about our conversation of Joris - that you think he is not good enough to care for me."

"Oh, my sister, I didn't mean that. I only meant . . ." Marie tried to finish.

"No, you did say that! You left me with the idea that I needed money to be happy and that Joris could not provide that for me," Catalyntje said boldly. "You are wrong. I want you to know that. I have never been happier, and what Joris and I can do together with our lives will be worth more than any money we make."

Marie didn't say a word as tears filled her eyes. "I am so sorry. I spoke when I shouldn't have. I have seen how you look at each other and how happy you are together. Joris is a wonderful choice for you, Catalyntje."

"Thank you," she said, hugging Marie tightly.

"What can I do to help you?" Marie asked, looking into her sister's eyes.

"Well, I need a witness for our marriage, and you are the only one old enough," Catalyntje answered. "But I did not want to ask until I knew your thoughts about Joris."

"I would be glad to do that for you," Marie smiled. "And I don't think you have enough time between posting banns and getting on that ship. Maybe Phillip and I can make an extra donation to the church to shorten the regular waiting period."

*****

Catalyntje and Joris needed a marriage license to bring to the church on Sunday. Neither spoke fluent Dutch, so they worried about communicating their information correctly at the recorder's office. They hoped he could understand them with their heavy French accents.

Catalyntje and Joris went together one windy morning to get their marriage license. When they reached the recorder's building, they opened the ornate door and walked across the room to a man busily writing at his desk. Joris explained the purpose of their visit, and the man led Catalyntje and Joris to a smaller room with a simple desk and two chairs. A balding man sat on the other side of the desk wearing a dark vest with spectacles balanced on his nose. He motioned for them to both sit down.

"So you're here for a marriage certificate?" the recorder asked.

"Yes, we are, Sir. We plan to marry and sail to the new colony the Dutch are creating. That is where we will start our lives together," Joris excitedly replied. The recorder grunted, looked at Joris, and said, "Let's begin with you."

Joris reported that he was nineteen years old and a textile worker who had come to Amsterdam from Valenciennes. As Joris spoke, the recorder kept his eyes on the page, nodding and writing in loopy Dutch letters.

Then, it was Catalyntje's turn. She had a more difficult time giving her information. When the recorder heard Catalyntje report that she was eighteen, he looked up at her from his paper.

"You are too young to sign this document and be married without a parent," he insisted.

"My mama is far away, and my papa died before I was old enough to know him," Catalyntje answered.

"Why should we proceed if this marriage can't happen?" the officer insisted.

"I have taken care of that. My sister will attend the wedding in place of my mama. She is nearly thirty and can stand as a witness," Catalyntje answered confidently.

"You have planned for this then, I see," the man responded, a bit bewildered. "Let us continue here. Where were you born?"

"I was born in Pris," Catalyntje responded.

"Paris, well, that is a fine place," the recorder said, writing on the certificate.

Anxious to ensure the document was correct, Catalyntje firmly replied, "No, I was born in Pris." She pronounced it more deliberately this time.

The man grunted and said, "I've seen that place on a map. It's not anything like Paris." He crossed out the word 'Paris' and put 'Pris' in its place.

After the recorder completed Catalyntje's portion of the document, he asked, "Can you sign your name or only leave a mark?"

"I will only leave a mark. I have not yet learned my letters," she responded.

"Here is the pen, then," the recorder said, handing it to Joris. "You can both sign at the bottom. It seems you don't have much to lose in this venture," the officer sneered in a judgmental tone. With that comment, Joris took the fountain pen and left his mark at the bottom of the page. Catalyntje followed, dipping the quill into the inkwell; she added her mark to the right of Joris'.

Saying Goodbye

Winter 1624- Beginning of the Year: 18 years old

Most of Catalyntje's life was uncertain, but her decision to marry Joris was deliberate. Since she knew she would soon be away from her sisters, Catalyntje spent more time with them, realizing how complete this separation would be. She didn't expect to see them again or even send a letter since she couldn't read or write.

Besides leaving her sisters, Catalyntje was saddened when she remembered her mama. When she and Margriet left Hainaut, she had supposed her mama would eventually come to Amsterdam. But now, if her mama made it to Amsterdam, Catalyntje would be far away in the New World. These thoughts weighed heavily on her heart, and she couldn't think too long about them, or they would quickly destroy her peace.

Catalyntje stayed with Margriet and Marie the day before the wedding for one last time. That evening, the two sisters helped her put the final touches on a ruffled apron she planned to wear. Marie bought her a fine hat, and Margriet embroidered a beautiful handkerchief to tuck in her pocket. After they talked and cried into the early morning, the three sisters fell asleep on the floor before the warm fireplace. They didn't want to go to separate rooms and miss their last few hours together.

*****

Catalyntje pulled her cloak tightly around her shoulders and wrapped the thin scarf around her head, careful not to stretch it too snugly since she wanted her hair to stay in place. She took a deep breath, stepped out of Marie's front door, and walked through the newly fallen snow. The town was quiet that morning as people headed to church instead of their ships. The snow added a stillness as a chilling breeze swept across the ice-covered canal. As she neared the end of Nes Street, the quiet was interrupted by the chime of a nearby church bell. She continued along the canal, and her face brightened when she saw Joris pacing near the church. He turned towards her, and his face lit up with a smile as he hastily walked toward her.

"Well, today is the day. Are you ready for all of this?" Joris asked.

"Of course, I am," Catalyntje replied with a smile as they linked arms and walked towards the church together. They didn't exchange many words but enjoyed a feeling of calm, knowing they would soon be husband and wife.

The Walloon Church of Amsterdam stood tall, its red bricks contrasting with the snow. It was built nearly two hundred years before but only recently became a place of worship for the Protestants in the area.

As the couple entered the church, Catalyntje's eyes followed the tall, sturdy pillars to the top of the arched ceiling and then over to the dim light through the colorful stained-glass windows. She couldn't help but smile as she and Joris sat down for the Sunday meetings, knowing they would truly belong to each other when they left the church.

The ceremony was simple. Joris didn't have any family in attendance that day. Catalyntje had Marie and her family, along with her sister Margriet. Marie was the only family member old enough to sign as a witness of the happy event. She proudly wrote her name on the marriage certificate to show that she was there with her sister.

*****

Catalyntje and Joris had three days to gather their belongings and get onto the ship *Eendracht*. The vessel, sponsored by the Dutch West India Company, was prepared to carry about thirty families to the Dutch colony in the New World. Many passengers were French-speaking Walloons from Valenciennes, Hainaut, Roubaix, and Nord-Pas-de-Calais.

Even though they had few possessions, Catalyntje and Joris were still uncertain about what they should bring. Shipwrecks, storms, and pirates could halt the safe delivery of provisions once they were in New Netherland. As Catalyntje looked at the small wooden crate on the floor, she knew it wouldn't hold much, but it would make a considerable difference if they brought the right things.

Catalyntje was thinking about having enough food once they got to New Netherland and had gathered seeds for the past few months. She still had some from her mama's garden in Hainaut and Griet's seed from Brussels. Some people who owned carts at the market also gave her some of their favorites. This simple gift was their way of wishing the young couple well in their journey and hoping their small offering would grow in the soil a world away. Catalyntje wrapped each group of seeds in small pieces of thick cloth and then rolled them again into a separate one.

As she refolded the seeds one more time before putting them into the trunk, she heard a knock at the door.

"Come in!" she called, quickly tucking the seeds away.

"Catalyntje!" Marie smiled and gave her a warm hug. "I wanted to see you before you packed everything," she confessed anxiously.

"Well, there is not much to pack, which is good because there is no extra room on the ship," she replied.

Marie gently hoisted a sack from her shoulder. "Uncle De la Grange gave this to me, and I promised to deliver it to you. He couldn't see you married but wanted you to have a treasure from his home." Margriet reached into the sack and carefully removed four small Delft plates. Catalyntje gasped when she saw them.

"Oh, Marie! Those are the ones I always looked at when we visited Uncle's home. They were not the fanciest he had, but they were always my favorite," she sniffled as tears formed. Catalyntje reached out her hand to examine one of them. The plate was medium-sized, and its painted pattern at the center was recognizably Delft Blue. The craftsman had painted a tall house with a chimney and a rounded door on the right of the plate. Near it were simple trees and a fence along both sides of the entrance to the front door. The back of the house disappeared along with the edge of the center design. In the middle was a waterway with several birds flying in a tight pattern over the water.

"Thank you, Marie. I will treasure these always. Please tell Uncle these have always been the ones I have admired. Please thank him for me. He must know this because I will not be able to tell . . ." and then her voice trailed off. Catalyntje didn't finish the sentence because she couldn't bear to think of never speaking with her uncle, sister, or friends again.

"I will tell him, Catalyntje," Marie promised as she began to sob. The two sisters held each other tightly and wept for some time. They both knew that things would soon change, and there would be no going back.

*****

The afternoon before leaving, Catalyntje and Joris wandered to the docks to look at their ship, which was made using the latest Dutch design, called a *fluyten*. These ships were superior to others because they were easy to maneuver on the ocean, inexpensive to build, and had a large cargo area. Surprisingly, there were no written plans for them. Instead, the ships' builders started by lining up blocks to set up the ship's keel, then added arched timbers for the hull and continued until completion. Every vessel piece was cut and shaped by hand. They built it perfectly so the ship would stay afloat, sailing for weeks with only water in sight. With its three masts, it seemed like it could catch every breeze it encountered on the ocean.

As they examined the ship, a sailor walked by. "Hello," Joris stepped forward to get the man's attention. "Is this a typical ship to cross the ocean?"

"She is over 100 feet long and 25 feet wide and is one of the best ships in all of Europe. We are loading up the ballast and cargo, too, since she will be sailing out tomorrow," the man confidently answered, setting down the crate.

"So, what are you loading into her today?" Joris asked, curious about what supplies would sail with them to their new home.

"So far, we have put in some crates of hand-wrought nails as I hear there aren't any houses in that place. We also put in some winnowing baskets for harvesting grain. By nightfall, we will load up the anchors, ropes, sails, rigging, and other necessities. The ship has already been well-caulked, but we still put in some barrels of pitch and tar in case there are problems once it's on the water," the man said confidently. "Tomorrow morning, we will put in the victuals for the folks on board. There is usually some brandy, a few pork and beef barrels, *zuurkool*, salt, and stationery. It's a long journey, and folks usually get anxious and miss their family even before getting to the New World, so writin' it down in a letter helps to ease 'em."

"We will be passengers on that ship when she sails out tomorrow," Joris replied excitedly, hoping for more conversation.

"Ah, yes. You will be living midship over the ballast and cargo. The officers will be on the top deck to keep their eyes on the winds and weather," he replied, nodding and disappearing into the ship's lower deck.

*****

As Catalyntje and Joris neared the room on Nes Street, their conversation was interrupted by a shout from behind.

"Catalyntje! Catalyntje! Joris!" the voice sounded.

"Margriet," Catalyntje smiled and hugged her sister tightly. "It is so wonderful to see you."

"I know everything will be in a rush tomorrow, so I wanted to come and say goodbye," Margriet replied, tears running down her cheeks.

Joris interrupted, "Why don't the two of you go to our room? Then you can talk for a while. I need to gather a few more items from the market anyway."

"Thank you, Joris," Catalyntje replied, holding Margriet's hand tightly. He kissed his new bride on the cheek and nodded.

"I will be back in a while," he announced, walking toward the market.

As they reached the door, Margriet had tears streaming down her face. "I will miss you, Catalyntje. I might never see you again," she exclaimed.

"I know, Margriet," Catalyntje answered tenderly as the two sisters embraced. Then, after sobbing together for some time, they stepped back and held tightly to each other's hands.

"I have never thanked you," Margriet admitted, "for bringing me safely here. It was such a long journey, and as I thought about it, I realized how dangerous it was. I relied on you to guide and protect us, and you did just that," she added gratefully.

"I will never forget our adventure together, and I am grateful we made it," Catalyntje said with a smile. They talked, laughed, and cried together until Joris returned. When Margriet left, they both knew this would be their last time together.

On the Ocean

Light snow began to fall as Catalyntje and Joris stood on the ship's deck, the chilled January air enveloping them. Catalyntje seized the ship's railing as a sudden jolt pulled her off balance. She held tightly with one hand and waved with the other to those on the dock. As the ship left the harbor, it rocked fiercely back and forth. Catalyntje stood beside Joris and looked back at Amsterdam, the place she had called home. Then she took a deep breath and turned towards the open water. *We will be alright*, she thought to herself. But as she watched, the familiar canal houses got smaller, and she could no longer hear the cheering crowd. Soon, the only sound was the deep water striking the ship's sides. She took hold of Joris' arm and looked up at him.

"We will be fine," he said with a confident smile. His assurance was all Catalyntje needed to quell the sudden apprehension she felt. *Goodbye, Amsterdam*, she thought with a tight-lipped smile.

There had been plenty of fanfare for such a brief journey before their first stop at Texel, a tiny island north of Amsterdam. Ships stopped to fill their barrels with drinking water before launching onto the ocean. The harbor on the far side of Texel sheltered ships as they waited for calm winds. The captain of their ship set sail as soon as the tides settled, confident that the east wind would blow them toward the New World.

*****

Catalyntje hadn't realized what continual rolling waves could do to a person. She'd heard of people getting seasick but didn't expect it to be so miserable; the carefree, indomitable spirit she'd felt earlier was gone. Nausea overcame her by early afternoon, forcing her to spend her day lying below deck. She only left her bunk to hurry to the vessel's top tier and lean over the edge. Unfortunately, heaving over the ship's railing only provided temporary relief before the wretched routine repeated itself.

Catalyntje usually felt better by nightfall and collapsed onto her straw mattress, exhausted, only to wake up with the sun and feel horrible again. After a few days, her sickness worsened, and her stomach even churned in the dark hours of the night. *How long could this go on?* She thought desperately one night, clutching her stomach in pain. She nudged Joris to let him know she was going to the top deck again to empty her stomach.

"I will go with you," he responded with slow, mumbling speech.

"No, Joris, you sleep. I have gone up and down that ladder many times; I will be fine," Catalyntje promised. He rolled over and muttered a reply.

As Catalyntje reached the ship's deck in the dark of night, she stopped and held onto the sides of the doorway before attempting to walk to the ship's edge. The dizziness soon passed, and she stepped with outreached hands until she grasped the cold railing. There was no rain, but the air was frigid as Catalyntje held her shawl around her shoulders. The fresh air helped the sickness in her stomach to subside as she drew a deep breath and looked around. However, she immediately realized there was nothing to see, only complete and utter darkness. She listened to the powerful waves below as they slid against the ship's side, accompanied only by the flag waving in the breeze.

As she stared into the blackness, fear and doubt crept into Catalyntje's heart. She wondered how the ship could keep from crashing into something without light; not even the moon or stars were visible. She was sure the deep, dark waters must be waiting for the ship to collapse and spill its passengers into its grasp.

Then Catalyntje began to think about her and Joris going to the New World. They were just ordinary people, so how could they make a difference in this faraway land? She thought they should sail back to their family in Amsterdam once they'd made it to New Netherland. As Catalyntje stared into the eerie darkness, she felt no comfort, only fear. Suddenly, her churning stomach forced her to lean over the railing to expel the wretched sickness from her body again. When she'd finished, she rested her forehead on the cold rail, thinking of how she could ask Joris about sailing back to Amsterdam.

*****

One morning, as the dim light peaked through the cracks between the boards overhead, Catalyntje thought about how miserable the day would be. She rolled over and pulled the thin blanket over her face, waiting for nausea to overtake her. But this morning was different; it never came. So, instead, she slept peacefully after being exhausted from sea sickness.

She didn't know how long she slept, but when Catalyntje finally awoke, her mind was foggy, and she couldn't remember how long she'd even been on the ship. Finally, she went to the top deck and found Joris talking with some of the other passengers. Catalyntje quickly ran her fingers through her hair and smoothed her clothes with her hands as she approached him.

"How long have I been down there all alone?" she asked, grabbing Joris around the waist from behind.

"Oh, you surprised me! You are feeling better?" he asked hopefully.

"I feel wonderful! I never thought that dreadful sickness would end. It is lovely to feel the ship sway under my feet but not have to run to the edge," she replied.

"Catalyntje, meet Guillaume Vigne. He, his wife, and their three daughters are from France," Joris announced, pointing toward the man standing by him. "They are brave souls like we are, trying their hand at a life in the New World." Catalyntje nodded politely at Guillaume and suddenly remembered her thoughts during the night about returning to Amsterdam. It had been such a miserable night, alone in the darkness; she brushed it from her mind and decided to think about it later.

After a brief conversation, a woman dressed in fine clothing and a warm shawl joined them.

"We have finished our reading, so the girls are walking their youngest sister, Rachel, around the ship," the woman reported to Guillaume without looking at Catalyntje or Joris.

"Thank you, my dear," Guillaume replied. "Meet Joris' wife, Catalyntje," he announced.

"You are feeling better now, I hope? I am Adrienne, and Guillaume is my husband. We have three daughters on this ship. Somewhere," she nodded and smiled as she spoke.

"It is good to meet someone else on this ship. I have not enjoyed the journey so far," Catalyntje replied.

"Half of the passengers are sick," answered Adrienne, "and I am glad not to be one of them. It has been enough to take care of my children. I worry about them on the edges of this ship as it tosses about."

"I've worried about falling off the edge myself," Catalyntje laughed. They talked for several minutes, then went their separate ways. Catalyntje hoped to visit with Adrienne again. She was interesting to talk to, and Catalyntje felt calmer having a female friend on the ship. She could learn a lot from Adrienne about how to run a household, and maybe they could even be neighbors once they reached New Netherland. This thought comforted Catalyntje, and for a moment, she felt she would be alright living in the New World.

Catalyntje spent part of the afternoon on the ship's deck. The air was crisp and cold, but the sun warmed the dark blanket around her. She had a skein of wool yarn from one of the merchants at Dam Square and was grateful for it since she'd probably have to spin her own when she got to the New World. As she knitted, Catalyntje heard footsteps coming in her direction. She turned to see Adrienne walking towards her with a stool in her hand.

"How are you this afternoon, Catalyntje? It looks like you have a project today," she said, sitting down and facing Catalyntje.

"I am happy to feel the waves under the ship and still be able to keep my stomach," Catalyntje answered, setting the yarn in her lap.

"Oh, you may continue working. I just wanted some company as I enjoyed the fresh air. What are you working on?" Adrienne asked.

"I am making a pair of gloves for Joris," Catalyntje replied. Reaching into her pocket, she pulled out the completed glove and handed it to Adrienne.

"You do fine work. I have completed gloves for Guillaume but haven't started any for the girls yet. Maria and Christina are making their own, but I still must make a pair for my little Rachel. I brought some yarn with me, but for now, I am of a mind to read," she replied, holding up a book. "Guillaume bought this one for me before we left. It is called *England's Helicon* and it is filled with poetry."

"I don't spend any time with books," Catalyntje replied, picking up her yarn again. "I ask people for help to read me important messages. There is always much to do, and it seems that reading would take up time that I simply do not have," she continued, her hands busy with her knitting.

"Oh, you won't change my mind. I enjoy traveling to places in my mind while I sit on this ship. To me, it is time well spent," Adrienne replied. "If you ever want to learn to read or would like to be read to, I would be happy to help."

The next day, as Catalyntje and Joris climbed to the ship's deck, they saw Guillaume and Adrienne visiting with passengers Catalyntje hadn't yet met.

"Have you met Jacqueline?" Adrienne asked, motioning for Catalyntje and Joris to come closer.

"I remember seeing you at the beginning of our voyage, but Catalyntje took a lot of my attention since she didn't begin this trip well," Joris replied, winking at her.

"I was sick and do not remember much of anything," Catalyntje admitted. "It is good to meet you."

"Why, thank you, and it's wonderful to meet you. We came from France before we lived in Amsterdam. My husband, Jean Montfoort, is on board with our two sons, Pieter and Daniel," Jacqueline replied. "I discovered that Adrienne loves to read, so we talk about books together. We each brought a few with us and would be glad if you would join us, Catalyntje."

"I would love to hear your stories, and I could share a few of my own, but I have not taken time for books," Catalyntje admitted without hesitation.

"Well, maybe we can win you over," Jacqueline raised her eyebrows. "At least come and listen. There is much to share, and the days on this ship are long," she smiled.

"Yes, they are extremely long," Catalyntje agreed. "Joris and I were just preparing lunch, but I will look for you later. It is good to meet you and wonderful to see you again, Adrienne," Catalyntje replied politely.

Catalyntje and Joris walked to the other side of the ship and sat on two small stools to eat some *zuurkool* and dried beef. They talked about nothing in particular but enjoyed being together as they ate. Time alone was rare on a ship with such little space.

Now that Catalyntje felt better, she spent her time on the deck, away from the water that dripped between the cracks of the worn boards onto her clothes and hair. The smell of sweat, waste, and sour cabbage was unbearable, and Catalyntje often wondered if the stench had caused her seasickness. Joris was by her side most of the time, but he sometimes wandered off to talk with some of the men on the ship. One day, as Catalyntje sat on the deck, mending a pair of socks, the sun shone warm on her face. She paused from her work, closed her eyes, and faced the sun's warmth. Then she heard giggling, quickly forcing her to leave her relaxed state.

"Hello to you. We see you are finally alone. We have been watching you and your husband and wanted to talk to you," the woman with dark brown hair exclaimed excitedly. "My name is Jannetje, and these are my friends Mary, Joanna, and Hester. We all worked at the same tavern in Amsterdam and decided to try our luck at a new life. From listening to you and your husband talk, I think you speak French?" she questioned. Catalyntje was surprised by their aggressive introductions but was also excited to meet more women on the ship, and they began to talk. They discussed mending, recipes, Amsterdam, men, and even cats. When Joris returned to Catalyntje, she introduced him to her new friends. They exchanged quick pleasantries and went in different directions, promising to talk again soon.

That chance came early the next day. As Catalyntje and Joris ate breakfast on the ship's deck, Jannetje suddenly appeared with a smile and a quick curtsy.

"Well, hello, Jannetje; it is good to see you again," replied Catalyntje, standing up to talk to her. She offered Jannetje an egg, which she accepted with a nod, and they began talking.

Jannetje took a mitten from her apron pocket. "Would you mind if I worked here with you for a while? I could use some help since I have trouble keeping my stitches even. I need my work to be tight to keep my fingers warm next winter. I don't know what it will be like in New Netherland, but I am preparing for it to be colder than in Amsterdam," Jannetje explained.

"I certainly hope it is not colder in the New World," Catalyntje answered with a shudder as she remembered the biting cold along the canals. Soon, the two friends were busy with their projects as they shared stories from their past, punctuated with laughter.

That night, Catalyntje talked about Jannetje to Joris and retold many of the stories Jannetje had shared. "I am glad you have found a friend," Joris responded with a genuine smile. "We have each other, but having friends in New Netherland will be nice.

"I agree," Catalyntje assured as she leaned over and put her head on Joris' shoulder.

*****

Catalyntje and Jannetje became better friends as they spent time together each day. Although there were no opportunities to make meals, Catalyntje could tell through their conversations that Jannetje was a brilliant cook.

Jannetje was so excited to tell Catalyntje about her culinary creations that her vivid descriptions stayed in Catalyntje's mind, and she hoped to try some of them once they reached land.

Jannetje was interested in hearing how Catalyntje created clothes for the children in Agnes's home. They each had a small collection of sewing supplies, and as they talked, their hands were busy preparing items they would need in New Netherland.

One morning, Catalyntje found Jannetje on the ship and greeted her with a smile and hug as they sat down together.

"How are you today?" Catalyntje queried with a smile.

"I have no complaints, but I admit I am a bit anxious this morning. Rem is a passenger on this ship and worked at the warehouse near the tavern I cooked at. We have been spending more time together the past few weeks, and I think we have fallen in love," Jannetje answered soberly.

"That is such wonderful news! Why are you so concerned?" Catalyntje asked.

"Because I think he will ask me to marry him," Jannetje replied.

"That is exciting!" Catalyntje exclaimed, nearly jumping up and down.

"I know it is good news, but it happened so fast. I have thought about it and already know that I will answer 'yes' when Rem asks me to marry him," Jannetje said with a smile. "I've also thought how wonderful it would be to be neighbors with you and Joris once we arrive in the New World. We could help each other in our homes and learn how to live in a new place together!" Jannetje said with excitement.

"That would be lovely!" Catalyntje replied, "And please tell me when Rem asks you. I will not tell another soul, well, except for Joris. I cannot keep things from him."

"Of course, I will. I am excited about all that has happened to me. Thank you for your friendship, Catalyntje. Watching you and Joris made me feel that marrying Rem will work out well."

Jannetje had been right; before two days had passed, she and Rem announced their intent to be married and didn't plan to wait until their feet were on land so the wedding would take place on the ship. The excitement spread, and the other three single women Catalyntje met soon announced they would also be married. When they were together, they often joked with Catalyntje that they decided to find their own man because of her and Joris. She knew it hadn't been all her doing but felt some satisfaction, knowing that as these women had watched them, they saw happiness and wanted it for themselves.

*****

After the weddings, the five couples continued to spend time together, and their conversations always focused on life in the New World. As they talked, the women planned how to set up their homes and help each other once they landed. Each evening, Catalyntje filled the air with excited chatter about plans for life in New Netherland; Joris usually just nodded and smiled.

*****

"We should spot land some time tomorrow!" the captain announced confidently, looking over the passengers gathered to hear him. The sun was close to the western horizon as he waited for the chatter to quiet before he spoke further.

"The area we are to colonize is large. I will take a minute to let you know where you'll each be going once we reach land. The Dutch West India Company has divided you according to your skills to make this a strong settlement. So, please listen for your assignment and wait until I have finished before you ask questions," the captain declared.

Catalyntje felt cold as she reached for Joris's hand. The thought that they might be in a different place from their newfound friends had never entered her mind. Surely, the captain had seen her and Jannetje talking and would want them to live in the same place since they worked well together. She glanced over at Jannetje, and her furrowed brow told Catalyntje that she, too, was concerned about this announcement.

Catalyntje tried to focus on the captain's words. When he announced those who would be living near Fort Orange, Catalyntje heard her and Joris' names, along with a few other families and several men who worked for the Company. She held her breath and listened intently for Jannetje's name but realized that the captain was now listing names for a different location. *This could not be correct. He had most certainly made a mistake.* Catalyntje would ask him to reread the list to be sure that she and Jannetje would live by each other in New Netherland.

Part 2: Wilderness
Spring 1624 - Summer 1626

Up the Noort River

Spring of 1624: 18 years old

The passengers and crew of the *Eendracht* had spent nearly four months sailing across the ocean. Each day of the journey, Catalyntje continually thought about the endless possibilities for her life with Joris in New Netherland. But the captain's recent announcement that Jannetje would be sent to a different part of the colony weighed heavily on Catalyntje's mind. She usually spent the mornings looking out over the endless ocean, trying to sort through her thoughts.

One morning, as she studied the horizon, the captain walked by Catalyntje. She turned and asked, "How much longer until we reach land?"

"Before the sun goes down," the captain answered cheerfully.

"That is good news," Catalyntje replied flatly. "I had a question about where we will all live once we reach land. I heard Rem and Jannetje will be staying near where we will land, and Joris and I will be further north, up the river. I do not know if you have noticed, but Jannetje and I are good friends. So, having us live in the same place would be most useful."

"Well, we decided all of this before leaving. The Company chose where the men would go before setting sail. I am just following their orders. Maybe Jannetje should have picked a different husband," the captain laughed, showing little care about Catalyntje's concern.

"I am sure the Company would trust your judgment if you made a change," Catalyntje offered, feeling she was losing the debate.

"The orders are already given. You will run into each other at some point, and there will be soldiers to deliver messages between settlements," the captain replied. Suddenly, a worker hauling a barrel along the deck interrupted their conversation. "Oh, I must see to this man," the captain responded, walking away from Catalyntje.

As she watched the captain follow the crewman without even a second thought to her concerns, Catalyntje didn't want to go to New Netherland, and she didn't want to be seen by anyone else. Tears filled her eyes as she hurried to her quarters to help Joris pack.

*****

Before too long, the captain announced he'd spotted land. The passengers anxiously gathered at the deck's railing to glimpse their new home. Catalyntje strained her eyes to see this new place, noticing a small hill that rose to the left along with endless trees, more than she'd seen her entire life. In the distance, a few thin lines of smoke curled toward the sky, but these were the only signs that anyone lived there.

*****

One at a time, Catalyntje and Joris lowered themselves down the rope ladder to the small boat, bobbing up and down in the water beside the ship. There was no easy way to get into the vessel except to let go once you reached the end of the ladder. Catalyntje firmly gripped the side of the smaller, unstable boat as it made its way to the river on the west side of the island in front of them. The man who was rowing called it the Noort River. Once they were close to the shore, there wasn't a dock, so Catalyntje and the others waded through ankle-deep water to reach land.

Once on dry ground, Catalyntje threw her arms around Joris' neck and shouted, "We made it, Joris!"

"I'm happy to be here with you, Catalyntje," he answered as they walked hand in hand, trying to take in everything they saw. As Joris breathed in the fresh air, he could tell it was a different place. There were no smells of the market, only the scent of soil and trees.

"We truly are in a whole other world," Joris replied slowly, "And we are far from where we started," he added solemnly.

*****

Everyone was up early the following day. Catalyntje had dreaded this day because she knew she and her friend would soon leave for different places. She would have to say goodbye to Jannetje, and she couldn't bear thinking about it. The captain organized them into groups according to where they would live. Jannetje and Rem were in the group going to the Delaware River, and Catalyntje and Joris were in the group headed north to Fort Orange. After giving brief instructions, the captain announced it was time to say their goodbyes. Catalyntje didn't waste a second getting to Jannetje, and they hugged each other tightly for a long time without saying a word. When they separated, Catalyntje pulled something from her pocket.

"I have a gift for you, Jannetje. Since you are such a wonderful cook, I made you an apron so you will not forget me when you are busy at the hearth," Catalyntje replied, handing her the apron. Jannetje carefully unfolded it, and tears rolled down her face as she saw the beautifully stitched design along the bottom hem.

"Oh, Catalyntje, I will treasure this forever. But you needn't worry about me forgetting you," she replied.

"I also have a gift for you," Jannetje admitted with a smile, taking something from her pocket. Catalyntje took the gift into her hands, and her eyes widened. "Your mortar and pestle! I am not skilled enough for this," she   admitted.
"Well, I told you enough stories of my days cooking in the tavern. I hope you remember something," Jannetje replied with a teasing voice.

"I will," Catalyntje said.

The captain shouted orders, and the two friends knew it was time to say goodbye. They embraced once more, hoping the distance between their homes would not be far.

"Goodbye, my friend," Catalyntje uttered with a brave smile.

"I will see you soon, Catalyntje," Jannetje assuredly replied. Then, they each stepped toward their separate groups, but after a brief pause, Catalyntje ran to Jannetje and hugged her one last time.

"It has been wonderful to have you as my friend, Jannetje. Thank you," she whispered because he knew her voice would crack if she spoke out loud.

*****

As Catalyntje's sloop released from the dock to sail up the Noort River, she fixed her eyes on Jannetje and did not look away until she could no longer see her. Then she just stared at the churning water behind the sloop until Joris came and sat by her, saying nothing.

After a few hours of sailing upriver, Arien Jorise, who was in charge of the Fort Orange settlers, gathered them together to give instructions.

"This is a significant event for the Dutch. It will be the first time that women and children will live in this colony," Jorise said with the wind blowing his hair. "I will be in charge of the area, and you can come to me with any concerns," he said. "We will be on this ship for a few more days before we reach the fort." His speech was one-sided since no one on the ship knew what questions to ask. Once he finished speaking, the group went back to their quiet conversations. Joris looked over at Catalyntje and saw tears running down her cheeks.

"What's wrong?" he asked with concern.

"I did not think we would be this far away from the other colonists," she groaned, then added, "from Jannetje. I thought we would be close enough to take a day to visit each other, but this place is not like Amsterdam. There are no paths or roads or homes or people. There are only trees and this extremely long river," she answered in a discouraged voice.

"I know this is difficult, but I will see what we can do to visit Jannetje and Rem. We can get settled in and then journey down the river," Joris promised.

"Being here is so different from what I thought it would be," Catalyntje admitted resignedly. She looked up at Joris, and he leaned over and kissed her. After that, they stood without saying anything for a long time.

*****

Excitement spread throughout the little ship when they first saw Fort Orange. It took some time for everyone to get off the boat with their supplies, but once they were back on land, their leader, Jorise, led a brief tour, talking and pointing at far-away structures.

Catalyntje wasn't sure what she expected to see, but it was a different experience from when she and Margriet had traveled to Amsterdam. No houses lined the river, no markets were in sight, no people walked about, and there were hardly any animals. But it did have a beauty that she had never seen before. Growing up in the idyllic town of Hainaut, fields were sprinkled with trees, but this place was different. It was vast, and the trees towered over every place. The only sounds were steady hammering, the wind in the trees, and birds overhead.

It was underwhelming as a soldier led the colonists to Fort Orange for the first time. The workers from the Company had just begun to build it in a small clearing surrounded by endless trees in all directions. The unfinished fort did not instill confidence. There were no apparent supplies, firewood, food, or animals. A few tools were stacked along the side of a wall, but not enough for everyone and certainly not enough to start a settlement in such a short amount of time.

As Catalyntje looked about, she realized the soldier from the fort had been talking to the group. "The walls will eventually house the Company soldiers and supplies. You will each receive a generous portion of land to raise crops and build a home. We have had good dealings with the Natives of the area, and you will trade furs with them since trade is the Company's main focus." The soldier seemed bold in his proclamations. As he spoke, Catalyntje's mind wandered back to the months before she'd left the bustling streets of Amsterdam to settle here. Then, she hadn't realized the overwhelming challenge of living in this distant place.

As Catalyntje looked around, she noticed a worn-looking structure in the distance, south of where they stood.

"Excuse me," Catalyntje interrupted the soldier, "What is that building over there?" The soldier paused with a questioning look; Catalyntje had interrupted him mid-sentence.

"Ah, yes. That is what remains of Fort Nassau. It was built about ten years ago as a trading post with the Mohawks and the Mahicans," he replied self-assuredly.

"Why don't they still use it?" Catalyntje asked with concern in her voice.

"Well, when they built it, the Company wasn't aware it was in an area that flooded, so most of it was destroyed," the soldier answered.

Catalyntje didn't know what to say, but his answer wasn't enough. *What would happen if she and Joris spent all their effort making a home, and the river washed it away, too?* She reached over and took Joris' hand and squeezed it firmly. He knew she wasn't satisfied with the soldier's answer. Finally, he let go of her hand and put his arm around her waist, pulling her close. She flashed a brief, forced smile and stared at the broken-down fort in the distance, tears filling her eyes again.

*****

The next day, the colonists started working to make a place to live. First, they had to clear an area to build a house. But clearing the land required cutting trees, digging the soil, and wrenching the stumps from the stubborn ground; this was hard work and took several days to make any progress. Once they had cut the trees, the colonists selected ones that would be suitable for building their winter shelter. This process was challenging since many of them had never built a house.

Most colonists dug a four-foot-deep hole about ten to fifteen feet square. Then, using the trees they'd harvested, they roughly planed the lumber to line the hole, which became the floor of their dwelling. Next, they cut more wood into planks and stacked them along the hole's edges to make walls for their one-room house. They would use the room for sleeping, cooking, and eating. Once the settlers had stacked the planks, they hoped they would remain standing throughout the winter and be close enough to keep the cold out.

Next, a simple door was added, along with a roof of rough planks from nearby trees and a chimney made of clay from the ground. Catalyntje and Joris slept under the stars, near the hole they'd dug for at least a month until they had a roof over their heads. None of the colonists got much help with these tasks since everyone was working hard to make their own places to live before winter. While the colonists worked, the Company men built a mill near the river and worked to complete Fort Orange.

After a few months, small gardens appeared near each dugout with the hope that the colonists could grow enough food for the winter months ahead. No one had ever lived in the New World, so they didn't know what to expect for a growing season or how much food they'd need to make it through the winter.

*****

As the weather grew warmer, the rain became a continual companion, bringing threads of mist that wove through the tops of the trees each morning. Catalyntje enjoyed this view as she worked in her garden. One morning in late June, she dug a scant row with a stick and then counted twelve bean seeds. Beans were sensible food because they provided easy-to-collect seeds and would last through the winter. She had planted twenty-four seeds the week before. This way of planting would allow her and Joris to have a steady food supply into the fall. As she carefully patted the soil over the seeds, she noticed Joris speaking with a soldier from the Fort. Once she finished covering the seeds, she got up and walked quickly to where they stood. She reached Joris just as the man left.

"What was he here for?" Catalyntje asked, wiping her hands on her apron.

"The next ship has arrived already. A month faster than it took us to sail here. I suppose the winds are more favorable this time of year," Joris replied.

"What did they bring? More supplies, more food, more tools? We need more of everything," Catalyntje replied anxiously.

"Well, the ship—they call her the *Nieu Nederlandt*—brought our first director, Cornelis May. He had explored this place before we arrived, but now he has returned to help us. The Company also got a few more tools and supplies. And they also brought thirty more families, mostly Walloons," he answered.

"They brought thirty more families? How will we manage?" she asked in disbelief. "Joris, we do not have extra to share."

"We will be alright. We are working hard, and the Company will look out for us," he said, embracing Catalyntje as tears wet his shoulder.

The Natives

Summer of 1624: 18 years old

Clearing the land was exhausting work. Catalyntje and Joris spent the entire day removing rocks and digging around stumps. This was more grueling than either of them thought possible. Each tree they felled was an exercise in agony as they cut the branches and trunks into usable portions for firewood, furniture, and foundations. They'd worked hard before, but nothing could have prepared them for the endurance this activity required. Unfortunately, this wasn't the impossible part of the process. Removing the roots and stumps from the ground was an unimaginable task. It took every ounce of strength to dig, hack, and pry whatever pieces remained in the ground from the once towering trees.

The summer weather was now humid and unbearably hot in the afternoons. After a seemingly endless day, Catalyntje and Joris worked until dark and then went inside for a simple meal of bread and thin soup. After they ate, Catalyntje went outside again and peered at a nearby field; she took a deep breath, closed her eyes, and squared her tired shoulders. She smelled the freshly dug earth and felt a warm breeze on her face as her dry, cracked hands hung by her side. She could hear the insects announce the evening, and as she slowly opened her eyes, she glimpsed the full moon rising from behind the trees. She surveyed the work she and Joris had done and admitted they still had much to do to prepare for winter; hopelessness crept into her mind. *Why had they decided to come here? Wouldn't it have been easier to make a home in Amsterdam?* Catalyntje's heart squeezed in her chest as she swallowed back the tightness in her throat. She was afraid, but they had chosen to come to New Netherland. So, they would keep working and make the best of their situation. As she listened, the frogs and birds slowed their evening calls. She looked over the land again, and in her mind, she could see a garden filled with food, enough to be stored for the winter. She also saw herself talking to neighbors and sharing what she had with them. Her wrinkled brow relaxed as these thoughts crossed her mind; she smiled, turned, and went inside, knowing she would sleep deeply.

*****

It was now the beginning of September, and Catalyntje began to worry about what winter would bring. She and Joris had done all they could to gather crops and had worked tireless hours making their home strong enough to withstand the wintry elements, whatever they might be.

Catalyntje went to her garden, where there were three rows of turnips and some carrots to dig and store for the winter. As she worked, her mind drifted so far away that it crossed the deep ocean and settled in the market near her home in Amsterdam. She had forgotten how much she enjoyed gathering food for meals in the Old World. She also enjoyed talking to the women and men who sold the produce she had so carefully selected. The colors, the smells, the people. Oh, how she missed every bit of it. The casual conversations she had with others while shopping at the market, all of this she had taken for granted. New Netherland had no markets and no people milling about the streets. There were no familiar faces yet, no exchanges of recipes or light-hearted conversations, only constant work, worry, and crushing isolation.

Another unsettling thought in Catalyntje's mind was the obligation to trade with the Mahicans. She had talked with many strangers when she and Margriet made their way to Amsterdam but talking to the Natives seemed more intimidating somehow.

One warm afternoon, Catalyntje and Joris sat down for a brief rest after they had cleared a narrow place for another garden. Joris was the first to spot the slender Mahican man who walked purposefully towards them. Catalyntje felt a sudden rush of fear. She stood without moving as Joris stepped towards the man, tipped his hat, and smiled. Catalyntje studied the visitor intently, not daring to meet his gaze. She noticed his foot coverings were made of leather, which closed around his toes, then went up to his knees and tied with a colorful band of thick woven threads. His clothing was plain, except for his belt and the bands around his forearm, detailed with brown, white, and deep red shells beautifully woven together.

He also wore three necklaces. The longest one had a sheath with a blade, but only the weapon's smooth wooden handle was visible. Shells decorated the sheath, along with leather and feathers that hung around the edges. The second necklace laid on his chest and contained a smoothed white circular shell, drilled with a hole for a thread of leather to keep it about his neck. The last necklace fit tightly around his throat, created using shells and beads in balanced patterns. Catalyntje noticed his black hair was pulled back, allowing his face to be visible, and nearly a dozen feathers, tied together, trailed down his neck.

As she gathered her courage, Catalyntje stared into his face. His skin was a striking brown, accented by his black eyebrows and deep brown, kind eyes. His face also had a black line, put there purposefully. While her hands tightly clutched her apron, Joris attempted to communicate with the Mahican, but neither understood what the other was saying.

*****

After several more visits, Joris figured out some hand signals and even a few words to communicate with the Mahican men. But for Catalyntje, speaking with them was too much to think about. Instead, she stood to the side as Joris talked with the Natives. She was happy to watch these dealings and impressed that Joris made it look so easy. He and the men would smile and laugh together; it seemed they had become friends.

*****

One morning, while Joris was away hunting, Catalyntje began her day in the garden; she enjoyed the calm routine of working in her garden. After filling her apron with beans, she suddenly noticed a Mahican man approaching her. She dumped the freshly picked beans on the ground and took a deep breath, trying to hide her fear. As the Native reached the area where Catalyntje stood, she wiped her hands nervously on her apron and slowly extended her hand in greeting as she faced him. He reached out with both hands for her outstretched one and shook it firmly; Catalyntje wanted to run. Finally, he released his grip and reached into a pouch hanging at his side. As he took his hand from the bag, he opened his palm to show Catalyntje a handful of dried berries. He looked at her and nodded. She smiled nervously and reached out slowly, taking the berries from him. "Thank you," she whispered and bowed to convey her gratitude to the man.

The man returned the smile, stood there, and looked at Catalyntje; she wasn't sure what to do next. After the awkward silence, she decided to show him what she had done in her garden and motioned for him to follow her. She pointed to the tiny leaves coming up from the dirt, and the man excitedly nodded and spoke words she didn't understand. Next, she led him to where she'd dropped the beans earlier, carefully gathered them, and handed them to the man. He nodded at Catalyntje, then turned and walked towards the woods.

She stood motionless in the middle of her garden and watched until he disappeared into the tall trees. After he was out of sight, Catalyntje stood there, thinking about what had just happened. It was a positive encounter, and she thought of what she would say the next time he returned. She took the dried berries from her apron pocket, went inside, and put them in a small dish on the shelf near the hearth.

*****

Catalyntje and Joris continued to work hard. Every day was exhausting and always the same; even the meals Catalyntje prepared lacked variety. One morning, as she readied for the day, she remembered the dried berries the Mahican had given her. She took them from the bowl and added them to her bread dough. Then, she set the rounded loaf on the wooden slat near the fireplace to rise and went outside to help cut more trees.

That afternoon, Catalyntje gathered a few crops from her garden and took a break to prepare an evening meal for her and Joris. She started baking the bread and unwrapped some of the remaining cheese the Company had given them earlier in the week. Then she took two bowls from the wooden shelf as the smell of fresh bread floated through their home, the berries adding extra sweetness.

Once Catalyntje cooked the soup, she gingerly removed the fresh bread from the fireplace, carefully using her apron to shield her hands from the heat. As she placed the loaf on the small table, she heard the door open and turned to see Joris and the lean Mahican who had visited a few days earlier. The three had talked in the fields, but this man had never been in their home; it seemed too close. Joris showed no worry as he motioned for the man to enter. The man saw Catalyntje, smiled, and nodded; she responded similarly. Her mind raced, trying to decide what to do next, but then she remembered the bread she had just baked, filled with the berries this man had given her. She stepped to the table, picked up a slice, and walked towards him. She pointed to the pouch at his side, then to one of the berries in the bread. His face lit up as he took a bite, then quickly ate the entire piece.

70

That night, when Catalyntje and Joris sat by the fire and talked about their day, she mentioned how frightened she had been that Joris brought the Native into their home.

"I am slow to realize that the Mahicans do not bring us danger but are as gentle as baby lambs," Catalyntje observed, trying to convince herself as she spoke.

*****

As summer ended, Catalyntje and Joris tallied all they had done since they'd arrived in New Netherland. One of the tasks they were proud of was a path they'd cleared through the tall hemlock and fir trees behind their home. It led to a grove of smaller trees they could use to build a lean-to or a fence. It was a narrow trail, but the towering trees on each side made it seem more majestic and beautiful.

Hope

Fall of 1624: 18 years old

The sky was nearly dark, and the air was crisp as Catalyntje gathered a pile of sticks under one arm and kept a lantern in her other hand. This would be her last load of twigs for the evening. As she walked towards the house, a sudden breeze blew her lantern out just as she passed through the corridor of trees, she and Joris had cleared. She stopped to let her eyes adjust to the darkness and gazed into the impenetrable blackness. She recognized she was suddenly standing in the middle of a giant forest, on the edge of a completely different continent, from nearly everyone she had ever known. There were no noises of closing doors, rambling carts, or distant laughter, only the sound of wind dancing through the trees. The quietness reminded Catalyntje of her home in Hainaut and of her mama. She wondered if she was safe, if she'd planted her garden, and if she was even aware that Catalyntje was so far away. Looking up, she noticed fluffy snowflakes slowly falling from the sky. She should have been frightened, out in the darkness, alone, but she wasn't. Standing among the tall, tall trees, she felt safe and at peace.

She thought about those trees and how long they'd stood as silent witnesses to the history of this faraway place. They had survived storms, droughts, and terrible winds but had remained firm. Catalyntje thought she could keep standing tall no matter what came her way.

*****

Winter had arrived, and Catalyntje and Joris had finally finished their home. However, it wasn't a proper house; it was only a simple shelter from the elements. The floor was a square hole in the ground lined with wooden slats. The walls, made of boards, were set vertically along the edges of the plank-lined hole, and the primitive structure had a thatched roof. Joris cut a place for two small windows to allow light in during the day and added shutters to keep the cold out.

Not having a completed house was a concern for Catalyntje. Some days, when snow fell gently from the sky, she remembered her winter in Amsterdam: the frozen river, the falling snow, and the heated rocks. Those had been difficult times, but she had made it through. These memories gave Catalyntje hope for the difficulties she faced now.

Winter

End of 1624-Winter: 18 years old

Catalyntje had seen snow in the Old World, but here in New Netherland, it was much more persistent. Excitement filled their primitive home as the flakes entirely covered the ground, turning the world a brilliant white. That evening, Joris walked along the rough inside walls of their house and pressed pieces of cloth into the cracks to help keep the warmth in. Catalyntje walked to one of the windows, lifted the heavy cloth that covered it, and peered outside. The snow had stopped, the clouds had blown away, and a full moon hung over the landscape. Her eyes examined the wintery scene beyond the window, with the moon illuminating every branch of the tall trees near their home. Catalyntje had never seen anything like it in her life. She stayed at the window for some time, trying to remember every detail.

*****

After a few weeks, the uniqueness of the snow wore off, and Catalyntje and Joris braced themselves against the cold that forced its way through their coats as they trudged to the woodpile. Before they went outside each time, they made sure there was a fire in the hearth to return to so its heat could warm them and dry the puddles left under the peg shelf where their outdoor clothes hung to dry.

One clear morning, after a few days of constant snow, Catalyntje went outside to see what the cold had done to her little garden beside the house. Each time she stepped outside, the cold nearly took her breath away. It usually only walked several steps before her feet numbed to the icy cold.

She expected that their house would protect her garden from the weather. She'd even built a simple fence around the small patch of ground to keep snow from covering the fragile plants. But, when she reached the garden, she saw that the fence hadn't protected the plants at all. Catalyntje realized she'd wasted the seeds she had planted at the end of the summer. She had saved food for the winter but had planned to use the side garden as a fresh food source when it was cold. Settling in New Netherland had seemed like such a wonderful chance to start on their own, but now they had nowhere else to go, no one to rely on, and no ships coming anytime soon with supplies. They simply had to make it work because to fail here could mean death, far from any family or friends. Catalyntje went back inside, filled with discouragement.

*****

One wintery day, Catalyntje and Joris spent the morning working inside since neither wanted to face the frigid temperatures outside. First, they built up the fire, then started some soup in the kettle. Hot food would keep them warm and lift their spirits when it grew dark. Next, Catalyntje made more candles with a few supplies she had been given from the fort the previous week. Suddenly, a bold knock at the door interrupted her work.

"Soldiers from the fort!" a demanding voice bellowed. Joris stood up and opened the door to let the soldier in. A harsh gust of glacial air and snow followed the soldier inside.

"Have a seat if you'd like. Can I get you something to warm you?" Joris asked.

"No, I have much business to conduct today. I am here to share a message with everyone living near the fort. The river has frozen. Frozen up solid, so we will not be getting any more supplies from Fort Amsterdam until spring," he reported with a stern face.

"Joris, what are we to do?" Catalyntje asked in a startled tone, turning towards the soldier, "You must still help us; we are not completely prepared for winter."

"We will share what we have, but we may all need to use less so that supplies will last. The winters here are harsher than what you were used to in Amsterdam; I won't mislead you," he answered, trying to quell her fear.

"But when will we get more help? From the southern Fort?" Catalyntje asked fearfully.

"Most likely by late April is the word we have. There may be some breakup of the ice before then, but we shouldn't expect it," the soldier replied matter-of-factly. Catalyntje said nothing but returned to her candles and continued her work. *How would this tiny bundle of candles last through April? Why wasn't the Company more prepared?* She heard the door close and knew the soldier had gone. She felt Joris' hands on her shoulders.

"It will be fine, Catalyntje. We have some supplies, and the Company will share what they have. We will manage," he assured.

"Well, I do not think it will be alright, Joris!" Catalyntje snapped as she turned to face him. "We do not know how long this winter will last. We do not know if we will freeze, starve, or stay alive. I do not like it here, Joris! I do not know why we thought this would be a good idea," she replied through her tears. She turned away from Joris and walked to the other side of the room to gather her thoughts and courage.

*****

After another long week of continual cold, Catalyntje sat at the table cutting carrots for porridge and heard a knock at the door. She froze, trying to brace herself for more bad news as Joris opened the door. She glanced over her shoulder and was startled at seeing a Mahican standing in their doorway. He didn't enter but motioned for Joris to join him outside. Joris grabbed his coat and followed the man outside. Catalyntje didn't join them but walked over to the window and pulled the thick curtain aside to see what was happening.

She watched as the Native pulled a long covering from his foot and handed it to Joris. It was about three times the size of a shoe with a woven pattern on the bottom that you could see through. There were also two sets of ties on each side. Catalyntje watched Joris put the long shape underneath his foot while the man bent down and helped him attach it around his boot. Joris put the next one under his boot, stood, and smiled. The man pointed to a nearby snowbank, and Joris stepped towards it. To Catalyntje's surprise, Joris stayed on top of the snow without sinking. She watched as he laughed, and the man smiled and nodded with delight. After they talked and gestured to one another briefly, Joris motioned for the man to come inside. Catalyntje hurriedly closed the curtain and stood near the table.

As the two entered, Joris described all he'd learned about the shoes that helped him walk on the snow.

"Catalyntje, we won't have to get our shoes filled with snow anymore with these!" he announced, handing her one of the shoes to inspect. "We will call them Indian Shoes," Joris said proudly.

"Can we make some for ourselves?" Catalyntje questioned as she examined the deerskin ties.

"He said we could keep these," Joris answered, looking at the Mahican standing near the door.

"That is a great kindness. Let me get him something in return," Catalyntje said, reaching into the wooden box by the wall. She pulled out a blue wool scarf and, bowing her head, offered it to him. He took it with a smile and placed his closed fist on his chest, showing gratitude.

*****

The following morning, Catalyntje and Joris took turns using the Indian Shoes to work outside. They stacked wood beside the house and brought more inside. Then they spent the afternoon inside, working by the fire. Catalyntje knit socks while Joris sharpened tools. In the evening, they enjoyed a simple meal together and then went to bed once it was dark to save their candles.

After a few weeks of the comforting monotony, the air outside changed. A chilling wind kept Catalyntje and Joris inside the entire day with their coats on. Each evening, after eating bread soaked in hot broth, they retired to their built-in bed even earlier than usual. When they awoke the following day, neither wanted to get out of bed because of the piercing cold that filled the house. They could see their breath as they talked to each other, huddled side by side under every quilt they owned. Joris finally got the courage to take the now cold heating stones from underneath the covers and put them into the coals of the fire.

When he returned from the hearth, Joris carried two cups of hot tea and announced that he couldn't open the front door because of the snow. After they warmed up with the tea, Catalyntje and Joris decided to inspect their situation further. They left the warmth of their bed, bundled up as much as they could, and went to the door to try and open it, but it wouldn't budge. Earlier in the season, Joris had plugged up a large gap in the wall above the door. So, he brought one of their rough-hewn stools to that part of the room.

"I think if I pull the cloth out of this hole, I might be able to see outside," he suggested, standing on the stool. "Hold this for a moment," he added, handing the fabric to Catalyntje and standing on his tiptoes. "I want to see what it looks like outside."

"What do you see?" she asked.

Joris was silent for a moment before answering. "You need to look for yourself. I've never seen anything like this in my life," he said slowly, stepping down from the stool. He held Catalyntje's hand and helped her up onto it. Standing as tall as she could, she peered through the bottom of the gap. She couldn't believe the sight that met her eyes. The gardens, piles of logs, and bushes had all disappeared beneath the white snow, and what was more astonishing was that the snow nearly reached the bottom of their thatched roof.

"Joris, how will we ever get out?" Catalyntje asked.

"I'm not sure how long it will take for all this snow to melt," he answered, helping her down from the stool. "We will need to ration what food we have left," he said with concern. "We don't have much wood inside to keep us warm either."

"We still have some dried food in the baskets hanging from the ceiling beams, Catalyntje offered.

They followed Joris's advice and were careful not to burn too much wood and to only eat what they needed. A few times each day, Joris checked the door to see if it had thawed enough to open; it hadn't. As they sat near the fire, they could hear the wind raging outside and feel the coldness of the air in their house. The freezing weather continued for two more days without a break.

On the third morning, Catalyntje and Joris stayed bundled in their outside clothes and worked on indoor projects without much conversation since their minds were filled with worries, which neither dared say aloud. They noticed that the wind outside had ceased when they ate their midday meal of bread and a shared apple.

"I think I hear voices outside," Joris said, quickly carrying the stool back to the door. He pulled the cloth from the hole to see where the voices came from.

"Hello! We are over here!" he yelled. "Catalyntje, grab me that hoe blade I've been sharpening. The Mahican are here!"

Catalyntje ran across the room, grabbed the hoe, and handed it to Joris. He quickly tied a cloth around its top and put it through the opening. Then, he waved it back and forth as he called out to get the men's attention.

"They have wooden tools to help us out," Joris cheered. He got down from the stool, and then he and Catalyntje stood motionless inside, listening to the Natives dig snow from around their door. Finally, after a long time, they heard scraping around the door. Joris grasped the door handle and tried to loosen the frozen snow from its edges. After several pushes, it came open, and two Mahicans fell into the room along with a pile of snow. Everyone seemed stunned for a moment, and then the conversations began. Joris talked to the men without much trouble while Catalyntje stood back and watched. One of them took a pair of Indian Shoes off his back and motioned to Catalyntje, smiling. She stepped over and gratefully accepted them from his outstretched hands. Another one of them handed her two dried fish. She nodded with gratitude. It had been some time since they had eaten meat; she was grateful for their generosity and kindness.

One of the men motioned for Joris to follow him outside. Catalyntje didn't want to stay inside any longer and put on an extra coat and the Indian Shoes. They were clumsy to wear, and she swayed as she walked towards the door. Once she was outside, she breathed in the cold, fresh air. She watched as the two men helped Joris make long steps down to their front door. Catalyntje smiled and remembered her fear the first time she met them. How could she have ever been scared of these generous men?

*****

Each day felt more hopeful when Joris pulled back the thick canvas curtains to let the sun shine through the windows. The winter had stayed for a long time, and one thought that worried Catalyntje during those cold months was having enough food. It had been a struggle, and many nights, they went to bed hungry. She planned to grow more crops in her garden next summer. As she laid her seeds on the rough-topped table, she counted them and made plans for each. The thought of having fresh food was something she looked forward to.

*****

Catalyntje walked to the baskets of dried food to see what was left; many were empty. She felt bad that she usually prepared the same foods for Joris and her. She took a small wooden bowl from the top shelf to cut some cabbage into, and as she set the bowl on the table, she was surprised to see a tiny handful of dried berries the Mahicans had given her. They knew she appreciated them, so they had brought her more before Winter arrived. She remembered the delicious flavor they added to the bread she'd made with them earlier in the year. But as Catalyntje looked into the bowl, she realized there weren't enough berries to add to a loaf of bread. Disappointedly, she scanned the lower shelf and saw the mortar and pestle Jannetje had given her.

Catalyntje smiled and remembered the sunny afternoon on the ship when Jannetje rolled out one of her cooking tales about creating flavored biscuits. She had described how she ground up dried onion with her mortar and pestle, so the crushed pieces spread through the biscuits, filling them with flavor. That was the answer! Catalyntje could use this tool to grind up the berries and add flavor to the entire loaf of bread. As she ground them with Jannetje's tool, her mind floated back to days, conversations, and laughter with her dear friend. Those had been hopeful times, and as she remembered them, she smiled and realized that one day, when the weather was warmer, she would see Jannetje again.

Changes

Spring of 1625: 19 years old

Spring finally arrived after a frigid winter in the snow-covered colony of New Netherland. Catalyntje and Joris enjoyed being outside and talking with the others who lived near Fort Orange. Soon, word traveled through the colony that the next ship, the *Orangenboom*, would arrive in New Netherland around May. It would carry their new director, Willem Verhulst, and Bastiaen Krol, who was returning to the colony. This was wonderful news for Joris since he had become friends with Krol before he had returned to the Old World. Now, he would serve as a comforter of the sick in the Dutch Reformed Church. When Krol arrived at Fort Orange, Joris invited him for an evening meal.

*****

Catalyntje had gathered fresh peas from her garden for the soup and baked a loaf of bread. Just as she set the bowls on the table, she heard a knock at the door; Krol had arrived. After some small talk, they sat down to enjoy the meal and discuss the colony.

"Mr. Krol," Catalyntje spoke up, "it took our ship close to four months to get here. Joris told me that your journey was longer. Did you meet with difficulties along the way?" Catalyntje asked.

"Yes, I thought you'd heard of our misfortunes. We were struck with a sickness of the worst kind, the plague. We kept our ship near Plymouth, hoping for a chance to heal. Eleven of our members died there, and twenty more were on the brink of death. Many didn't know if God's grace would bring us to this land," Krol admitted, slowly lifting a spoon of soup to his mouth.

"I am sad to hear you endured such tragedy. Did you stay well?" Catalyntje asked.

"Yes, I was healthy and helped those who were in need. But it was a difficult way to end our time on the ship. Once we landed, we had to remain on board for nearly a month to keep from bringing sickness to New Netherland. Then, just as we thought illness had left us, a few more passengers got sick, which kept us on board for another two weeks," he said. "At least we didn't travel on the *Mackerel*."

"I hadn't heard of their journey. Did they fall ill as well?" Joris asked with concern.

"No, they didn't have time for the plague. They left Texel at the end of April, and within two days, the Dunkirk pirates robbed them of their goods and stole their ship," Krol explained. Catalyntje didn't know what to say. She thought about how sick she'd been on their journey, but it seemed insignificant compared to plagues and pirates. To lighten the conversation, Joris asked, "What will those who arrived with you be doing here?"

"Six of them will be farmers in the settlement. The Company hopes to ease the burden for colonists like you who are trying to get started so the next ship they send will carry animals to help work the land," Krol added. "Before I left Amsterdam, I heard a report that this colony was doing well with the fur trade. The Company reported a returning cargo of 500 otter skins, 1,500 beaver pelts, and a few other parcels. It amounted to nearly 28,000 guilders."

"We have all been doing our part," Catalyntje said proudly.

*****

Krol's ship wasn't the only one to arrive that year. Two other vessels brought fifty more people, along with horses, hogs, cattle, and sheep. One even brought supplies to begin building a small dairy farm. Catalyntje was grateful for the supplies and animals which made their lives easier.

She was also interested in any news about family or friends she had left behind. She heard some men talking about her Uncle De La Grange's successful investments. Even though he didn't send a personal message to her, it was good to hear his name spoken.

*****

Fort Orange was built where the Mohawk and Mahican tribes lived, making it an ideal location for a fur trade between the colonists and the Natives. Once the Dutch settlers built their homes near the fort, these two tribes moved across the river from them. However, this new opportunity for trade caused some contention between the two tribes.

One evening, as Catalyntje and Joris finished stacking a pile of logs, they heard sharp cries from the woods. As they returned home, they noticed a soldier from the fort approaching them.

"Joris, I am sure you've heard the sounds from nearby this afternoon," the soldier replied.

"Yes, we have. We are going inside earlier tonight just to be safe," Joris answered.

"Well, there is no need to worry that harm will come to us. The fort sent out spies, who returned with word that the Mahicans were attacking the Mohawks. Their fighting occurs off and on, but lately, it has happened more often," the soldier reported.

"Thank you for letting us know about this," Joris nodded. He and Catalyntje clasped hands and headed toward their home.

*****

Taming the land required days filled with constant work, but Catalyntje still took time to get to know the other women in the colony. There weren't as many women as men, and most homes were far apart. But Catalyntje understood that women needed to be with women, so she tried to reach out to others whenever she could. Margot was one of her friends who lived the closest to her and Joris.

One sunny day, Catalyntje walked to the fort to borrow supplies for her garden. On her way there, she saw Margot also approaching the fort. She smiled and quickened her pace when she recognized Catalyntje.

"I am glad to see you this morning. How have you been?" Margot asked sincerely.

"I am well enough," Catalyntje answered. As the two talked, Margot proudly described the wood shelter she and her husband had built near their house. Then Catalyntje told Margot about her new, garden near their front door.

"Since we are talking about gardens," Margot said excitedly. "I have been carrying these around for a few weeks, hoping I would see you," she replied, reaching into her apron pocket and pulling out a cloth bag of seeds. "I saved these for you."

"Thank you," Catalyntje said excitedly as she opened the small cloth bag and poured some of the seeds into her palm. "What kind are these?"

"They are pinks, a type of flower," her friend answered.

"Flowers?" Catalyntje responded, "I have been so focused on having enough food that I did not think to grow flowers. What a delightful idea."

"I brought them from my garden in the Old World; they remind me of home," Margot replied wistfully.

"Thank you for sharing them. I look forward to the color they will add to my gardens," Catalyntje replied, tucking the bag into her apron pocket.

"I am glad you like them. How have you and Joris been?" Margot asked.

"Honestly, I have been quite tired and do not feel well. I know I have been working more than usual, but I think," Catalyntje paused. "I think I might be with child."

"I have been with child before," Margot responded softly.

"You have had a baby?" Catalyntje asked, a bit confused.

"My baby died within me after only a few months," Margot stammered sadly.

"Oh, Margot, I am sorry. I did not mean to bring up . . ." Catalyntje started.

"There is no need to apologize," Margot answered kindly. They continued discussing how Catalyntje felt, and Margot confirmed that she was probably expecting a baby.

As the two women approached the fort, they saw three soldiers in serious conversation. Naturally, Catalyntje was curious to know what they were talking about.

"My friend and I are here to borrow some tools for our gardens, but first, may I ask what you were talking about? Does it involve the fort?" Catalyntje inquired.

"No, but it does involve our friends across the ocean," the soldier answered. "I don't know if you've heard of the city called Utrecht," he replied solemnly. "We just got word that they have fallen on hard times. Scurvy and dysentery have crippled the entire area, and the plague has also visited them."

"Klaas!" Catalyntje exclaimed with surprise. "I know that place. My sister and I traveled through there on our way to Amsterdam. We met a delightful young boy, Klaas, with a goat named Pieter. I hope he was spared from the plague."

"I'm sure he is fine," Margot interjected quickly. "It would have spared many."

"I don't agree with you," the soldier responded. "Now, what tools can I get for the two of you?"

Catalyntje mindlessly took the tools from the soldier as a strong sense of grief overcame her. Klaas had been such a cheerful and helpful lad, and it pained her to think that disease could take him away from his dear Pieter. Then, Catalyntje began to think about her own situation. She was expecting her first child in a place far from the home she grew up in, and her family would probably never even know. No other woman from across the ocean had given birth in this place. Catalyntje would be the first, and there was no one to help her or the baby; she was suddenly paralyzed with fear.

*****

Catalyntje continued to visit Margot whenever she could, and as her abdomen grew, she hoped to ask her friend more questions. She felt exhausted and useless since she couldn't work as before. With her stomach in the way now, she moved awkwardly, which made Joris more protective of her. She spent many tired evenings sewing small clothes and tiny socks for their baby, which helped pass the time.

*****

After working outside with Joris for most of the day, Catalyntje came inside to rest her sore feet. She went to the bench near the wall, sat down, closed her eyes, and soon fell asleep. Suddenly, a sound at the door awoke her. She slowly opened the door, surprised to see Margot standing in the doorway. The two usually met near the fort but never at each other's homes.

"I'm glad to see you and hope you are well," Margot began. "I spoke with another woman here in the colony, Anne Marie, to see if she would help with the birth of your baby. I hope I haven't misspoken since I didn't ask you beforehand."

"I welcome your help and anyone else willing since I do not know how to give birth to a baby. I was young when I left my mama and have never helped with such things," Catalyntje admitted.

"Unfortunately, Anne Marie has never had a child either, but she did help her older sister once. That is all the experience I could find," Margot sighed.

"I suppose the three of us can figure out what to do," Catalyntje murmured nervously. After her friend left, she took the flower seeds off the shelf near the hearth. They would brighten up her garden and remind her that she had a friend who cared about her.

Sarah

Summer of 1625: 19 years old

It was a quiet morning as birds sang in the nearby trees, and the sun warmed the day. Catalyntje put some food into Joris's shoulder pack before leaving to work with some of their neighbors, who were helping him clear trees. As Catalyntje peered into the basket on the floor, she saw there were enough plums for Joris to share with the other men. As she bent down to add them to his pack, a sharp pain tore across her lower abdomen. Catalyntje froze and slowly lowered herself onto a nearby stool.

"Joris!" she called, her voice fearful. "Joris, I need you to go get Margot. I think our baby is coming."

Joris ran out the door, leaped on the horse, and galloped to Margot's house to get her help with Catalyntje and the baby. Once he returned, he sat with Catalyntje until Margot and Anne Marie arrived. Then, he quickly went outside to chop wood, hoping it would relieve some of his worry. There he spent the whole day, only stopping for a drink now and then, and before he knew it, night had replaced day. But he still had no word from within his home about Catalyntje or the baby. He felt a cool breeze rustle the nearby trees but didn't dare go inside. He leaned against the base of a towering tree and soon drifted into a fitful sleep.

His dreams flowed in and out of places he'd been and wove themselves between memories. He dreamt he was standing in Dam Square back in Amsterdam. He talked with people he knew there who wanted to trade for some of his cloth. As he spoke with them, someone in the distance began yelling his name so loudly that he couldn't hear what his friends were saying. A bit upset, he turned to see who was interrupting his conversations and suddenly realized that Anne Marie had been calling his name. He wasn't in Amsterdam talking to friends but was sleeping against a tree in the dark.

"Anne Marie, I am over here. Is Catalyntje alright? Has the baby come yet?" he called out. He searched the darkness until he saw the dim light from Anne Marie's lantern bobbing up and down. "I'm over here!" he hollered again, stumbling through the field towards the light.

"Catalyntje is doing wonderfully!" Anne Marie called out to reassure him. They reached each other, and Joris grabbed Anne Marie's arm.

"Catalyntje is well, you say?" he asked frantically.

"Yes, she is tired, but she is fine. Now go in and meet your new little daughter," Anne Marie said with a smile. He ran as fast as he could to the door of their home.

*****

Anne Marie fixed breakfast for everyone the following day, then cleaned up and returned home. Margot stayed to help Catalyntje and her new baby while Joris remained close and continually checked on them. Since Margot planned to stay the night, Joris gathered as many quilts as possible. Unfortunately, they didn't yet own a straw mattress, so he didn't have a comfortable place to offer her, but she graciously accepted the quilts.

That night, by the light of a lantern, Catalyntje and Joris spoke quietly so they wouldn't wake up Margot. As they talked, they chose Sarah as the name for their new baby.

"That was a brave thing you did, Catalyntje," Joris said, looking at her tired face in the flickering lantern light. "You are the first one to have a child here. No one knew what to do, and they helped the best they could. But it was you, my dear. You did this thing for us and gave us our dear baby Sarah," he said, leaning in and kissing Catalyntje's forehead.

*****

It had been nearly a week since Sarah was born, and it surprised Catalyntje how much she had already changed their world. Sarah took so much attention, making it impossible for Catalyntje to accomplish anything during the day. She remembered Jannetje, her kindness, cooking, and energy as she struggled with exhaustion. She wished her friend would show up at her doorstep, and they could talk to each other like they had on the ship long ago. Jannetje might even have a baby of her own by now.

Catalyntje thought about making a fresh loaf of bread and working in her garden. But she couldn't do any of that right now, which caused her to wonder if she could ever work like she used to. Her worries upset baby Sarah, who began to cry softly. As her small whimpers grew louder, Catalyntje became more frustrated. She didn't know how to be a mama, and no one around her could help. Suddenly, she burst into tears as she walked back and forth, trying to get Sarah back to sleep. As the baby's cries grew louder, Catalyntje continued to talk to her in a sing-song voice, trying to calm her, but nothing worked. Then her voice began singing a song she'd forgotten she knew:

Slaap, kindje, slaap
Daar buiten loopt een schaap
Een schaap met witte voetjes
Die drinkt zijn melk zo zoetjes
Melkje van de bonte koe
Kindje, doe je oogjes toe.

It was the song Catalyntje had learned when she helped Agnes's children. The Dutch words danced through the air as she sang them repeatedly until Sarah fell asleep. It seemed the song had soothed Catalyntje as much as it had Sarah.

Looking out the window, Catalyntje saw the pinks she had planted from Margot's seeds. They were just starting to bloom, and she smiled at the simple sight. With her smile came remembrances from her past. She remembered her bravery escaping to Amsterdam with Margriet and her courage in crossing the ocean to this land. With all Catalyntje had accomplished so far in her life, she felt she was probably brave enough to raise a child in the New World. She hadn't known what she was doing all those times before; she just did her best to figure out what needed to be done. She realized that Sarah's cries signaled a change in this isolated place. It was evidence that New Netherland wasn't merely a business deal but a home for her, Joris, and Sarah.

*****

Catalyntje was exhausted for the next several weeks. She and Joris worked during the humid summer months to prepare for the cold winter. The never ending, backbreaking work seemed impossible this season since having Sarah. This sweet baby had taken many hours from Catalyntje's days and nights, making it difficult to finish any tasks.

Early one morning, as the sun was still low in the sky, Catalyntje quietly stepped outside to see if her gardens needed water before the day grew too hot. Sarah had just been fed and was asleep inside, so Catalyntje worked quickly while she had both hands free. She carried a basket on her left arm and kept her right hand free to collect any vegetables that were ready to harvest. First, she went to the row of carrots and looked for the small, tender ones. As Catalyntje examined them, she saw the orange tops just above the soil. The sight reminded her of the market in Amsterdam when the sight of orange carrots had first captured her attention.

As she recalled that day, she realized she didn't know what was ahead of her. If someone told her she would travel across the ocean, she would have shaken her head and walked away from such an absurd idea. But here she was! She proudly picked more carrots, dusted them off on her apron, and ate them as she stood in her garden an ocean away from where she'd begun.

*****

Near the end of summer, word reached Fort Orange about the arrival of the ship Mr. Krol had told Catalyntje and Joris about—the one that would bring animals. The three vessels, *Het Paert*, *De Koe*, and *Het Schaep*, had sailed together to New Netherland. Six families and some freemen were also on the ships, so there were now about 200 people in the colony.

One afternoon, with Sarah on her back, Catalyntje walked through the field with Joris to the edge of the woodpile. Holding her hand, he asked, "We should go to the fort and see if anyone knows more about the three ships that have arrived?"

Catalyntje turned, "Yes, we could use the help of those animals," she replied as they reached the massive pile of logs. They loaded their small wagon with cut lengths and exhausted themselves before hauling the timber toward their house. The weight of the logs and the uneven ground made it nearly impossible to move. They took turns pushing and pulling the load; thoughts of the animals that had just crossed the ocean were at the front of their minds.

*****

As Catalyntje and Joris approached the fort, they saw Mertijn, the soldier who usually delivered the news. They always looked forward to his visits because he was always interested in seeing their work to improve their house and land.

"Mertijn, what news do you have about the three ships?" Joris asked, squinting in the bright sun.

"Both the people and the animals are living in places nearer to Manhattan than to our fort," he reported.

"How many animals did they bring?" Catalyntje asked, keeping pace with the two men.

"There were about 100 cattle, along with some mares and stallions," he replied.

"I cannot imagine such a chaotic journey," she added. "How would they do it?"

"Well, they separated the animals, one ship for the cows, one for the horses, and one for the sheep and hay. I've yet to hear stories of how they got the hay to the other ships," Mertijn laughed.

"With so many animals, how did they decide where to send them all?" Joris questioned.

"The Head Farmers each got four cows and four horses; the others will be sent to different places around the colony," the soldier answered.

*****

Often, when Catalyntje was alone with Sarah, her thoughts floated down the Noort River and into what she imagined to be Jannetje's house. She would love to talk to her, hear about the meals she was cooking, and let their little ones play together, grow up together, and become friends. There had been many challenges and successes, and Catalyntje wanted to celebrate these with her friend. But for now, she would have to treasure stories in her mind to share once their paths crossed again.

*****

Catalyntje had worked hard at the beginning of the summer, planting row after row of vegetables so they would have enough food. One cool morning after baby Sarah had been fed and seemed content, Catalyntje swaddled her tightly in a thin blanket, brought her outside into the garden, and laid her gently on a thick quilt in the shade of a small bush. Catalyntje worked quickly, filled her apron with beans, dumped them onto the blanket beside Sarah, and then filled it again. Next, she picked a dark green squash that had ripened. She had planted them the previous year, gathered, dried, and saved the seeds for the plants she was now harvesting.

It was late in the season, but Catalyntje knew she could get one more crop of peas before the snow began to fall. As she walked up and down the rows, she noticed a low sound in the distance, one she didn't recognize at first, but as it grew louder, she realized it was the sound of animals. As she peered around the corner of the house, she saw a man leading two tall horses toward her. She leaped over to where Sarah was asleep and picked her up. Then, she walked to the front of the house and waved at the approaching visitor. It was Mertijn from the fort.

"Catalyntje, how would you like extra help with that wood this afternoon? Where is Joris?" he asked. "Look at these strong and healthy animals, perfect for dragging logs. They have been working along the Noort River, and the director said it's our turn to use them. Joris is the first person I thought of to try them out."

"This is wonderful! We need help to get the wood to the house before the snow begins to fall. But, with sweet little Sarah, I am afraid I am not much help this season," Catalyntje admitted.

"No need to feel bad. You have a job to do there with that little one. Joris and I will have some fun with this," he replied with a smile as he spotted Joris in the distance.

"I'll head over to see him now," Mertijn said, walking towards Joris and waving his hat above his head. Catalyntje sat down beside the row of peas she had just planted. *The use of these animals would be the help we need*, she thought with a smile. She looked into Sarah's perfect little face and said quietly, "It will be alright, little one. We will take care of you, and you will be toasty warm this winter."

Danger

Summer of 1626: 20 years old

Catalyntje and Joris's lives finally calmed down. They made it through another winter in the New World with enough food and warmth to be comfortable. Finishing the house required them to work continually, but they wanted it to be perfect for Sarah. So, after nearly two years, it was finally a comfortable place. Many of their initial fears were behind them since they'd now experienced the weather, the food, the tribes, and the colony's isolation.

As Catalyntje played outside with Sarah, she suddenly heard unexpected shrieks in the distance. She quickly took Sarah inside. Before too long, the front door flew open, and Joris joined them. He'd been in the far field turning the soil and had returned to see that his little family was safe.

"What was all of that noise past the woods?" Catalyntje asked in a frightened tone.

"I don't know," answered Joris slowly. "I suggest we stay inside, and then later, I will go to the fort and see if they know what has happened." After some time, the noise quieted, so Joris went to the fort while it was still calm. When he arrived, he found at least a dozen other men assembled, all worried about the same thing.

"Gather around," the director of the fort ordered. The small crowd quieted, and he began to speak. "The two tribes in the area, the Mahicans and the Mohawks have been fighting. This has happened before, but we may be a bit to blame this time. Both tribes trade furs with us, which has caused some rivalry between them. They aren't bent on harming us; they each just want to be the favored tribe we trade with," he added. "We will keep our eyes on the situation and let you know of any possible danger."

Joris didn't stay long because he knew Catalyntje would be waiting for news.

*****

One morning, after a few days without any disturbances, Joris took Sarah to the field with him after she woke up from her nap. When she realized she would be going with Joris, Sarah jumped excitedly onto Joris' back and wrapped her tiny arms tightly around his neck. She loved the trees and constantly chattered about what she saw when she was out among them.

With the two of them gone, Catalyntje had a chance to sweep the floor and plant more in her garden. She hadn't kept up as planned and was worried about having enough food for the winter. Catalyntje hummed as she swept, then stepped outside carrying some beet seeds her neighbor had shared. The weather was perfect for them to grow.

Catalyntje turned the soil with a small metal shovel and chopped the pieces of dirt that stuck together. Next, she grabbed a thick stick from the side of the house and made rows just deep enough for the beet seeds. She got half of them planted when a sound in the distance made her stop; she held her breath as she listened. Catalyntje heard screams, painful screams, along with a chorus of angry voices. They seemed nearby and reminded her of what she and Joris had heard a few days before. Then she stiffened, remembering that Joris and Sarah were in the woods. She forgot the garden and dropped the remaining seeds on the ground. She lifted her skirt and quickly ran into the forest to find them.

As she neared the trees, unable to see clearly through her tears, Catalyntje heard another loud howl and noticed movement to her right. Blinking her eyes, she focused and recognized Joris running towards her with Sarah in his arms.

"Run to the house, Catalyntje!" Joris yelled without stopping. She stared at him but couldn't move. Then, she willed herself to turn around and run toward the house. When she reached the garden's edge, she turned to see that Joris and Sarah had almost caught up with her. She held the door open until they were safely inside.

"Joris, I was so scared. You and Sarah were out there and so far away," Catalyntje sobbed. "Were you hurt?"

"No, just frightened," Joris answered, holding her close. She could feel his body shaking from exhaustion and fear. "I heard a sound in the trees near us and then saw several Mohawks run about a wagon's length past us, so I picked up Sarah and started running before the shouts began."

"Joris, this is how I felt when I left my mama's house. We came here to be away from this worry," Catalyntje stammered.

"I know we did. The Mohawks aren't after us; they are fighting as they always do," he tried to reassure her.

"I know they are not trying to attack us, but something could still happen. If they are fighting nearby and an arrow went where it was not meant to go . . ." Catalyntje couldn't finish her thought.

It wasn't until later the next day that she got up the courage to go to her garden and gather the seeds she'd dropped. She put them in her apron pocket and went back inside. She would plant them another day.

*****

Troubles continued between the two tribes, and by late summer, the Mahicans had attacked the Mohawks again. This time, the Mahicans asked Daniel van Crieckenbeeck, who worked at Fort Orange, to fight with them. Until then, the colonists had not taken sides with either tribe.

Van Crieckenbeeck paid careful attention and realized the Mahicans had been wronged. Even though the Dutch West India Company had explicitly told the colonists to remain peaceful with the Natives, Van Crieckenbeeck felt he understood the situation better. He expected the Company would soon thank him for his brilliance in handling the problem.

Van Crieckenbeeck and six other men left Fort Orange with a small group of Mahicans to search for the Mohawks. As they cautiously stepped along the bank of the Beaverkill, one of his men heard a twig snap to their left. As he turned to look up the forested hill where the sound came from, a shower of arrows emerged from the trees, and the small group soon realized they had walked into an ambush. This surprise attack left them at a disadvantage, and before long, four men, including Van Crieckenbeeck, were lying dead on the forest floor.

Word traveled quickly about what had happened, and a sudden fear blanketed the area. Even though it was a sweltering day, Catalyntje kept Sarah inside with the front door tightly closed. While they waited, Joris went to the fort to find out what they needed to do to stay safe. As she waited, Catalyntje paced about, seemingly busy with tasks but accomplishing nothing.

Catalyntje gathered a few items as she paced, trying to pass the time. She knew she could pick up these things quickly if she needed to run into the tall trees with Sarah until Joris could find them. Endless scenarios filled Catalyntje's mind, and she tried to develop solutions for each one, no matter how unlikely they were to happen.

Joris had been gone most of the morning when suddenly Catalyntje heard a sound at the door. She gasped and crept swiftly to the far corner of the house near the back door. Holding Sarah tightly, Catalyntje remembered she hadn't grabbed any of the items she'd planned to take with her if she and Sarah had to escape. If she had to run, she was unprepared. The door opened suddenly, and Joris walked in. Catalyntje ran to him and nearly collapsed in his arms with relief.

"What has happened? Will we be safe?" she asked without pausing for an answer.

"Sit down, Catalyntje. I'll share with you what they told me at the fort. Van Crieckenbeeck is dead, along with three other men. They thought they knew better than the Company and set out with some of the Mahicans to fight against the Mohawks. When Van Criekenbeeck's group was about a mile from the Fort, the Mohawks met them with a barrage of arrows. One man swore he saw the Mohawks leave with a few human arms to prove they had won the ambush," Joris' voice trailed off as he watched Catalyntje's eyes fill with horror.

"Joris, we were supposed to be friends with the tribes. We were not to take sides. Why did Van Crieckenbeeck do this? He put us all at risk," Catalyntje replied through her tears.

"I don't know." Joris's answer was empty. "They have buried Van Crieckenbeeck and his men near where they fell. That is all they told me." Joris pulled Catalyntje and Sarah close to him, and no one spoke for a very long time. This terror was beyond anything they'd ever experienced.

All the commotion and gossip filled them with fear, and for the next week, Catalyntje was anxious to hear any new information about what had happened, but it took too much energy to worry about it all. Finally, she decided she didn't want to hear about it anymore and instead wanted to be left alone with Joris and Sarah, harvest her garden, and prepare for the winter.

So, she did just that: she gathered food from her garden, helped Joris cut and stack more wood, began making an extra blanket, and knitted a new little cap for Sarah. These projects helped her feel a sense of control and hope. It was early August, so Catalyntje also spent much time watering her gardens and harvesting winter squash. In addition, she worked on the mounds of corn she'd grown and harvested some to eat and some to dry for planting next spring.

As Catalyntje worked in her garden with Sarah, playing in the dirt beside her, she noticed two soldiers from the fort walking towards them. A sense of dread filled her heart, and she pretended she hadn't seen them to let Joris deal with the matter. As she watched through the corner of her eye, she saw them greet each other and talk briefly before one of the men started walking in her direction. *Why would Joris do this?* He knew she didn't want to hear more about the violence that had occurred. Then Joris called out Catalyntje's name, and she pretended to be surprised they were there.

"Well, hello; what brings you to our home today?" Catalyntje asked, rising to her feet and picking up Sarah.

"Catalyntje, this man said he would like to speak with us. It is about a matter that has come up," Joris uttered apprehensively.

"Yes, I have come to share some urgent news from the Company with both of you," the man said. "As you know, there has been some violence in this area. The first incident is over, but things haven't settled much. The Company is worried for the colonists' lives here near the fort," he replied.

"Have threats been made at us? We have only shown kindness and friendship to both tribes and have traded as the Company has asked. Who has threatened us?" Joris asked, taking a deep breath and facing the soldier.

"No one has threatened us, Joris. Not directly. But Director Minuit is worried for our safety, not violence from the tribes, but from being in the middle of their fighting. If we are in their way when they settle matters between themselves, we may be in danger," the soldier said.

"That makes sense," Joris replied calmly. "So, how do we keep from getting in the middle of their fights?"

"Minuit suggested that all the families and most of the men here at Fort Orange move south to New Amsterdam, where you landed when you first arrived. There is already a fort there, and they are expecting our arrival and will help us with winter preparations. We are in a dangerous place here and are too far away to get help quickly enough to save us," the soldier replied. Catalyntje could not believe his words, and her lips clenched tightly.

"When will this move happen?" Catalyntje asked a bit sarcastically. "I have spent the entire spring and summer working in my garden to prepare for winter. I have planted seeds that I have saved for this very purpose. Joris and I have spent countless hours in the hot sun cutting wood so we would have enough to keep our little Sarah warm during the winter. We have worn ourselves out while building this fine home, and it is where we want to raise our daughter. I have used every minute to make enough clothing to . . .," but the soldier's words ended her rant.

"Catalyntje," he interrupted, "we have all worked hard but must still move south. I'm certain you have many questions since this change is sudden. I will let you talk alone and return in a few days to discuss the details, but we will leave within a few weeks. We don't know when the two tribes will have another scuffle, and we must get everyone settled down south before autumn arrives. I'm sorry to bring you this news," he replied, tipping his hat as he left.

"I won't go!" stormed Catalyntje emphatically, "Joris, we have worked too hard to just leave our home. There is no way to pack enough to make it through the winter in a new home we have not seen. The plants must be harvested, and more seeds put into the ground for the fall," she paused, then continued, "I need you to take Sarah," Catalyntje snapped in a tight voice as she sat Sarah down by Joris, turned around quickly, and headed to her garden. Joris knew better than to follow her. He took Sarah and walked to the front of their little house. Joris sat on the ground, holding Sarah close and rocking her, trying to keep a smile on his face

.

New Amsterdam

The unexpected move south shortened the harvest Catalyntje had planned on. When she had planted seeds in the spring, she never imagined she wouldn't see them to fruition. She wouldn't even be able to gather seeds from many of her plants for next year's crop. Catalyntje hoped there'd be a place for her to have a garden in the southern part of the colony but was uncertain what the weather would be like there since they would be closer to water.

Catalyntje and Joris only had about three weeks to gather their hard-earned belongings and move to a new place. They wouldn't arrive in the spring, as they had at Fort Orange, but would reach the island's southern tip at the cusp of chilly autumn days. Where would they live? How would they get everything prepared in such a short amount of time with little Sarah? Catalyntje loved Sarah more than anything, but tasks took twice as long to accomplish with her.

The only thought that gave Catalyntje hope about this situation was being closer to her friend Jannetje. She hoped they would be close enough to share many stories and smiles. This hope was the one thing keeping Catalyntje from collapsing.

Finally, after constant days of work, Catalyntje and Joris had all their tools and supplies gathered. They had a wooden chest that Joris had made their first winter at Fort Orange. It was packed with extra clothes, towels, dishes, utensils, and bedding. Catalyntje carefully set the four glass plates from her uncle de la Grange between the clothes to keep them from breaking during the journey. Next, Catalyntje had a deep basket filled with the extra cold weather clothing she'd made-scarves, hats, mittens, and socks. In the center of the basket, she tucked away all the seeds she could save, each wrapped carefully in tiny pieces of cloth. A soldier from the fort brought them a second wooden chest to carry food in, but Catalyntje knew it wasn't large enough to store what the three of them would need for the winter.

*****

Between the preparations, Catalyntje worked on a gift she wanted to have finished before they left Fort Orange. She wanted to make something to give to Jannetje when they finally saw one another. Catalyntje was usually exhausted each evening and could hardly think of doing anything else. Still, the thought that she could surprise Jannetje with a gift was enough to give her one last burst of energy before falling asleep. Jannetje had always admired Catalyntje's handwork, so she worked to create a small bag for seeds - beautiful and practical. It had a drawstring top, with carefully stitched small purple flowers with yellow centers along its front side. She finished the project with her eyes strained under the dim candlelight; she couldn't wait to see Jannetje's face when she gave her the little bag filled with seeds from her garden.

*****

The day to travel south arrived too soon. Catalyntje, filled with worry about being ready, hadn't thought about what it would be like to leave their house. It was the first place she and Joris had called home. Weighed down with worry, she finished her work and realized this would soon only be a memory; she'd likely never return to this fair land.

"Can you take Sarah for a moment?" she asked Joris as the morning sun came through the window. "I want to take a quick walk before we board the boat."

"Of course, Sarah and I will walk around to make her sleepy before our journey, hopefully," he replied with a kind smile.

"Thank you," Catalyntje replied quietly and walked toward the area behind their home. As soon as she closed the door, her eyes filled with tears. She'd learned to love this place and didn't want to go. She'd learned about living and surviving here and much about herself. She loved her garden dearly and closed her eyes briefly as she reverently walked through it.

The place Catalyntje wanted to see one last time was the forest behind their land; those tall trees still held her attention. The path she and Joris cleared had been a place of comfort and peace, and Catalyntje didn't know if there would be another place like this at the next fort. She walked deep into the trees along the path, stopped, and stared at their noble tops. She held still and gazed up at them, trying to burn this image into her mind so that she could take it with her. Then, finally, she took a deep breath, blinked the tears from her eyes, and walked back towards her family- towards the next part of her life.

*****

Catalyntje hadn't expected to get onto a ship again this soon. As she and Joris carried little Sarah towards the sloop that awaited their arrival, memories flooded her mind about their previous voyage. The last time she'd sailed, it took at least two weeks before she could even stand up and look over the rails to enjoy the uniqueness of what she was experiencing. Seasickness had been her companion for the first part of that trip, and she hoped it wouldn't be the same this time. But this boat was much smaller, and even though the Noort River was tidal, the tossing and churning of the waves wouldn't be as intense as the journey across the ocean had been.

Catalyntje was nervous and kept a tight hold on Sarah because she had just begun to run. She loved moving quickly, but this newfound independence couldn't be allowed on the river. Only one other family was on the small sloop, along with a few soldiers. It didn't take long before the anchor lifted, and the sloop gently rose and fell on top of the water. The craft's movement felt familiar to Catalyntje, and now, with everything packed, she was excited about this new place. She had made peace with the idea that they would leave most of what they had worked for behind. They'd become exiles once again.

*****

Catalyntje hadn't remembered much about the river's voyage to Fort Orange when they first arrived in New Netherland. She had been too excited to reach their destination and hadn't taken time to enjoy the sights. But this time, she carefully observed every detail she could and realized it might be the only time she would see this all again. Catalyntje had recognized the need to appreciate experiences as they came because situations could change unexpectedly.

Sarah was fussy the first evening on the water and couldn't sleep. Maybe she was having some of the same problems Catalyntje had when she'd sailed on the ocean. Catalyntje sat down towards the front of the ship, a few feet from the edge, and watched the water gently glide along the side of the boat. Even though the night was warm, she wrapped Sarah in a blanket and held her close, rocking her back and forth to help soothe her to sleep. As the light left the sky, Catalyntje could no longer see the water's movement below and soon tuned her senses to the sound of the water instead. The gentle gliding noise of the water as it broke along the ship's sides calmed her thoughts; the sound reminded her of the rhythmic spinning of the windmill's fins in Amsterdam. She could hear Sarah's soft breathing, signaling her lapse into sleep, but she didn't hurry to lay her down. Instead, she allowed the cadenced sound of the rippling water to fill her soul with quiet contentment.

As they continued down the river the following day, Catalyntje noted the endless thick forests of trees on both sides of the water. The sight of smoke curling into the air also signaled the presence of tribal villages. Joris was the first to see the mountains in the distance, known as the Catskills. They rose solidly and added stability to the wildness of the area.

Catalyntje and Joris each took turns looking after Sarah, which allowed time to admire the picturesque surroundings as they drifted by. Early the second evening, Sarah fell asleep in Joris's arms as the three sat along the railings towards the front of the ship. Catalyntje noticed a sudden widening of the river, and then, to her right, a solid cliff rose magnificently upward. *How had she missed this the first time?* Just then, the captain walked by, "What is the name of that mountain?" Catalyntje asked.

"Why, that's Hook Mountain," he replied with a smile. "When we see that, we know we are almost to the bay — to New Amsterdam."

"We are getting close?" Catalyntje asked.

"Yes, we are. I'll let everyone know once we start to see the town," the captain replied confidently.

"Thank you," she said with a nod. "This has been a fine trip, but I am anxious to get to land and see where we are to live."

"I heard another ship arrived from Amsterdam about a week ago," the captain reported.

"Were there a lot of people?" Catalyntje asked. "Will they still have room for us?"

"Madam, there is so much space here that we will never fill it all up," the captain replied confidently and walked on.

Catalyntje's worries were not unfounded. When they reached New Amsterdam, it was in commotion. The Company had only recently found places to build houses for those who'd arrived from Amsterdam a few weeks earlier. These new arrivals had already gathered most of the shared food and supplies. The Company hoped that the settlers from Fort Orange would have most of their own supplies and food.

Once they landed, Catalyntje, Joris, and Sarah went to Fort Amsterdam, where they shared their concerns and reported what they had brought with them. After about a week, they chose a piece of land and started building another house. Catalyntje didn't want to be too far from the fort, so they selected a small lot to the southeast. More soldiers were here at Fort Amsterdam and helped the settlers from the north build their houses before the cold weather arrived.

Catalyntje took Sarah to the fort each day to get food to store for the winter. Getting to the fort was closer to their home than it had been up north but lumber to build with and burn was not. Getting wood required Joris to spend long hours riding on wagons with other men to bring it back to their home. As Catalyntje spent time outside with Sarah on sunny days, she noticed the coolness of the constant breeze from the nearby water. She was glad they would have some logs to burn when the weather got cold.

Catalyntje made it a point to get to know people when she was at the fort. She knew they would need to help each other through the winter, and since there hadn't been many others to rely on near Fort Orange, this comforted Catalyntje. She also began to ask about her friend Jannetje. Once she found her, they could spend time together, and the winter months would go by much more quickly.

*****

On Thursday morning, Catalyntje got Sarah ready and headed to the weekly market near the fort. The busyness of the market reminded Catalyntje of Amsterdam, and she enjoyed being there. She'd brought some seeds from the flowers Margot had given her and, knowing they were unique, hoped to trade something of use for them. Under a nearby tree, a woman and her husband sat by a small stack of round, green squash they were trading. Catalyntje knew the squash would last through the winter and painfully remembered she had left at least two dozen ripening in her garden up north. With this thought, she approached them for a trade.

She introduced herself and Sarah and told the merchants about their journey down the river as the couple listened with interest. Catalyntje also took out her seeds and described the beautiful pink blossoms they brought to an early summer garden.

"I would love to trade with you," Catalyntje suggested. "I enjoy this kind of squash; it makes a fine soup at the end of a long winter."

"Oh, you are right about that. A young woman about your age used to make the best soup I've ever tasted. She knew exactly which herbs to crush up with a mortar and pestle she'd brought from Amsterdam to make every spoon filled with flavor," the woman replied. The mention of the mortar and pestle caught Catalyntje's attention, and she stared at the woman.

"I might know her!" Catalyntje responded with excitement. "I have a dear friend who settled here when I settled up north. We traveled across the ocean together to get here. Jannetje is her name. Does she come here often?" Catalyntje asked, barely able to contain her excitement. The husband and wife looked at one another without saying a word.

"Oh, my dear girl, yes, it was sweet Jannetje, but I'm sorry, she didn't make it through the winter," the woman groaned as she walked towards Catalyntje. "She had a high fever with the chills, too, and she only lasted a few weeks before she was gone."

"I do not think I will be trading today. Thanks to you both, and have a good day," Catalyntje blurted. She heard the woman call after her as she walked blindly through the streets, with Sarah in her arms and tears blocking her sight. Catalyntje wandered through the crowded streets, then suddenly realized she was near the water. She saw a windmill near the fort to her right, slowly and methodically spinning around and around and around. She forced her breath to match the motion of the windmill to try to calm herself. Jannetje was gone. She was gone, and nothing could bring her back. Catalyntje would never see her again.

The only hope Catalyntje had when she packed up her home at Fort Orange was seeing Jannetje, but now she felt nothing but utter loneliness. *New Netherland is a cruel land. It has taken my friend and left me without hope.* Catalyntje finally gained her composure and realized Sarah had been fussing for a while. She gently rocked her, trying to calm her, then slowly returned to their partially built home.

Part 3: Pearl Street
Fall 1626 - 1636

A New Home

Fall of 1626: 20 years old

The end of the summer was different than Catalyntje and Joris had planned. They had lived in the New World for a few seasons and knew what to plant to keep them fed during the winter. However, the unexpected move from Fort Orange to New Amsterdam forced them to leave most of their crops behind. Joris had also spent much of his time finishing their one-room home and fixing it to make sure it would keep them warm during the winter. These efforts were also left behind up the Noort River.

It had been about a month since they left Fort Orange. They chose to build their house on Pearl Street, near the fort, but it still wasn't ready for winter. Catalyntje, Joris, and three hundred other colonists worked through the end of September to prepare as much as possible for the upcoming winter.

While Joris was away cutting firewood some days, Catalyntje used her time to organize and clean their new home. Once the sun warmed the afternoon air, she and Sarah enjoyed sitting on the front stoop. There, she stitched blankets, hats, and scarves while Sarah picked up little rocks and put them in rows.

One day, when Joris returned home from cutting wood, Catalyntje asked him to watch Sarah so she could go to the market. He sat on the floor and got Sarah's attention by rolling a rag ball in her direction. She squealed with excitement and immediately sat down to play with him.

Catalyntje took the small bag of wampum from the shelf near the hearth. When she made purchases at Fort Orange, she had traded beaver skins for what they needed. But here in New Amsterdam, she used wampum as currency. The Narragansett and Pequot tribes crafted the wampum from purple and white quahaug clam and periwinkle shells. They shaped them and drilled holes through them with a stone awl; then they polished and strung them on a hemp cord for use within their tribes and in the colony.

At the market, Catalyntje stopped for a minute to notice the variety of people who lived in New Netherland. They'd come from all over Europe and walked peacefully with the tribes who had lived there longer than anyone could remember. Since it was a sunny day, Catalyntje decided to walk home along the shore. She stopped and looked over the bay once she arrived at the water's edge. A large ship was near the shore; a few sloops were further out, and several Native canoes were floating nearby. She recalled the first time she'd seen a large ship when she and Margriet had passed through Antwerp. She distinctly remembered thinking how lucky the people who lived there were because they could watch ships come and go each day. Catalyntje smiled as she realized she was now one of those lucky ones.

Cold

Winter of 1626: 20 years old

The first snow came, signaling the beginning of cold weather, and Catalyntje and Joris were not yet prepared for it because of their move late in the summer. To deal with this, Catalyntje didn't add as many vegetables to their soup when she cooked, hoping this would help their food last. She was glad she'd used her time making winter clothes since she often kept the fire burning low to make the wood last longer. Each morning, Catalyntje dressed Sarah and herself in extra layers of clothing and then worked to keep her mind from the cold air that crept into their home. It was more frigid in New Amsterdam than at Fort Orange. There was more snow up north, but the air near the water cut through the walls of their unfinished house. On these cold days, Catalyntje often remembered walking upstairs to her room in Amsterdam, weighed down by the heated rock in her coat pockets.

She usually held Sarah close after rocking her to sleep for her nap. This kept both of them warm on ice-cold days. As the two of them rocked in the chair, Catalyntje often closed her eyes to listen to the wind outside; sometimes, she could hear waves splashing. As she listened, she pictured the windmill spinning in the fierce wind and imagined ships bobbing up and down at the water's edge. Then, her mind drifted across the ocean and back to the ship she and Joris had sailed on. She remembered laughter and friendship with Jannetje, as well as Amsterdam's full markets and tall, thin buildings. Sometimes, her thoughts remained there for a long time as she reveled in the abundance and hopefulness of that faraway place. It wasn't until Sarah moved abruptly that she was brought back to the starkness of their situation.

Every evening, Catalyntje was exhausted after working all day to keep her family warm and fed. Because of the constant work and worry, she didn't initially recognize the cause of the weariness. After a month, she finally realized some of her tiredness was because she was expecting another baby, probably in the spring. She wasn't as worried about having another child because New Amsterdam had more women living close by her. There still wasn't a midwife in the colony, so she would have to rely on her previous experience and the help of others.

*****

The winter days gave less sunlight and warmth to the world. Catalyntje had done her best to make the wood last, but they ran low once the new year came. Joris asked neighbors about getting more wood to keep his family warm, but there wasn't much extra to share. Since many colonists arrived in New Amsterdam at the end of the summer, most weren't ready for the bitter weather that descended on them. It was exhausting to be cold all of the time, and soon, Catalyntje and her family were relegated to sleeping fully clothed with extra socks, coats, and scarves. It was a cumbersome way to sleep, but at least they didn't wake up from the cold in the middle of the night.

Every morning, Catalyntje realized one problem with sleeping in most of her clothes was that she didn't have any more to put on once she got out of bed. She had to force herself out from beneath the quilts each morning, overwhelmed by the dread of being unbearably cold. The only thought that motivated her was that Sarah would need to be warm. As she continued this cold routine each day, she kept reminding herself that spring would eventually come.

Marretje

Spring of 1627: 21 years old

Catalyntje was right about the arrival of their new baby; in early March, a second daughter joined their family. Catalyntje and Joris named her Marretje Jorise. Sarah was now two years old and delighted with her new sister; she often sat on Catalyntje's lap when she held Marretje. She loved softly touching her little hand and smiling at her.

One morning in early summer, Catalyntje dressed her two girls, and the three of them headed to the fort to trade for some items they needed. The colony's market reminded her of Amsterdam's market but on a much smaller scale and without the option of frivolous purchases. Despite its size, she enjoyed the ever-changing displays, the noise, and the activity of the place. On the way, she stopped to watch the windmill and let Sarah run around. As she looked out on the waters, she was startled by a sudden boom of a distant cannon. Sarah screamed and ran to Catalyntje's side.

"It's alright, dear. That sound means a ship is coming to the harbor. Do you want to see it?" Catalyntje asked, and Sarah nodded, keeping her eyes focused on the water. Catalyntje put her arm around her daughter as they sat side by side, watching the great ship slowly reach the edge of the land.

"Watch for the people getting off the ship. They will be excited to walk on land again," Catalyntje said as she reminisced about how she felt when they landed in New Netherland. Before long, Marretje had fallen asleep while Catalyntje and Sarah continued to watch the sailors from the ship unload supplies. As Sarah chattered, Catalyntje realized that being in New Netherland was part of something significant. The massive ship in the harbor had brought supplies from a world away and delivered them to Catalyntje and others living in New Amsterdam. Next, the ship would be loaded with beaver pelts and sailed back to the Old World, where the Company would sell them. Catalyntje smiled as she thought of her small part in this worldwide venture.

The Taproom

Spring & Summer of 1628: 22 years old

It had been two years since Catalyntje and Joris moved south to New Amsterdam. Their clapboard house on Pearl Street was large enough for their growing family, and Joris worked on the docks, helping to load and unload supplies from across the ocean. Although Catalyntje and Joris were doing well, they discussed owning a taproom. Catalyntje could grow food in her gardens and was a skilled cook, and Joris could carry on a conversation with anyone. They hoped that, by combining their talents, a taproom would be the perfect option.

Catalyntje and Joris were eager to start work on this new idea. So, when spring arrived, they started building a small taproom on their property. It was in the back, near the southwest corner of the fort. They gathered lumber and built the small structure together. Then, they traded for dishes, cutlery, extra pans and kettles. The taproom mantle was made of stones they'd gathered near the water, and Joris built a small lean ti next to the building to store wood. Once it got cold again, they'd need a warm fire to keep the patrons happy. A few days before the taproom opened, Joris put the finishing touches on four small tables and several stools.

By late summer, the taproom was ready to open for business. On that day, Joris spent the entire time at the taproom while Catalyntje went back and forth between preparing food and serving patrons. One of their neighbors cared for Sarah and Marretje, which helped tremendously to make the first day successful. That night, after Catalyntje tucked the children into bed, she and Joris collapsed on the bench near their own fireplace; it had been a busy and wonderful first day.

Since the taproom was near the docks of New Netherland, plenty of people stopped by for rest and refreshments. As Catalyntje and Joris served meals, they spoke with sailors and passengers recently arriving at the colony. They both asked these patrons for news from the Old World, and Catalyntje always waited to receive letters or news from her sisters. Marie sent two letters about her family, and Margriet and Catalyntje's uncle also sent a short letter mentioning that one of his children might be coming to New Netherland. He also sent an apple tree with its roots wrapped in rough cloth and eight small clay cups, which surprisingly all arrived unbroken.

Catalyntje could only sign her mark when she left Amsterdam, but she already knew her numbers from going to the market with her mama in Hainaut. Recently, however, she had studied to read and write a few simple words, mainly those dealing with trade. She still needed friends to read letters from her family and then write back to them. Catalyntje also saved a bit of currency to pay for the delivery of these precious letters since most Old-World traders charged a small fee for delivering them. But there was no guarantee they would ever reach her family since these sailors focused on business and trade, not simple letters from ordinary folk. Catalyntje always asked about her mama in her letters, and she also sent news about herself, hoping her mama would receive it one day. Catalyntje hoped her mama had received word that she and Margriet had made it safely to Amsterdam and that she had married Joris. How she wished her mama could have met Joris.

*****

Owning the taproom required more water, so Joris built a wooden cistern to collect it for drinking, washing, and watering the gardens. It was about five feet long and had an open top, permitting it to fill with rainwater. This supply usually lasted until mid-summer, when they had to go to Collect Pond for more.

Collect Pond was about a mile north of Catalyntje and Joris' home. The Lenape tribe used it as a water source, but once the colony expanded, the tribe had to move to other areas to obtain water. Collect Pond was a beautiful place near the tallest hill in a small, lush area. Catalyntje and the children often went with Joris when he hauled water from there to fill their cistern. The water always tasted fresh and clean.

Joris thought it would be good to have some entertainment in the taproom so the patrons would stay longer and buy more drinks and food.

116

To help keep the visitors occupied, Joris made wooden game boards with pieces for simple games. Sarah enjoyed watching him work and loved lining up the small wooden pieces he'd made. He built two trick track boards rather quickly, but it took him an extra week to carve pieces for a chess set. Knucklebones was another game the patrons enjoyed, so Joris traded for some sheep's ankle bones to use as dice.

One of their regular taproom patrons was Jonas Michaelius, the first minister of the colony. One sunny day, Michaelius entered the taproom with a leather bag slung over his shoulder. He nodded at Joris and walked to the far corner of the room where a lone man was drinking. Joris watched them talk excitedly back and forth, and soon, Michaelius opened his satchel and took out a piece of parchment, a quill, and some ink. Then, Joris heard Michaelius clear his throat and begin reading to the man across from him, who listened intently and nodded occasionally.

Joris decided it was time to find out what they were discussing and walked over to the table with a newly filled pitcher.

"Can I fill your glasses today?" he offered.

"Why, of course," Michaelius answered. "Can you stay briefly and listen to a letter I am writing to the Company?"

"I would be happy to," Joris answered, placing the pitcher on the table and sitting down.

"I have observed the colony as the Company asked and want to report what I have seen here. I sent a letter describing the land, weather, plants, and rivers on the last ship that left here. I told them about the thick woods in this area, too," Michaelius replied. "I wrote about the tribes, how they live, hunt, and trade."

"It sounds like you have been thorough in your letters," Joris noted.

"Yes," the man seated at the table replied, "but he is concerned about this letter because he sees a few things that must change here in the colony and doesn't want to offend the Company."

"Let me listen to what you've written," Joris encouraged.

"It seems that all of you work your hardest but still can't provide enough for your families. I think the Company should give you more help, both in manpower and goods," Michaelius reported. "I've suggested how they could better help all of you."

The man seated at the table spoke up, "Michaelius plans to suggest to the Company that they recruit skilled farmers to settle just south of here, in the Zuid River area."

"You are all doing your best, and I don't mean any disrespect, but as I've shared meals with many colonists, I find the food 'scanty and poor.' And at times, it lacks flavor since there aren't as many fine spices here as in the Old World," Michaelius said, tilting his head.

"And then there is the worry of not even receiving the supplies," the other man with Michaelius added. "If a voyage ends in shipwreck, we could be without supplies for some time."

The taproom door opened, and an older man walked in. He looked around for someone to help him, and as Joris got up, he looked at Michaelius.

"I like your idea, and I think it is useful to suggest a solution to the problems you see," he reassured him as he greeted his newest customer.

*****

Two neighbors came to the taproom one summer evening just as Joris lit the lanterns. They had journeyed for most of the day and were hungry, so before returning home, they needed a place to have a meal and talk. "As they sat down, Joris brought a small loaf of rye bread with cheese and dried salmon to their table.

"Where have the two of you been today?" Joris asked.

"I am looking to get more land from the Tappan tribe over by the Noort River," the taller one said.

"How is that going, Hans?" Joris asked. "I know we've been told to offer a fair price to keep the peace here."

"Yes, we've kept that in mind. I brought Laurens with me; he is a first-class blacksmith, and it seems the Tappans like metal items," Hans answered.

"I made some kettles and hatchets for them, and they seemed agreeable with these trade items, but I worry it isn't enough," Laurens admitted.

"I've realized we think differently from the tribes in this area. For example, when we buy land from them, we claim it as our own. But it seems that when they sell us land, they think they are only sharing it with us," Joris said.

"Even though I gave the Natives the items they wanted in exchange for their land, I think I'll still need to let them hunt and fish and maybe even farm on parts of it to make the trade fair in their eyes," Hans said.

"I agree, and I think you'll need to keep paying them in goods as well," Joris added.

118

"I'm prepared to do that," Hans said with a nod.

The colonists quickly learned that the tribes in New Netherland were not simply a backdrop to the daily life of the colony. Instead, they were at center stage because this was their home. Catalyntje, Joris, and most other settlers treated them well, often even welcoming them into their homes. When Natives came to the settler's homes to trade, they usually enjoyed sharing goods and stories and sometimes sitting together for a meal.

*****

As the humid summer neared its end, Catalyntje and Joris' third child was born in their home on Pearl Street. The birth was uneventful, and there was still no midwife to help, but neighbors happily assisted. Catalyntje had decided, without hesitation, to name their new baby Jannetje in memory of her dear friend, whom she still missed terribly. She hoped her new daughter would grow up to be as full of kindness and love of life as her friend had been and that she'd also be an excellent cook.

Trijn

1630: 24 years old

Sarah, now five years old, was able to help Catalyntje with little Jannetje, who was only just learning to walk. Smitten with her newest little sister, Sarah took every chance to carry her around, feed her, and wrap her up in blankets. Jannetje had started to respond to Sarah's conversations, and Sarah was delighted by her little sisters' babblings. Marretje, left in the middle of things, often followed Sarah around the house, mimicking her and attempting to help. When Catalyntje spent time outside, her three little girls always stayed close to her, dancing and chattering.

*****

As Catalyntje pulled weeds in the bright sun, she paused to look at her garden. The girls were inside with Joris that afternoon, which gave her some time alone. After she planted two more rows of beets, the sun hid behind a cloud, and Catalyntje decided to walk along the water alone. When she reached the shoreline, she stared along the horizon where the sky and water meet, and there she saw a large ship.

While it neared the harbor, its cannon fired to signal they were ready to be boarded and have their cargo inspected. As Catalyntje watched, she could tell the people who worked on the ship from those who had just arrived. Those who came to stay in New Netherland did as she and Joris had done they seemed to be preparing to make this their new home. She paid particular attention to the ship's crew who had sailed it across the Atlantic's rough waters. She knew she would probably see many of these people later that night at the taproom, where they'd come to eat, drink, and talk about their travels.

Catalyntje watched as each of the passengers slowly lowered themselves down the rope ladder from the side of the ship, then clumsily drop into a smaller boat that rocked up and down beside the larger one. As each small vessel filled with people, it sailed to the shore, finally allowing the passengers to walk on solid ground. As Catalyntje watched the second boat reach land, she noticed a young couple with a little boy jumping up and down excitedly beside them. He looked to be about Sarah's age and seemed very interested in everything that was going on around him. Next, her focus shifted to a woman with them, who looked older than Catalyntje; she was holding a baby. As she watched, she realized the couple with the young boy and the woman carrying the baby were together. Possibly, the older woman was the grandmother to the young boy and the baby she was carrying. Catalyntje watched as the five went along the dock toward Fort Amsterdam.

*****

It had been a week since Catalyntje had seen the ship come into the harbor with supplies and colonists. She'd enjoyed the stories told by the men who visited the taproom as they narrated what life was like in Amsterdam. She loved life in New Netherland but still longed to hold onto what she knew and loved from the Old World. Catalyntje remembered her first months in Amsterdam, filled with chaos and wonder, as a place that had taken her in and helped her feel at peace during a difficult time. Unfortunately, as she listened to the men talk, there was no word from anyone she knew well in Amsterdam; she had to be satisfied with general news.

*****

A few days later, after Catalyntje had finished cleaning her dishes, she went outside to sweep the front stoop, surrounded by her three children, who jumped around as she worked. Then, she heard Sarah talking to someone and turned around to find her chatting with the little boy she'd seen coming off the ship the week before. His parents were behind him, holding the baby the older woman had carried when they got off the boat.

"Come now, Aalf. We must let these girls help their mama." The young boy scowled and looked away. His papa soon stepped in, grabbed the boy's arm, and apologized to Catalyntje for the disruption.

"Oh, it's quite alright," Catalyntje replied. "It looks like those two might be about the same age," she said, pointing to Sarah and Aalf.

She propped her broom up outside her house, quickly wiped her hands on her apron, and nodded to introduce herself, "My name is Catalyntje, and these are my three children, Sarah, Marretje, and Jannetje. My husband Joris and I live here and own a taproom. I think I saw you come from a ship recently."

The man stepped forward, "My name is Roelof Jansen, and this is my wife, Anneke. And you've already met Aalf," he replied with a laugh. "We came here from Sweden. We heard about this colony and hoped it would be a suitable place for us to settle."

"We are happy to have you here," Catalyntje said. "This place is not without its difficulties, but we find more success each day—with a lot of hard work."

"We hope to find it a good place, too. We came with my mother-in-law, Trijn Jonas. She practiced as a midwife in the Old World and thought she might have some skills that would be appreciated here in this isolated place," Roelof replied.

"Yes, she is needed here! We are all so busy with our own families that there is no guarantee we will have the help we need when our delivery time comes," Catalyntje responded thoughtfully.

"It sounds like we've chosen a good place then," Anneke remarked. "It is good to meet you, Catalyntje, and we appreciate your patience with Aalf. I think he didn't get to run around as much as he would have liked to on the voyage here."

"Please stop by any time. You are always welcome," Catalyntje offered with a smile as Aalf hugged Sarah and waved.

The following week, as Catalyntje was washing Jannetje's face after she had eaten her lunch, she heard a knock at the door and opened it to find Anneke standing on her front stoop.

"It is good to see you again," Catalyntje smiled.

"I am glad to find you home," Anneke said. "Would there be any way you could help my mother, Trijn, with the birth of a baby over on Broad Street? The woman is having twins. I know we have hardly met, and you have never met my mother, but she needs help and doesn't know people well enough to ask."

"Of course, I will help," Catalyntje answered, looking at her children.

"I can watch your children if you don't mind them coming to my house. My baby is still too young to be left very long, and our two oldest seem to be friends already," Anneke commented.

"That would be helpful," Catalyntje responded. "Can you help me gather their things?"

"Yes," Anneke replied, reaching down to pick up Jannetje. Within several minutes, the two women had the children ready to go. Catalyntje kissed them goodbye, gathered her things, and stopped at the taproom to tell Joris where she would be.

*****

When Catalyntje knocked at the door where she was to help, she heard a strong voice say, "Come in." She sat down her things and walked to the birthing chair where a woman sat, tightly gripping the handles at the side.

"Good afternoon; I am Catalyntje Trico, your daughter sent me," she said with a nod.

"Catalyntje Trico, I am happy to meet you. I suppose you have children of your own?" the kindly woman asked.

"Yes, I have three," she answered.

"Then you will be a great help to us today. Please get another kettle of water boiling. And thank you for coming," the woman paused. "My name is Trijn."

Catalyntje and Trijn worked through the night and were exhausted when the two babies were finally born early the next day. They were well, but their mama was overwhelmed because this was her first birth, and having two babies to care for was much more than she had planned for. Trijn helped her feed the babies while Catalyntje cleaned the room and cooked a batch of savory muffins. Then, as she finished stacking more wood by the fireplace, Trijn entered the room.

"I appreciate your help with this one. I don't know many folks here, and I don't know your situation but thank you for taking time from your family," Trijn replied sincerely.

"I would be happy to help again if needed," Catalyntje offered.

"I would welcome your help. And, if you ever want to visit at a less stressful time, you can stop by my home any time. I live near the fort at the end of Pearl Street," Trijn replied.

"Pearl Street?" Catalyntje asked with excitement. "We also live on Pearl Street, on the east side, facing the bay."

"Well, this is an interesting way to meet a neighbor," Trijn laughed. "I hope to see you soon."

*****

As Catalyntje gathered some beets from her garden, another light rain began to fall. It reminded her of the rain in the Netherlands, near the North Sea. It was rain that you couldn't see or hear, and it gradually engulfed you like a thin web, entirely covering your skin and clothes.

Catalyntje brought the basket of beets inside and prepared a piece of bread for herself and her children. As they ate, the rain slowed, and the sun shone brightly through the window. Catalyntje decided it would be an excellent time to visit Trijn and share some of her freshly picked beets. She gathered her children and put the beets into a fresh basket before they headed to Trijn's house along Pearl Street. When they reached the last clapboard house on the right side of the street, Catalyntje peered into the back part of the lot, where Trijn's house was, and saw her planting garlic.

"Trijn!" Catalyntje called out. "Is this a good time for my girls and I to visit?"

"Yes, I am so happy you came. I just baked some sweets your girls might want to try," Trijn offered as all three girls looked at her with a smile. They all went inside, and Trijn put freshly cooked *oliebollen* on a plate for everyone and invited them to join her outside. It was a beautiful summer day. Trijn and Catalyntje sat on a small bench beside a freshly planted tree and talked while the three girls chased each other nearby.

*****

Catalyntje and Joris worked hard that summer to get more items for their home. To do this, Catalyntje made extra hand-sewn items and gathered baskets of vegetables to trade for things they needed.

A few of Catalyntje's neighbors had purchased mirrors for their homes, but she had never had one. She imagined how much the girls would enjoy it. But before she traded for a mirror, she needed two chimney cloths, one for their home and another for the taproom. She wanted a chimney cloth to cover the blackened fireplace. Besides hiding the smoke-stained mantle, it would keep the smoke from filling their living space on cold days when the windows remained closed. Joris had already hung an unusually straight branch across the top of the mantel, which would be ideal for hanging the cloth.

Catalyntje also traded for more dishes for their home and the taproom. She had a few pieces of tinware she'd brought on the ship, some wooden plates and cups Joris made at Fort Orange, and more they had traded for when they first opened the taproom. This time, Catalyntje traded for redware dishes created from clay in nearby riverbeds.

Life in New Amsterdam

1632: 26 years old

Catalyntje's garden flourished again, and all her spring vegetables were nearly ready to harvest; rows of peas, lettuce, and spinach. She needed to take care of her garden before her day filled with chores, but the house felt cold, so she built up the fire before going outside to work. The outside air was crisp, but Catalyntje felt warm as the smoke from the fireplace drifted through the air, reminding her she had a warm place to return to when she finished outside.

Once she'd completed her work in the garden, Catalyntje swept the front stoop. Since the girls were with Joris, she rested on the bench in front of their home until she was interrupted by Marretje, who ran out of the front door.

"Mama, can we go see the boats? Papa said we could," she asked hopefully.

"It is a good day for a walk to the water. Go tell your papa we can all walk down there," Catalyntje instructed. Before long, they were all on their way down the street near the corner of the fort, where they could see the windmill and the water. Sarah counted the boats she saw but kept losing track as they floated in different directions. Marretje and Jannetje drew pictures in the dirt and threw rocks at the water.

*****

Life in the colony continued to improve for Catalyntje and Joris. One evening, Trijn offered to take the three girls so the two of them could work together in the taproom, cooking, cleaning, and serving guests. As Catalyntje dished up a big bowl of soup, she noticed Joris talking with Michaelius, the minister in town, so she quickly brought the soup out to the waiting guests, along with several spoons.

"You will be missed, Michaelius. You have done much good for the colony," Joris commented.

"Thank you. I sail back to Amsterdam in a few weeks," Michaelius paused. "I'm glad the Company listened to my idea to bring more farmers here. They are using the land upriver to build patroonships."

"What is a patroonship?" Catalyntje interrupted.

"It is a large parcel of farmland given to a patroon, but for them to receive it, they must bring at least fifty adults to cultivate that land for four years," Michaelius explained. "It will help give all of you a more stable food supply."

"That is a fine idea," Joris added.

"Yes, it is. But unfortunately, I also have some unhappy news to share," Michaelius changed to a serious tone. "Do you remember Mr. Vigne from your ocean voyage?"

"Yes, he and his wife were wonderful to Joris and me," Catalyntje answered.

"Well, I am afraid he has passed on. His wife and children are now alone in New Amsterdam," Michaelius said sadly.

"That is sad news. It seems there aren't many colonists left from that first ship," Joris responded thoughtfully. "I've heard of a few others who have died and some that have returned to Amsterdam."

"This is a harsh land, my friend, and I am sorry to bring such news," he apologized.

"No need for an apology. Please be safe on your trip back across the waters," Catalyntje said, turning to see a man waving his hand for service. She nodded and walked across the room to refill his glass.

The colony continued to grow, and with it, diversity increased. It took Catalyntje and Joris some work to understand the twenty different languages spoken in New Amsterdam. Not all were from the Old World; some spoke African dialects and many Native languages. However, the one language that was common among everyone was Dutch. So, if understanding faltered, nearly everyone in the colony could rely on speaking some Dutch.

*****

Trijn invited Catalyntje to go to the market with her at the end of the week. It had rained every day the week before, but now the clouds were gone, and the sun was high in the sky. This warm, sunny day would be one of the last before the winter weather arrived. Joris planned to take the girls with him that morning to prepare the taproom for the day. They enjoyed pushing in stools, sweeping, and stacking dishes. All three were old enough now that they were a big help.

Catalyntje set two pairs of mittens and an apron on the table. Then, she gathered the lettuce, carrots, and small onions she had collected the night before to bring to the market to trade. She placed them in her basket, put on her coat, and wrapped a scarf around her head and neck since the recent rain had chilled the air. Finally, she bent down, hugged each girl, and kissed Joris before stepping out the door and heading toward Trijn's house.

Catalyntje enjoyed looking at the gardens she passed, and neighbors greeted her as they cleaned their stoops. She had only passed three houses when she saw Trijn approach her, also carrying a basket of trade items. She quickened her pace and waved.

"I delivered another baby two nights ago, up north on Broad Street past the canal," Trijn announced. "They just moved here from up north by Fort Orange."

"That is a beautiful place. I so loved the trees there," Catalyntje said.

"The mother told me about that place and described how she loved it there too. Did you trade with the Natives much while you were there?" Trijn asked.

"We did, and I must admit, I was a bit nervous at first. Joris was wonderful about speaking with the men from the tribes, but it took me some time to warm up to the idea. They helped us in many ways, though," Catalyntje answered with a smile.

"The woman I helped said that trade with the tribes wasn't going well, which is part of why they moved here," Trijn said.

"That seems odd. When we lived there, the Natives always brought furs to trade. We did not move because of a lack of trade; we moved because the Mohawks and the Mahicans were fighting each other, and the Company did not want us to get caught in the middle of it all," Catalyntje responded.

"The Company wants this colony to do well, especially with trade, since they make money that way. I heard they sent Harmen van den Bogaert to look into the problem. He will spend the winter up north and come back with a report for the Company in the spring," Trijn noted.

"I hope he can help. It was a wonderful place for us to trade," Catalyntje said as they reached the market.

Growth in the Colony

1635: 29 years old

Three years had passed, and another hot and humid summer arrived, especially for Catalyntje, who was expecting their fourth child sometime in the middle of summer. Trijn planned to help with the birth and doted over Catalyntje, continually checking that she was comfortable and doing well. In addition, Anneke, Trijn's daughter, volunteered to watch Catalyntje's three children during the birth.

Before dawn one morning in early July, Joris showed up at Anneke's house with his three sleepy daughters. Then, he went directly to Trijn's house to tell her that it was time for their baby to be born. After that, he went straight to the taproom to keep himself busy while the women worked to get the new baby into the world.

It was eight o'clock that evening when the woman helping Trijn with the birth burst happily through the taproom door to tell Joris he had another daughter, Judith Jorise. He shouted this grand news to everyone in the room and announced drinks on the house for everyone there. Then he left his friend in charge and ran home to meet his new baby girl.

After the birth of Judith, Catalyntje stopped working at the taproom for a while because she had her hands full with three children and a new baby. Sarah, the oldest, was now ten years old and loved to be in charge. Marretje was two years younger than her and always followed Sarah, copying everything she did. Jannetje liked to play alone and was delighted to have a baby in the house. Catalyntje continued to work in her garden and cook, but she couldn't stand long without getting too tired. Harvesting her garden and preparing for the winter was now more problematic since she had a two-month-old baby. She knew they wouldn't have enough food for the winter if she didn't take the time to store it properly. Joris was usually more help, but he had taken over nearly all the tasks at the taproom while Catalyntje kept up with the children.

After about three months, Catalyntje returned to help at the taproom three or four days a week. Better weather brought more ships from Amsterdam and more patrons to the taproom, which increased the number of dishes to clean and food to prepare.

One morning, Catalyntje and Sarah prepared food for the taproom while Marretje played with Jannetje and little Judith. First, they baked four loaves of bread and three dozen *koekjes*. Then they sliced cheese Catalyntje had traded at the market the day before and gathered dried fish from the baskets hanging on the broad beams overhead. Next, Catalyntje picked carrots, turnips, and cucumbers from her garden, which Sarah washed. While Sarah finished cleaning the vegetables, Catalyntje carried buckets of water to her garden to keep the plants growing. As she walked toward the house, she noticed colorful flowers blooming on the edge of her garden. *I will set some of these on each table at the taproom to brighten the place up,* she thought, picking a few dozen of them.

Once the food and flowers were ready, Catalyntje and Sarah brought everything to the taproom, where Catalyntje stayed to help. She gathered a few tall cups, filled them with water and the flowers she'd picked, and set them at the center of the tables. As she finished, she heard someone call out, "Those flowers add a nice touch. Have you heard of the tulip sales in the Netherlands?"

Catalyntje turned and walked towards the man who had called out to her. He wore a light green shirt and sat with several other sailors who had recently arrived at the colony. "No, I have seen the tulips of Amsterdam but have not heard any news of selling them."

"You look like someone who would enjoy a good story about flowers," the man said, pointing to the flowers Catalyntje had just placed on his table. "Tulips are changing the lives of those who sell their bulbs in Amsterdam. Some families gain more wealth than they will need their whole lives in one day."

"They sell the bulbs even before they are out of the ground," the second man added. "The price continues to rise each season."

"They can even predict what color the flowers will be the next year. Some are ruffled or double-petaled, and those get the most money," the first man added. "One man died of a fever but left a basket of rare tulip bulbs to his children. Then, one afternoon, they sold them at an auction and gained enough wealth to last them the rest of their lives."

"One of the men deep in the tulip trade, Van Goyen, who has a good hand for painting. He often paints pictures to show his buyers what they will get the next season from the bulbs he sells," the second man reported.

"I would like to see some of those tulips. Will anyone be bringing them to our colony?" Catalyntje asked.

"I think they are too valuable to risk bringing them across uncertain waters," the first man answered. Catalyntje thanked the men, and as she prepared food and cleared tables for the next few hours, she imagined the unique colors of each tulip. Oh, how she wished she could have a few bulbs for her garden.

*****

Early one crisp fall morning, on market day, Catalyntje sent the three oldest girls to work with Joris at the taproom while she and Judith went to the market. On their way, she stopped at Trijn's house to bring her beans and squash from her garden. As she approached Trijn's stoop, Trijn called through the top of the Dutch door, "Come right in!"

"Good morning. I was on my way to the market and wanted to bring these to you first," Catalyntje replied, holding the vegetables to Trijn.

"It is good to see you this morning. I haven't had a birth to attend to for over a week, so I am well rested and enjoying this morning air," Trijn said, setting the vegetables on her table. "Do you want to sit for a while? My tree has a lot of shade this time of the morning."

"Of course, and I even brought a small blanket for Judith to sit on; she is always happy to be outside," Catalyntje said, laying the blanket on the ground. "Your tree has grown larger in the past few years, and I see you have added others, too."

"I planted some fruit trees on the side facing the fort. It gives me a break from everyone over there," Trijn responded.

"What is that bench for?" Catalyntje asked, pointing to one that was outside of Trijn's property.

"I had Roelof build it for people to sit on. I don't know everyone in this town, and I figure I have a fine tree that provides shade. When you sit on that bench, you have a perfect view of the water, the ships, and the windmill," Trijn said with a sigh. "I guess I just want people to be able to enjoy the beauty of this place."

"What a thoughtful idea. I might come and sit while you are helping with babies," Catalyntje admitted. "New Netherland has become rather busy, especially here, near the fort; it reminds me more and more of when I lived in Amsterdam."

"I have noticed that, too. Just last week, I delivered a baby to a couple, and the man wore a kippah; he was Jewish," Trijn reported. "I've also helped a few women from Africa, mostly free African women."

"I have also seen more Native traders on market days," Catalyntje said. "They bring items to trade just like the rest of us."

"You mentioned this place reminds you of Amsterdam. It is similar, but to me, it seems rougher," Trijn said.

"I think you are right," Catalyntje responded. "I've noticed that as I have watched the visitors that come to the taproom lately. Of course, we have the usual settlers and sailors, but lately, those who deal in piracy have come through our doors, and I am always a bit uneasy about them." She raised one eyebrow.

"With so many types of people, it is an unusual place. But when I go further north to help with births, I'm reminded that we are on the edge of the New World, kind of a lonely thought," Trijn said with a distant look in her eye.

Part 4: Troubled Times
1637-1646

The Wallabout

1637: 31 years old

As the colony grew, so did the number of people who visited the taproom. Catalyntje and Joris were glad to see more guests, hoping to increase their earnings so they could trade for more land. They enjoyed their home on Pearl Street but realized having more land could supply them with additional food and wood for their growing family. After searching the settlement for several months, Joris finally found some land he wanted to trade for. It was across the Oost River but would give them space to produce what their family needed.

After talking to the Natives for a few months, Joris finalized a trade agreement with the Canarsie for more than 300 acres of their land.

The vast Oost River flowed between their home on Pearl Street, and this newly acquired land. The Oost was a tidal river, so its waves were sometimes unpredictable, but owning a boat wasn't necessary. The colonists could use the services of Cornelius Dirckson, who ran a ferry back and forth across the river. He owned land on both sides, so anyone who wanted to cross would blow a horn that lay on the side of the river they were on, and Cornelius would meet them and row them across.

Catalyntje and her family frequently traveled on the ferry to work on their new land. Sometimes, they crossed with piles of cabbage and other times with several hogs. The heavier the weight of the ferry, the further it would lean from side to side as if trying to throw its passengers into the water. Sometimes, the waves lapped over the edges when it rode low in the water, soaking the bottom of Catalyntje's dress. Other times, dark clouds and strong winds created waves that rose high over the vessel's edge, keeping everyone focused on the other side of the river as if their intent looks had the power to bring them safely to it.

Catalyntje and Joris's new land was part of Wallabout Bay in Breukelen and named for its winding shores. None of the settlers built permanent homes there because of recent problems trading with the Canarsie tribe. These new problems between the settlers and the tribes had replaced friendship with mistrust.

During the first part of the summer, Catalyntje and Joris spent time wandering around their new land to see what it had to offer. Catalyntje selected a place that didn't have many trees that would need to be cleared, making it ideal for a garden much larger than the one behind their home on Pearl Street.

Catalyntje spent as much time as she could spare, working the dirt into soft soil that could grow seeds. After a month, it was ready to be planted. So, Catalyntje traveled alone to her garden and planted several rows of crops. It was time to plant more and see how the seeds she had already put into the ground were doing. This time, Catalyntje wanted some company and decided to take Marretje with her. She gathered her saved seeds from the shelf near the mantle and put them in a cloth bag. Then she tied the bag closed and pushed it deep into her apron pocket. Then, she and Marretje walked across New Amsterdam to board the ferry. They each carried a small hoe and a skin of water with them.

The weather was pleasant, so the ferry ride was uneventful. Once it reached the Breukelen side, where their new property was, Catalyntje paid Cornelius, and she and Marretje began walking to the garden. It took some time to get there, but once they reached the garden area, Marretje stopped.

"Mama, this is the biggest garden I've ever seen," she exclaimed, wiping the sweat from her forehead.

"It is, and I think there is no end to what we can grow here. Do you see the small rows already coming up?" Catalyntje asked, pointing to the tiny plants.

"I do. What are we planting today?" Marretje asked. "I can start making more rows."

"Today, we will plant differently. It's what I learned from the tribes up north when your papa and I lived near Fort Orange. They call these seeds the Three Sisters," she replied.

"That's a funny name; it's like our family before Judith was born," Marretje laughed.

Catalyntje smiled, "The Three Sisters are corn, beans, and squash. They are each planted together in mounds instead of rows. As the corn grows, it provides a place for the beans to climb, while the squash shades the ground, so the water stays with the plants longer."

"That makes sense," Marretje said.

It took Catalyntje and Marretje the rest of the morning to finish making fifteen dirt hills, each separated by about three feet. Then, at the center of each one, they planted and meticulously covered a few seeds of each of the Three Sisters.

"So, were the Mahicans and the Mohawks up north helpful?" Marretje asked as she worked beside her mama.

"Of course, they were very kind and always offered their help. They even freed us from a snowstorm that trapped us in our house," Catalyntje recalled.

"The snow trapped you inside?" Marretje asked, pausing to look at her mama. "Why didn't you ever tell me that story?"

"I am not sure," Catalyntje admitted.

"So, if they are so helpful, why are they fighting with the setters now?" Marretje asked.

"I have had the same question. When Papa and I lived near Fort Orange, there were more Mahicans and Mohawks than settlers. At first, I was quite fearful of them. But now that we are in New Amsterdam, there are more settlers than Natives. I wonder if they might feel fearful of being outnumbered?" Catalyntje asked with a distant look in her eye.

"If there are more settlers in New Amsterdam than people from the Munsee tribe, where did they go?" Marretje asked.

"I assume they are moving further west. They traded so much of their land to us that we have not left them much choice," Catalyntje responded.

"Maybe they are afraid now and fight because we took their place," Marretje added.

"You could be right, dear," Catalyntje answered.

By mid-afternoon, the two were back on the ferry. The wind was lazy, and the river was smooth as it crossed back to New Amsterdam.

*****

Summer progressed, and Catalyntje and Joris enjoyed the new resources from their land across the river. Catalyntje remembered the first cold winter they'd spent in New Amsterdam, and to her relief, the Wallabout, near

Breukelen, offered an endless supply of firewood. However, the river made it challenging to get the wood to their home on Pearl Street. Joris spent many hours cutting and splitting firewood on their newly acquired land. He left stacks of it and loaded it onto a wagon to get it to the ferry. Cornelius was always patient when there was wood to be loaded. The more carefully they stacked it, the less likely it would fall off the ferry once they were on the water. Joris waited for a day when the wind was calm, and the sky was clear to sail firewood across the river.

One humid morning in mid-July, when Joris stepped outside, the leaves on the trees were still, and the sky was completely blue. It would be a perfect day to ferry wood to their home on Pearl Street, and since it was early in the day, he could get three loads if he worked quickly. After breakfast, Joris walked to the ferry, which took him across the river to the Wallabout. Once he reached the other side, he rode a horse he'd borrowed from a neighbor a few miles to get to the stacks of previously cut wood and loaded his cart. Then he urged the horse forward, pulling the load to the ferry. He had transported enough timber shipments across the river to know precisely how much to put into the cart. He waved at Cornelius as he halted the horse, then walked to the ferry with a load of logs in his arms.

"It's a nice day to cross the river with a heavy load, my friend," Cornelius shouted to Joris, waving his hat in the air.

"Yes, it is, and I plan to make at least two more trips today," Joris responded, carefully piling the logs onto the ferry.

"That sounds like a good plan. I don't seem to have many other folks who want a ride today, so I will stay on your side of the river to save you time," Cornelius said with a smile.

"Thank you," Joris replied as he continued to load the logs. Cornelius put down his hoe and began helping Joris; as they worked, a slight breeze blew in from the river to cool them. Once they finished the task, Joris tied the horse to a nearby tree, fed him an apple from his pocket, and got on the ferry.

Once they left the shore, they realized the breeze had suddenly turned stiff. The river quickly became angry, covered with white waves, and the sky almost instantly turned gray.

"I certainly didn't see this coming," Cornelius said with concern, pointing to the darkening clouds.

"I didn't either," Joris replied, tightening the rope that held the wood. The wind increased, and rain began to fall from the sky in heavy droplets. Cornelius tried to control the sail and steer the ferry between the rising waves. Unfortunately, the waves grew steadily larger, throwing several pieces of wood into the water. Joris couldn't retrieve them.

Within a short period, Cornelius couldn't keep the ferry on a steady path, and Joris had abandoned holding onto the wood. He desperately hung onto the ferry with one hand while placing a foot on the pile of logs nearest him. They continued to juggle the situation as the ferry approached the dock.

"I think we are going to make it, Joris," Cornelius hollered over the sound of the wind, "Hold on to those . . ." but Cornelius was unable to finish his thought as the rope that connected to the ferry snapped, and the sail dipped into the river. The quick change in direction launched the remaining logs into the water. Everything happened so fast that there was no time for Joris to respond, and he watched in disbelief as the logs followed each other over the edge of the ferry. For an instant, they all disappeared, then rose to the surface and bobbed up and down on the waves.

Once Joris and Cornelius reached the other side of the river, they quickly jumped to the dock, pulled up the injured ferry, and tied it to a nearby tree. Joris looked at the logs he could still see bouncing up and down in the water and then turned to Cornelius.

"I am sorry about your ferry," he said, staring across the river.

"I didn't see the storm coming, my friend. Your wood is gone! I am sorry that . . .," but Cornelius couldn't finish his sentence as Joris interrupted him.

"You don't owe me an apology. You and I both know that sometimes the river has its own plans. I am glad we both made it safely to this side. Come to my taproom. You and I need to walk away from this for now," Joris said with a sad smile. Cornelius nodded as they turned towards New Amsterdam. Their stride was automatic as they silently walked, water dripping from their clothes.

Marretje and Sarah, now ten and twelve, helped with many chores. As the end of summer drew near, Catalyntje, who was close to having their fifth child, taught her daughters new skills to help her manage the household once the new baby arrived.

Although Catalyntje was uncomfortable, she still enjoyed her garden as a place to collect her thoughts while she dug through the soil. At the end of the summer, she sent Joris, Marretje, and Jannetje, who was now eight, to gather crops from the Wallabout since she didn't feel confident standing on the swaying ferry.

*****

Shortly after the winter squash began to ripen, Catalyntje gave birth to their fifth child and first son, Jan Jorizen. Again, Trijn offered friendship and support and even stayed a few days to help keep things in order. Sarah and Marretje also helped immensely, even without being asked.

After the birth of her child, Catalyntje didn't have as many visitors as she usually did. The increased animosity between the Wappinger tribe and the settlers seemed to keep people indoors more. Being separated like this was a challenge, and freedom to be with each other was not always an option.

Time at the Wallabout

Spring of 1638: 32 years old

It had been several years since Catalyntje and Joris had settled in New Amsterdam, and now they were preparing for their daughter Sarah's wedding. Hans Hansen Bergen had arrived from Norway about five years earlier as a ship carpenter in New Netherland. He spent his days near the water and evenings at the taproom, where he met Sarah.

Life in the colony required constant work, so when Sarah and Hans had looked for a companion, they knew they'd need someone to contribute to their home's economy together. The bride's family collected the required items, so Sarah and Hans could set up their own household. Catalyntje traded for many of these necessities, and Joris added to the preparations by building a sizeable and well-crafted kast. He had already made one for Catalyntje, and she'd filled its shelves with extra clothes, towels, and bedding. Sarah and Hans chose to get married in the spring. By then, the snow would have melted, and the rains would have slowed.

Catalyntje divided her days between caring for her five children, working at the taproom, and helping to prepare for Sarah's wedding. Her children ranged from one to thirteen years old, and the two youngest still needed constant care and supervision. As Catalyntje watched Sarah and Hans together, she could tell they enjoyed being together, but Sarah was only thirteen. How could she be prepared to be a wife and a mother in this faraway place? As Catalyntje thought about it, she realized that New Netherland was the only place Sarah had ever known.

Catalyntje knew she would miss Sarah after she set up a home with Hans since she'd always been good with the younger children and a great help at the taproom. Sarah was also often interested in what was happening outside of New Netherland. She enjoyed cleaning tables in the taproom so she could hear the latest news from other parts of the world. Even though Sarah had never seen these faraway places, the pictures she painted in her mind as she eavesdropped were fabulous. Sarah often told Catalyntje her magnificent stories, but soon, she wouldn't be there each day to share them anymore.

*****

Sarah and Hans's wedding was a simple affair. Three weeks before, they posted banns, their intent to marry, and the Domine came to Catalyntje and Joris' home to perform the ceremony. They had decorated the beams overhead with branches covered with fresh green leaves. Everyone stayed after the ceremony and enjoyed a delicious meal cooked by Catalyntje. Joris served ale from the taproom, and the candles burned long into the night with laughter and conversation.

*****

Catalyntje went to the northeastern part of town for some trading business one afternoon. She was glad to be out in the spring weather and looked forward to the walk home along the river and the bayfront, which wasn't a place she often went to, so she took her time and stopped by the river. Looking at the reflection of the trees in the water, she heard a rustle of leaves and noticed a small group from the Munsee tribe fishing nearby; she sat down at the water's edge to watch them. Each man had a woven net tied at his waist, and then, as Catalyntje watched, one young man untied a leather pouch that hung at his side, from which he retrieved a stone and tied it to the rope he held. She could see the stone had grooves carved into it, making it easy for the cord to stay tied around it. These grooved stones weighed the nets down to sink deeper into the river.

Next, the men threw the net into the water, and after several minutes, the young boy who'd carried the stones began to move about excitedly; he'd noticed the net filling up with fish. Then, four other men quickly grabbed the edges of the net, pulled it up, and tossed it onto the shore; it was a successful catch. Catalyntje only regretted that she didn't have bread with her to trade; fish would have tasted delicious for dinner. After the men put the fish in their baskets, Catalyntje picked up her own basket and continued home.

As she walked, she thought about the tribes in the area. As a group, they all shared their ideas, and no specific person made all the decisions like the Company did for the settlers. The tribes were also very generous to each

148

other and shared what they had, even giving away more than they kept sometimes. She also thought about their sense of beauty; they ate from pots they'd made from clay and decorated themselves. It reminded her of the beauty of the paintings and vases she had seen in Amsterdam years ago.

*****

Sarah offered to care for the children the following day so Catalyntje and Joris could spend time on their land at the Wallabout. The ferry ride was smooth, and the windless sky showed only a few clouds along the horizon. Once they reached the other side, they walked through the low trees along a path they'd worn from previous visits; the path's shape matched the water's edge. Before they stepped into the taller trees, they stopped and looked back at New Amsterdam.

"I like the view from here," Catalyntje commented. "I like watching the ships; I've always liked them since I first saw them with Margriet."

"Then this would be a nice place to build a bench. Let's gather some wood today; then you'll have a place to watch the ships," Joris said with a smile.

"I would love that," Catalyntje replied as they headed into the trees. They followed the path to the cleared garden area, where Catalyntje examined the seedlings grown from what she'd planted a few weeks earlier. Next, she and Joris continued through the woods along a small creek, enjoying the birds' songs overhead, until unexpectedly, Catalyntje tripped on a branch in the path.

"Are you alright?" Joris asked with concern.

"I am fine," she answered, trying to gather her dignity as she continued, but she halted after a few steps.

"I think a piece of that branch stuck in my shoe," she replied, leaning against a nearby tree and removing her shoe. She discovered a stick poking into one side and pulled it out.

"Are you sure that's it?" Joris asked, walking to where she was leaning against a tree, her hand resting on a smooth surface. She turned to examine the tree more closely and noticed a shape carved into its trunk. It was a long, straight line with a circle on top and three curved lines coming out from the straight line.

"What is this, Joris? Someone has been here," she said, somewhat startled.

"I've heard about these. It is a sign left by the Canarsie tribe to let others know that there is a grave nearby. They often bury their people near water because it symbolizes life," he replied.

"So, there are Canarsie people buried here?" Catalyntje asked reluctantly.

"Well, it was their land for a very long time. I don't know that they ever expected to trade it. I'd say we leave this part of the forest alone," Joris said. "I've seen Canarsie on the land a few times while working here. They traded it to us, but they still want to use it. I am fine with that, but not everyone thinks that way."

Catalyntje and Joris continued wandering around the area. As promised, Joris chose some pieces of wood to make Catalyntje's bench by the water. When they returned to the garden area, Catalyntje filled the baskets she'd brought with food.

"If we decide to move onto this land, I think this clearing would be a fine place to build our home. We would be close enough to the ferry, and your garden is already here," Joris said. Catalyntje stood up from her work, looked around the area, and smiled.

"I like that idea; this would be a wonderful place to settle down. I enjoy New Amsterdam, but I like the peace of this place," she agreed.

*****

Joris was frustrated. He had broken the blade on his favorite saw again and didn't have time to bring it across town for repair. Catalyntje had just returned from the market with fresh cheese and a bucket of shellfish. Before that, she'd spent the morning baking bread for her family and the patrons at the taproom. After she put the bread into baskets, she went to the taproom to help prepare it for the evening meal while Marretje stayed home and tended to the other children. Jannetje was already at the taproom helping Joris.

That afternoon, people filled the taproom, talking and enjoying delicious food. Catalyntje busied herself with the customers and always liked talking with the regulars who came in. She glanced at the door as it opened, and a young man who looked to be about twenty years old walked in. Since Catalyntje didn't recognize him, she walked over to see what he wanted to eat and drink. He had a pleasant smile, wanted to visit, and seemed like he was there alone. As they talked, Catalyntje discovered he had only recently come to New Netherland and started to work with a blacksmith in town. He was an apprentice, but Catalyntje soon realized he was willing to help Joris with his broken saw blade. What a lucky turn of events!

She sent for Jannetje, who had been cooking for most of the evening. When she reached the table, Catalyntje introduced her to the young man, Rem van der Beeck, and asked her to fetch her papa to come and meet him. Jannetje bowed her head towards the young man and left to find her papa. She looked forward to introducing Rem to him.

Kieft

Fall of 1638: 32 years old

As fall approached, Catalyntje and her family prepared for winter by setting aside food for the cold months as they'd done ever since they arrived in New Netherland. Catalyntje also spent her evenings knitting and sewing extra clothes for her family to use on colder days.

This particular fall brought speculation and excitement as a new leader came to New Amsterdam. In late September, a ship arrived carrying Willem Kieft, their fifth director. There had been much conversation at the taproom about him since he was new to the colony. Some were excited that he might have fresh ideas to help the colony succeed, but others believed he wouldn't know how to lead the settlement. Catalyntje heard he was a brilliant businessman but had no experience with governing people. She wasn't ready to make any judgments yet and hoped for the best.

*****

Kieft had only been in New Amsterdam briefly, and the colonists' attitude toward him was already unfavorable. Catalyntje heard constant discussions of how he demanded that the colony function in a certain way — his way. In addition, Kieft hadn't requested help from anyone living in New Netherland. After a few weeks of negative results, Catalyntje realized Kieft wouldn't be the leader she'd hoped for, and she watched as his overbearing attitude turned away the support of many of her neighbors and friends.

One afternoon, serving hot soup and cheese, she noticed David de Vries entering the taproom. He had come to the area before it was officially New

Netherland but had not met with success because of attacks from the Natives. Several years after Catalyntje and Joris arrived, De Vries returned to the colony and became involved in what was happening there. She tried to catch bits of conversations as De Vries met in the corner with a few other men from the settlement talking about Kieft.

"He is very authoritarian in his leadership," De Vries said. "And this makes the colonist oppose nearly everything he suggests."

"We have done well for ourselves so far. Kieft has never lived in a colony and doesn't know what it takes to succeed here," the man sitting near De Vries said.

"The Company suggested that he form a group of men to help with decisions, but he hasn't followed through with that," De Vries reminded the men sitting near him.

"He is obstinate; he won't listen to a word they'd say anyway," the man at the far side of the table blurted out.

"I agree with you; Kieft isn't the friendliest of fellows. He has already made enemies with the Swedes by the Delaware River and the English along the Connecticut waters," De Vries added. "And don't get me started on how he treats the Munsee tribe. Mark my words, Kieft will cause a great calamity here with his hostile attitude towards the Natives," De Vries said angrily, standing up from the table and pinching his lips tightly together.

Unfortunately, De Vries had been correct in his assumptions about Kieft. He was more concerned with himself than the colony he was supposed to lead. He took no advice and often surprised everyone with his proclamations, which were self-serving and detrimental to most aspects of the colony. Kieft did not understand equality. He looked down on the Wappinger and Lenape tribes, viewing them as a mere business opportunity.

Changing and Remembering

1639: 33 years old_

Catalyntje's life had changed a lot since she and Joris had traded for the land at the Wallabout. Besides the large garden, they also sowed an entire field of corn and wheat and had a few heads of cattle, horses, goats, and pigs grazing there. The marriage of their oldest daughter, Sarah, had been another adjustment. She was now a farmer's wife and had plenty of responsibilities of her own. And besides all of this, an underlying worry continued to build as Kieft changed life in the colony.

In the middle of this uncertainty, Catalyntje and Joris welcomed their sixth child, Jacob Jorizen. He was born near the end of May and christened at the Dutch Reformed Church a few days later. He was cheerful and easy to care for, so Catalyntje took him on errands because he was never fussy or needy. She appreciated his relaxed disposition, which helped her cope with the many new changes and responsibilities.

As Catalyntje and Joris' family grew and number, their little house on Pearl Street became more crowded. To help with this, Joris made more items to keep their belongings organized. After Jacob was born, Joris finished another kast and three new peg shelves. Catalyntje used the kast to keep clothes for the offseason and extra aprons, caps, and handkerchiefs. The family used the peg shelves to hang their everyday clothes on at night to air them out for the next day.

Recently, Catalyntje relied more heavily on her children for help. She'd always done all she could, but having a new baby and not having Sarah around was more than she could keep up with. Jannetje spent most of her time helping with the taproom. She was only ten years old but was good at cleaning, and she loved to help Catalyntje cook. Marretje also stepped up to fill the void Sarah left. She was always interested in patrons from other parts of the world and enjoyed listening to their conversations. She usually brought the taproom gossip home to Jannetje, who didn't understand most of what she was talking about, and honestly, Marretje didn't either, but it made her feel grown-up to share what she'd heard from the adults.

Late one afternoon, Catalyntje was at home with all the children. The younger ones played near the beds while Marretje and Jannetje helped prepare vegetables for dinner.

"Yesterday, I heard a man talking about being in the Dutch West India Company building in Amsterdam. He sounded important, so that's why he got to be in it," Marretje announced. "I think it is probably like our courthouse in the fort, except it's made of bricks."

"I don't think I've been in a brick building," Jannetje said.

"I didn't understand all he talked about, but I liked to listen and felt important that I was near someone who had been in such a grand place," Marretje said proudly.

Catalyntje smiled, "I have been in the Dutch West India Company building in Amsterdam," she said as both girls turned to her without saying a word. "It is not like our courthouse here in New Amsterdam; it is one of the finest places I have seen in my life," she admitted. "Most of it is at least three stories high, with some windows taller than our house and floors made with stone patterns that shine like water."

Marretje was still speechless, but Jannetje piped up and asked, "What did you do that made you important enough to be there, Mama?"

Catalyntje laughed, "I wanted to marry your papa and sail here to the New World. We met with a man dressed in fine robes who knew his letter well, and he wrote our names on a paper so we could get married."

Marretje looked at Catalyntje in disbelief, "Every day, I have been by someone who was in that building; it was you!" she said, pointing at Catalyntje. "Mama, where else have you been?"

"So many places, Marretje, places far away from New Netherland. They were part of my life long ago, but I am content to be here now," she said, hugging her two daughters.

*****

Besides eavesdropping at the taproom, Marretje had to understand how the patrons paid for their daily food and drinks. Visitors from across the ocean often paid with coins, which came in endless forms from the Old World. The town's regulars paid with *wampum*.

The Algonquin tribe made wampum, used as currency in New Netherland and beyond. Since this tribe lived near the coastlines, where the shells were, they were the bankers of the area and had been for years. They gathered white and purple shells from the coastal waters, then used their small hand drills to create a long hole through the center of each one. Once prepared, the wampum was strung on thin pieces of animal sinew to keep it together.

*****

Joris entered the dimly lit room through the door to find Catalyntje knitting a small cap.

"I'm glad you're safely home," she said, putting her knitting in the basket beside her chair.

"I spent some time talking to the man we met who lives over on Broad Street, the one that knows the Montfoorts," Joris replied. "He had bad news; Mrs. Montfoort, Jacqueline, died last night. She had a fever and chills for the past few days and didn't make it."

"That is dreadful. I remember Mrs. Montfoort's kindness and how she enjoyed reading on the ship. What will her family do?" Catalyntje asked.

"Her children are older now, and all but one is married," Joris answered.

"Many people with us on that first ship to New Netherland have died or moved back to the Old World," Catalyntje slowly replied. "It makes me feel lonely somehow."

*****

It was nearly December, so it was time to prepare for St. Nicholas Day. Catalyntje enjoyed this holiday in the Old World and shared it with her family each year in New Netherland. They had spent the past month making gifts for each other and trying to keep them a secret until the night Sinterklaas would visit. After finishing each creation, they carefully wrapped them in a piece of cloth tied up with string, then hid each one in a corner of the loft. Jannetje also worked to write poems to go along with her gifts.

157

Finally, the first week of December arrived, along with St. Nicholas Day. Jannetje, who was now ten, remembered the fun she'd had in years past and couldn't stop talking about it with her younger sisters. That morning, the three children gathered grass to leave for Sinterklaas's horse.

"Be sure to get enough," Jannetje instructed Marretje as they wandered around the space behind their house. "We don't want Sinterklaases' horses to be hungry."

"I put some in my apron pocket," Marretje replied, pulling out the grass as most of it fell to the ground.

"No, keep it here until we go inside. Mama won't let us go back out once it is dark," Jannetje warned. After some time, the two went inside to show what they had gathered.

"Do you think this will be enough for the horse?" Marretje asked.

"I think you have just the right amount," Catalyntje said. "You can put it beside the table." The two girls jumped up and down as they put their grass in a small pile by the table. "Now, get your shoes to sit by the grass you have gathered. That way, Sinterklaas can fill them with surprises," It would be hard to wait until morning to see what treasures Sinterklaas would leave for them.

When morning finally arrived, the children were not disappointed. Sinterklaas had filled everyone's shoe with cookies and gifts. The day was spent with cheerful voices by a warm fire.

Oma and Opa

1640: 34 years old

In July, Sarah and Hans had their first child, Annetje Hansen Bergen, and this meant that Catalyntje and Joris became Oma and Opa for the first time. Catalyntje had traveled with Trijn across the river to Flatbush for the delivery and stayed five days to help Sarah. Then, Joris and the other children took the ferry to meet the newest family member and attend her christening. During the service, Catalyntje held one-year-old Jacob close to her. She remembered the same ceremony for him, which hadn't been that long ago.

*****

Catalyntje and Joris' family continued to grow. In November, thirteen-year-old Marretje, their second daughter, married Michael van der Voort, an employee of the Company. The colony had also grown, with the population now reaching five hundred. With this increase, more settlers built houses, so there continued to be more patrons at the taproom.

Since Catalyntje now had a grandchild, she often wondered more about her own mama. She loved being a part of her grandchild's life and felt sad that her mama would probably never meet her grandchildren, at least those in the New World. She would have loved to play with them, teach them songs, and have them help in her garden. Sometimes, Catalyntje spoke aloud to her mama and hoped that somehow her words would travel over the ocean and across the land to the little cottage where she pictured her softly humming near the fire as she knitted a pair of mittens for the winter.

*****

Kieft's leadership continued to stir up trouble in the colony. His violence against the Munsee tribe brought retaliation from them and put the colonists in danger. Kieft only worried about himself and believed his proclamations would make him look good in the Company's eyes. But his decisions worried Catalyntje.

One day, as she cleared the tables at the taproom, Catalyntje overheard some men discussing an absurd new idea Kieft had proposed.

"He isn't showing much of a profit for the Company; I suppose he's trying to get money any way he can," a man in a dark hat replied. "He doesn't seem to care about how he gets it."

"He hasn't been here long enough to know what will even work, and he brushes away ideas other than his own. A poor method of leadership if you ask me," a thin man added.

"I agree with you there! He isn't cut out to be a leader," the first man added.

"His latest announcement has me worried. He's taxing the Lenape and the Munsee tribes," the lithe man said excitedly.

"What does he think they should be taxed for?" the first man asked with a scowl.

"He thinks it's their payment to the colony for protecting them, but I'm not certain what they are being protected from. They were here long before us and seem to do fine on their own," the man answered.

"I don't think the Munsee, or the Lenape will agree. I just don't see this going well," the man said, shaking his head.

A sickening sense of dread filled Catalyntje's mind. *Why would Kieft come and destroy everything they had worked so hard for?* She wished he would just return to the Netherlands and leave them alone, but she feared he might have already caused irreversible problems for their growing settlement.

Unfortunately, she was correct about Kieft. He got angry when the Munsee and the Lenape refused to pay taxes, and what made him more upset was that they wouldn't acknowledge his power in this territory. Since he hadn't bothered to build a relationship with them as the settlers had done, they ignored what he had to say. As a result, he tried to bully them into obedience. To do this, he gathered soldiers who worked for the Company and ordered them to attack the tribes. He wanted to teach them a lesson and let them know that he was in charge, that this was his land, and that they must obey him or suffer the consequences.

As word of these massacres reached the colonists, their disapproval of Kieft escalated. They wondered why he would march into their colony and destroy it. His violence against the Lenape now threatened to destroy New Netherland, putting the colonists in danger. The attacks on the tribe didn't change their attitude towards Kieft but only made matters worse, and they began to question why the Dutch had suddenly turned against them.

One morning, as Catalyntje carried the ashes from the fireplace, her frustration with Kieft became too much to handle. The month before, she had realized she was expecting again, which was good news, but she also feared what life would be like for this new little child in this now violent place. She took a short walk to free her mind from the sickening situation she was now living in. Catalyntje often went to Trijn's house, at the west end of her street, when she needed to think and refocus.

The tree that Trijn had planted along the edge of her property nearly a decade ago had grown into a splendid tree where anyone could sit in the shade of its sprawling limbs. A gentle breeze from the water moved the leaves overhead as Catalyntje sat breathing in the moist air. Behind the tree stood the solid and stable walls of Fort Amsterdam; stable, like Catalyntje hoped her life could be despite Kieft.

Tensions

1641: 35 years old

Grumblings from the community reached Kieft's ears, and he realized the settlers didn't like his one-sided decisions of dealing with the Lenape. He finally decided to form a council like the Company had suggested when he first arrived. This Council would include twelve men from New Amsterdam, Breukelen, and Pavonia, and Kieft claimed they would help him make decisions.

On a hot day near the end of summer, Joris sat outside fixing a bench near the front stoop of their home. He was startled when a soldier from the Company approached him and requested his presence at the fort. He promptly left and was gone for nearly an hour before returning home.

"What was that about?" Catalyntje asked as soon as Joris returned.

"I've been asked to serve on the Council of Twelve Men. With Kieft," Joris answered, "He said I knew many people here so that I would understand their thoughts about his decisions. Since I've been successful at our taproom, I suppose he sees me as a leader."

"I hope that will be good," Catalyntje responded. "Do you think he will listen to your counsel?"

"I don't know if he will. But I have some strong opinions about how he has treated our friends, the Lenape," Joris answered.

"I know you will speak your mind and share with Kieft what we are all worried about," Catalyntje said confidently.

"I want to be able to move things in a different direction here in the colony," Joris replied.

*****

Kieft had only a few followers who sang his praises. Most of the colonists nervously watched for what he might do next, and many were worried he was too bullheaded to listen to ideas from the Council of Twelve Men he had appointed. Joris found it was a delicate situation as he carefully balanced between keeping Kieft happy and improving the colony.

One of the first responsibilities of the Council was to suggest punishments for the Lenape accused of violence against the colony. This clash had resulted from the hostilities initiated by Kieft. As the Council discussed this matter with him, it became apparent to Joris that his opinions wouldn't align with Kieft's way of thinking. Joris had always enjoyed positive interactions with the tribes and wondered how he could ever be part of a decision that would alienate him from them.

Other colonists were also worried about Kieft's attitude toward the tribes. Many letters were sent from settlers in New Netherland to the Old World, focusing on the worry Kieft was causing them. Anneke's friend Maria wrote one such letter to her sister living in Amsterdam.

Dearest Sister,

We have had much distress in the colony of late, and I do not see an end. I have previously mentioned our new director, Willem Kieft, who is not leading the settlement well. He appointed twelve men to help him make decisions, but I feel it is all for show since he doesn't listen to their ideas.

He has unfairly taxed the Munsee and the Lenape and brought violence to their villages as a punishment for their non-payment. When they are in battle, it is a terrifying sight. Many colonists left their homes and went to Fort Amsterdam for protection, but all they could do was huddle fearfully in the corners, waiting for help from the soldiers. At the same time, the tribes killed cattle, pigs, and chickens and even destroyed some of the colonists' homes.

I fear to share the worst with you. We are fine for the moment, but brutality has visited many of us. Since the attacks, some women and children have been taken captive and not seen since. I heard this morning that five men were taken down with tomahawks by the tribes. They rightly call this the Kieft Indian War, for he is the cause of it all.

Pray for our safety, dear Grietje, and Godspeed,
With best love, your sister
Maria

164

*****

Life continued to move forward despite the horrors surrounding them. On the twentieth of March, Catalyntje and Joris had their seventh child, Catalyntje Jorise. Trijn helped with the birth and was always a positive constant for Catalyntje.

*****

Parents living in the colony tried to keep their fears about the situation they were all in from their younger children. But, this was no small task as the smell of smoke from burning farms filled the air most mornings and led to questions from the children. Additionally, it was difficult to explain the screams that pierced the air. There was also an influx of settlers living around the fort. Some came to the taproom for food but couldn't always pay because the Wappinger had destroyed their homes and crops. Sometimes, Sarah came to New Amsterdam from Flatbush and brought Catalyntje's son Jacob home for a few days to get him away from the violence. Sarah's daughter, Annetje, and Catalyntje's son, Jacob, were both two years old and always enjoyed playing together, so this was a good distraction for him.

A Small Joy

Summer of 1642: 36 years old

Life in New Netherland continued to be filled with anxiety and worry under Kieft's rule. Then, as summer arrived, Sarah struggled to feel well for another reason. She was expecting her second child near mid-summer, and the weather was scorching. Her husband, Hans, tried his best to ease her discomfort, but there was so much else he had to do to keep the crops growing with the lack of water that summer. Because of the heat, Sarah often stayed home with Annetje, who was nearly three years old now. She was full of energy, and Sarah had difficulty keeping up with her.

Once July came, Trijn often stopped by to check on Sarah. She wanted to be sure that, besides exhaustion, Sarah was doing alright. Catalyntje and Trijn usually went together, giving them time to talk.

One day, near the end of July, Sarah suddenly felt extreme pain in her abdomen and sent Hans and Annetje to get Trijn. When they reached Trijn's door, Hans' sharp knock startled her. She quickly set the dried herbs on the table and walked swiftly toward the door. When she opened it, she saw Hans standing there with Annetje in his arms.

"Sarah isn't doing well this morning and asked that I come and get you," he said in a matter-of-fact voice. "I am also stopping at Mama's house on my way back. I will meet you at our house."

"Let me get my things, and I'll be there shortly," Trijn responded, "Do you have cloth and water nearby?"

"Yes, we do. As soon as I arrive home, I will start heating the water. Sarah is in bed now. I told her to lie down and wait for our return," Hans reported as he quickly left the stoop.

Next, Hans and Annetje went to Catalyntje's house. As he entered holding Annetje, Catalyntje knew what was happening. Annetje jumped out of Hans' arms and ran to her, squealing, "Oma! Oma! I will stay with you!" Catalyntje hugged her tightly and kissed her cheek.

"Well, what a fun time this will be. You can help me wind the thread. I needed a helper today," Catalyntje said with a warm smile. Next, Jacob burst through the door and hugged Annetje tightly. The two instantly ran off to play and quickly forgot the thread winding.

"That was easy," Hans said with a sigh.

"How is Sarah?" Catalyntje asked in a concerned voice.

"She is in a lot of pain and asked me to fetch Trijn. I have already spoken to her; she will be at our house soon. Sarah was curled up in pain in bed when I left. I'm worried about her," Hans said.

"You are right to be worried. Having a baby is not an easy business, but it seems like you have taken good care of her," Catalyntje said, reaching over to hug Hans.

"Before you go, let me gather a few items to send with you for Trijn," Catalyntje requested, walking to the shelf near the fireplace. She took a small loaf of bread wrapped in beige-colored cloth along with a handful of little purple plums.

"Please give these to Trijn," she insisted, "She always takes care of others, but I worry that she does not look out for herself."

"I will do that, Mama. Thank you for taking Annetje. I will come for you when we know the baby is coming because you know Sarah wants you to be there," Hans replied.

"Of course, we will work out the details when I get word from you," Catalyntje said, placing her hand gently on his shoulder. "Tell Sarah she is in my thoughts."

"I will," Hans nodded and hurried out the door. His walk quickly became a run as he headed towards the ferry to get home.

Catalyntje waited for news of the birth of Sarah's new baby while Annetje and Jacob played together. Soon, Joris arrived home and asked about Sarah, but Catalyntje had nothing to report.

"You should gather the things you need and go help. Sarah wanted you to be there, and it would give me some time to play with this little mouse," Joris suggested as he playfully tickled Annetje.

"Opa!" Annetje squealed with delight and ran away, looking over her shoulder to be sure he was chasing her.

"That is a good plan," Catalyntje agreed quickly. "I will collect my things and return home, probably by tomorrow. What can I prepare for you before I leave?"

"Nothing at all. Just bring me home word of a sweet new grandchild," Joris said with a big smile.

"I will be happy to do that," Catalyntje replied. She picked up the basket by the table, went to the kast to get extra towels, and placed them in the basket. Next, she put on a fresh apron and took a small piece of cheese and some hard rolls. She also brought a blanket since she probably wouldn't return before nightfall. Finally, she bent down and squeezed Annetje tightly.

"Please take good care of Opa for me. Make sure that he does not stay up too late. You and Jacob have fun together, too," Catalyntje smiled.

"I will, Oma," Annetje said in a serious tone. Catalyntje gave Joris a firm hug. She never liked to leave him for very long.

"I will see you soon," she said softly to Joris, giving him her kindest smile. When she arrived at Sarah's home, it was early evening. Catalyntje opened the door without knocking and walked in to find Sarah and Trijn near the fire. Sarah was asleep on her side, facing the fireplace, and Trijn was sleeping nearby. When Trijn heard Catalyntje enter the house, she instantly sat up, blinking her eyes.

"How is Sarah, and how close is the baby to coming?" Catalyntje asked with an anxious whisper.

"I am afraid there will be no baby today," said Trijn, standing up and folding the small blanket that had covered her. "Sarah was in pain for a few hours, and then the travail ended. She is sleeping peacefully now and should be alright for at least another week. She will need to be careful not to do too much, though," Trijn instructed. "Thank you for coming. Come sit with me while I finish up here."

"I am glad you came to be with my Sarah. I brought some food to eat while you prepare to return to your own family," Catalyntje offered, unwrapping the rolls and cheese from the cloth. She set them on the table beside the book and pencil Trijn had placed there. Catalyntje got a small knife and began slicing the cheese into thin layers. Trijn opened her book and started writing in it.

"Why do you always write things down?" Catalyntje asked. "It seems there is nothing to write down today, especially since Sarah has not even had the baby yet."

"Keeping details is important to me," Trijn answered. "I can't remember everything that happens, so this helps to remind me who I have helped, what medicines I gave them, how long they were sick, and things like that," she added with a smile. "Sometimes, I just sit and read what I've written, then I see who I've helped, and it makes me feel like I've done some good in my life."

"It is nice that you do that, but there is always so much to get done, which I think would be more important than writing things down. I learned my numbers and use them to keep our taproom records, but I have never taken the time to learn many of my letters," Catalyntje said, glancing over her shoulder at Sarah. Trijn didn't reply but began writing as Catalyntje tiptoed over to Sarah. She bent over and gently kissed her on the forehead. "Rest well, sweet Sarah. I will stay here with you for the evening."

"Ah, Mama, thank you for coming," Sarah replied sleepily. "Trijn said the baby wouldn't be here today, though. There's no need to stay."

"I will stay. I have talked with Trijn, and she said you need to rest. Annetje is with your papa; you can enjoy a good night's sleep. I will prepare some food, but for now, drink a bit more and continue to rest," Catalyntje instructed as she lifted a cup to Sarah's mouth.

"Thank you, Mama," Sarah said as she slowly turned to her other side, groaning as she moved. Catalyntje walked back to Trijn and helped her tuck away her belongings for the journey home. Trijn planned to tell Hans about Sarah's progress so he would be home soon.

After Trijn left, Catalyntje tidied up the dishes and swept the front stoop. Then, she gathered fresh handfuls of lettuce and pulled beets from the garden for dinner. Next, she prepared the dirtied towels for cleaning the following day. It had been much hotter than she expected, and as the sun lowered in the sky, a light breeze moved the warm air. She opened the top of the door to let the draft come through and freshen the air in the house. Sitting on a bench beside Sarah, Catalyntje closed her eyes and thought about all she had done that day. She relaxed in the quiet room and fell asleep on the bench against the wall.

*****

Catalyntje carried an apron filled with slender green beans into her house and realized it had been a week since she'd left Sarah's home. She expected to return soon to help with the birth but busied herself with chores that needed to be done for now. As she separated the beans into two piles, one for her family and one for Sarah's, she heard a voice call through the opened top of her door. It was Trijn.

"Hurry along, Catalyntje. The baby is coming. Hans just came and asked that I go and help," she called out.

"I have my things ready and will catch up with you in a moment," Catalyntje answered as she quickly stepped outside to tell Joris she was off to greet their new grandchild. He dropped his shovel and ran to hug her.

170

"Safe home, Catalyntje," he said, kissing her cheek. She smiled at him, hefted her basket of items, and lifted her skirt to run faster and catch up with Trijn.

*****

Once Catalyntje and Trijn arrived, everything happened quickly, and soon, the tiny cry of a newborn filled the humid room. Baby Breckje had entered the world. Catalyntje peered down at her tiny features, which reminded her of when she first saw Sarah's petite hands; it didn't seem that long ago. Breckje wiggled, and her quiet cry signaled that she needed food. Catalyntje kissed her forehead lightly and gently handed her back to Sarah.

"I am proud of you, Sarah," Catalyntje said, walking to the small table where Trijn sat.

"Thank you for your help, Trijn," Catalyntje said, watching Trijn rummage through her satchel for supplies. Once she found them, she set her pen, ink, and worn notebook on the table.

"You are most welcome," Trijn answered with a smile. "Helping babies into the world is one of my favorite things," she said as she carefully removed the lid from the ink bottle, dipped in her pen, and began to write. Catalyntje watched Trijn's pen glide on the paper and noticed the writing left a fainter trail as it slid across the page. When that happened, Trijn dipped the pen back into the ink and then back to the page for more writing. Once she finished, she blew on the page to help dry the ink before closing it.

"Could you read me what you wrote about Sarah and Breckje today?" Catalyntje asked in a curious voice.

"Why, of course!" Trijn replied with a smile. She began:

July 27 at Mr Bergens
A hot morning. I was called the 10th hour morn to Mrs bergen who was in travail for the second time this month. I walkt there with her Moether Catalyntje wo helpt. Birth Breckje Hansen Bergen daughter.

Once Trijn had finished reading, Catalyntje sat quietly and looked out the window before speaking. "You wrote about me," she said in surprise.

"Of course I did; you were a part of this," Trijn said, putting her writing supplies into her satchel. Catalyntje said nothing but couldn't stop thinking she was in Trijn's book. Because of that, someone might see her name there one day, think about her, and know she was there to help Sarah bring a new baby into the world on a hot summer day.

*****

The day after Breckje's christening, Catalyntje went out to her garden early in the morning because the heat and humidity were already overpowering. She carried water to the squash and pumpkins that grew rampant in the hot weather; after that, she was overheated and tired. She sat for a minute and thought about her life. She was thirty-six years old and had a wonderful husband, and together, they owned a successful business. She had seven children, two of which were married, and she now had two grandchildren. Catalyntje had taken a risk by coming to New Netherland, but her family had grown and been happy here despite their challenges.

Continued Troubles

Fall of 1642: 36 years old

New Netherland wasn't the only place burdened with conflict. The pilgrims in the neighboring colony of Massachusetts had colonists who didn't follow the pilgrims' strict religious ideals. Because of these differences in belief, the leaders banished them. The one place that welcomed the outcasts was New Netherland.

In New Amsterdam, the violence continued between the colonists and Natives. Sometimes, when things calmed down briefly, Catalyntje took advantage of the peaceful situation to run errands. One of these seemingly quiet mornings, she left her children at home with Joris so she could return quickly if a problem arose.

As she approached the market, she saw Johanna, a friend who lived a few streets away. They hadn't seen each other for some time because of the fighting between the Lenape and the settlers.

"Johanna," Catalyntje called, approaching her friend.

"It is good to see you," Johanna replied. "How has your family been? Are they all well?"

"We are all well. Sarah had another baby, and we will visit her when it is peaceful again," Catalyntje answered.

"I just had another son and am doing well, but I needed supplies from the market, so I left him with my husband to get what we needed and be home quickly," she said.

"I did the same thing. Our town has become unpredictable, and I do not much like that," Catalyntje replied.

"But even with our problems, more people are coming to our settlement. Just the other day, a pilgrim woman, Anna Hutchinson, moved here because her people wouldn't accept her religious ideas," Johanna reported. "She brought nearly fourteen people with her."

"I had not heard of that. Where is the family living?" Catalyntje asked.

"They are just north of New Amsterdam. They have permission from Kieft to be in that area," Johanna answered. "She is aware that we have a war here in our settlement, but she is religious and believes that God will protect her during these unsettled times."

"Did she trade the Lenape for her land?" Catalyntje offered.

"I don't think she did. She is relying on Kieft's permission to be sufficient, and she doesn't think she needs to talk with the Natives," Johanna said sadly.

"That is not good news. I do not mind her being here, but I wish she would work with the tribe because it will only add to their anger against us," Catalyntje responded.

The two women continued to visit as they approached the market, then parted ways to quickly and safely complete their errands.

Another Wedding

Winter of 1642: 36 years old

With the arrival of winter, Catalyntje and her family stayed inside their clapboard house more than usual. It was a comfortable place since they'd lived there for several years. Smooth, hand-planed beams across the ceiling held baskets filled with dried food in the main room. Along the far wall was a fireplace with a tiled backdrop, without jambs or sides. A large hood hung over the fireplace to catch the smoke and send it up the chimney. Along the other wall was a built-in box bed, a warm place to be on a cold night. A narrow cased-in stairway led to a small loft above the main dwelling. Near the center hung the children's rope beds, made from wood slats hanging from the ceiling with rope. Each had a mattress made of a sack stuffed with hay. In the loft's corner were baskets full of nuts, bags of dried beans and apples, broom corn, seeds to plant at the Wallabout, and candle molds.

Before the year ended, Catalyntje and Joris' third child, Jannetje, married Rem van der Beeck. The joyous event occurred at church on December 21st; Jannetje was thirteen years old, and Rem was twenty-three. He was a hard worker and self-employed as a blacksmith and a farmer. Catalyntje still remembered the first day their family met him when he'd offered to fix Joris' broken saw blade. Rem always did quality work, was polite to the family, and never expected anything extra. He had enjoyed the companionship of their family, and now he had become part of it.

Unspeakable Horrors

Late Winter/Early Spring of 1643: 37 years old

Fear crept through the streets of New Amsterdam as hostilities between the settlers and the Lenape grew. Catalyntje was expecting again for the eighth time, and their baby would arrive near the end of June. Her friend, Trijn, the midwife, checked on her often, and Catalyntje always welcomed her visits. She felt well enough during this pregnancy and knew what to expect since she had already had seven babies, but she felt exhausted. Part of her fatigue came from being nearly forty years old, and the other part from the instability of having Kieft in charge of the colony.

Being a member of the Council of Twelve Men, Joris spent long hours debating with Kieft about what should be done with the growing contentions in the colony. The Council vehemently fought against Kieft on his continued desire to retaliate against the Munsee and the Lenape tribes, but he couldn't be reasoned with. The Council suggested treaties and talks, but Kieft wanted to show his power with violence instead. By February, he had taken action in direct opposition to what The Council suggested and ordered a retaliatory attack on the Lenape, Wappinger, and Munsee. He then dissolved the Council of Twelve Men and forbade them from meeting without his permission, fearing they would gather colonists against him.

Kieft's attack on the tribes quickly led to more fighting against the settlers, and soon, there weren't many safe areas in New Amsterdam. The families living there usually filled the streets with hard work, trade, and cooperation, but now it was overshadowed by threats and an uncertain future. As the fighting escalated, New Amsterdam began to shut down. Businesses were afraid to stay open for fear of attacks, and people stayed in their homes to be safe and close to their families. Staying alive and out of harm's way quickly became the focus of each day.

Joris and the other colonists had previously experienced positive interactions with the Lenape, and it pained them to see such anger hurled at those who had been his friends. Joris remembered the kindnesses of the Mohawks when he and Catalyntje first came to the New World. He also recalled that they had shared their knowledge of the land and seasons to help him and Catalyntje when they arrived in New Netherland.

Everything changed rapidly once Kieft decided to exact vengeance upon the Lenape. Additionally, the Munsee tribe now faced two foes, Kieft and the Machicans. By the end of February, hundreds of frightened Munsee Natives flooded New Amsterdam, seeking safety from the attacking Machicans. When they arrived, they'd traveled many miles through the deep February snow in freezing temperatures to reach safety.

Once there, the colonists set up encampments for the Munsee to obtain food and shelter. They showed humanity and care, and the Munsee were relieved to find safety until Kieft had other ideas.

When he saw the kindness shown to the Munsee, Kieft recognized he wasn't the one receiving thanks, so he gathered what few allies he could and, in early March, ordered another attack on two Munsee camps. He decided this would happen at midnight when everyone was asleep to ensure success. What followed was beyond description, as the still night air was suddenly sliced with the Munsee's shrieks, announcing the violence that came to them by Kieft's command. Cries of terror filled the crisp night as men, women, and children were assaulted and murdered without warning.

A member of the disbanded Council of Twelve Men, David de Vries, crept out of his house to see how he could assist the Munsee. As he ran towards Fort Amsterdam, he recognized their leader, Penhawitz, waving a white flag, showing his willingness to stop the mayhem and find a suitable solution. But Kieft would have nothing to do with him, so De Vries secretly went to Penhawitz and planned a meeting to find a peaceful resolution; they agreed to talk the next day.

Throughout the dark hours of that night, screams and cries filled the air. The colonists weren't aware of Kieft's planned attack as they huddled together in the dark corners of their homes, anxiously awaiting the sunrise and, hopefully, news about what had happened. When the first dim light of the day pierced their covered windows, they cautiously peered out one by one. Once a father or a mother stepped outside, they quickly closed the door behind them to keep their children inside and away from any horrifying sights that might fill the streets in front of their homes. It soon became evident that there were two groups in New Netherland: those who wanted to share Kieft's power and the colonists who wished for a peaceful place for their families to live.

As the sun lit the sky, horrifying news traveled throughout New Amsterdam that more than one hundred Munsee were mutilated and slaughtered that night, with many of their bodies being thrown into the water or burned. Men of the colony kept the curtains of their homes pulled tight over the windows, and women kept their children inside, away from the sight of Kieft's haughty soldiers proudly carrying Munsee heads through the streets to the fort where they received praise from Kieft.

David de Vries stopped by Joris' home early that afternoon, and together, they went to the taproom to secretly discuss matters with a few other members of the disbanded Council. At their meeting, De Vries described the horrors he'd seen the night before, and then the small group made hushed plans to oppose Kieft.

Later that evening, De Vries went to the Munsee village to meet Penhawitz as promised. The tribe welcomed him, and after much discussion, both parties agreed to remain partners and continue friendly terms. They gave De Vries a large amount of wampum to show their acceptance. He quickly returned to Fort Amsterdam to discuss what had happened with Kieft, hoping to devise a peaceful plan. But when he reached the fort, he realized he was too late. While De Vries talked with the Munsee, Kieft planned to exterminate them.

Kieft's continued attacks on the tribe resulted in raids and counter attacks against the entire colony. Because of this violence, the Munsee planned to attack the colonists and take captives to exact revenge.

Because of this, Catalyntje and her family's lives changed drastically. They no longer kept their taproom open and only used it to hold secret meetings against Kieft. Catalyntje wouldn't allow her children to play outside. Instead, they had to be inside, away from the windows and doors, playing quietly so Catalyntje could hear any sign of danger that might unexpectedly come to them. She and Joris had enough food, wood, and supplies, but they continually worried about what might happen on the other side of their front door.

Catalyntje constantly worried about Sarah and her family because they were too far away for her to check on them. She could only hope they had what they needed and were out of harm's way.

Catalyntje still needed to keep her family fed, so she cautiously brought her children outside to work in the garden behind the house on days when everything was silent. She needed help to work quickly, and they enjoyed the fresh air. She was close to the delivery of their next child, so carrying buckets and heavy baskets were strenuous tasks for her. Joris also brought the older children to the taproom for short periods to prepare for the secret meetings. At least once a week, he walked with Catalyntje to see Trijn. Catalyntje used the excuse that the visit was a check-up for herself, but truthfully, she was worried about Trijn. The midwife had become recognizably older in the past few months, probably from ill health and the worry that had become everyone's constant companion.

Of all Catalyntje's children, Jacob had the most challenging time staying inside during the endless violence. When warm spring days arrived, he was always the first to jump at the chance to help in the garden. His four-year-old body needed to jump, throw things, and play in the dirt. He was too young to go to the taproom with Joris, so he usually stayed home and helped Catalyntje outside. He usually spent a little time helping in the garden before getting distracted by every bug and stick he could find.

As Jacob leaped about the garden one hot sunny afternoon, Catalyntje called him to help weed the squash. The squash's large leaves made it easy to tell the weeds from the plants. As Jacob weeded, he suddenly called out, "Mama, I found us some food for supper!" Catalyntje walked over and looked where his chubby finger was pointing.

"You are right, Jacob. That is a squash," she said with a smile, stooping beside him.

"I will bring it inside to eat," he proudly announced, reaching for the unripe squash.

"We need to wait for that one. It is not yellow like the ones we usually have for dinner. The sun needs to warm it up a bit so it will taste good inside. It needs more water, too," she added, raising her eyebrows.

"Can I water it then so we can eat it soon?" Jacob asked, turning to get water behind the garden.

"You certainly can, and that will be your job every day when I am out here with you. You keep it watered for us, and then you can pick it and bring it in for dinner one night. It will be ready after the baby comes. Will you do that for me?" Catalyntje asked.

"Yes, Mama! I will feed it all the water it needs, and no one else will pick it," he said proudly, jumping up and down.

Jacob kept his word. Every day, he begged Catalyntje to go outside to water his squash. His persistence paid off, too, because that squash grew faster than any of the others.

In the meantime, life remained uncertain in New Amsterdam. A few days passed peacefully, and sometimes Catalyntje forgot about the problems Kieft had caused. But the calm never lasted; since their home was close to the fort, they often heard soldiers clamoring about on nightly raids. Other times, they smelled smoke in the middle of the day and could see flames devouring nearby buildings.

With all the commotion, some of Catalyntje's neighbors began to run out of food. She kept her garden growing the best she could, and because they didn't have the taproom open, Catalyntje had more than she could use. Sometimes, her neighbors would come quietly to her door and ask for any extra food she might have to share with them. Catalyntje always gave as much as she could and hid vegetables from her garden or a loaf of bread near the edge of her front fence.

Jacob enjoyed putting the extra food in the front. On quiet days, Catalyntje allowed him to go outside and look in the basket by the fence to see if they needed to refill it.

One summer morning, there were no gunshots or screams, but an uneasy feeling had settled over New Amsterdam. Catalyntje hurried about preparing in case there was another attack. Sometimes, the raids could last a few days, and she needed to be ready to keep her family fed, comfortable, and distracted. She had some of her children go to the back and gather food and water while the others helped Joris in the taproom. They each had their assignments, and Jacob was on his daily errand to check the status of the food situation by the front fence. As Catalyntje cooked, she watched him bound out the front door, leaving it wide open as usual; she smiled. He was always happy to help, so she didn't mind that he'd forgotten to close the door - again.

Then suddenly, without warning, she heard a rush of people outside, accompanied by screams that sounded too terrifying to come from a human. Her children, who had been in the garden, burst through the back door, their eyes wide with fright. It was another swift attack in the middle of the day. *Why does this have to keep happening to us?* Catalyntje wondered as she gathered her children in her arms to hold them close so they would feel safe. She closed her eyes tightly to keep the tears back.

Then suddenly, she heard a cry from the front stoop, "Mama!" she heard Jacob's voice call out. Catalyntje had forgotten that he was in front checking the food basket when everything started to happen. Terror gripped her as she ran for the front door, her legs like lead. When Catalyntje reached the stoop, she saw Jacob's tiny body lying on his back with an arrow through his chest. He was motionless. She screamed and dropped to his side, trying to protect his small body with hers. Everything was a blur. She remembered one of her children running past her out of the door. Next, she heard gunfire up the street and then Joris gathering her from the front porch. Now she was inside her house staring into the fire, unable to keep any thought in her mind except one: her precious Jacob was gone.

*****

Joris helplessly watched as grief consumed Catalyntje. Her beloved smile was gone, and now she seemed more stern and often stared into the distance, only wanting to sit quietly alone. She hadn't been hit by an arrow that day, but her soul was deeply wounded.

Word traveled fast throughout the colony, and soon, everyone who lived near Catalyntje and Joris came to buoy them up as much as possible. Catalyntje refused to leave their home as long as Jacob's lifeless body was there, so Trijn came early the next day to stay with her. When she reached the door, she didn't knock since their friendship allowed them to always be welcome in each other's homes. Trijn found Catalyntje preparing food for the younger children when she walked through the door. At the sound of the door closing, Catalyntje turned, and when she saw Trijn, she gasped and ran to her with swollen eyes. Trijn hugged her friend tightly for a very long time as she sobbed, her body shaking, and Trijn wept with her. After several minutes, Catalyntje looked at her friend and, with a tear-stained face, quietly said, "Thank you for coming. I needed you to be here."

Trijn put her arm around Catalyntje and guided her to sit down while she finished the food for the children and settled them down to eat. She offered Catalyntje food, but she refused because she had no appetite. As the children ate, Trijn and Catalyntje sat by Jacob's body and talked about nothing and everything.

Trijn stayed long after the sun had gone down. She cleaned the house, fixed more food, and helped the children into the loft to their beds. As she prepared to leave into the dark night, Catalyntje pressed several pieces of wampum into her friend's hand and asked a favor. She still needed to acquire the pall to put over Jacob's coffin for the funeral but didn't want to leave his side. Trijn accepted the task and promised she would be back the next day. Joris walked Trijn to the door, thanking her for the comfort she'd given their family, especially Catalyntje.

Refugees

Summer of 1643: 37 years old

A week and a half had passed since Jacob's ruthless death, and Catalyntje tried to stay busy to keep her mind from the horrors that haunted her thoughts. She wouldn't spend time in her garden because her mind always wandered back to Jacob there.

However, after a few weeks of avoiding it, Catalyntje knew the neglected plants needed attention. So she went outside late one afternoon, gathered a few beans into her apron, and placed them in the basket she'd brought outside with her. Another head of cabbage was ripe, and Catalyntje put it on the ground beside the basket to keep it from crushing the beans she had just picked. Finally, she pulled the spindly tops of the parsley and thyme that had gone to seed and considered saving them for next summer.

The sky started to dim, and Catalyntje realized it was time to go inside for the evening, where she could keep busy with something that needed mending. She reached down to pick up the cabbage, and her eye caught sight of the round yellow squash, Jacob's squash. The one he had watered, the one he claimed as his own, the one he would pick for dinner when it was ready. Tears filled Catalyntje's eyes. She dropped the cabbage she had just harvested and walked over to the squash. With tears streaming down her face, she ripped the squash from the vine, flung it to the ground, and stared at its core splattered across the other plants in the garden. Catalyntje took a few deep breaths, returned to the cabbage, picked it up, and walked silently into the house. She was no longer hungry. One of the children could make dinner if they wanted anything to eat. Without a word, she set the vegetables on the table by the hearth, went to bed, and sobbed for a long time.

Catalyntje's soul was numb each morning, and she often couldn't concentrate. Her mind replayed the tragedy, hoping she could somehow change what had happened. She understood the stories of heaven she'd listened to at church and often heard of "the better place" people went to after they died. Catalyntje believed these ideas but wondered how Jacob could be in a better place if he wasn't with his family. Her mind couldn't understand where he was, even with the Domine's words still fresh in her mind from the funeral. The idea of Jacob roaming around alone in "a better place" worried Catalyntje endlessly. *How would he understand what had happened, and who would help him?* These questions crowded Catalyntje's thoughts and made her unable to carry out daily tasks or care for her family. Joris noticed this again late one afternoon and came home earlier than he'd planned from the taproom. He gently put his arm around her shoulders and kissed her cheek.

"I will cook something for dinner. You go for a walk. Come back when you are ready," Joris said, his voice filled with kindness. Catalyntje couldn't speak as she embraced him, and tears filled her eyes again.

Catalyntje stepped onto the front stoop, only to be reminded of the horror of the past weeks. The streets weren't as clean as usual, and there were broken items and random stones lying everywhere, evidence of the violence that had taken over their town, especially of the needless brutality that had taken Jacob from her. Angry tears came instantly to her eyes as she mindlessly walked along Pearl Street. Then, without thinking, Catalyntje realized she'd walked to the water's edge; her feet had carried her there as they had often done.

As she recognized her surroundings, Catalyntje stopped, took a deep breath, and tried to clear her mind of the overwhelming sadness that consumed her. *Just listen to the rhythm of the waves,* she thought to herself. After several deep breaths, she finally relaxed her mind and focused on the consistent rhythm of the waves that ran to touch the shore, then quickly withdrew over and over again. Finally, Catalyntje closed her eyes, matched her breath to the rhythm of the waves, and began to relax.

As she did this, her mind cleared, and a most unusual view filled her thoughts. In her mind, Catalyntje could see Jacob running in a field, skipping happily without a care. Unharmed. Carefree. Unconcerned. Then, another figure entered her mind, and she gasped. Closely walking behind Jacob was her friend from long ago, Jannetje! As she watched, Jannetje also seemed content and delighted to walk with Jacob, enjoying the grass and the sunshine. Catalyntje held Jacob and Jannetje in her thoughts for as long as she could, feeling their joy until it spilled over into her soul, and her sadness was gone. Catalyntje felt that Jannetje would help Jacob until she could get to where he was one day. These peaceful thoughts filled her heart and mind as she focused back on the sound of the waves.

"Thank you, Jannetje," Catalyntje whispered as she turned to walk back to her home and family. Somehow, everything would be alright.

*****

Although tragedy had visited their family, time continued to march on, and in late June, Catalyntje and Joris' eighth child, Jeronemus Jorizen, was born. Trijn and Sarah were there to help Catalyntje, and the birth occurred without complications. Sarah did most of the work while Trijn sat on a stool and directed her on what she should do since she was more tired lately. When Sarah handed Catalyntje her baby for the first time, Catalyntje looked at Jeronemus' sweet face, and he grasped her finger tightly with his tiny hand; she felt hope.

*****

By the end of the summer, more settlers from the surrounding area had come to New Amsterdam for protection from the continued violence caused by Kieft's War. Many of them moved into the fort, and since Catalyntje and Joris' taproom was officially closed, they spent their time comforting and helping those who were displaced instead of keeping up with their business at the taproom. Catalyntje assigned the older children to work in the garden so they could keep food in the taproom for those in need. The refugees had been forced to flee their homes and didn't have wampum or goods to trade for meals, but Catalyntje and Joris didn't turn anyone away.

Violence was more prevalent at the colony's borders, and as homeless settlers came for protection, they shared their tales. One evening, a woman who'd lived across the river came into the taproom with her three young children. Catalyntje immediately went to her with food.

"Here is some bread you can share with your children. Please let me know what else you need. I will be back shortly," Catalyntje offered.

"Thank you," the exhausted woman replied in a hollow voice.

"I am glad you are here," Catalyntje said, sitting beside the woman.

"We will be alright. Thank you for your kindness. I don't know what we will do," the woman said, sobbing.

"You do not need to know. Just sit for now. We will help you get to the fort," Catalyntje replied.

"My husband is missing. We were attacked, and he told me to run with the children. As we ran past Anne Hutchinson's homestead, her home was on fire. Bodies were lying about, and we saw one of her girls being carried off on a horse by one of the Natives. I should have helped her," the woman said, sobbing uncontrollably.

"You did the right thing to keep your own children safe. You are here now; it will be alright," Catalyntje replied as she gently stroked the woman's hair.

A Cold and Cruel Winter

Winter of 1643: 37 years old

By October, both the violence and the weather had worsened. Many settlers didn't have enough food for the winter and only had drafty shelters to live in during the brisk cold months. Late one evening, a few men came to the taproom for a place to meet privately. Joris was happy to allow this, especially when he discovered they were writing a letter to get help from the Company because of the damage Kieft was causing.

Joris watched as they raised their voices and stood to emphasize their words. While he cleared a nearby table, the man who seemed to be in charge of the group signaled for Joris to come to the area where they were talking.

"Joris, I trust your opinion. Would you be willing to take a minute to hear what we've written to the Company?" he asked.

"Yes, something needs to be done about the injuries Kieft has brought to our town," Joris answered, turning toward the group of men.

The man in charge stood up and read aloud, "The fort is defenseless and entirely out of order and resembles a molehill rather than a fort. The Munsee who attacked the fort consisted of about fifteen hundred men, while those in the colony were only about two hundred strong. The colonists are trying to protect their families while living in straw huts outside the fort since the Natives have destroyed most of their homes," the man looked up from his reading. "What do you think, my friend? Is this a fair description of our situation?" he asked.

"Unfortunately, it is, and I hope your letter gets to the Company soon. Then we can be rid of Kieft, and maybe our lives can return to what they once were," Joris replied.

*****

Winter was overly cruel that year, and Catalyntje couldn't remember being so cold. The sun hadn't shone as usual, and there were fewer clear days as thin gray clouds continually hovered over New Netherland. Catalyntje had always been aware of rainfall and when the ground would freeze because she had always worked in her gardens. But this past year, she'd noticed her winter crops hadn't grown like they usually did. Not as many squashes and pumpkins had ripened, and some tomatoes and corn hadn't grown to maturity. This change probably happened because the ground hadn't warmed up enough during the day because of the constant cloud cover. It was too cold for plants and people.

Trijn

1644: 38 years old

Life in New Netherland continued with uncertainty and fear. The men who'd written to complain about Kieft hadn't yet received word about the possibility of new leadership. While waiting, the settlers kept looking out for each other since their leader would not.

The winter had been long and lean, and many families didn't have enough food, wood, or heart to carry them through. But Catalyntje and Joris kept the taproom open for those who needed help. A few times each week, an entire family would arrive, and Joris could sense their timid spirit and shame that they needed food but had no way to pay for it. He always offered them a bowl of soup and a warm fire and let them stay as long as needed, never asking for payment. Occasionally, these refugees offered to split wood or clean dishes at the taproom, and he gratefully accepted their help.

Catalyntje spent most of her time at home with the children, who helped bake bread and prepare meals for themselves and those who came to the taproom. She also saved a portion of food each day to share with Trijn. Joris walked with Catalyntje every afternoon to Trijn's house, where they stayed to talk and enjoy time together. Catalyntje had been worried about Trijn for some time now because her steps were not as steady, and she'd lost the stamina she used to possess. Her family still cared for her, but Catalyntje wanted Trijn to know she was her friend.

*****

When spring weather arrived, Catalyntje spent more time sitting on the bench underneath the large tree in Trijn's yard. She could see the windmill spinning from there and enjoyed the tree's shade. On quiet days, she sat and watched the smaller leaf-covered branches sway back and forth in the wind and listened to the slosh of the waves against the shore; Catalyntje knew she could sit there and let her mind and soul rest. Sometimes, she'd bring young Jeronemus with her. He was only a year old and was rather fussy, so breathing in the cool ocean air usually calmed him.

When Catalyntje sat under the shady tree, Trijn usually came out of her tiny house to sit with her. They often talked and sometimes just sat silently together.

*****

Once summer came, Trijn quit her midwife work to give her more time to rest and enjoy her family. Catalyntje had noticed a sizable decline in her energy and strength. She listened as Trijn told story after story of her adventures as a midwife, which Catalyntje realized wasn't just about delivering babies. Trijn often testified in court to identify the father of a child she'd delivered. Trijn also frequently traveled in the dark of the night with only a lantern to get to the home of a new mother who needed help. Trijn was a strong woman, and Catalyntje appreciated her vigor; it was difficult to see her less involved in the lives of others.

*****

Every tree in the colony had ripe peaches, so Catalyntje took advantage of this bounty to make three pies. Since peach pie was Trijn's favorite, one was for her. As the pie cooled, Catalyntje picked flowers from her garden to bring to Trijn along with the pie. When she reached Trijn's house, she quietly opened the door and walked in. Trijn didn't look at who had entered but calmly said, "Hello, Catalyntje."

"Good afternoon, Trijn," she responded, walking to the bed. Trijn rolled over to look at Catalyntje.

"Those are beautiful flowers, dear. They will brighten up this room," Trijn smiled.

"I also brought a fresh peach pie," Catalyntje added.

"Oh my, that is worth sitting up for," Trijn answered carefully, pushing herself into a sitting position. Catalyntje gathered two spoons from the shelf by the fireplace, and the two friends enjoyed the pie as they talked. Catalyntje always liked talking to Trijn, but she could tell her old friend was getting tired after a while.

"I will wash the spoons and the dish, and then I need to return home," Catalyntje said.

"You have a lot of people relying on you, don't you?" Trijn said with a weak smile. "Before you leave, get my book from the little table over there."

"Here you are," she said, holding the book to her bedridden friend.

"I want you to have this book," Trijn replied with a weary smile. Catalyntje instantly recognized it was the book her friend, Trijn, had written in after every baby she delivered. Catalyntje carefully opened the pages and began to look at the words.

"I know you've done more reading since we talked about this book when I helped your Sarah deliver one of her babies. I thought it might help you to read even better. You know all of the people I wrote about here, and if you remember, I wrote about you too," she said with a faint smile.

"This is a treasure, Trijn. I do not know what to say," Catalyntje responded. "It seems that it might be better for the record keeper or another midwife to have."

"I know it's filled with useful information, but it's also filled with people and memories; that is more important to me than information," Trijn answered firmly. "I mentioned to you that writing things down helped me remember them. I don't think I need to remember for much longer, but it will help you remember me."

"I will never forget you, Trijn," Catalyntje answered, tears filling her eyes.

"I won't forget you either, my friend. You are a strong and determined woman, Catalyntje. You have been here, in New Netherland, since it started, and I think you will be here much longer. I have always admired you and am honored to have been your friend," Trijn added, reaching over to hold Catalyntje's hand.

"You have brought such sweetness to my life. I will treasure this book forever and learn to read all of it," Catalyntje promised.

*****

Catalyntje heard a knock at the door just as the sun was barely up in the sky. She cautiously opened it, and there stood Anneke, Trijn's daughter.

"My mama is gone. She died early this morning, and I wanted you to be the first to know," Anneke said with red, swollen eyes.

"Oh!" Catalyntje gasped. "I knew it would be soon. How can I help you, Anneke?"

Catalyntje invited Anneke to come in and sit down, and then the two women planned how to say their final goodbyes to Trijn.

*****

By the end of the week, more violence visited the settlement near the fort. Catalyntje and Joris stayed inside for long nights with their children wrapped in blankets to calm them from the terrifying sounds that filled the night air. The following evening, the screams and shots had subsided, so they decided to look around before darkness covered the scene.

"I do not like all of the death and destruction, but I must know what is happening near our home," Catalyntje admitted softly.

"I feel the same way, and I want to know how to help our neighbors," Joris said, carefully stepping over broken windows and destroyed baskets abandoned in the streets. There were streaks of blood in the dirt, and when Catalyntje saw these, she pulled her bonnet tight, nearly covering her eyes as she held onto Joris' arm for guidance. Once they reached the end of the street, they paused and looked toward the fort.

"Joris," she gasped, pointing near the fort. "It is broken! The windmill is broken!"

"There is more destruction than I have ever seen here," Joris said

"The windmill is broken, Joris. You do not know how often the spinning of its fins has calmed me. They must fix it," Catalyntje sobbed.

"I will see what I can do," Joris responded, hugging his wife.

*****

In mid-April, Catalyntje and her daughter, Jannetje, went to Sarah's home to help with the birth of her third child, Jan Hansen Bergen. Trijn was noticeably missing during this process, and her absence left a tangible hole. After the birth, Sarah and the baby slept while Jannetje cleaned the house.

Catalyntje sat at the table and carefully took out the book Trijn had given her. She opened it to a blank page and added her own words.

Mid-April 1644

Berth of Jan Hansen Bergen, my 3 granchild. Jannetje was heer to help but Trijn was not.

*****

Late in December, the Company finally replied to the letter sent to them by the upset colonists. They dismissed Kieft as the director and requested his return to the Netherlands to defend his actions. When Kieft became aware of this, he immediately sent a letter to the Company, reporting that the men had written nothing but slander and lies.

Legal Matters

1645: 39 years old

Winter came strong again that year, and with the added troubles they'd experienced, the colonists were unprepared. That winter, the fierce winds' chilling fingers slipped through every tiny crack in the walls, and the temperatures were even more frigid than the last winter because the colonists had now endured three consecutive years of continual cloudy skies. With so many problems in the colony, Joris had given away a fair amount of firewood to those without, and he worried he hadn't gathered enough for his own family to make it through another bitter winter.

Catalyntje spent every spare moment sewing quilts and extra clothing. Her handwork basket overflowed with creations of socks, mittens, and hats, all at different stages of completion. Judith helped with these projects since she had learned to sew and knit at a young age. Catalyntje was also careful to burn just enough wood to keep her family warm without running out.

As the cold increased, Catalyntje pushed worn clothes under doors and around the windows to keep any heat from escaping. On nights when the strong wind blew in from the water, Catalyntje often lay awake, unable to sleep, as her mind reviewed her worries. She wondered about her children keeping warm enough, their wood supply, the continued violence surrounding them, and their food situation.

Joris worked and worried also. He usually spent late mornings at the taproom, helping those who needed food and a fire, while Catalyntje was home with the younger children, trying to keep them busy and warm. Late one afternoon, as Joris arrived home, he could sense tension as soon as he walked through the door. "Mama is in bed," Jan reported.

Joris immediately went to their built-in bed, fearing what might be wrong with her. As he pulled back the curtain, Catalyntje turned, and he saw her tear-stained face.

"What has happened?" he asked.

"Sarah was here a while ago and shared some upsetting news with me," Catalyntje replied.

"What has happened? Is she alright? Are the children well?" Joris asked without giving Catalyntje time to answer.

"The surgeon that came to the colony last year, Paulus van der Beeck," she said.

"I know him. He worked for the Company and married a widow just last year," Joris said.

"He went to Sarah's home to help and ended up arguing with her, and before he left her home, he hit her! Joris, he hit our daughter," Catalyntje snapped. "She was in tears when she told me. Hans was not home, or he might have hurt Van der Beeck."

"Catalyntje, I don't know what to say," Joris replied.

"I have already made up my mind. My family will not be mistreated, and I will tell Van der Beeck this," Catalyntje sputtered.

"You are going over there?" Joris asked.

"Yes, I am. Women have the right to speak their minds in this colony, and I will tell him what I think about all of this," she said, blinking back her tears. Then she got up and gathered her coat, gloves, and scarf. "I am going there now so it will not fill my head all night while trying to sleep."

The crispness of the air sharpened Catalyntje's thoughts as she walked to Hans Kierstede's house, where Van der Beeck worked during the day. Her bold knock brought Keirstede immediately to the door.

"Good day, Catalyntje. What brings you here?" Kierstede asked politely. "Come in."

Catalyntje walked into the large room and answered, "I am here to speak with Van der Beeck." As she spoke, he entered the room and nodded to greet her.

"I will be brief in my visit. I am here to ask why you beat my daughter," Catalyntje demanded.

"You lie. I would never do such a thing, and besides, you have no proof," Van der Beeck answered, not expecting a response.

"You lie. You lie like a villain and a dog!" Catalyntje shouted out, pointing her finger for emphasis. Van der Beeck's anger instantly rose in response to her accusation.

"You are a whore and a wampum thief," Van der Beeck yelled as he lifted his hand and struck Catalyntje across the face, "Leave this place at once!"

"You have not heard the end of this!" she shouted back at Van der Beeck as she spun on her heel and headed back home. Once she was a few houses away, she began sobbing.

*****

Since Kieft's arrival, too much negativity has been allowed in New Amsterdam, and Catalyntje was determined to stand up and combat such behaviors. Kieft's leadership changed many things in New Netherland. His decisions brought violence, divided the people, and replaced peace with tension, as evident in Catalyntje's interactions with Van der Beeck. The next day, when Catalyntje and Joris talked about the problem with Van der Beeck, she told Joris she was going to the provincial secretary with Van der Beeck to resolve the matter. Since she was a woman in a Dutch town, she had the right to approach the court and settle things just as men could. So, on a cold morning early in January, Catalyntje went to the office of the provincial secretary to have her case against Van der Beeck heard. Over the next few weeks, the secretary recorded the court proceedings in his loopy Dutch letters.

Register for the Provincial Secretary: 1645, January 5
Catrina Trico, plaintiff, vs. Paulus van [der] Beeke, defendant, for slander. Plaintiff complains that the defendant called her a whore and a seawan thief. Ordered that written testimony be produced.

Register for the Provincial Secretary: 1645, January 10
Egbert van Borsum, aged about 30 years, at the request of Catelyn Trico, attests, testifies and declares, in place and with promise of a solemn oath if necessary and required, that Catelyn came to the house of Master Hans and asked Master Pauwel: "Why do you beat my daughter?" He, Pauwel, answered: "You lie." She replied: "You lie like a villain and a dog." She, Catelyn, raising her hand, Master Pauwel struck Catelyn and then called her a whore and a wampum thief, which she called people to witness.

Egbert van Borsum
Willem de Key
Surgeon Hans Kierstede.

Surgeon Paulus van der Beeck, or Becke

Council Minutes for 1645, January 12

Catalyn Trico, plaintiff, vs. Pauwel van[der] Beeke, defendant, for defamation. Plaintiff demands satisfaction for the injury done to her [character], which she proves by two witnesses. Defendant is ordered to prove what he said or, if he can not do so, defendant shall acknowledge that he knows nothing of the plaintiff that reflects on her honor or virtue. Defendant declares that he cannot prove the slanderous remarks made to her and that he has nothing to say against her that reflects on her honor or virtue. For the blow struck by the defendant he shall pay [fine of 2 ½ guilders] and Pauwel is warned not to do so again on pain of severer punishment.

*****

Catalyntje was pleased the court had listened to her and required payment from Van der Beeck for his disrespectful words and violence. She didn't appreciate spending her time seeking restitution for the damage done; however, she was grateful to live in a place that allowed her some rights as a woman.

*****

After the cold, bleak winter, spring finally arrived, with the hope that the colony would soon see the end of Kieft. As the days warmed, the people of New Amsterdam began to go to the Munsee and discuss possible peace solutions. But with lost trust and Kieft still ruling, the progress was sluggish. Finally, by the end of the summer, and after many discussions, a peace treaty was decided upon. Some settlers gathered with the Munsee "under the blue canopy of heaven" at Fort Amsterdam for this much-anticipated event.

Catalyntje, Joris, and their children were among those who gathered to witness it. Along with others, their family had endured irreversible damage since the Kieft Indian War had begun. Many settlers had even returned to the Netherlands, losing all hope for a peaceful life in the colony. By the end of the war, nearly sixteen hundred Natives were killed, and much of the settler's land and property was destroyed. Worst of all for Catalyntje and

200

her family was the unforgivable death of their dear son, Jacob. Everyone had suffered from Kieft's authoritarian command, but this day brought hope that it would soon end.

Another Winter

1646: 40 years old

Blowing wind and snow ushered in the following winter, but it wasn't as severe as the past three years. This change probably happened because the cloudy skies had finally cleared up, so the temperatures weren't as cold.

Late on a dark evening in early February, Joris wrapped a scarf around his neck and faced the blowing snow to get help from a neighbor. He and Catalyntje's ninth child would soon be born, and she would need some help. When the women arrived, Joris bundled up the younger children and took them to the taproom while the neighbor women assisted with the birth. Unfortunately, neither Sarah nor Marretje could come through the storm to help, but Jannetje stayed to assist, so she was there to see her new little sister, Annetie Joris, come into the world. Catalyntje was prepared with plenty of blankets and clothing for little Annetie because Catalyntje knew it was a hard time of the year to begin a new life in New Amsterdam. Catalyntje and Joris christened their baby a few weeks later. It was a frigid time, but adding Annetie's name to the church records was important to them.

*****

As spring timidly returned to New Amsterdam, the colonists spent more time outside. Winter also kept them further apart, more than usual, so it was good to renew friendships and share stories about how they'd survived the cold months. The people of New Amsterdam also wondered when it would be warm enough to send a ship back to the Netherlands with Kieft. He was still serving as the colony's interim leader and continued to make dangerous declarations.

As the colonists emerged from their winter homes and into their gardens and businesses, they recognized the improved changes in the colony. It was as if the icy winter had frozen the difficulties and melted them away with the sun. Kieft was still there, and the Indian Wars he caused had finally subsided. Because of these positive changes, more families moved to New Netherland, and it slowly returned to a place of profit and peace.

*****

Shortly before the Sinterklaas season, Sarah and Hans had their fourth child, Michael Hansen Bergen. Catalyntje couldn't be at the birth because of the frozen river but planned to visit her fourth grandchild once the weather cleared. She and Joris also planned to spend more time on the other side of the river once the weather cleared. There, they would be closer to Sarah and Hans and could spend time working their land at the Wallabout, growing gardens, and cutting timber - the continual cycle of survival that was their life in New Netherland.

Part 5: Across the River
1647 - 1663

Changes

1647: 41 years old

Fear continued to surround New Netherland, but as Catalyntje's family grew, life moved forward. Kieft had started wars with the tribes near the colony, but gratefully, a ship would soon take him back to the Old World, where he would account for his reckless leadership in New Netherland. With these changes, business at the taproom increased as people cautiously returned more regularly.

That summer, Kieft was released from his duties as director of New Netherland. Finally, one bright summer morning, Catalyntje watched *Princess Amalia* fill with a dozen men from New Netherland. After they boarded, soldiers from the Company escorted Kieft onto the ship. Knowing that Kieft would be sailing far away from New Netherland brought relief. Catalyntje felt guilty as she watched Kieft board the ship because she wished for nothing good to come to him.

Fifty-four-year-old Petrus Stuyvesant replaced Kieft. Previously, Stuyvesant had led a settlement far away in the Caribbean. The first thing most colonists noticed when he arrived was his wooden peg leg. Word spread that he'd lost it in an unsuccessful attack on the island of St. Martin when a cannonball exploded and shot it off. Stuyvesant wasted no time exploring the problems Kieft had left and called many of the colonists to answer questions about his predecessor.

*****

Within sixteen days, Stuyvesant had established a court of justice and organized a council to meet regularly to discuss important colony matters. He was very orderly, businesslike, and somewhat unapproachable, and many colonists did not like his stern mannerisms. His organized ways reminded Catalyntje of Kieft, but Stuyvesant seemed more level-headed and less likely to argue with the tribes.

Stuyvesant had a specific way he wanted New Netherland to operate. He ordered the strict observance of the Sabbath and prohibited selling alcohol and weapons to the Natives. He also wanted to rebuild New Amsterdam after its destruction from the Kieft Wars, so he encouraged the colonists to rebuild their homes and businesses. Under Stuyvesant's direction, the colonists also added a cattle auction to the weekly market and built another school.

With more ships returning to the colony, Joris took on extra work as a chief boatswain at the docks. With this job, he oversaw assigning men to keep the vessels seaworthy and looking respectable. This included organizing the men to clean and paint the hulls and fix any damage from their journeys across the ocean. His primary responsibility was for the cargo rigging, including the booms, ropes, and sails. The textile skills he had learned in the Old World were valuable at this new job.

Joris also learned much about what was happening in the settlement, being near the sailors and workers. One sunny afternoon, he helped a few men paint the hull of a boat that had arrived a week earlier; one was named Gysbert. He had worked on the docks since arriving in New Netherland and seemed to know everything happening there.

"I remember my journey in one of these sea monsters," Gysbert joked, dipping his brush in the paint. "When did you come over, boss?"

"I was actually on the first ship that landed here," Joris answered proudly.

"You're not that old. I haven't known anyone who was here on the first day," Gysbert added with surprise. "Why haven't you returned like some of the others?"

"My wife and I found that we rather like this place. But it hasn't been without its problems and hard work, mind you," Joris answered.

"Do you have many new neighbors since more people are moving here?" Jaep, the other worker, asked Joris.

"I have one new neighbor you may have heard of; his name is Stuyvesant. He moved to a big house near us, and I can see its silhouette when I look out towards the water," Joris laughed.

"He is a stuffy fellow," Jaep said, standing up to stretch. "He sure seems to have a lot of rules for us to follow."

"Jaep, you weren't around when Kieft was here, messin' the place up. I'd choose a few rules over an Indian war any day," Gysbert admitted. A shadow fell over the area Joris was painting, and he turned to see a man standing by him. Joris stood and extended his hand, "Good day, my name is Joris. How can I help you?"

"Good to meet you; my name is Claes Bordingh. I have a ship coming in this week and would like to hire you and your men to fix her up before she sails back," the man replied.

"Bordingh, I have heard that name," Jaep said. "Glad to see you for myself."

Bordingh ignored Jaep and looked back at Joris, "So, can we talk about the cost sometime soon? "

"We certainly can. So, what part of the colony are you moving to?" Joris asked.

"I am moving to the middle of Pearl Street, the side that faces the water," he answered.

"The middle of Pearl Street, well, we will be neighbors. My wife and I can come over to help if you need it," Joris offered. And tomorrow would work fine to discuss your ship. Would you like to meet here at the dock before lunch?" Joris asked.

"That would be fine. I will see you then," Bordingh nodded and walked off.

"I've heard tales about that man," Gysbert said after Bordingh left. "I hear he sells guns."

"No," Jaep said, raising his eyebrows, "he smuggles them. He's a pirate of sorts, and I've heard it said more than once that he is the wealthiest man in the area."

"Well, he will surely make for an interesting neighbor then," Joris added.

News from the Old World

1648: 42 years old _

Fear and despair left on the ship with Kieft, so the new year brought hope to New Amsterdam. The colonists were anxious to hear what punishment the Company would give Kieft, and several of them greeted every ship that entered the harbor, waiting for news about his sentence.

Finally, on a windy morning in early spring, a ship sailed to the docks of New Netherland. The usual group gathered around to hear any word about Kieft, but they were disappointed when the captain stoically left the ship and walked towards the fort. With no gossip to pass on, the men dispersed and went back to their own business.

By the time the sun was overhead, the fort bell began ringing. Catalyntje left Judith in charge at home, promising to return as soon as she could. When the fort bell rang, all the settlers were required to go to the fort and hear whatever important announcement would be shared. Joris greeted Catalyntje as she stepped onto the front stoop; he had just closed the taproom. He smiled when he saw her and reached out his hand as they walked towards Fort Amsterdam together.

A buzzing crowd surrounded the fort, and Catalyntje grew nervous and began to worry. Surely, there couldn't be more attacks from the tribes; Kieft had caused those, and thankfully, he was gone and suffering somewhere, she hoped, for all the misery he had caused.

At the sound of a man's voice, everyone's attention turned to the fort, and the crowd immediately quieted as Stuyvesant stepped forward.

"Greetings to you this day," he announced, looking over the crowd. "Thank you for gathering. The ship's captain has a brief proclamation you will be interested in hearing, and then you may return to your duties.

Captain, you may speak," Stuyvesant said, nodding at the captain and pointing to where he should stand.

"Good people of New Netherland, I have information that the Company wanted me to share with you as soon as I landed. Your former director, Willem Kieft, was lost at sea and is presumed dead. The others from the colony on the ship were also lost; there were no survivors. Their ship went down in a storm off the coast of Wales," as the captain finished, he took a step back.

"Thank you, captain. I appreciate those who have gathered. You may return to your work," Stuyvesant replied.

After a few minutes, the astonished crowd began to disperse without a word. They didn't know whether to cheer or weep. Kieft was dead; he had been the cause of so much needless suffering, pain, and death in the colony. As they walked home, no tears were shed, only guilty smiles, which they tried to cover with their bonnets and hat brims.

News spread quickly about Kieft, and those in New Amsterdam wanted to share it with the settlers living further north in Beverwyck. Messages usually traveled between these two towns along the river in sloops during the warm months. But at this time, the river remained frozen in spots, and there was no chance to send the news by water.

During the cold months, the Tappan tribe usually delivered messages between the two places. Traveling by foot from one place to the other took them a few days since they could travel quickly through the thick forests.

*****

As the weather warmed, spring brought signs of good fortune to New Netherland. First, Catalyntje and Joris welcomed the birth of their tenth child, Elizabeth Jorise, which was a much happier time to have a baby than when Annetie was born a few years ago.

The settlement also received news that the Eighty-Years War in Europe had finally ended, an event to be celebrated since most early settlers made New Netherland their home because of this lengthy war. It had been a long time since Catalyntje had lived in the Old World, and she had forgotten the fears she had escaped from there. When she heard that the war had ended, she wondered about Margriet, Marie, and her mama and hoped their lives would be more peaceful.

*****

Catalyntje and Joris continued to improve their home. They could purchase many fine things because of their work at the taproom and Joris's position at the docks. They could finally trade for leaded window panes and green-glazed tile for their floor.

Catalyntje was content with her home and its furnishings, but she often noticed the exquisite items that entered Bordingh's house since her new neighbor was presumed to be the wealthiest man in the settlement. Catalyntje wasn't bothered by his wealth; what didn't sit well with her was that he was a pirate who earned money through gun smuggling. Of course, it wasn't her business how people made their money, but she didn't like the boisterous and drunken manner of the pirates who had made New Amsterdam their home. Additionally, pirates and smugglers usually conducted their business in the dark hours of the night. Since Bordingh was in the smuggling business, Catalyntje's family was often awakened at night by arguing, loud laughter, and sometimes, even gunshots.

Better Days

1649: 43 years old

Summer came quickly, and Catalyntje's life was soon filled with the work required to get her family through the sultry months and prepare for winter. She spent more time in her garden growing extra food for Sarah's family since Sarah was expecting another child in July. Catalyntje knew how uncomfortable summer pregnancies could be and often sent Jan and Judith with a basket of chard or beets and a round loaf of bread to Sarah's home. Sarah's sisters, Marretje and Jannetje, also offered extra help by bringing her younger children to their homes to enjoy the day with their own children.

One hot summer morning in the middle of July, ten-year-old Annetje, Catalyntje's granddaughter, came to Catalyntje and Joris' home. As she approached the half-opened Dutch door, she saw Joris and walked in.

"Well, how are you today, Annetje?" asked Joris.

Without answering his question, Annetje said, "I came to get Oma to help Mama have her baby." Joris' face lit up as he motioned for Annetje to go to the garden where Catalyntje was harvesting carrots. Catalyntje smiled when she saw her oldest grandchild walking toward her. She put the carrots into her basket, wiped her hands on her apron, and hugged her.

"It is always such a treat to see you, Annetje," Catalyntje said cheerfully. "You're just in time to help me finish pulling up this row of carrots, and I have some seeds saved that we can plant after lunch."

"I can't help you today, Oma. Mama needs you; she said the baby is coming," Annetje announced.

"Let me put on a clean apron and bring these carrots inside. Planting new ones can wait until later. It sounds like we have more important things to do today. Does Opa know?" Catalyntje asked.

"Yes, he does. I told him right when I got here, and he sent me out to tell you," Annetje answered.

"Can you please get some fresh towels from the kast? I need to talk to Opa, and then we can go," Catalyntje said.

It didn't take her long to get ready. Before she left, Catalyntje hugged Joris and was off with Annetje to help Sarah.

*****

Joris Hansen Bergen entered the world that evening without difficulties, but Catalyntje stayed with Sarah and her family for a few days before returning home. Two weeks later, the entire family traveled across the river to witness the christening of their newest family member.

The end of summer was an excellent time to go to the market to trade and buy goods. Catalyntje's family went together that day since they needed many things, and Catalyntje wanted their help carrying them home. As they approached the market, Jeronemus ran to a man selling ripe, oblong watermelons near the fort.

"Mama, we need many of these; they are my favorite," he exclaimed.

"Those are delicious, but remember, they will not keep, and I do not have a recipe for watermelon pie," Catalyntje joked.

"Can we get two? I will carry one home," Jeronemus offered.

"Well, we could eat them both in a few days and maybe even get a third one for the taproom," Catalyntje said, looking at Joris.

"That sounds like a fine plan to me," he responded. After purchasing the melons, they stopped for flour, shellfish, and spices. Then, weighed down with their purchases, they headed home.

"Catalyntje, let's go around the far end of our street to get home," Joris suggested.

"Do you think that's a good idea? We are all carrying so much. Look at Jeronemus. I think he chose the largest watermelon there," Catalyntje laughed.

"There is something I want to show you. I saw it yesterday when I was working at the docks. It will be worth the extra effort," Joris promised. "Children, you can run along home. Your Mama and I will be there shortly." They turned and continued to lug their items home. As Catalyntje and Joris reached the end of the street, Joris stopped, pointing towards the fort.

"Look past the fort. What do you see?" Joris asked. Catalyntje set her basket down, squinting in the direction he was pointing.

"They repaired the windmill," she gasped.

"I told you it would be worth the extra few steps," Joris said with a smile. "They have been working on it for the past week, and I noticed yesterday that it was nearly mended."

"That is a good sign that this place is shaping up to what it used to be," Catalyntje said, kissing Joris on the cheek before they headed home together.

A Growing Family

1650: 44 years old

The weather was perfect for Catalyntje to work each morning in her garden. She had four children who could help, even though the three youngest usually spent their time chasing each other. Young Catalyntje, now nine, usually followed Elizabeth since the curious two-year-old was always trying to pick the blossoms from plants. Catalyntje was extremely tired because she was expecting their eleventh child and appreciated the help. Even going up and down the dirt stairs of the cellar was exhausting, and bending over to work in the garden was extremely uncomfortable.

Catalyntje sent seven-year-old Jeronemus to follow thirteen-year-old Jan to the small dugout cellar behind the house. She had saved two dozen cabbage roots in the cellar from the year before. After three trips down the cellar steps, the two boys retrieved all the cabbage stumps. As Catalyntje examined each one, she found several were too rotten for replanting, so Jan gathered them up and carried them to the hogs. Jan loved to feed these animals leftovers and usually made a game of it, throwing each one high into the air and watching where it landed. He always waited to throw another one until at least a few hogs fought over the first one. Judith and Annetie helped their mama gather the healthy cabbage roots from the cellar and put them into a pile. Then Judith and Catalyntje dug two rows of small holes while little Annetie followed and put one cabbage root into each hole. Sometimes, the roots stood upright, and other times they leaned sideways. Young Catalyntje usually went back to check the direction of the roots her four-year-old sister had planted before covering them up.

Within weeks, Catalyntje had small cabbage leaves to harvest. This year, they wouldn't produce full heads of cabbage, but their primary purpose was to provide cabbage seeds for the following year.

Catalyntje and her children also planted two short rows of turnips. These were always a treat because they were one of the first plants ready to eat in the spring. She usually planted two rows each week for about a month; that way, they would have a steady supply of turnips.

*****

Just before Christmas, Catalyntje had their eleventh child, Daniel Joriszen. Jannetje and Marretje were there to help her. Catalyntje had aged, but giving birth after having ten children wasn't as difficult. As she labored to bring Daniel into the world, she remembered her distressing situation long ago when she had Sarah in the isolated forest of Fort Orange.

Many Things to Do

1651: 45 years old

A continuous stream of ships sailed between New Amsterdam in the New World and Amsterdam in the Old World. Vessels filled with furs, timber, and the coveted beaver pelts offered the Dutch continual income on both sides of the ocean. Catalyntje and Joris' efforts were divided between their home, the taproom, and their land at the Wallabout. All three places required more and more of their time.

"I certainly appreciated Jan and Judith helping at the taproom yesterday. The work just doesn't seem to slow down over there," Joris said, sitting down to eat breakfast.

"I am glad they can help. How was business last night?" Catalyntje asked, sitting down with Joris to eat some bread and milk.

"There has been much talk lately about the English moving in closer," Joris reported. "They are doing more business with us and seem to be threatened by the success of our colony."

"Well, we treat the tribes kindlier than they do, even though we have had wars and quarrels," Catalyntje replied.

"I agree, even though some people from our colony get tired of the tribes roaming on the land they traded with them. The tribes assume we only borrow the land and should still share it," Joris responded.

"We have worked hard to repair the damage between us and the Natives. It seems they chose us over the English when it comes to trading," Catalyntje smiled.

"You are right there. The Natives still speak Dutch when they trade; that's a good sign," Joris answered.

"I have heard Sarah tell how the English are moving closer to the Dutch land on Langt Eylandt. They seem to be surrounding us," Catalyntje said. "Do you think they would ever try to take our land from us?"

"I'm not sure about that. We don't have an army here in this settlement; it would be an easy task if they set their minds to it," Joris said with a frown. "I hope that day never comes."

*****

As fall approached, Catalyntje and her family worked hard to finish their final preparations for the coming winter. She still had three small children underfoot but often got the help of their older siblings to tend to them. Little Daniel, her eleventh child, was only one year old and needed near-constant care.

Part of their winter preparations included getting firewood. Joris had learned that patrons would stay longer to avoid going out into the cold if he kept a warm fire in the taproom. During the winter, the wind from the bay pierced through their cloaks, and one more drink or bowl of soup could delay the inevitable. Catalyntje and the older children worked continuously to prepare food because they wanted the taproom to feel like a place of abundance where people would be comfortable staying as long as they wanted.

Catalyntje also took time to help her daughter Sarah, who had her sixth child, Maritje Hansen Bergen, in October. When Catalyntje went to help Sarah, she brought a basket of vegetables, crisscross rolls, and a fresh quilt for the new baby. Sarah's sisters stayed to help her for a few weeks after the birth, but Catalyntje did not; she had young Daniel at home, who needed her attention.

Shortly after Maritje's birth, Judith married Peter van Nest, who had moved to the colony from Friesland. The marriage was a happy occasion, and Catalyntje and Joris provided a generous wedding meal with a warm fire in their taproom.

Unexpected Events

1653: 47 years old

Stuyvesant continued to set regulations to improve New Amsterdam, hoping this progress would impress the Company overseas. One cold afternoon early in February, the people of New Amsterdam heard the bell ringing and gathered at the fort. The last time they were called, they heard about Kieft's shipwreck, so they were interested in what Stuyvesant had to say this time.

First, he raised his hand to silence the crowd. Once they quieted, he announced that the Company had granted city rights to New Amsterdam, which meant more independence for the settlement. Cheers went up all around, and the buzz of conversations began. Stuyvesant also announced that the inn, built a few years ago, would become the town hall.

"That makes us sound rather important, doesn't it?" Catalyntje replied.

"I think it does. I suppose we can call this place our city now instead of our settlement," Joris replied. "And we can call ourselves citizens, not settlers."

"It is still the same place, Joris, but it is quite a milestone, especially as I look back and remember how wild and untamed it was when it first arrived," Catalyntje mused.

"Yes, and we were part of that beginning. We got off the ship together and were among the first to change this place into a respectable town," Joris replied. "Are you glad we came here?"

"I am. I cannot imagine any other way life could have been, and I am delighted I am here with you," Catalyntje added, leaning on Joris' shoulder.

*

Once the days began to warm, people spent more time on their front stoops, cleaning the steps and talking to their neighbors. Catalyntje looked forward to the times she helped Joris at the taproom. She worked on her own, doing many things for the success of their home and business, but it was most enjoyable when she could work side by side with Joris. Daniel, her youngest, was now three, so twelve-year-old Catalyntje could tend him while her mama worked at the taproom. One morning, after sweeping off the front stoop and placing a jar of flowers near the front door, Catalyntje took three loaves of fresh bread and went to the taproom to help Joris.

"You work with the customers this afternoon, and I will cook for a while," Joris offered.

"I would like that," Catalyntje said as she walked to where the patrons were seated. She asked what they each wanted to eat and drink, then helped Joris prepare it and brought it to their table. On one of her trips back to get more plates of food, she noticed a man in the corner writing. This intrigued her, so she walked to his table.

"Good day. Can I get you anything to drink?" Catalyntje asked, but she received no indication that the man had heard her since he kept writing. She stood motionless for a bit until he stopped writing, and a pleasant smile covered his face.

"Oh, yes, I'd like a drink and some bread if you have it," he answered. "My apologies for being preoccupied. My name is Jacob Steendam."

"Good to meet you, Jacob. I do not think I have seen you here before," Catalyntje replied.

"No, I just arrived here, and my supplies are being brought to my house as we speak. I've come here to spend time alone and collect my thoughts. I am a writer, or a poet, to be more precise," he answered.

"I saw you were writing, and that caught my attention. My friend Trijn wrote all about the women she helped as a midwife," Catalyntje added excitedly.

"I would like to meet this Trijn you speak of. Maybe we could share some of our writings," Steendam suggested.

"She has passed on," Catalyntje spoke sadly. "But she gave me her book of writings before she died. I have learned to read more since I came here, and always enjoy reading what she wrote in her book," Catalyntje added.

"Well, it is fine to write words for others to enjoy," Steendam replied.

"So, do you live nearby?" Catalyntje changed the subject.

"Yes, I live near the fort, second house from the end," he answered.

"Then we are neighbors. My husband Joris and I live a few houses to the east of there; you are right by where my friend Trijn lived," Catalyntje said.

"Well, let me get settled in, and you can come over and tell me all about New Amsterdam. I heard many fine things about it, so I decided to make it my home," he said, picking up his pen again.

"That would be wonderful. Now let me get that drink for you," Catalyntje said.

*****

The next day, Catalyntje and Joris sat down to lunch together before he went to the taproom.

"I almost have some pretzels finished. When they are done, I will have Jeronemus bring them over to you," Catalyntje said as she sat at the table.

"The patrons will be glad for those," Joris answered. "What do you think about our taproom? We've been at it a few years now."

"I think nearly thirty years," Catalyntje responded thoughtfully. "We have made a good life here, and I have enjoyed the chance it has given us to visit with our friends and neighbors."

"I think our whole family has worked together to make it successful," Joris said, putting cheese on his bread. "But what would you think of selling it and moving to our land in Breukelen at the Wallabout?"

"I did not expect that question this afternoon. What has brought this to your mind?" Catalyntje asked.

"Sarah and Hans are over there, and we spend much of our time on that side of the river helping them and working our land," Joris answered.

"It would be nice to keep the firewood on that side of the river; I always worry about you carrying it over on the ferry. Also, Sarah and Hans have their hands full with their growing family, which would make it easier for me to help them," Catalyntje smiled. "It has become busy in New Amsterdam, and we are in the middle of it all here on Pearl Street. I remember living among the trees near Fort Orange when we first came. It was a wild place, but it was peaceful to live there. I like the idea, Joris."

"Then I will see what needs to be done so we can move there," he smiled.

*****

Sarah was expecting her seventh child near the end of November, which meant that Catalyntje might not be able to help her with the birth since cold weather during the winter often froze the river. So, she took every chance to see Sarah when Joris went to the Wallabout to prepare for their move. When Catalyntje was there, she worked in Sarah's garden, cooked food, played with the children, and did extra mending. Sarah wasn't incapable. It was just that this pregnancy was different. Besides having a large plot of land and six children to look after, her stomach had grown much faster, making it difficult to get around. She was also exhausted all of the time, especially in the hot summer weather.

*****

Late one afternoon, as the autumn leaves fell outside, Catalyntje pulled four loaves of bread from the oven for the taproom. Then she looked up when she heard Annetje and Breckje, Sarah's two oldest children, calling through the Dutch door.

"Oma! Mama needs your help with her baby. Papa is in the field, so she sent both of us to take the ferry to come and get you," Annetje announced anxiously.

"What did you say?" Catalyntje questioned as she carefully set the loaves on the table. "I thought we still had some time. Did she call for anyone else?"

"No, she wants you to come as quickly as you can," Breckje answered with a concerned look. "Will Mama be alright?"

"Yes, she will, my dear. You return home, gather some towels, and then play with the younger children. Do you have a neighbor who could watch the younger children at their home?" Catalyntje asked.

"Mrs. Wolphertsen talks with Mama a lot and lives close by," Breckje answered.

"Before you go home, go to her house and ask if she can help with your little brothers and sisters. Tell her that your mama said the baby is coming. She will understand," Catalyntje instructed.

"We will do that, Oma," Annetje said seriously.

"Now, take this bread with you to eat along the way," Catalyntje said, holding out a freshly baked loaf wrapped in cloth. "I will stop by the midwife's house and bring her along. Safe home, girls."

"Thank you, Oma," Annetje said, hugging Catalyntje tightly. Then, the two young girls were gone.

Catalyntje gathered her children and gave them instructions on how to care for each other. She put a few supplies in a basket and went quickly to the taproom to tell Joris what had happened. After talking to the midwife, she headed for the ferry. On the ride across the water, Catalyntje didn't visit with the other passengers as she usually did. She was lost in her thoughts and wondered what could be wrong. Sarah wasn't due to have her baby for another month. She was glad the midwife would be there.

Once she arrived at Sarah's house, Catalyntje saw that the older children had done as she had asked. Mrs. Wolphertsen was leaving with the younger children and had sent her husband to the field to let Hans know what was happening. Catalyntje talked with Sarah as she prepared boiling water and gathered the birthing stool. As she tightly hugged the towels Annetje had gathered for her, she thought about Trijn and wished she could be there to help. She was always calm, kind, and knowledgeable during these situations.

Before long, there was a knock at the door, and to Catalyntje's relief, it was the midwife. She thanked Catalyntje for her preparations and then began to examine Sarah. After some discussion, the midwife stood up and looked around the room.

"Ladies, I think we will have two babies coming this evening. Sarah, you are going to have twins," she announced.

"What?" Sarah asked in an unbelieving tone.

"Twins," she responded. "Everything points to it: the larger stomach, the early labor, and I can feel two distinct heads."

"Will they be alright?" Catalyntje asked, wishing she hadn't brought doubt into the tense room.

"They will be much smaller, but we will do everything we can to help them," the midwife said.

By the light of several candles, Jacob Hansen Bergen and Catalyn Hansen Bergen entered the world, one right after the other. Catalyntje gathered extra blankets and little gowns to clothe each of them, and after the births, Sarah settled back into bed and started to feed them with the midwife's help. Catalyntje made her way to the barn with a lantern to invite Hans inside for the surprise that awaited him.

Catalyntje and the midwife spend the next day helping Sarah. Catalyntje also sent word to Joris about their two new grandchildren and told him she would stay for at least a week before returning home.

These births surprised the entire family, and they soon realized that two babies at once were a lot of work. Sarah had many friends and family who came to help in her garden, bring her food, and prepare for the winter. The babies were tiny and weak, which made them fragile, but within a month, Sarah noticed Jacob's little cheeks began to fatten, and his cry grew louder. However, little Catalyn didn't seem to grow as quickly. She wouldn't eat as much and didn't move around like little Jacob. She seemed content to lie calmly, swaddled in a blanket.

Jacob was christened in September, while Jannetje, Sarah's sister, stayed home to watch over Catalyn. This allowed the rest of the family to witness Jacob's christening while Catalyn could be kept at home where it was warm.

Little Jacob kept improving. He was eating on a schedule and sleeping well. Baby Catalyn, on the other hand, was still struggling; she seemed eager to eat but had difficulty keeping food down. She was feeble and had a faint, weak cry that continued day and night. Catalyntje spent as much time as she could helping Sarah care for her new babies and her six other children. Sarah was exhausted from feeding the babies, losing sleep, and the weight of constant worry for Catalyn.

As the snow fell and the river froze over, Catalyn's situation still didn't improve, and Sarah worried because she hadn't been christened yet. By November, Sarah and Hans decided they couldn't wait any longer, so they brought Catalyn to the church for her christening. Unfortunately, most of the family couldn't attend because of the cold weather and deep snow. The underlying worry for Catalyn dampened the spirit of celebration that should have been there.

Shortly after Christmas, their fears were realized when, on a frigid winter night, Catalyn grew too delicate and died in her sleep without a sound. When word reached Catalyntje and Joris, they went across the ice to visit Sarah and Hans, utterly devastated. Joris stayed for nearly a week before returning to be with their children back home and reopen the taproom. Catalyntje stayed with Sarah for three weeks, spending her days caring for and comforting her grandchildren, along with cooking and cleaning. Most days, she ran Sarah's household with a smile until she collapsed onto the straw mattress on the floor each evening, tears watering her pillow.

Her granddaughter's death was devastating, but it was equally difficult for Catalyntje to watch her grown child suffer so much with this heartbreaking loss. Catalyntje had lost her sweet Jacob and watching Sarah sob endlessly brought back painful feelings to her own heart. Their family's grief matched the darkness of the season and overpowered the light that shone each day. Every week went by more slowly than the one before it, and joy had stepped out of their reach.

Across the River

1654: 48 years old

Catalyntje and Joris continued their preparations to move to the Wallabout and hoped to be there by the middle of the summer. For several years, Joris had been building a house for them across the river. It was now livable and would only need a few more additions for the family to live there comfortably. The land was already cleared, gardens established, and a barn built. This would be the most prepared they'd ever been when moving to a new home.

The warmer weather thawed the river, allowing Catalyntje and Joris to make weekly trips on the ferry to their new home. Their property was up against Sarah and Hans' acreage, and their homes would be within walking distance.

At the end of April, Catalyntje and Joris sold their home on Pearl Street to Hendrick Hendrickson, a drummer at Fort Amsterdam. By the end of June, he would move in, and Catalyntje and Joris's family would move to their new home at the Wallabout in Breukelen.

*****

Catalyntje and Joris' neighbors were saddened to hear they would be moving across the river. Joris didn't want to go without saying a proper farewell, so he and Catalyntje planned a party at the taproom and invited everyone who frequented there. With the help of her daughters, Catalyntje baked pretzels, cookies, and loaves of bread. Their son, Jeronemus, gathered food from the garden, and Joris made sure to have plenty of drinks. That night, the taproom was filled with the laughter of friends enjoying their final evening together.

Catalyntje and Joris had decided beforehand that they wouldn't charge for anything that evening; it would be their treat. However, by the end of the evening, once the room was empty, coins and wampum from their dear friends filled the wooden bowl on the mantle.

"I will miss this taproom, especially seeing all of the folks we have come to know," Catalyntje admitted, sitting down at a table with Joris. "We have many friends and memories from this place."

"Yes, they are wonderful people. We will still come and visit once we've settled across the river. Then, maybe we can enjoy being here without working," Joris smiled.

Suddenly, a forceful knock interrupted their discussion. Joris rose to his feet and looked questioningly at Catalyntje.

"I am sorry to bother you at this late hour," the young man at the door started. "Your daughter Sarah has sent me here. Her husband, Hans, fell off a ship at the dock today. He bumped his head rather hard and . . . well, he is dead."

Joris stood without saying a word; Catalyntje gasped, her hand reaching for her mouth.

"What did you say, young man?" Joris asked.

"Your son-in-law is dead," the young man said timidly. "Can I help you in any way?"

"No, son. Thank you for coming to tell us in the dark of the night. Is the ferry still running?" Joris questioned.

"Yes, I asked them to watch for you to cross even though it is late; they are waiting for you," the young man replied.

"Thank you for your thoughtfulness. We will follow shortly," Joris said.

"I live across the river, so I will alert the ferryman that you are on your way, and we can all cross together," the young man offered, turned, and was gone.

Joris looked at Catalyntje, whose head was on the table, her audible sobs filling the empty room.

"Joris, Sarah cannot be asked to go through this! She cannot handle another loss!" Catalyntje sobbed.

"I know; it was just last year that they lost little Catalyn," Joris responded, tears filling his eyes.

"She is young, Joris, not even twenty-nine, and she and Hans have been happily married for fifteen years. She is too young for such tragedy," Catalyntje stammered.

"She is. Let's gather our things and go to the ferry. I will wake up our young Catalyntje and see that she watches over the children," Joris replied.

*****

A few days later, at the end of May, Hans was buried near the homestead where he and Sarah lived. The funeral was solemn, and Sarah could not be comforted. She was overwhelmed by the prospect of running the four hundred acres she and Hans had traded for and raising their children alone. Catalyntje offered her love and help but couldn't keep Sarah from being overcome by her tragic situation.

*****

When the end of June arrived, Catalyntje and Joris were ready to move to the Wallabout with their five youngest children, who were between four and thirteen years old. Catalyntje looked forward to the change, but as she packed the last items, she looked around their home. This place held countless memories, good and bad; it was difficult to say goodbye. Her garden, the taproom, the windmill, and the market were all there. And then there were the ever-present memories of Trijn and little Jacob that always kept a tight hold on her thoughts and feelings. The events surrounding these two people she loved were etched into her heart.

As the family crossed the river on the ferry, Catalyntje remembered the worry that accompanied their move from Fort Orange to New Amsterdam, but this time was different; they were prepared, and there weren't many unknowns. New Amsterdam had been a fine place, but now they were ready for a quieter life with a slower pace. Working on their new homestead would still be a lot of work, but it wouldn't be at the bustling center of New Netherland. Catalyntje lifted her gaze to the other side of the river and was ready to move on.

*****

Moving everything to their new home at the Wallabout took a few weeks. This new place reminded Catalyntje of their home near Fort Orange because they were surrounded by trees. After the work of moving, Catalyntje and Joris were glad Sunday had arrived so they could rest. The entire family walked to the nearby Dutch Reformed Church in Flatbush, where they were delighted to see Sarah and her children. Catalyntje was grateful they now lived closer to her newly widowed daughter. Since Joris had spent much of his time working on this land the past few years, he was pleasantly surprised that he already knew many people in the congregation. After the meeting, the Domine led those at the church to the newly established cemetery on the church grounds, the Flatbush Cemetery. Death was still fresh in Catalyntje's mind, so she appreciated this new addition to the church.

New Neighbors

1655: 49 years old

Catalyntje and Joris were settled comfortably into their new farm at the Wallabout in Breukelen. With Stuyvesant in charge, the colony had improved dramatically by establishing city councils and courts in the settlement. Joris was appointed to serve as a magistrate of Breukelen in April under Stuyvesant's direction.

Catalyntje and Joris had much to do once they had moved into their new home. Besides working and improving their place, they helped Sarah as often as possible. Early on a hot July morning, Joris took Jeronemus with him to help plow Sarah's land while Catalyntje and the other children worked in the garden and moved the animals to another pasture. After working all day, Catalyntje prepared a hearty soup to enjoy once they returned home together. As Annetje set the table, Joris and Jeronemus walked wearily through the door.

"Jeronemus and I just washed up outside, and it smells like it is time to eat," Joris said, hanging his hat on the peg shelf near the door.

"Yes, it is nearly ready," Catalyntje replied, hugging Joris. "Sit down; it is almost ready."

"Elizabeth, Annetje, come and help serve dinner," Catalyntje called out; both girls came quickly to help.

"We got many things done today," Catalyntje said to Joris, sitting across from him. "The garden, the animals, and even some repairs to the barn door."

"Thank you for what you have done. It was good that Jeronemus went to help Sarah. Although we may not need to spend as much time there in the future," Joris said, raising his eyebrows. "She has a suitor."

"What?" Catalyntje replied excitedly.

"His name is Teunis Bogaert. He came here a few years ago as a sailor from the southern part of Holland. He is a good fellow with solid business sense," Joris reported.

"That is wonderful. I look forward to meeting him," Catalyntje said.

*****

Joris had been correct in his assumptions about Sarah. In the middle of August, she married Teunis. He was a good husband, loved Sarah and her children, and quickly took over the farm duties. Catalyntje hoped that this union would bring Sarah and her children happiness again.

*****

That fall, Stuyvesant led many of the able-bodied men who worked for the Company south to the Delaware River. The Swedes had taken Fort Casimir in the southern part of New Netherland, so Stuyvesant was determined to get it back. He filled several ships with men to accomplish this, and they all sailed south. The Susquehannock had been watching Stuyvesant, and once they saw his men leave, they banded with other nearby tribes to watch New Netherland more closely, still wary from previous wars with the settlers.

One morning, while Stuyvesant and his men were away, Hendrick van Dijck got out of bed, stretched, and pulled on his trousers to step outside and breathe some fresh autumn air. To his surprise, he saw a Susquehannock woman eating peaches from his tree. This intrusion was a surprising way to wake up; without thinking things through, Van Dijck ran out to his garden and killed the woman for her thievery. One of her nearby companions saw what he had done and shot Van Dijck with an arrow. The commotion woke Van Dijck's neighbor, Paulus van der Grift, who ran over to help him but didn't make it before a tomahawk sunk into his skull.

Awakened by the disturbance, men living nearby rushed outside to see what was happening. When Cornelis van Tienhoven saw the fighting, he quickly gathered men to battle against the Susquehannock. Van Tienhoven was known for his leadership against the Natives and had previously joined with Kieft in this cause, but since he was not well-liked among the settlers, he couldn't gather enough men to make a difference against the attacking tribes.

First, the Natives crossed the river and invaded New Amsterdam from the shoreline to the northern border. After damaging homes and yards, they went back to the other side of the river, setting fire to Pavonia and taking nearly one hundred fifty hostages.

The following day, just as the sun rose, sixty-four canoes, carrying around six hundred Natives, landed silently at the southern tip of New Amsterdam. The settlers were still asleep when the tribes noiselessly scattered themselves throughout the city's narrow streets.

Next, the Susquehannock continued up the Noort River, destroying farms and forcing people to flee to Fort Amsterdam for protection. Several years ago, Kieft's unexpected violence had surprised the tribe, so they decided it wouldn't happen again. This time, they would strike first and control the situation.

Catalyntje and Joris were alerted to a problem when they saw smoke rising across the river in New Amsterdam. It was too far away to tell what was happening, but word traveled quickly, and soon they learned of the devastation. After a few messengers visited their home, they realized that the Natives had killed at least one hundred people in the raid and taken more as prisoners. With the sudden flow of people seeking shelter in New Amsterdam, they expected there would be even more deaths and many more people without homes.

Terrifying memories flooded Catalyntje's mind as reports of the destruction reached their home. Her fear and desperation during the Kieft War had overwhelmed her. It had happened nearly ten years before, but the horror was still painfully etched in her very being. Once Stuyvesant got word of the violence, he and his men sailed back to New Amsterdam, where they found numerous crops burned; this would hurt the entire settlement since they probably wouldn't receive any more supplies for at least five months. Additionally, the territory lost nearly five hundred head of cattle, which were stolen or killed by the Susquehannock.

Catalyntje's heart broke for those in the middle of this violent situation, and although she was across the river, she still wanted to help. Joris planned to take the ferry to New Amsterdam immediately to offer his assistance. As he gathered his coat and a few tools, Catalyntje and Annetje got other items for him to bring. Jeronemus, now twelve years old, got ready to go with Joris. Catalyntje set out a loaf of bread from the previous evening; Annetje wrapped it in a clean cloth. Young Catalyntje gathered onions from the cellar, and Elizabeth chose a blanket, three soft scarves, and two pairs of wool mittens from the kast for those who now had nothing.

Catalyntje carefully packed all the items into two baskets and handed them to Joris. He could see it was difficult for her to hear about these attacks. As he leaned down and kissed her forehead, she smiled and whispered, "Safe home, Love."

Catalyntje stood in the doorway and watched Joris and Jeronemus until they were out of her sight. Then she slowly closed the door and turned around to see Annetje, Elizabeth, and young Catalyntje standing motionless where they were when Joris and Jeronemus had left. She could see the fear in their eyes, so she knelt and held out her arms. They all gathered close to her and began to cry.

*****

Catalyntje and her daughters kept themselves busy the entire day. As they worked, they didn't say much to each other because worry filled their minds. Because it was a quiet day, they were startled when Elizabeth shouted, "Papa and Jeronemus are coming!" With that announcement, Catalyntje set down the spoon she was stirring soup with, wiped her hands on her apron, and followed her daughter out the door.

"It is good to be back home," Joris said, putting down his bag and hugging Catalyntje tightly. She was relieved to have him home and appreciated the strength she felt from having him beside her. The entire family stood around Catalyntje and Joris, anxious to hear any news about what had happened across the river.

"Thank you for the supplies you all gathered. Many people needed help, and what we shared with them was appreciated. Sadly, there are many badly damaged homes near where we used to live, and unfortunately, the news we heard was true. Some people in New Amsterdam were killed yesterday, and some were taken north as prisoners," Joris reported. No one responded, so Joris continued. "I have volunteered to help, but it will take all of us to do this. Some families lost their homesteads because the Susquehannock burned them to the ground. Stuyvesant said there were at least thirty families without a home now." Catalyntje closed her eyes and slowly shook her head.

"How many more times will we have to deal with this violence?" she asked. "We got along well with the tribes until Kieft arrived."

"I worry about the same thing, and I'm glad we are farther from where most people live. Since we are in a safer place now, we can share with those in desperate need," Joris said.

"Those who lost homes will not have time to build new ones or prepare for the winter," Catalyntje said.

"Your mama is right," Joris replied. "It is too late in the season for them to rebuild or plant any crops. But we have plenty of land, two barns, firewood, and food. So, I volunteered to have one of the families live in our extra barn this winter until they can build a new home in the spring. Of course, it will only be for this winter, and I know it will make our supplies tight, but I can't leave them without help."

Tears filled Catalyntje's eyes as she slowly nodded, "You did the right thing, Joris. I remember being forced to leave Fort Orange at the end of the summer. We had difficulty gathering enough supplies for the winter and struggled so much," she recalled.

"I remembered that too," Joris said. "I don't know when this family will arrive, but if we could start early in the morning, I think we can have things ready to make them feel at home."

Everyone was up with the sun the following day, preparing for their new neighbors. Jeronemus and his sister Catalyntje cleaned the barn while Joris moved extra benches and shelves into the space. Catalyntje gathered winter clothing and blankets, along with yarn and knitting needles. She didn't want their soon-to-be neighbors to feel pity; instead, she wanted to give them a place to heal. She also had Annetje collect food the family could keep in the barn where they would be staying.

After spending the entire morning preparing for their guests, everyone was tired. So, they took a break under the apple tree, and Catalyntje brought out bread and salted meat to eat. Just as she sat down, Elizabeth jumped up and announced, "I think I see our new family coming!"

"I think you are right," Joris said as they all stood.

Once the family reached them, Joris offered his hand to the man standing before him. "Welcome. My name is Joris Rapelje, and this is my family: Catalyntje, my wife, and our children, Daniel, Elizabeth, Annetje, Jeronemus, and Catalyntje. We are happy to have you join us here at the Wallabout," he said with a nod.

With tears in his eyes, the man grasped Joris' hand and humbly said, "We can never thank you enough for your kindness, Mr. Rapelje." The woman beside him was looking down and couldn't meet the gaze of Catalyntje and her children.

"We are glad to have some new friends. Please call me Joris," he said with a smile.

"Thank you," the man paused, "Joris. I am Cornelius van Deusen, and this is my dear wife, Elizabeth, and our three children, Roelof, Gerrit, and Isabel," he said. "You are more than kind to allow us to live here with you for the winter. There just isn't enough time to build a new home before the cold weather arrives."

"You must be prepared for when it gets cold here. Follow me. I will show you what we have come up with," offered Joris as he walked towards the barn. "This is your home for now, and you are always welcome to spend time with us in our home. Unfortunately, I don't have the means for you to cook out here; you'll have to come in and eat meals with us. My wife is an excellent cook and gardener, so we will have delicious fare to offer."

Catalyntje stepped forward, "Please let me know what other supplies you might need for clothing and food. I didn't know how old your children were, so I haven't given you everything you'll need yet," Catalyntje offered Elizabeth.

"You are generous; I will help with meals and sewing and gardening and . . ." Elizabeth started.

"I know you will help," Catalyntje interrupted, "but for now, just take some time to rest."

"Thank you," Elizabeth said in a shaky voice.

"We will have dinner ready before sundown, but you are welcome to visit sooner if you'd like. You have had a painful day, so there is no hurry," Catalyntje said gently.

They walked inside the barn, and Joris talked with Cornelius about things he would like to fix up for them to be warm enough in the winter. The children jumped up and down and chased each other happily, immune from the pressures their parents felt.

After the family settled in the barn, Catalyntje added more carrots to the soup and picked more turnips from the garden. She had enough bread but decided to bake an apple cake to sweeten the evening. The Van Deusen family joined them after a few hours, and together, they enjoyed the evening, eating and laughing.

"I'm glad to have a new friend," Daniel said, hugging Gerrit. "Stay here before you go to your new house," he replied. After a few seconds, he returned proudly carrying his spinning top. He handed it to Gerrit and said, "I don't think you brought your toys; this is yours now." The room went silent with the kindness they had just witnessed.

240

Catalyntje and Joris spent the next few weeks making the Van Deusen family comfortable and ready for the winter. Joris and Cornelius patched holes that might let the cold air slip into the barn, improved the chimney, and strengthened the fireplace. The two men also cut and split wood and stacked it close to both homes.

Catalyntje enjoyed time with Elizabeth and appreciated her help. Elizabeth was about twenty years younger than Catalyntje and relied on her for advice. The two women cooked and knitted together, and Catalyntje even learned some new stitches. While the preparations continued, the children played endlessly, enjoying their newfound friends.

*****

Since this was Catalyntje and Joris' first winter living across the river from New Amsterdam, things were different than they were used to. Catalyntje enjoyed the clear days when she could walk outside and look over the white, untouched snow. She missed the ships that frequented New Amsterdam's harbor but could still see them when she was out of the forest and near the river. Ever since she had seen the great vessels in the Old World, their size and movement on the water had captured her attention.

Now that they lived in Breukelen, Catalyntje missed the waves' soothing sound and the windmill's slow spinning near Fort Amsterdam. They had always brought focus to her life during difficult times, but here, she found other sights to keep her centered. There were more trees than in New Amsterdam, and they reminded her of when they lived at Fort Orange. She remembered how amazed she was seeing those tall trees for the first time and couldn't believe the endless number of them standing near their first home. That feeling returned to her as she walked about their land at the Wallabout.

*****

Before the year ended, Sarah and her new husband, Teunis, had their first child, Aertje Teunisen Bogaert. Catalyntje helped with the birth and was glad that this time, she lived on the same side of the river as her daughter. A few weeks before Christmas, they all traveled to the Flatbush Dutch Reformed Church for the baby's christening.

Repair and Rebuild

1656: 50 years old

The Van Deusen family appreciated having a safe place to spend the winter with Catalyntje and Joris. Then, when spring arrived, Cornelius van Deusen looked for land in Breukelen for his family to settle on. They had grown accustomed to the quiet life at the Wallabout and chose not to return to New Amsterdam.

*****

The people of New Netherland had spent the winter healing their hearts from the recent violence that had enveloped their area. Once spring came, they were busier than usual, rebuilding and repairing what they'd lost. This brought a feeling of hope that floated through the territory once again.

When the snow melted, the Van Deusens worked tirelessly to build a house on land they had traded for with the Canarese. During the summer, their children played and worked under Catalyntje's watchful eyes while they and Joris prepared their new home.

*****

Early September marked an entire year since the Van Deusens had come to live with Catalyntje and Joris, and now their new home was ready. Elizabeth had planted a garden near Joris' barn to provide her family with food for the upcoming winter. Since she was often away helping construct their new home, Catalyntje usually tended Elizabeth's garden along with her own. Without mentioning it to Elizabeth, Catalyntje also grew extra food in her garden, which she planned to send with them when they moved.

Pirates

1657: 51 years old

Stuyvesant continued working to restore peace to New Netherland. The changes in policies he'd made helped the area look better and allowed the citizens to focus their energies on more peaceful projects. Stuyvesant saw these successes as a reason to celebrate and announced an upcoming day of worship and thanksgiving. It was held on the first Wednesday in March and was a delightful occasion. Businesses remained closed, and everyone gathered to spend the day with family and friends, eating and playing games.

A week after the celebration, Catalyntje and Joris returned to New Amsterdam for a few days to visit their old friends. Catalyntje gathered flowers and vegetables from her garden, and Joris took some handmade tools. These would be gifts to share once they arrive.

Catalyntje and Joris spent the day visiting their friends' homes, and when evening came, they went to their old taproom. They spent time visiting with their old friends from this familiar place there.

"What do you think of your old taproom, Joris?" one of his friends asked.

"It is wonderful to be back and not be working this time. Don't get me wrong, I loved being here, but I like where I am now," Joris answered, taking another sip.

"Glad to hear it, my friend, and glad you're back to visit," the man replied loudly over the singing in the room. Then, suddenly, the door swung open so hard that it hit the wall behind it.

"What is happening here tonight, and why wasn't I invited?" a loud voice boomed as the room quieted and two men entered.

"Who is that?" Joris asked as Catalyntje went to his side.

"Those are the Van Salee brothers. Pirates they are," his friend answered quietly. "Anthony brings fear, but his brother Abraham isn't as bad. Their father is the king of the Barbary Coast Pirates." Catalyntje paid careful attention as the older pirate started to rant about a ship full of rotted wood.

Then, her attention shifted to the younger man who had entered with his brother. He said nothing but stood to the side and nodded at various times as his brother bellowed.

"They are from Morocco," Joris' friend said.

"I don't know that I've ever met anyone from that part of the world," Joris admitted.

"And they aren't Christians either. They read a different Holy Book; I think they call it the Quran. Anthony brought a copy when he came to the settlement; they worship here in town."

"I've never seen the book, but I've heard tell of it," another man said.

As Catalyntje watched, she realized that there was also a small child, maybe three or four years old, standing behind the younger of the two brothers, and she wondered why pirates would bring a young boy to a taproom. Soon, the oldest brother stopped speaking, and they both went to the counter to get a drink while the boy silently followed behind. After getting their drinks, the two men looked around until their eyes settled on Catalyntje and Joris. Then, the older man laughed as they walked towards them.

"Well, I haven't seen you at this taproom before. You must be fresh off the ship," Anthony remarked.

"No, I am very familiar with this taproom. I started it years ago. My wife and I are here to visit old friends and wanted to see how the place was holding up," Joris answered.

"My brother, Abraham, and I come here quite a bit and rather like this place when we aren't taking Spanish ships," he said with a boisterous laugh.

"Good to meet the both of you," the younger brother spoke up, walking to another table with the young boy still following behind. As Catalyntje watched, she realized that the little boy didn't speak with anyone or eat anything. At one point, he sat on the floor by the men, looking rather tired, while they talked.

"Joris, I am worried for that young boy. He has not had anything to eat or drink all night, and he looks exhausted," Catalyntje said with concern.

"I noticed that too," Joris responded. "The two pirate brothers seem wrapped up in their own world. Maybe we could offer to help."

"I like that idea," Catalyntje answered. As the night continued, Joris kept talking with his friends, but most of Catalyntje's acquaintances had left for the evening to care for their families. Watching the tired little boy, she decided she wouldn't wait for Joris to talk with the pirate, and even though he was frightening, she would approach him.

"Excuse me. Abraham, I think it was?" Catalyntje spoke as firmly as she could.

"Good evening to you. Ah, yes, you and your husband started this fine establishment," Abraham responded.

"Yes, we did," Catalyntje answered timidly. "My husband is still visiting, but we are staying nearby with a friend. I noticed the young boy with you. It looks like he could use some rest. I mean no offense, but I wondered if I could take him with me to get some sleep while you enjoyed more time here."

"I don't know you, but you seem to have a goodly heart, and I would enjoy being here until this place closes for the night," the pirate responded. "The boy's mother, Fortuyn, we ain't married, was supposed to look out for him this week but changed her mind, so he is with me. I can pay you for your services."

"Oh no, I just wanted to help so you could enjoy your evening. I will not require any payment," Catalyntje replied.

"When we are finished here, where can I find him? Where is your house again?" Abraham asked.

"We are just visiting. My husband and I live across the river now, but we are staying with a friend on the south side of Pearl Street for the night," Catalyntje spoke more boldly.

Abraham looked down at his son and said, "Hey, my little sea dog. Do you want to go with this nice woman? She will take care of you until I'm done here."

"Yes," the little boy responded. Catalyntje put out her hand, and the thin boy reached for it.

"We will get you a bite to eat before we leave," Catalyntje told him; his face lit up.

"I can get him in a few hours," Abraham offered.

"He will just be asleep then. Why don't you come and get him in the morning? Then he can have a good night's sleep," Catalyntje offered.

"I thank you. The boy's name is Frans. What was your name?" the pirate asked.

"Catalyntje. My name is Catalyntje Trico," she answered. The boy smiled at his father and looked up at Catalyntje, waiting for her to fulfill her promise of food. She spoke briefly with Joris, took the boy to get some food, and headed to her friend's house, where Frans fell asleep within minutes.

Catalyntje and Joris let the young boy sleep as long as he would the following day. The sun had been in the sky for at least three hours before Frans peered around the corner of the main room where Catalyntje and her friend were talking.

"Hello, Jadda," he said quietly, walking to where Catalyntje sat. She looked at him questioningly.

"I have not been called Jadda before. How did you think of that name?" Catalyntje asked.

"It means Oma in your language. You act like an Oma or a Jadda because you looked after me," the young boy replied.

"I like that name, then," Catalyntje said, smiling. "Would you like some breakfast?" she asked.

"Yes, I would," he answered, clapping his hands. Then, he waited quietly beside the empty stool as Catalyntje brought him food. After he ate, he began to talk about everything. He spoke about his father's ship and his mother being gone most of the time. He also mentioned playing with a pile of gold coins. He was a delightful young boy, and Catalyntje enjoyed learning about his life since it differed from hers.

It wasn't until after lunch that Frans' father, Abraham, came to pick him up. Catalyntje and Joris listened as he told them about his most recent ship attack. Then the conversation shifted to Catalyntje and Joris, who shared a bit about their story in New Netherland.

"If you are ever on the other side of the river, you are welcome to come to our home," Joris offered. "Your young Frans would have a good time playing with our little Daniel."

"I will remember that. Frans doesn't get to play with children very often. He spends his time on ships or moving about with his mother," Abraham said, bowing his head.

"I think we need to be going, my little sea dog," Abraham said, looking at Frans, who grabbed his father's hand.

"Goodbye, Jadda," Frans called out happily as he skipped out the door with his father.

*****

Each year, as the children grew older, they could help Catalyntje and Joris more with the chores and duties of the homestead. Now, the entire family was busy with the usual preparations for the winter. The days hadn't been as hot that summer, but Catalyntje still kept her gardens and trees well-watered. One morning, before it grew too warm, she and Jeronemus spent time pulling the water wagon back and forth between the stream and the area around their house. Finally, after their third trip, they were tired and headed inside for some cheese and dried fish. When they reached the door, young Catalyntje met them and said, "We have some visitors. I do not know them."

"I will be right there," Catalyntje replied, wondering who it might be. Then, as she entered the house, she saw Abraham and Frans.

"What a surprise," she gasped, pulling up a stool to sit by them.

"Hello, Jadda. Do you remember me?" Frans asked with a big smile.

"Of course, I remember you. Let me get you some food, and we can talk for a bit," Catalyntje replied, instructing Elizabeth to go outside and get Joris to join them.

As they talked about the past few months, Catalyntje's children couldn't pull away from Abraham's stories of the sea. It didn't take long before Daniel asked if he could play with Frans, and soon, they were outside and up in a tree. After a few of Abraham's stories, Joris took him outside to show him their farm.

To everyone's delight, Abraham and Frans stayed for dinner and continued talking about their land and sea adventures.

"I know it may seem strange for a sea-faring man, but I recently purchased some land," Abraham announced proudly. "I want a place for Frans and his mother to stay if something happens to me while I'm away on my ship."

"I think that is a grand idea. A man needs a place to call home," Joris replied, taking another biscuit from the plate. "I could even help if you'd like. I have quite the collection of tools and animals."

As the conversation continued, they decided Joris and Jeronemus would help Abraham for a few days and leave Frans to play with Daniel; everyone liked that idea.

The two families became better acquainted since they saw each other at least once a week. Then, as winter grew closer, Joris realized Abraham's home wouldn't be finished in time, so he offered to have Abraham and Frans stay in their barn for the winter. The Van Deusen family had their own place now, and the barn was still furnished for simple living. Abraham gratefully accepted, and Frans was delighted to spend time with the family. They all passed the winter together, their evenings filled with warm soup and tales of pirate adventures around the hearth.

*****

Just before the end of the year, Sarah and Teunis had another child. They named her Catalyntje Teunisen Bogaert. Catalyntje was there to help as her namesake was born. It was a hard time to enter the world, so Sarah took extra care to keep their home warm, and many neighbors made their way through the snow to bring food and handmade blankets for them. Abraham and Frans attended the christening with the rest of the family, filled with curiosity since it differed from their Muslim ways. As they left the church after the ceremony, Abraham slipped a small gold coin into Sarah's hand.

"For the little Catalyntje," he said with a smile. "Her Jadda is a kindly woman."

The Orphan

1659: 53 years old

For the past two years, Joris and Abraham continued working on Abraham's home. It took more time than expected because Abraham's pirating activities kept him away more and more. When he was at sea, Frans spent most of his time with his mother, Fortuyn. Until one day, Abraham brought word that the boy's mother had caught a fever and died. With this tragic change, Frans spent even more time at Catalyntje and Joris' home. Catalyntje never knew when they would show up at her door, but she always welcomed them. Even though Frans was young, he was eager to help and was a great friend to her eight-year-old Daniel.

*****

Once the snow began to melt, Abraham and Frans helped plant the gardens and replace the stacks of firewood that had kept them warm during the frigid winter. Each day started with breakfast and a plan for the day's chores. The chickens had started laying more eggs, so Catalyntje usually cooked a pan of eggs with salted pork each morning.

"Daniel, can you please set the table?" Catalyntje called.

"But that is Frans' job, Mama," Daniel complained.

"I know it is, but we worked hard yesterday, and he and his Papa have not come in yet; I need you to do it," she replied.

"Alright," Daniel said in a low voice, walking to get some dishes. After a short time, everything was ready to eat, and Catalyntje wondered if the two in the barn would be joining them or if they'd taken off again since the weather had improved.

"I'll go out and see if they are still here," Joris offered, walking towards the door. Before he reached it, the door swung open, and six-year-old Frans entered abruptly. Everyone turned to face him as he stood motionless in the doorway.

"My papa won't wake up. I told him we could eat, but he won't wake up," Frans offered in a shaky voice.

"Did he talk to you when you tried to wake him?" Joris asked, kneeling in front of the young boy.

"No, he wouldn't talk to me," Frans replied.

"Catalyntje, why don't you all sit down for breakfast? I will go to the barn and help Abraham," Joris said with concern. Catalyntje quickly busied Frans with meal preparations and worried about what Joris might find in the barn.

When he returned to the house, he instructed the children to finish eating and clean up the dishes. Then he took Catalyntje gently by the arm and guided her to the far corner of the room.

"Abraham is dead," Joris replied. Catalyntje raised her hand to her mouth and gasped. "There doesn't seem to be any foul play. He is just gone."

"He lived a rough life, but Frans is so young, and his mama is gone too. What will he do, Joris?" Catalyntje asked with concern.

"I'll take Frans outside and tell him about his papa. I think he already knows. We will keep him here as long as he needs to stay," Joris replied. "Our first duty is to care for him and make this as easy as possible. As you remember, Abraham put me in charge of his land and house if anything should happen to him," Joris replied.

"Frans can live here until we sort things out," Catalyntje replied.

"That is a fine idea; now I'll go talk to Frans," Joris said.

The next few days were spent preparing for the burial of Abraham and comforting Frans. Joris and Jeronemus made three trips across the river to locate the pirate's brother, Anthony, which took nearly a month. He was too busy to take in Frans, so the little boy spent his days with Catalyntje, Joris, and their family, where they offered love and comfort to this young orphan. After a few more weeks, Joris went to the house he and Abraham had been working on. When he arrived, he saw people surrounding the building, going in and out.

"Greetings to you," Joris offered, walking towards the front stoop, his face etched with concern. "What business do you have here today?"

"Greetings," said a man in a nice coat. "I am with the church. We received word that the man who owns this house has passed on. We are here to seize it for our congregation's needy members."

"That is interesting because Abraham, who owned this place, put me in charge of his land and home. In his testament, he left this property to his young boy Frans," Joris insisted.

"We haven't seen that document," the well-dressed man suggested. "You might want to inform the council about it."

"I will do that soon. But you need to leave this place be. Abraham and I have worked hard on it, and I want to be sure that it ends up in the right hands," Joris replied.

"We will finish a brief inventory here, and then we will be on our way," the man said, reaching out to shake hands with Joris.

When Joris arrived home, Daniel and Frans welcomed him, calling from the top of a tree. Inside, he found Catalyntje working near the hearth; the smell of fish chowder floated through the room.

"Sit down for some bread and chowder, and tell me about your day," Catalyntje said.

"I will be honest. Deacons from the church were at Abraham's house; the council had sent them. They were taking an inventory and were under orders to seize the property," Joris replied.

"They cannot do that," Catalyntje jumped in, setting her spoon down loudly on the table. "You are in charge of that property. Tomorrow, I will go and talk to them. I will take the ferry across the river and show them the papers Abraham left you," Catalyntje insisted.

Catalyntje kept her word, and early the following day, she walked to the ferry. Once she reached the bench near the water's edge, she sat and drank from the water skin she'd brought while she counted four ships docked at New Amsterdam and watched faint smoke trails stretching to the sky. She felt confident the council would listen to her.

*****

Catalyntje sat on the hard wooden bench at the back of the council room until they called her name. Then she walked forward with Abraham's will in her hands.

"Thank you for hearing me," Catalyntje began. "I am here to speak on behalf of the dead - Abraham van Salee. He died at my home over a month ago. He and his six-year-old son lived with us while they worked to complete their house. My husband, Joris Rapelje, went to the homestead yesterday and found deacons from the Dutch Reformed Church preparing to seize his home."

"It seems right that they take an inventory and see how they can disperse the remains to the poor since Abraham is now dead. And is the child's mother still alive, or does he need someone to look after him?" a councilman asked.

Catalyntje cleared her throat and reached for the folded paper in her apron pocket. "Abraham left this paper putting my husband in charge of his land. He wanted his son to have his homestead."

"And who is the boy's mother? And where is she?" a councilman asked.

"Her name was Fortuyn," Catalyntje answered.

"Wasn't she an enslaved woman? She helped my neighbor with his flax field last season," the councilman replied.

"Yes, she was, and the boy's papa was from Morocco; he is a Muslim and does not attend the church, so they are not on its records," Catalyntje said.

"Let me see that paper you have," the first councilman requested, reaching out his hand. Catalyntje gave it to him and observed his face as he read it. "Well, it seems you are right; your husband is in charge of the property since Van Salee is dead. Because the boy isn't with the church, the Orphan masters should handle this matter. Here is your paper; we have written some details about our discussion today. Now talk with the Orphan masters to settle this."

"Thank you for your help," Catalyntje replied respectfully, walking out the door.

She arrived home just as the sun set in the western sky. Joris listened anxiously to what had occurred and was relieved there was no contention over the matter. Catalyntje spent the rest of the evening assigning jobs to the older children since she planned to be away the next day to meet with the Orphan masters.

*****

When Catalyntje left the following day, Jeronemus was busy helping Joris sharpen tools while Daniel and Frans picked apples from the tree beside the house. Elizabeth and Annetje were in the garden, putting cut

254

herbs into their baskets to be dried for the winter. Catalyntje didn't have to cross the river this time since Breukelen had an Orphan master. She knocked firmly when she reached the orphanage's door, and a kindly older woman answered and invited her in.

"I would like to speak with the Orphan master," Catalyntje requested.

"He is in discussion with a few of his council right now, but I will see when he will be finished," she answered. Catalyntje stood purposefully near the door until an older man approached her from a back room.

"I am the Orphan master. How may I help you today?" he asked sincerely.

"I need to speak with you about an orphan and some matters relating to the land his papa has left him," Catalyntje answered.

"Certainly, come in. A few members of the orphan council are here, and we would be glad to listen to your concerns," he replied kindly. As Catalyntje entered the room, the men welcomed her.

"My husband, Joris, and I have an orphan living with us. He is the son of the pirate Abraham van Salee and the enslaved woman Fortuyn. Both have died, and their son, Frans, is supposed to inherit his papa's homestead. I have the paper and the will stating this. Frans is only six years old, and he cannot keep the place on his own, but we were concerned because the church has taken steps to seize it and use it for the poor," Catalyntje reported.

"I know the young boy is an orphan, but have you gone to the director-general and council yet? They can decide this matter," the Orphan master answered.

"I talked with them yesterday, and they said you would handle this," Catalyntje said as the men seated around the table mumbled.

"I am, well, I am not certain how to decide this matter. The orphan is not," the Orphan master paused. "Well, he would be different from us since his mother was enslaved and his father was a pirate. I am familiar with his father and think he is a Muslim," the Orphan master noted.

"I know this, but the young boy still needs to be allowed to claim the land that is his. I have come to you for help," Catalyntje said firmly.

"You see, we have never had anyone come to us on behalf of a mixed-race child. Therefore, we are unsure if this matter should be handled differently," a council member spoke up.

"But he is a child, just like any other!" Catalyntje demanded. "He may look different from us, but he needs love and help. So, he should not be treated differently from any other orphan."

"You are most likely correct," the Orphan master replied. "But since we have not handled a situation like this before, it seems right that you go back to the director general's council. We cannot claim jurisdiction over this matter since we have not handled a case like this one."

Catalyntje scowled and thanked the council for their time. As she walked back home, she didn't understand why they would suggest treating Frans differently from another orphaned child.

*****

Catalyntje spent the next two weeks presenting this matter to the council in Breukelen and then to the director general's council in New Amsterdam. No one wanted to decide on the issue, and she felt she was getting pushed from one place to another just because Frans' parentage was not common. Finally, she received the desired results during her last visit to the director general's office. They agreed that the land would go to Frans when he was old enough to live there independently, but until then, he was to stay with Catalyntje and Joris.

Once Catalyntje returned home, she and Joris went for a walk while she told him about the council's decisions. "Catalyntje, you have spent much of your time helping Frans; I am glad it has turned out well," Joris said.

"It has puzzled me, though, Joris. Since when have people in this settlement minded how someone spoke or what they looked like?" Catalyntje responded in a sharp tone.

"I have noticed more of that, too. I think the English have been getting closer to our borders, and they aren't as welcoming as the Dutch," Joris offered, kicking a pinecone out of the path.

"I agree. The British have purchased more and more land to the east of us, and I think they have had more influence on the Orphan master than we realized," Catalyntje responded.

"I, for one, will keep a keen eye on their actions," Joris replied, continuing silently for several steps. "Do you mind taking in Frans until he can move to the place his papa left him? It will be several years."

"I do not mind at all. He is such a sweet boy and always willing to help. He and Daniel have become good friends; they are like brothers," Catalyntje smiled.

"I have noticed that as well. I appreciate that you have a generous heart, Catalyntje," Joris said, reaching for her hand.

256

More Changes

1660: 54 years old

While the snow was still on the ground, Sarah had another child, Neeltje Teunisen Bogaert. Joris brought Catalyntje over the snowbanks in their sleigh to Sarah's home to help with the birth. Unfortunately, Catalyntje could only stay for a week before returning home to care for her own children.

Catalyntje and Joris noticed that New Netherland was undergoing many changes due to its growing population. Additionally, the English were moving closer to the edges of New Netherland, which made it increasingly difficult for the tribes in the area to have enough space to live comfortably. Since the Dutch were losing more land to the English, they had become more demanding about their land rights with the tribes. As a result, the Natives had become more easily agitated and less willing to share what they had.

Besides the problems between the settlers and the tribes, nature had also turned against the city of New Amsterdam. Over the past several years, the people living near the coastline noticed the land slowly eroding. So, Stuyvesant dealt with this problem as the Dutch would. First, he had a seawall built in front of the Stadt Huys. Then, he had men from the Company construct a canal down the center of Broad Street. This allowed the extra water from the bay to flow into the canal instead of eroding the shores.

Besides the continual renovations to New Netherland, Catalyntje and Joris also had changes within their family. A new daughter-in-law joined them when Jan married Maria Fredericks Maer in the spring. She was a gentle and kind young woman, and it was evident that Jan was smitten with her. She wasn't as physically strong as most women her age, but she and Jan lived close to family, so they got extra help when they needed it. Catalyntje regularly brought them vegetables from her garden, loaves of fresh bread, and baskets of cookies. Maria was always appreciative of her visits and enjoyed talking with Catalyntje.

Marretje and her husband, Michael, visited Catalyntje and Joris a few days after the wedding. The four walked about the property as Joris described the improvements he'd made, and Catalyntje showed off her gardens. The sun was warming, so they took a break underneath the peach tree in the front.

"We wanted to talk to you," Michael started. "As you know, we have thought about moving south."

"I remember you mentioning that a few times," Joris admitted.

"New Amsterdam is going through some difficult times. Its success in trade has led to much growth here, but possibly all too fast," Michael replied. "So, we wanted to let you know that Marretje and I will be moving to the South River within a few weeks."

Catalyntje tried to keep calm as Michael presented his idea. "I hear they are giving land away there if you improve it," she said calmly.

"Yes, Mama, they are. We have thought about this for a long time and feel that it is the chance we have been waiting for," Marretje replied.

"I would be lying if I said it did not make me sad," Catalyntje said with a weak smile. "It is over two hundred miles from this place, and I'm not sure how often we will see you."

"I know. We have thought about that, too. We will do our best to send you letters to let you know how we are doing, and I hope we can still see one another at least once a year," Marretje answered.

"I can't fault you in your ambitions. Your mama and I did the same thing for the same reason," Joris replied, looking at the two. "We wish you both the best."

"Thank you, Papa. We will do well there; you and Mama will be proud," Marretje said with a weak smile.

"Thank you for your blessing," Michael responded, reaching to shake Joris' hand.

"We will have none of that handshaking," Joris laughed as he embraced Michael warmly, blinking back the tears that filled his eyes.

After Marretje and Michael left that night, Catalyntje and Joris walked along the path to the bench by the water. "How do you feel about all of this, Dear?" Joris asked Catalyntje.

"I am happy for them, and I know they are doing what is right for their family, but oh, how I will miss them and all of their sweet children," Catalyntje said, trying not to cry.

"I will, too," Joris admitted.

"We cannot stop them from following their dreams. We did the same thing. They are not moving as far away as we did, but two hundred miles is a considerable distance," Catalyntje replied.

"Yes, especially with the winter weather, our crops, the Indian wars, and the English. Many things are happening around us right now," Joris said.

"I have often wondered if Mama or my sisters still think of me," Catalyntje replied. "I wonder what they would think if they could see my life. I wonder how many children they have and if Mama ever made it to Amsterdam to be with them. I have always had these questions and realized I will never find the answers. I fear we will lose track of Marretje and Michael as our families did of us back in Amsterdam."

"I have the same worry. Of course, we will try to visit during the warmer months and send letters, but I know this is a difficult change," Joris admitted.

"It is, but I am glad we still have each other. Our children are meant to go out on their own, but we get to stay together. I am not going anywhere," Catalyntje said, squeezing Joris' hand.

"I'm not either, my love," he answered.

Added Responsibilities

1661: 55 years old

One crisp afternoon, Daniel, now ten years old, and Frans, who was eight, were outside helping Joris move firewood from the barn to the lean-to near the house; the snow squeaked under their boots. They had already dragged three loads of firewood to the lean-to and unloaded them. Once they did this, Annetie and Elizabeth stacked it tightly in rows along the back of the lean-to. The boys only had one load left and kept their eyes closed against the blinding sun as they walked, leaving a crooked trail behind them. Then, to their surprise, they heard an unfamiliar voice.

"Whoa," the voice said with a laugh. "Where might you be going with your eyes closed?" The two boys immediately opened their eyes and stood at attention.

"Good day, Domine," Daniel replied. "We didn't see you coming."

"Of course, you didn't. You had your eyes closed," he laughed. "Where is your Papa?"

"He is in the barn, chopping the last load of wood for us to haul. He said if we work while the sun is shining, we will be ready before the next storm," Frans said.

"He is absolutely correct," the Domine replied, getting down from his horse and helping the boys pull the sled to the barn.

"The man from the church is here," Frans announced as he pushed open the barn door. Joris put down his ax and walked over to welcome the Domine into the barn.

"What brings you this way?" Joris asked, wiping the sweat from his forehead.

"Our friend, Pieter Montfoort, has passed on," the Domine announced. "We will have his funeral next Saturday at the Church in Flatbush."

"That is not good news. Pieter served our settlement well," Joris replied.

"Yes, he did, as both a deacon for the church and a magistrate for the settlement," the Domine answered.

"Please come in and enjoy a bite to eat before moving along to the other farms," Joris offered. "If you can't stay, I'm sure Catalyntje will have something to send with you," he promised. The Domine spent nearly an hour warming himself by the fire, eating, and talking with the family.

*****

Joris always helped others, and he appreciated being with other people. Whether it was building a barn, cutting firewood, or hauling crops across the river, Joris was there to offer his assistance. His eagerness to help endeared him to many people who owned nearby farms. Conversations and friendships effortlessly wove together when people came to the taproom, but at the Wallabout, Joris no longer had daily interactions with others. As he thought about this, he realized it wouldn't take much effort to visit some of his neighbors and see how he could help them.

Once spring came, Joris prepared his horse once a week and rode off to visit some of the settlers who lived close by. When he did this, Catalyntje always wrapped some bread and cheese in a cloth for him, and he filled his waterskin before leaving for the day. He had no other goal except to get out and talk to people. He enjoyed hearing how they fared during the winter, what they planned to grow this season, and how many new animals they expected that spring. He always returned home before dark and filled the evening with stories that lasted longer than the candle's wick. But no matter what his day had been like, Joris always came home happy.

As they attended church each Sunday, Catalyntje noticed that folks always surrounded Joris, waiting to talk to him. She soon realized that many of them were the people he had come to know on his weekly trips around Breukelen and the Wallabout. She had always admired his ability to talk to anyone about anything. When the two of them first met in Amsterdam, she remembered watching the animated way he spoke with those who came to his cart to purchase cloth. She'd often teased him that they bought his cloth just because they liked talking to him. She also recalled the afternoons at their taproom in New Amsterdam, where Joris had always been surrounded by neighbors sharing stories and laughs. Now, he had found a way to continue connecting with people.

Catalyntje wasn't the only one to notice Joris's interest in others. One spring day after their Sunday church meeting, Catalyntje and Joris lingered afterward while he exchanged watering tips with those owning farms in the area. She noticed the Domine outside, watching them talk. After the last family left, Catalyntje and Joris prepared for their ride home. As Joris fed each horse an apple, the Domine called out to him.

"Joris, may I have a word with you?"

"Yes," Joris said, walking towards the Domine. "You spoke fine words today. It was good to be here, as usual," he complimented.

"Thank you, Joris. May I visit with you? Catalyntje may join us as well," he said, nodding toward her.

"I will," Catalyntje replied respectfully.

"More settlers continue to come to this fine area, which is a pleasing thing, but the church needs more help to keep up, especially with the passing of our good brother Montfoort. As you know, we assist orphans, widows, and those in need. So, Joris, the church has requested your service as a deacon to serve God and help those who need extra help," the Domine announced.

Joris was quiet for a moment and looked surprised at the request. "I would be pleased to help others, but I don't see myself as one to be a deacon in the Lord's church," he responded modestly.

"You are just who the Lord needs, my friend. You know the people here well, and you know how to help them. I've watched how they respond to you," the Domine replied.

"Thank you for your belief in my abilities. Catalyntje, what do you think?" Joris added, turning his head towards her.

"I think Domine has chosen the right man," she replied, smiling.

"With Catalyntje's approval, I will help as a deacon in the church," Joris said, standing a little taller.

"I knew you would help us. May I come to your home to talk more about this in the coming week?" the Domine asked.

"Yes, and you can join us for dinner. The garden is doing fine, and Catalyntje always has fresh food to share. Can we see you in two days?" Joris asked.

"That would be wonderful. I look forward to it," the Domine said, shaking Joris' hand and nodding to Catalyntje.

Joris' new position with the church came with the added responsibility to help those in need, and the summer proved to be a time of need. The previous winter had been much milder than usual, which meant less snow and ice. This was nice in the winter but became a problem in the summer when ponds began to dry up earlier. The rivers were lower than anyone could remember, and the lack of water made it difficult to irrigate the gardens and crops properly. The drought also affected the animals; they had to be herded to other areas to survive without their regular water holes. Catalyntje and Joris lived in an especially hard-hit area, so Joris spent most of his extra time helping neighbors move their animals to different parts of Breukelen, where there was more water.

By the end of the summer, Joris had even more responsibilities when the Company appointed him to be a magistrate for the city of Breukelen. He gladly accepted this position as well, and Catalyntje took on extra duties at home while he was away.

*****

Near the beginning of November, Aaltje Teunisen Bogaert was born to Sarah and Teunis; she was Sarah's twelfth child. A few weeks after her birth, she was christened in the Dutch Reformed Church in Flatbush, where Joris served as a deacon. They all stayed at the church to celebrate this happy occasion and kept warm by sipping steaming tea and warm soup. The adults talked near the hearth while the children played outside in the snow. They were careful not to make too much noise and alert their parents that they were being too lively on the Sabbath.

"Thank you for the pretzels you brought today, Mama," Sarah said, sitting beside Catalyntje.

"Of course, Dear. I was happy to do it, and it gave me a chance to see Aaltje for a bit longer. May I hold her once again?" Catalyntje reached out her arms.

"Yes," Sarah answered with a smile. Catalyntje gently took her newest grandchild and snuggled her close. The baby stirred and squeaked, then settled down into her arms. "She loves her Oma already."

Difficult Times

1662: 56 years old

For Joris, serving as a deacon at the church in Flatbush came with extra work. He filled his days visiting the poor and the widows and checking in with the orphanage in Breukelen. He enjoyed his added responsibilities but was weary by each day's end. Catalyntje and the children attended to the extra chores to help ease his load.

During the winter, the cold began to bother Joris when he traveled to check on folks in the area. The constant work and frigid temperatures were catching up to him. He wasn't ill, but something wasn't right with him. Catalyntje noticed the change in Joris during the coldest months, and they both blamed his exhaustion on the relentless freezing temperatures. In years past, he would bundle up and keep going, often outdoing his sons-in-law at most tasks they set out to do, but this year, the cold seemed to hold onto him. For Joris, it was a different kind of weariness that came sooner and lasted longer than it once had. When he arrived home in the evenings, he was content to sit by the fire and quietly work on a project while Catalyntje added extra logs to the fire to keep him comfortable.

Catalyntje herself was endlessly busy with tasks at home. As the summer ended, her gardens were nearly harvested, and bright leaves from the trees littered the ground. She looked forward to helping with the birth of another grandchild since Maria and Jan were expecting their first baby and had asked her to assist with the delivery. Her children were old enough that leaving them was no longer a hardship.

*****

"I have three more baskets to be brought down," Catalyntje called into the dark cellar as she set down the last basket of apples.

"We have them all lined up as you said," Frans reported, squinting as he walked up the stairs from the cellar and into the light with Daniel close behind him.

"You two have been a great help today," Catalyntje said as Frans grabbed another basket and disappeared back into the darkness of the cellar. Catalyntje could bring the baskets down, but she let the young boys do it. Instead, she sat on a stump near the opening of the cellar and watched them carry the last baskets down the dirt steps. Then, a movement along the road caught her attention, and she recognized Jan riding toward her on his dark brown horse.

"You look concerned, my son. Is Maria ready to have her baby?" Catalyntje asked.

"I think so. Can I get the horse ready?" he offered.

"That would be helpful. I have already gathered my things in a basket to bring with me. Let me get them and tell your papa that I am leaving. I will be right out," she said. Everything was ready to go within several minutes, and Catalyntje and Jan rode side-by-side to help with the new baby. Once they arrived at Maria and Jans' house, Jan went to the field to keep busy. Catalyntje and two other women prepared for the birth of Maria's child.

Outside, a cool breeze blew among the trees, and a light rain dampened the ground. Once the sun hid behind the western hills, the rain became more incessant while Catalyntje and the others helped Maria. This birth wasn't going as the others had, and the rain on the roof made Catalyntje unusually tense. Just before the sun rose, Maria finally had her baby, whom they named Frederick. As soon as Catalyntje saw him, she knew he wasn't well. He didn't cry and was limp. She tapped his chest to get him to breathe, then carefully laid him on his stomach over her hand and patted his back. She had seen Trijn use all of these tricks, but nothing worked. Frederick never made a sound, but Jan heard Maria's cries all the way to the barn. Her sobs brought him running to the house. As he threw open the door, he could tell by the look on Catalyntje's face that something was terribly wrong. He ran to his wife, and together, they held the lifeless baby, their tears matching the ceaseless rain.

*****

266

Before the snow got too deep, Catalyntje and Joris' grandchild, Annetje, married a fine young man from Holland. The wedding was a happy occasion at the little church in Flatbush, with light snow covering the ground outside.

Joris

1663: 57 years old

Decisions made in the Old World would soon affect the lives of those who lived in New Netherland; decisions that Catalyntje and the others wouldn't recover from quickly. King Charles II had returned to England, bringing his dislike of the Dutch with him. The Netherlands' success with global trade, which included New Netherland, filled King Charles with envy, and he planned to take over the Dutch settlement. He gave his brother, James, the Duke of York, a birthday gift to hasten this process. It was a large piece of land in the New World, which happened to include New Netherland.

*****

February was always difficult, with the cold in the air and the snow blanketing the ground. During this part of the year, Catalyntje's family always spent as much time indoors as possible. But there was still work to be done outside. When the woodpile in the lean-to ran low, the family had to refill it.

One morning, as the sun warmed the air, the day was perfect for moving firewood closer to the house. Working together always made the job more enjoyable. After the word was done, the day ended with a snowball fight and a partially constructed snow cave. Then, as evening came, they all enjoyed the warm fire while eating hot soup and bread. Once it was dark, the wind began to blow outside as they each returned to their indoor projects by the flickering lantern light. Joris opened the front door slightly and peered out; he could see thick flakes of snow covering the tracks they'd made earlier and was glad to be inside.

Joris had already planned the next day. It was time to elect new church officers, which had been part of his duty since he had served there. He looked forward to meeting with the others, especially after the long winter months that separated them more than usual. Joris felt tired again and kept coughing more than he had been, but he was ready to go to the church by late morning. His travels on church business usually took most of the day, so Catalyntje got some bread from the night before and dried meat to carry with him. The snow had stopped, and the sun was shining again; it would be a pleasant day to travel. As Joris stood by the door and finished wrapping his scarf around his neck, Catalyntje brought him the bundle of food.

"Safe home, Love," Catalyntje said, kissing his cheek.

"You enjoy this warm fire today. Thank you for the food; I will appreciate it, especially on the trip home," Joris said. "Thank you for looking out for me. You have always taken care of me, Catalyntje," he hugged her. His embrace lasted longer than usual, and Catalyntje enjoyed the warmth of his body against hers.

"I filled the lantern and put it in the wagon, Papa," Daniel said.

"Thank you, Son. I don't think I'll be too long, but the daylight leaves quickly this time of the year. Take care of your mama for me," Joris added, winking at Catalyntje as he walked out the door. She watched him from the window as he left new footprints in the fresh snow.

*****

Catalyntje spent the afternoon baking rye rolls and a pie from apples, which she kept in the corner bucket. She knew Joris would appreciate the smell of warm food when he returned. She finished the pie and settled down to work on some knitting, wondering why Joris hadn't returned home yet. She frowned, looking at the darkening sky, until she remembered that Daniel had filled Joris' lantern; he would have enough light to make it home. She could stop worrying. The clouds were gone, and a nearly full moon was up, reflecting on the snow, adding even more light to Joris' journey home.

"I see Papa's lantern," Elizabeth announced, standing by the window.

"Help me get the rolls, Daniel. I'm sure your papa will be cold and hungry," Catalyntje replied, dishing up the soup into bowls. She heard a knock at the door as she filled the last one. *I wonder why Joris would knock?* She wondered as she walked to the door. A cold wind blew into the room as she opened the door.

There stood one of the other deacons from the church. Then, information came too quickly, and Catalyntje didn't comprehend what had happened.

"He had collapsed during the election of the officers . . . the surgeon came, but it was too late . . . it was so sudden . . . he wasn't in pain . . . He called your name, Catalyntje."

The man helped her to a nearby bench. Catalyntje stared questioningly around the room. All talking stopped as she looked at the man with a furrowed brow.

"Joris is fine. Yesterday, we worked all day together. There is still much to do; he said he would see me tonight. He will be home soon," she said haltingly, staring forward. Elizabeth pulled a stool near Catalyntje and put an arm around her shoulder.

"It will be alright, Mama," Elizabeth said as Catalyntje sat silently staring at the door.

*****

Life didn't make sense to Catalyntje for the next few days as family and friends made their way through the cold snow to gather at her home. Preparations were made for the funeral, and food was cooked on hearths of friends and brought to Catalyntje's table, but hunger had left her. She told and retold the story of the deacon coming after dark with news of Joris' death. She told of the bread she sent with him and the warm meal he didn't eat. She told of their day of work together and that Joris was feeling fine and shouldn't have died. He was only 58 years old and was tired but hadn't been sick. The only solid idea that would stay in Catalyntje's mind was that none of this had happened because she and Joris still had plans. They had spent every day together in New Netherland, and she still needed him by her side to keep building their dreams.

Catalyntje was acquainted with death, but this time, it was Joris—her Joris, her friend for as far back as she could remember. He had always been there, but now that had changed.

After the funeral commotion passed, only the cold days of February stood before her. She knew that March would soon arrive. It was a time to sit at the table with her carefully saved seeds and choose which ones she would plant first. But now, none of that mattered. Joris was gone, and going forward with plans for a future without him was unbearable.

Early one morning, the sky showed signs of continual storms. Catalyntje wanted to accomplish at least one thing, so she gathered the eggs from the barn before more snow fell. It wouldn't be much, but it would be at least one thing. As she headed out the door with the egg basket, Frans asked, "Can I help you, Jadda?"

"Yes, come along before the snow starts," Catalyntje replied matter-of-factly. Ten-year-old Frans quickly put on his jacket and pulled a hat over his dark, curly hair. The air was cold, so Catalyntje promptly closed the door once they reached the barn. They gathered the eggs in silence for a few minutes before Frans spoke up.

"I heard what they said about Papa going to heaven at the funeral meeting," he offered.

"Yes, they talked about that a lot at his funeral. It is supposed to make us all feel better, but it is difficult to understand. I miss him so much that I can't see past what I feel," she said.

"I've been thinking about what the Qur'an says about Janna, which is what we call heaven," Frans replied.

"So, you have?" Catalyntje asked. "And what does the Qur'an say about heaven?"

"Well, I think it's a place you'd like. You get to be with your family so that you could be with Papa," Frans offered encouragingly. "And the place you meet each other is a really pretty garden. You like gardens, so I think you'd like Janna."

"Frans, I think I would like that very much. Thank you," Catalyntje said with tears in her eyes.

*****

Frans, Elizabeth, Annejte, and Daniel took over most of the chores and duties of the home and farm. They hadn't seen their mama so hopeless and hoped their work would help her heal. Catalyntje mindlessly watched as they completed her chores around the house. She watched Annejte prepare a meal each evening but wasn't hungry; even the thought of food sickened her.

It had been nearly a month since Joris' death. One evening, as Catalyntje watched the girls prepare dinner, she looked out the window and noticed the sky was growing dark.

"I am going for a walk," Catalyntje said, pulling on her mittens.

"Do you want to take some bread with you?" Daniel asked, reaching for a lantern and handing it to Catalyntje.

"Thank you, Daniel," she replied, grasping the lantern handle with a weary smile. "I just need to walk. I will return after I get some fresh air."

"Safe home, Mama," Elizabeth replied, hugging Catalyntje tightly.

"Yes," was the only reply Catalyntje could manage.

Once she closed the door, her eyes filled with tears, blurring her vision as she stumbled through the snow. Catalyntje needed to be alone where she could sob without restraint.

Suddenly, she was at the bank of the Oost River but didn't remember how she'd gotten there. Chunks of ice silently floated by as Catalyntje looked out over the darkening water and listened to the sound of the river lapping on the edge of their land. But now it wasn't their land; it was only Catalyntje's land. The constant rhythm of the water had always comforted her, so she focused on that sound, hoping to feel some peace.

As she stared blankly into the dark river, the memories returned: the extraordinary life she and Joris had enjoyed together, the visits at Dam Square, the journey across the ocean, their first home in the middle of the wilderness, the births and lives of their children and grandchildren, and the taproom—so much life and so many memories together. Coming to New Netherland had been their dream. Together. So, how could she go on without Joris? They had struggled through failures and fears and made it through. Together. More than the struggles, though, Catalyntje remembered the good times. But their lives together had happened too fast. Was it over already? Was this it? Who would she plan with? Who would she love?

Catalyntje knelt at the water's edge, her face in her hand, and there she sobbed uncontrollably for a very long time. *Joris, you can't leave me here alone. We had such a good life together. Our children and grandchildren need you. I need you. Joris, I cannot go on without you by my side.*

Catalyntje hadn't noticed that the sky had gone completely dark while she'd knelt by the river. Light snow began to fall slowly and quietly; she shuddered with cold and lifted her head. She felt nothing. She stared out at the water until the coldness of the night enveloped her. Then, she lit her lantern with shaking hands and stiffly stood up to begin her trudge home. After she had walked for some time, she saw the light from her house in the darkness - her house without Joris. It was a tiny, lonely speck of light, far away from anything and totally isolated.

*****

As one cold day followed another, Catalyntje struggled without Joris being there by her side. Out of necessity, she tried to return to her regular chores and activities. Her children had been mourning, too, but had worked to pick up the loose ends where Catalyntje had faltered. Each task she completed, and each conversation boosted her ability to return to her former self.

Late one afternoon, a strong wind began to blow, and she remembered that the barn doors needed fastening, which Joris usually did. She bundled up and gathered a knife and some extra rope. When she entered the barn, the chickens scattered and screeched at her invasion of their area. She waved her arms and swished past them with her long skirt. As she fastened the shutters over each window, Catalyntje realized she wasn't sure if she'd done it right. She wasn't incapable, but Joris and the boys usually did this while she was inside, cooking a warm meal for them. This simple thought was a painful reminder that Joris was no longer there; this would be one more task she would have to add to her list of duties. She missed Joris' conversations, his smiles, and his love, but today, she missed him for his work on their farm. As she struggled to fasten each shutter tightly, she felt angry at Joris for leaving her so soon. She was angry at him for giving her extra chores, and she wondered why he had abandoned her.

As her mind waded through these thoughts of despair, the barn door suddenly flew open. Catalyntje turned around to see Daniel.

"Mama, I wanted to see if I could help fasten the shutters. The wind is picking up, and I think it might start raining," he said, walking to the nearest opening.

"Thank you, Son. I could use the help. I am not going as quickly as I should," Catalyntje admitted. The two of them worked their way around to each shutter until they were all tightly fastened.

"I think Papa would be glad you are taking care of the barn," Daniel said. "You have both worked hard to build this place and now you are the one left to keep it as you and Papa planned."

Daniel's last comment made Catalyntje think. He was right; she and Joris had worked to make this place, and now it was up to her to continue their dream. This idea gave her a bit of hope as if she'd caught the end of a rope in a raging river.

The winter was harsh and brought sickness across New Netherland. Two young girls who had traveled by ship with Catalyntje and Joris on their way to New Netherland also died that winter. When she and Joris first met them, Rachel and Christina Vigne were little girls who read during the entire ship's voyage. Once they reached New Netherland, they grew up, married, and moved to Breukelen. Sickness took both of them the same week Joris had died.

*****

Life continued to move along, which was one of the cruelest things for Catalyntje to understand. She often thought that since Joris wasn't here to enjoy life, why should she? Even though spring had arrived and the garden needed planting, Catalyntje couldn't imagine seeds sprouting and growing without any regard for Joris' absence. She felt that all life should pause and acknowledge that he was no longer there, but everything continued.

Not only was nature moving forward, but Catalyntje and Joris' children also continued progressing. Their eighth child, Jeronemus, married Annetie Tunise Nyssen, followed by the marriage of their ninth child, Annetje, to Martin Ryersen. These spring weddings were beautiful, and many people came to celebrate at the Flatbush Church. Some of Catalyntje and Joris' friends from across the river joined in the celebrations, and Catalyntje wondered if they had come to support her, as well as her children. She smiled and greeted each guest while struggling to keep back the tears; the hole left by Joris was tangible. After each wedding, Catalyntje was exhausted from forcing herself to play a role. Each time, she went home and collapsed on her bed in tears.

*****

Although Joris' death absorbed Catalyntje, she couldn't help but be concerned for Jan's wife, Maria. From the first time she and Jan met, Maria had been frail, and this winter, she had caught a horrible cold, which turned into a fever. The fever weakened her even more, and by March, she had joined Joris. Of course, young Jan was devastated that his bride of three years was gone, but Catalyntje didn't have the strength to comfort him. She left that to his siblings; she still needed time to heal.

By the end of the year, Catalyntje had reached another milestone. Her first grandchild, Annetje, had her first child. Catalyntje had become a great Oma.

Part 6: Alone
1664 - 1689

The English

1664: 58 years old

The winter was long and lonely without Joris. Catalyntje had extra time to think about him as she sat alone in her chair by the fire, sewing, and knitting while the wind blew outside. Joris had left her with enough food, wood, and tools, but Catalyntje would trade all of those for a chance to have him whittling by the fire next to her. Life continued moving forward, but Catalyntje wasn't ready to move. Without Joris, her energy and happiness was gone.

Once February's wind and snow passed, spring arrived again. Catalyntje spent more time in her gardens, hoping this might bring some joy back into her life.

One bright day, just as she finished planting another row of peas, Catalyntje noticed someone approaching her home. As the figure got closer, she realized it was an old friend, Adrianna, who lived near her and Joris on Pearl Street. She was with her husband and their younger children.

"Greetings. It is good to see an old friend," Catalyntje called out, walking toward Adrianna.

"It has been a long time since I've seen you, and much has happened in your life," Adrianna said, embracing Catalyntje. "How are you doing?" she asked with concern.

"I made it through the miserable winter. I've spent as much time as I could, busying myself in my garden, and the fresh air does me good," Catalyntje answered.

"You always had the prettiest garden on the street. I brought you some fresh cheese and a start from my apple tree. I didn't know if you had an apple tree, but one cannot have too many apples. Good for winter food, you know," Adrianna said, handing the cheese to Catalyntje.

"I have one apple tree, but they are my favorites," Catalyntje smiled, taking the bucket that held the small tree.

"Do you have a moment?" Adrianna's husband, Francis asked.

"Of course, I do; I have too much extra time these days," Catalyntje answered, leading her guests inside.

After getting tea and cookies, Catalyntje sat down to hear all the latest news from across the river.

"I don't want to worry you, but I figured you hadn't heard much news from New Amsterdam," Francis started. "I fear the English have encroached on our territory more than usual, and there is talk that they will try to take over New Netherland. I didn't want you to be taken by surprise."

"Oh, that is dreadful news. What have the English been doing?" Catalyntje asked, leaning forward so as not to miss a word.

"Just a few days ago, Stuyvesant received a letter. It reported that King Charles II gifted some of the land that belonged to the Dutch to his brother. King Charles figured he had enough people in this area to claim it as his own," Francis reported.

"Do you think the English will attack or try to run us from our homes?" Catalyntje asked with worry in her voice.

"I don't know," Francis answered. "But I wanted you to have time to prepare because this could happen very soon," he added.

"What do you think I should do?" Catalyntje asked.

"I don't know, and I am sorry you are alone. Maybe keep your family closer for the next little while," Francis suggested.

"I will do that," Catalyntje answered.

*****

Catalyntje tried not to think about the situation with the English, but it never entirely left her thoughts. She spent some time focusing on her daughter Catalyntje's upcoming wedding. She was their seventh child and would soon marry Jeremias van Westehout. Catalyntje had prepared for the marriages of her other children before, but one thing she couldn't prepare for was Joris not being there. Once the day of the wedding arrived, Catalyntje wore a smile and welcomed those who attended the event, but she felt unbearably alone. People and happiness surrounded her, but Catalyntje's heart still had a hole that wouldn't let her stay happy for long.

After the celebration, the newly married couple went their way. Catalyntje went for a long walk in the stifling evening air with tear-stained cheeks.

*****

Unfortunately, Francis had been right in his predictions about the English invading New Netherland. When Catalyntje went for walks by the river over the next few weeks, she looked towards the harbor of New Amsterdam and stared intently to see if she could distinguish the flags that stood proudly atop the ship's masts. Sometimes, when they were close to her side of the river, she recognized the Dutch flag's proud red, white, and blue horizontal stripes. Now and then, though, Catalyntje also noticed the pattern of the English flag.

That summer, Catalyntje spent time visiting her children who lived nearby. She planted more in her garden than she could use to have an excuse to share her produce with them, giving her time away from home. Each time she visited her family, Catalyntje recognized that there were more English citizens in the settlement.

One hot summer day near the end of August, Elizabeth van Deusen, whose family had spent a winter in Catalyntje and Joris' barn, came to visit. Elisabeth had purchased some cloth from the market and brought some to Catalyntje. This was an excellent excuse to let her see how Catalyntje was managing without Joris.

Catalyntje and Elisabeth wandered about the gardens and fruit trees, filling the air with continual conversation. Elizabeth had also brought her two youngest children, who ran around happily with Daniel and Frans, exploring and climbing trees together. That day, Elisabeth's oldest child was with her husband, Cornelius, trading cabbage at the market, and planned to join them when they'd finished.

Once he finally arrived, Cornelius looked concerned. He greeted his wife with a warm hug and shook Catalyntje's hand. Then, they sat on the bench under the tall apple tree.

"Dear, how was the market today?" Elizabeth asked.

"They have come to New Netherland; the English are here!" Cornelius replied anxiously.

"We heard they were coming closer; what has happened?" Catalyntje asked.

"There was no market today; the English colonel, Richard Nicholls, is at the fort. He is preparing to take over New Netherland and make it part of the English colony," Cornelius said with dread. "I was there when it happened."

"What is going to happen to New Amsterdam?" Elizabeth asked anxiously.

"Colonel Nicholls was at the fort with a document the English had written. It was a contract for how things would be when they took charge. I arrived just as Stuyvesant came out of the fort with the document. He read it and didn't seem pleased, then he walked out of the fort with it in his fist and declared, 'I hereby denounce these Articles of Capitulation from the English. Though they guarantee our religious freedoms and the preservation of our contracts and customs, I refuse to turn the Dutch land of New Netherland over to the English.' Then, he ripped the paper and threw it at the feet of Nicholls."

"What did the people do? Was there an uprising? Did they force the English to leave?" Catalyntje asked, unable to control her curiosity.

"Those who work with Stuyvesant moved quickly to collect the destroyed document and gathered Stuyvesant back into the fort," Cornelius reported. "I wanted to see what would happen, so I went to the market to trade my cabbage as planned. Many people at the market had the same idea, and with all of the standing about, I sold all of the cabbage I brought," Cornelius said, smiling. "After a few hours, Stuyvesant and his men left the Fort. One of the men carried the ripped-up paper, which they had somewhat repaired. Nicholls came forward, and then Stuyvesant made a brief statement saying the Dutch had decided to accept the articles proposed by the English, but I am not convinced that he was happy with the decision."

"What does all of this mean? Will we have to turn over our farm? Cornelius, what are we to do?" Elizabeth asked, desperately.

"I don't know, but I plan to return to New Amsterdam tomorrow to get more information," Cornelius replied sadly.

*****

Things happened quickly after that. Catalyntje knew that if Joris were here, he would go and see what was happening. So, Catalyntje took Daniel and walked to the ferry to see if they could tell what was happening across the river. As they strained to see the bay, a sobering sight met their eyes. Daniel looked at Catalyntje, and neither said anything, overwhelmed by the ships and swarms of people that filled the bay of New Amsterdam.

"Mama, those are English flags on those ships," Daniel said.

"I know, Dear. I am glad Cornelius warned us, but I do not know what we should do," Catalyntje said, unable to take her eyes from the scene across the river. As the two of them watched, they soon realized that a group of men had gathered along the water's edge just north of them, on their side of the river! The men were English and, most likely, lived east of Breukelen. They carried weapons and stood near the ferry with their boats.

"It looks like they are ready to cross the river and help the English," Daniel said, his voice quivering.

"I think you are right, Son," Catalyntje said, not daring to breathe. "I do not hear any cannons or gunfire; I suppose that is good, but we can do nothing here. We have seen for ourselves, and now we need to return home and keep things in order there," Catalyntje announced in a shaky voice.

"Let's go then," Daniel said, taking one more look at the ships filling the harbor. Their walk back home was filled with disconnected conversations, and neither heard the other's words since they were each lost in their own thoughts and fears.

Across the Oost River, Stuyvesant knew the Dutch wouldn't stand a chance against the English in a battle. Military training and supplies had never been a focus for New Netherland, and they were unprepared for such an event. Direction from the Company took months to arrive, so after accepting the articles the British demanded, Stuyvesant was left to decide the destiny of the settlement on his own. He and his council recognized that the citizens of New Netherland valued their lives, homes, and property. They had all worked ceaselessly to create a place they could call home, and fighting for the land would only result in losing everything. New Netherland would now belong to the English.

*****

As September approached, Catalyntje decided to visit New Amsterdam. Winter would arrive soon, and she needed supplies from the market. She also wanted to see for herself what was happening in New Amsterdam. News traveled to her home from neighbors, but Catalyntje wished to see it for herself. She chose to go alone so she wouldn't have to worry about anyone but herself, and she didn't want to put any of her family in harm's way. She gathered seeds to exchange at the market, a pouch full of wampum, and a basket. She paused momentarily before going to the kast to get Joris' flintlock gun from the back of the middle shelf. She didn't want to bring it, but she also didn't know what dangers she might find on the other side of the river. Catalyntje carefully hid it beneath her light cloak, waved goodbye to her children, and headed with determined footsteps to the ferry.

Catalyntje was lost in thought as the ferry gently rocked back and forth, and her eyes focused on the fast-approaching shore of New Amsterdam. When they reached the dock, she paid the ferryman and nodded without saying a word. There, she headed for the market near Fort Amsterdam, and as she did, she passed her old home on Pearl Street; its sight brought many wonderful memories to her mind.

As Catalyntje approached the market, she saw a large group of people facing a platform where British military men and leaders from New Netherland stood. Catalyntje instantly spotted Stuyvesant with his wooden leg. She walked toward the crowd and turned her ear towards the platform to hear what the British man was saying.

". . . and you will no longer be led by Petrus Stuyvesant as director general. This is Captain Richard Nicholls," the man gestured, turning to a well-dressed Englishman. "He will be your new governor over this land." Nicholls stepped forward and straightened himself, trying to look taller.

"Thank you, my good people. Let it be known that your land will no longer be called New Netherland but will hereafter be known as New York," Nicholls said with authority. His announcement didn't receive the enthusiasm he expected, but he continued to speak as the people walked away in different directions, giving him no heed.

Catalyntje didn't see anyone she recognized, so she headed for one of her favorite places, which she hadn't visited for a long time. When she reached the old windmill, she watched its fins spin steadily and breathed deeply as she had many times when she lived near it. Catalyntje enjoyed the view and the sound of the waves as the memories of those she had loved and lost in New Amsterdam filled her with emotion.

Living under British Rule

1665: 59 years old

After the English took over New Netherland, Catalyntje watched for changes that might affect her. The new English leaders made proclamations, but these didn't change things much for Catalyntje and her neighbors. It seemed to her that no one had lost their property, and everyone still enjoyed their usual Dutch conversations.

As the warmer spring days lured Catalyntje outside, she felt more capable. She still missed Joris every day, but grief no longer swallowed her thoughts. Instead, she welcomed the sunshine and fresh air as she slowly reclaimed her land from the winter.

On market day, Catalyntje gathered some of her unique items to bring to trade. The winter months had been long, and she'd kept busy, making socks, gloves, and aprons as she sat by the hearth each evening. She was precise with her handwork, and her delicate stitches always caught the attention of those at the market.

Catalyntje also brought her seeds to trade. She'd learned to save seeds of different colors or ones that could be harvested before the others. She also used what she'd learned about writing from Trijn to keep notes about each group of seeds she'd saved; otherwise, it was impossible to remember what was unique about them.

Most people had lettuce, turnips, and daffodils in their gardens by early spring. So, Catalyntje brought her harvest of unique varieties to the market, such as lettuce with thin strips of red through it or a delicate ruffled edge. She also saved the first of her tulip bulbs to bloom each spring and, over several years, had coaxed one to bloom two weeks before her neighbors.

Those bulbs usually sold quickly at the market since people wanted to be the first on their street to have a vase of tulips in their window.

One change Catalyntje noticed since the English had taken over was that more English families now traded at the market. The Dutch were always friendly and never afraid to speak their mind. However, the English were quieter, and conversations usually started more formally. Another difference Catalyntje recognized was that the men usually traded at the market while the women stood silently by them, nodding and smiling politely.

That day at the market, everyone talked about the Netherlands because a few days earlier, news had arrived that the plague had ravaged the Old World. Nearly 25,000 people had died from the plague in the Netherlands during the past few years, more people than Catalyntje had ever met. Hearing news like this always turned her thoughts to her family across the ocean, and worry settled in her mind as she hoped that her sisters and their families had escaped the deadly sickness.

Once the market was over, Catalyntje began to pack up what she hadn't traded. She had sold all her tulips and had only two small bunches of lettuce and one pair of mittens left. As she carefully tucked the mittens in the bottom of her basket and stacked the items she had traded for beside it, Trijn's daughter Anneke came up to her.

"Catalyntje, how have you been? It has been some time since I have talked to you," she hugged Catalyntje.

"It was a bitter winter, and I am glad for spring," Catalyntje said. "I've been wondering how the British leaders have treated those of you living here in New Amsterdam," Catalyntje said, wrapping a cloth around a new pitcher she had traded for.

"Well, they want us to think they are in charge but have let us keep to ourselves for the most part. The new leaders have their people coming into town more, and we interact with them. But I am most curious about their women. They don't seem as free as you and me, and I overheard that they aren't involved in business either. They just leave that to their husbands. I don't know if they aren't interested or are incapable," Anneke said thoughtfully.

"It seems unfair that the women are not allowed to choose for themselves. Joris and I always shared ideas and worked together; he never kept me from doing as I pleased," Catalyntje said, packing her basket.

"I don't know what Dutch women would do if they couldn't help with the family's land and business," Anneke replied.

"Nor do I. We have not seen many changes in Breukelen either," Catalyntje added, reaching into her basket. "Here is some of my ruffled lettuce. You can enjoy it with your meal tonight."

"Thank you. It has been wonderful to see you again. Safe home, my Friend," Anneke said.

*****

By the end of summer, Catalyntje's youngest daughter, Elizabeth, was married to Dirck Hooglandt. This was difficult for Catalyntje because she would miss having another woman around the house. But she still had Daniel and Frans to keep her company, and they were always coming up with something interesting to do. She was also grateful for their willingness to help. During the long summer days, after completing their chores at home, the two young men worked on the house Frans' father had started for him years ago. Frans was now old enough to work his own land, and Catalyntje could see that he was preparing to live on his own soon.

*****

Catalyntje didn't have the time she'd hoped to work in her garden and make winter preparations because Sarah was expecting her thirteenth child and wasn't doing well. She was much more exhausted, and Catalyntje wondered if her delivery date was off because she was much larger this time. She couldn't even get out of bed some days, so Catalyntje helped her by playing with her children and bringing the family food from her garden.

By the end of August, Catalyntje knew the baby would be coming soon and moved to Sarah's house. After being there for only two days, the baby was ready to be born, so Sarah's husband, Teunis, took their oldest son with the wagon to let Sarah's two sisters know she needed their help. Once they arrived, he and the other children kept busy outside. This time, the birth took much longer than usual, and in the end, Catalyntje discovered the reason. Poor Sarah had been carrying two babies, so two new grandchildren, Neeltje and Annetje, joined the family that day, Sarah's second set of twins.

A few weeks later, Sarah and Teunis proudly brought their two new baby girls to the Flatbush Church to be christened. They wore new dresses and matching bonnets that Catalyntje had lovingly made.

Living with Death

1668: 62 years old

A few years had passed since the English had taken over New Netherland and changed its name to New York, but Catalyntje hadn't noticed many differences. She still had her land and could travel from place to place to visit her children whenever she pleased. She also continued to speak Dutch and French to some of her neighbors, and she attended the same Dutch Reformed Church in Flatbush, where the Domine and patrons still spoke Dutch.

Catalyntje kept busy, but the loneliness she felt without Joris made her weary. Her family noticed this gradual change and began to help her more than they had in the past, at least as much as she would let them. She couldn't fall trees and cut them into pieces to fill her woodsheds anymore, so her children and grandchildren took over that responsibility. When they came to help, Catalyntje always had a hearty meal prepared for them to enjoy after she'd helped unload the carts full of wood. She couldn't move as fast as she used to and certainly didn't do most of the work, but Catalyntje loved working and talking with her family. They always left her house with baskets filled with bread and minds filled with tales from her adventure-filled life.

Catalyntje's family continued to grow; her oldest granddaughter, Annetje, had a second child, and Annetje's mother, Sarah, had another child, her fifteenth; they named him Gysbert Bogaert. Sarah was now forty-three years old, and gratefully, she didn't have many more childbearing years left.

As Catalyntje helped Sarah one day, she sat and held little Gysbert while Sarah slept. Looking down at the tiny infant in her arms, she remembered when she held Sarah as a baby; it seemed a lifetime ago. So many things had happened to her and her family during their time in New Netherland. Nevertheless, Catalyntje smiled and was glad she had crossed the ocean so many years ago to come to this land and make a life here.

Catalyntje knew all too well that along with birth came death. Her young friend, Elizabeth van Deusen, who had lived with them one winter, was visited by a tragedy when her youngest daughter, Isabel, became ill during the winter and died quickly. Catalyntje knew death shouldn't be handled alone, so she put on her cloak and hitched up the horses to attend the funeral at the Flatbush Church. As the Domine preached, he spoke of heaven and how the young woman, Isabel, was in a better place now. Catalyntje's mind drifted back to other funeral sermons she'd heard as he spoke.

She had experienced the anguish of death many times and found that grief went in cycles, like the crops that grew and the winter that followed after the leaves fell. She sat among those mourning in the church and wished to trade places with the young woman whose body was in the casket. Catalyntje had lived a long life. She was happy and had experienced many beautiful things, and it didn't seem fair that this young woman, who had passed on, would have to miss out on so much of life. *Why am I still here to live and breathe and move? What else must I accomplish in my life?* Catalyntje wondered as she sat on the hard bench with her thoughts. The Domine continued to talk, and her friends continued to weep.

After the service, the men carried Isabel's casket to the cemetery outside of the church and lowered her into the damp, rectangular hole. Catalyntje stayed close to her friend Elizabeth until other women came to her side to offer comfort. Then, without being noticed, Catalyntje slipped away to visit Joris, whose body lay in the same cemetery.

She walked alone to where his body was buried, under the leafless oak tree. The ground, covered with pale yellow leaves, announced her steps under the gray sky. Her heart tightened as she stopped at the final resting place of her dear Joris. She missed him so much that it still caused physical pain to her soul. Since she was alone, Catalyntje spoke out loud to Joris. She told him of the cellar she'd filled, the six scarves she'd made, and how his favorite old horse was still doing well. She described how the English had come to New Netherland and how she was doing a wonderful job caring for the house and farm. She told Joris that she made his favorite dessert every few weeks and still couldn't get the closure on the barn door to work. Suddenly, her words caught in her throat, but her thoughts continued. *Know that I love you, Joris. Keep our dear Jacob safe and say hello to Trijn; I'm sure she is there. Look for Jannetje, too; it has been so very long that I hardly remember her face. And if you can look for my mama, even though you never knew her, I am sure she will find you there.*

Catalyntje stood silent for some time. She felt comforted being close to Joris; it was the only way she could be with him now. She recognized that no one could ever really plan for what challenges would come to them, and she certainly hadn't intended to be without Joris. She took a deep breath and watched the mist float as she exhaled into the cool evening air. People were leaving the cemetery, carrying lanterns to light their way home. Catalyntje removed her mittens and kissed the palm of her hand, then stooped down and placed it gently on the ground over where Joris' body lay. "I will visit you again, my Love," she whispered, turning to find her way back to the wagon alone.

New Orange

1673: 67 years old

For the past five years, Catalyntje had continued her daily routines, even though it was more difficult for her to get around. Part of her routine included walking around parts of her land. She and Joris used to spend an entire day wandering around their homestead and exploring every corner. But now, since Catalyntje was alone most days and didn't want to bother anyone to walk with her, she was careful about walking too far.

Her favorite place to go was still along the path she and Joris had made, which followed the far west side of their land and touched the river. She always paused once she reached the water and rested on the bench, she and Joris had built years ago. She liked that place because it reminded her of sitting under Trijn's tree in New Amsterdam. From that vantage point, she could see Manhattan, or New Amsterdam as she still called it, and enjoyed watching the ships glide in and out of the harbor across the river. Catalyntje imagined each vessel filled with passengers and crates being loaded and unloaded before sailing back across the ocean. Watching the ships also reminded her of the first time she and Margriet had seen the tall ships in the Old World, and she remembered thinking that she'd probably never see a ship like that again. Catalyntje had no idea where life would take her when she was that young.

Seeing these tremendous vessels brought memories of when she and Joris traveled across the ocean, met Jannetje, and moved to New Amsterdam. When Catalyntje was alone with her thoughts, they reminded her that she didn't need to be weighed down by the hardships and heartaches that had come her way. Instead, she focused on the fact that she could still walk around her land, work in her garden, and bake apple pies.

*****

The weather had cooled enough by the end of August to make it perfect for working outside, so Catalyntje spent most of the week in her garden. She felt alive as the sun warmed her back, and she filled her baskets with the food she'd grown. August was usually a busy time, but now that most of her family was grown, she didn't have to work as hard to save food for the winter.

After a whole week of working outside every day, Catalyntje awoke one morning to find that the air had cooled from the previous day. Having no reason to stay indoors, she decided to walk to the river again to sit, look, and rest. She packed some bread, an apple, and a skin of water and went on her way. Catalyntje walked silently with only her thoughts as companions. It took her most of the morning to get to the river, but she was in no hurry. Her only purpose for the day was to sit under the trees and watch the ships across the water.

The bay seemed extremely busy that morning, more than Catalyntje had seen for a long time, possibly because winter was approaching, and the weather would soon limit the number of ships. But as she reached for her waterskin, she noticed several Dutch men of war in the harbor, an unusual sight. She squinted to see what was happening in New Amsterdam's harbor. "I certainly chose a lively day to come to the water," she said out loud.

As Catalyntje peered across the river, she could tell several ships were sailing toward the harbor that had cannons on their sides. She sat up, leaned forward, and watched the events across the water. She thought about hurrying home to see if anyone else knew what was happening, but then she thought again. Here on the bench, she had an excellent view of what was going on, and news wouldn't have traveled to her home yet anyway. Making herself comfortable again, Catalyntje watched all that was happening across the water near her old house on Pearl Street.

*****

As Catalyntje finally headed up the dirt path back home, Daniel and Frans ran out to meet her.

"Mama, are you alright?" Daniel asked excitedly.

"You won't believe what has happened," Frans added as he reached Catalyntje's side.

"You two are so excited. How long have you been here? I thought you were working on Frans' house today. And, of course, I'm alright. I have been down by the river watching the Dutch men of war in the harbor," Catalyntje said with a slight smile. Neither of the boys said a word but were amazed that she knew what was happening across the river.

"At first, I thought of coming back here and sharing the news, but then it was more interesting to sit and watch, so I did. It is not every day that my bench hosts a full view of a takeover," Catalyntje said. "So, share with me what you two know."

Daniel spoke first, "Well, from what we've heard, ships came from Zeeland to take back Manhattan for the Company."

"That is what it looked like to me," Catalyntje added. I counted eight ships with Dutch flags on their masts."

"I heard they landed, and troops flooded the fort and took over," Frans added.

"I think you are right," Catalyntje replied.

The three of them soon found their observations were correct when a soldier came across the river to tell them that Manhattan had returned to Dutch control. This reversal still didn't change much for Catalyntje and her family. The city of Manhattan reclaimed its original Dutch name, New Amsterdam, and the entire colony was renamed New Orange after Prince Willem of Orange.

Catalyntje thought the return to Dutch control deserved a celebration since she and her family had always been proud to be a part of New Netherland. So, the following week, she invited her entire family to her home to honor the occasion. The days were still sunny, so there was plenty of room for the adults to talk and the children to climb trees and play in the barn. Everyone brought baskets of food to share, and Catalyntje gathered fresh beans, peaches, and watermelons from her garden. She also had a basket of apples from the tree near her house and four loaves of fresh bread.

As her home gradually filled with voices and busy hands, Catalyntje sat quietly on a bench near the fire and enjoyed it all. She was content not to be at the center of all the activity. But as each family arrived through the half-opened Dutch door, they always headed straight to Catalyntje. She was loved and never left alone for very long.

When her children arrived, they greeted her with kisses on her cheeks, held her hand, and shared stories about their families. When the grandchildren and great-grandchildren came, they didn't pause for a greeting but ran full speed toward Catalyntje, throwing their chubby little arms tightly around her neck.

"I love you, Oma," were usually the first words from their mouths.

"What have you been doing today?" Catalyntje would ask them. And their excited replies rambled on about various things they'd done. She always listened with a smile, asked questions, and enjoyed their tales. This usually happened while at least two or three small children talked excitedly at once.

When everyone arrived, and the younger children were playing outside, Catalyntje got up from the bench to see how the meal preparations were going. She enjoyed working near the mantle near where her older granddaughters were, and as she worked beside them, they talked and laughed together.

Their conversation usually turned to a request for Catalyntje to share one of her stories, which she loved telling a captive audience. That afternoon, she sat on a stool near the table cutting carrots with two of Jannetje's daughters when one asked, "Oma, can you tell us about when you moved to New Amsterdam?"

"That was so long ago, but I still remember many things about that journey," Catalyntje began. "I remember I was worried that Opa and your Aunt Sarah would not have enough food when we arrived. I had gathered all the beans from my garden at Fort Orange, even the small ones. I put them in a basket and wrapped them in a cloth to keep them dry. Your Opa was good to help me tuck them away into the crate we carried on the sloop with us."

The entire day was filled with delicious food and conversations, and as the women served the pies, Frans called for everyone's attention.

"I want to make an announcement while we are all gathered here. As you know, Daniel has been helping me finish my house, which is finally completed," Frans said proudly. "You have all been so kind to me. You have accepted me as your brother, and I am glad to call you my family."

"Of course, you are family," a voice called out.

"I want to let you know I will move to my house within the next few weeks. I want to get settled in before winter comes," Frans added. After speaking, he was surrounded by handshakes, kind words, and warm hugs.

Catalyntje knew this change was coming, but it still left a hole in her heart. She had stood up to the leaders of New Netherland for that little boy long ago and had loved him as if he were her child. She was proud that he would be on his own now, but Daniel would be the only one left at home with her once Frans was gone, and Catalyntje suspected he would marry soon. The thought of being totally alone was difficult to think about. But for now, she would continue to enjoy the evening, surrounded by the cheerful sounds of a family that loved her.

Alone

1674: 68 years old

Across the sea, in the cold of February, the English and the Dutch argued over the Treaty of Westminster until both eventually signed it. A portion of this treaty required New Netherland to return to English rule, so a few months later, when word of the accord reached New Netherland, no cannons were fired; only men from both sides signed papers and traded places again.

*****

Even though the English rulers New Netherland again, Catalyntje continued doing things the way she always had. She continued to speak Dutch with most of her neighbors and sometimes enjoyed lively conversations while standing near an English settler to make them feel uneasy. She wasn't mean-spirited about it; she just wanted to let them know this was still her place.

Catalyntje's prediction about her youngest son, Daniel, came true when he married Sarah Klock that spring. The ceremony was in Breukelen, and Catalyntje's daughters helped prepare for the event. On the morning of the wedding, the church was filled with family and friends Catalyntje hadn't seen for some time. Her nephew Aldolphus de La Grange even attended. He had lived in New Netherland for the past few years and made a good living for himself. He always enjoyed Catalyntje's company; sometimes, he'd show up to spend the day with her.

Although Daniel and Sarah's marriage was a day of celebration, it carried some sadness for Catalyntje. Daniel was young when Joris died and had been such a support throughout the years. Of course, Daniel promised to come and help Catalyntje whenever she needed it, but she also knew that he would be occupied with his own land and family now. She wasn't above asking for help but was determined to do as much as possible for herself. She had accomplished hard things in her life and knew she could work through this challenge also.

Mere Bonte

1680: 74 years old

Daniel had been married for nearly six years, so Catalyntje spent many days alone. Her family checked on her regularly, but the weather sometimes kept them away for long periods. She had to continually bring wood inside to keep her house warm during the winter, but the fear of slipping on the snow worried her. So, she decided to use the inside wall by the door to stack kindling and firewood. That way, she didn't have to go outside on days when the snow and wind were relentless.

Catalyntje spent time making items for others during the cold winter months. There wasn't much she needed for herself, but she remembered long ago when she and Joris had a home filled with children, and it had taken so much effort to keep everyone clothed and fed. When family or friends visited, they never left empty-handed. She kept a basket of projects by her chair near the fire, and once she finished one, she stored it in the small chest near her bed. It was always filled with the mittens, socks, aprons, scarves, and candles she'd made. Catalyntje also continued to sort seeds for her garden. She organized some to share with friends when they stopped by and planned to put some in the ground once the weather warmed.

Catalyntje enjoyed sitting by the fire on cold, windy nights, listening to the trees blow outside, but this hadn't always been the case. The first few years after Joris died, she used to fear the nights when the wind blew. But after being alone for so long, she'd taught herself to be calm when the winter winds sang, breaking up the quiet of her lonely nights.

Even though Catalyntje tried to see the best in her situation, it wasn't always easy to be alone so much. Some days, her mind filled with memories, and even though many were wonderful, in the end, she remembered that she was still alone. She often took out the record book Trijn had given her and read through its pages many times, running her finger over the words Trijn had written many years ago. Catalyntje's eyes had grown weaker, but she could see well enough to read if she had at least three candles lit.

*****

When spring finally arrived, Catalyntje didn't take the ferry to New Amsterdam as much as before, but she still tried to walk along her favorite path to the river's edge at least once a week. She never tired of sitting on the bench near the water as the waves lapped the shore while she gazed at the city where she once lived. When she watched the ships in the bay, she often remembered how it felt to have the cool air from the ocean blowing into her face when she'd sailed across the waves long ago.

She enjoyed sitting on her front stoop most days in the spring, watching the robins land gracefully in the trees, their beaks filled with sticks for their new homes. These days, she didn't always have something to do when she sat out front; it was enough to breathe the fresh air and feel the sun's warmth.

*****

One day, late in May, as Catalyntje sat on her stoop, enjoying the fresh air, she noticed movement in the distance. Soon, her aged eyes could see three people approaching her house on foot. She didn't expect them to be her children or grandchildren because they usually arrived by wagons or on horseback. A voice called out to her as the visitors reached the path by her front peach tree.

"Auntie Catalyntje, how are you this fine day?" the voice asked.

"Oh, I recognize your voice, De La Grange," Catalyntje exclaimed excitedly. "It has been a few months since you have come by."

"Yes, it has been some time. I have been busy with work," De La Grange answered happily.

"Thank you for the yarn you brought me a few months ago. I have used it all for socks. It was some of the finest I've ever had," Catalyntje said, raising an eyebrow.

"I can make some good trades every so often and enjoy sharing when I can. I knew you would put it to good use," Catalyntje's nephew replied. "Auntie, I want you to meet two friends, Jasper Danckaerts and Peter Sluyter."

"Pleased to meet you both. And what brings you to Breukelen today?" Catalyntje asked.

Danckaerts stepped forward and took off his hat, "My companion and I are Labadist ministers and have come from across the ocean to see this fine land," he answered. "We were sent from Amsterdam to find an acceptable place to establish our church."

"All the way from Amsterdam? I have taken that journey myself. I am over seventy years old now, so that was long ago," Catalyntje said. "Amsterdam, what a wonderful place; I arrived there as a young girl with my sister. We were running from the Inquisition. I made it to Amsterdam, met my Joris there, and we came here together, not to this place but up the river from New Amsterdam. He helped our Flatbush Church and did such a fine job. You would have enjoyed talking to him," Catalyntje rambled on.

"I am sure you are right, Auntie," De La Grange interrupted. "I have had the honor of showing these men our settlement. We planned to cross the river and come to Breukelen today, and I told them all about you. They have looked forward to spending some time here if that is alright."

"Why, of course, it is. I always enjoy your company, and you know that I love to talk," Catalyntje answered with a twinkle in her eye.

"We do not wish to impose on your time," Danckaerts added.

"You are welcome to stay as long as you wish. I am fine here alone, but I always appreciate visitors," Catalyntje replied.

Sluyter, who had yet to say anything, stepped forward and opened his satchel. "We don't want to use your resources, so we brought some food to share with you," he said, pulling something from his bag.

"You can leave your things inside and unload your goods on the table," Catalyntje said, opening the door and beckoning the three to follow her. Sluyter walked to the table and unwrapped the parcel he had started to take out earlier. It was a round of cheese, some cured fish, and a bag of Dutch *oliebollen*.

"Oh! I have not been to a market for some time. This is quite a feast," Catalyntje exclaimed.

"Your nephew told us about your garden, so we brought things you couldn't grow," Sluyter responded.

"We did bring some garden items, though," Danckaerts added, opening his bag. He pulled out a bundle of bulbs and a small cloth, which Catalyntje could see contained seeds.

"Well, you boys are certainly spoiling this old woman today," Catalyntje said.

"These are daffodil bulbs, a new variety that is supposed to be more delicate in size. And the seeds are an early type of watermelon along with some extra beet and winter squash seeds," De La Grange added.

"You are welcome to come with this fare every day of the week," Catalyntje replied. She arranged the items on the table and invited her guests to walk outside with her. As they wandered around her homestead, they told stories about their journey to the New World.

As they walked to Catalyntje's barn, Sluyter talked about their journey from the Netherlands across the ocean. He shared tales of their days on the ship, writing in their journals and playing with the cat, a fellow passenger.

As he spoke, Catalyntje was reminded of her and Joris' journey, crossing the same path that Sluyter and Danckaerts had traveled. Before sitting under the apple tree, Catalyntje picked three mostly ripe apples and handed them to the three men while she told stories of her trip across the ocean. Next, she spoke of how she and Joris landed in New Netherland and went north because the Company wanted them to homestead there. She also shared stories of trading with the Indians at Fort Orange and bragged about becoming an expert trader. Finally, she explained the process of trading furs and having them shipped to the Old World and delivered to Russia for processing into the material used for the ever-popular beaver skin hats. Danckaerts was impressed with her knowledge of the entire process and took notes as she spoke.

After their visit under the apple tree, Catalyntje wanted to walk with the men to the edge of the woods near her home. It was a place where she could go to cool down on hot days. They walked along together, admiring various plants, until they reached a bench Daniel had built for her. When they stopped there, Danckaerts took his turn sharing a tale.

He told of the journey he and Sluyter had taken on foot near the end of December, describing the constant rain and the lack of places to sleep. He explained how they'd tried to sleep one night while standing up after walking more than fifteen miles. Danckaerts shared his story with such detail that Catalyntje couldn't help but laugh as he described Sluyter crossing the river, then falling and soaking his already wet clothes. And

302

how Danckaerts then put his breeches on his head and waded into the river to rescue his companion.

Catalyntje told her guests about walking to the edge of her land to watch the ships sailing into the harbor, and De La Grange suggested that they all get the wagon ready to see the place for themselves. Catalyntje liked his idea, and while De La Grange and Sluyter got the wagon ready, she took Danckaerts to the garden to gather food for the short journey to the river.

As they traveled along the well-worn path, Catalyntje filled the air with stories of her children, her life in New Amsterdam, her friends, and those who were no longer with her. Danckaerts recognized that her life had many challenging moments, but he could also sense it hadn't stopped her from living the happiest way she could.

When they reached the water's edge, they sat under the trees, discussing ships, ferries, and life in New Netherland. Then, finally, as the sun lowered in the sky, De La Grange suggested they return to Catalyntje's house. Once they returned and put the wagon and horse away, Catalyntje sensed that her visitors needed to return across the river before dark.

"Well, let's gather you up some goods before you leave," she insisted. Catalyntje led them to the garden, where she pulled up carrots and turnips. Then she sent De La Grange to pick apples from the tree. As they came inside to gather their things, she took out three pairs of socks she'd made.

"These are some I made this winter from the yarn you brought me, Nephew. I know it is late in the season, but you can always use a good pair of socks come winter. Tuck them away for the next cold season," Catalyntje insisted. "And I also have some extra dried berries. Put these into a loaf of bread; it makes a delightful treat, a secret I learned from the Natives up north," she said, smiling.

"You have shown such generosity, and we have enjoyed your stories," Danckaerts added sincerely.

"I am glad you would spend the day with me. My family often visits now that the weather is fine. You know, I have 145 people in my family living in this area and will soon have 150—quite a lot of folks to look after me. More than a few of them have invited me to come and live with them so they can watch over me. I am grateful for their concern, but I am fine enough here. I made my way to Amsterdam when I was very young. I sailed across the ocean. I had the first child in this land; I learned to trade with the Indians and clear the land. I am still doing well enough," Catalyntje said proudly.

"You have inspired us; if only we can be as lively as you when we reach your age," Danckaerts added.

"I have all I need here: my garden, my chickens, and my goats. These all provide more than enough food, and my garden keeps me happy and moving so I can continue to look after myself. I am much slower than I was years ago, but I can still get along. My children have helped me keep up the barn and built benches to rest on. I still have the tools Joris made, and I have many conveniences that I use to help myself enjoy each day that comes to me," Catalyntje said matter-of-factly.

"I nearly forgot, Auntie," De La Grange said, reaching into his leather pouch. "We brought you a few more items," he said, pulling out a piece of light brown fabric with small orange flowers printed on it.

"Why, this is beautiful. It will make a colorful new apron," Catalyntje said excitedly.

"And here is a new garden shovel. It is small, newly made, and sharpened," De La Grange said as he presented it to Catalyntje.

"I will keep gardening then; when you come back to visit, I will have more vegetables to share," she replied.

De La Grange hugged Catalyntje tightly, "Thank you for sharing such a fine day with us, Auntie."

"Thank you for remembering me. It is always a good day to spend time with family and friends," she said.

"You are rather exceptional, Auntie. I don't know of anyone who has done all you have and is still so pleasant to be with," he added.

"This has been a most delightful day. As we have traveled about this land, it has been one of my favorites," Danckaerts said with a slight bow.

"You are welcome any time. I am glad to find new friends," Catalyntje responded kindly.

That night, Danckaerts took time to write about Catalyntje in his journal. He removed his inkwell and dipped his pen after smoothing out the paper. He then penned: This aunt of de La Grange [our guide] is an old Walloon woman, seventy-four years old. She is worldly-minded, with mere bonte [goodness], living with her whole heart, as well as body, among her progeny, which now number 145, and will soon reach 150. Nevertheless, she lived alone by herself, a little apart from the others, having her [little] garden, and other conveniences with which she helped herself.

A Light in the Sky

After a month of constant snowfall, there were finally a few clear days where the sun shone brightly over the snow-covered ground. So, one afternoon, Catalyntje put on her heaviest cloak, wrapped a thick wool scarf around her head, and stepped onto her front stoop, closing her eyes. The blinding sun warmed her face for a moment before a biting wind stole it away. She knew the sunshine wouldn't last long and spent the afternoon moving wood closer to her door and into her house. As she pulled the sled filled with wood back and forth across the crusted snow, the movement warmed her, and she kept working, refreshed by the sun.

Since Catalyntje started late in the day, it wasn't long before the sun began to sink behind the trees. She stopped halfway between the house and the barn to enjoy the familiar silhouettes of the trees along the horizon, and as she did, a soft glow in the sky caught her attention. As it glowed in the sky, this dim light looked like a hen's egg but without distinct edges. It also had a faint tail trailing above it. The ribbon of light that followed made it look like it might crash into the ground, but it wasn't moving; it was just hanging motionless above the trees.

Catalyntje had never seen anything like it, and as a soft breeze brought a sharp chill to the air, she remained standing, trying to make sense of the curious light in the sky. Her legs were tired from working in the cold, so she sat on the wooden sled and watched. As the night sky darkened, the faint light glowed brighter, and Catalyntje wanted to stay outside longer, but her hands began to feel tingly, and she knew she needed to get inside. She left the wood and the sled where she had stopped to rest. Then she went into her house to get warm, her mind still thinking about what she'd seen in the sky, as she fell asleep in her chair by the fire.

The next day, the sun showed brightly overhead again, and Catalyntje went out early to finish her abandoned chore from the night before. She was deep in thought about what she'd seen the night before and didn't realize that Elizabeth was suddenly standing beside her.

"Mama, how have you been?" Elizabeth asked. "I baked some extra biscuits, and since the sun is shining, I wanted to bring you some."

"You startled me, Dear, but it is good to see you. Unfortunately, the weather has not allowed us much chance to visit, has it?" Catalyntje asked rhetorically. "I have been well. How are you and your dear family doing?" Catalyntje asked, grasping Elizabeth's hands.

"We are staying warm and have food to eat," she answered.

"That is good to hear," Catalyntje responded. "I was working outside last night and saw a strange light in the sky. Did you happen to see it? It rested above those trees," Catalyntje said, pointing in the direction where the light had been the previous night.

"I didn't see it, but my neighbor came over this morning and couldn't stop talking about it," Elizabeth answered. "She said she'd seen it for the past few evenings.

"Well, I am going outside again tonight to get another look," Catalyntje said as they walked inside together.

*****

Catalyntje couldn't wait for the sun to go down, and as soon as the sky darkened, she bundled up and sat outside on a stool she'd put out earlier in the day. As she searched above the trees from the night before, she saw the oblong glow in the sky again, but tonight, it was even brighter than the evening before. She wasn't sure why she enjoyed watching it. There was no movement or change in color, but it differed from anything she'd ever seen. As she sat looking, she wiggled her toes in her boots, trying to keep them warm for as long as possible. But once the temperature dropped, she had to go back inside to warm herself by the hearth.

Catalyntje spent the next few nights outside, enjoying the companionship of this new phenomenon. But after several days, the glow grew dimmer until one night, she could barely see it. When she returned inside that evening, she knew it would be the last night she would spend with the mysterious light.

*****

After a few more days of cold sunshine, Catalyntje's neighbors, Hannah, and her husband, came to visit. They asked if she'd seen the glow in the sky, and she excitedly told of her evenings outside.

"Well, I've come over to see you because of that light," Hannah's husband replied. "This morning, the Domine visited our home and asked me to deliver a message to you and other neighbors. That light you saw," he paused. "It was a sign from God to us, a sign that we need to repent," he said knowingly.

"Oh, it is?" Catalyntje replied.

"Domine has called for a day of fasting and humility so that we can show our deep repentance before God," he responded.

"Thank you for that message, my friend. Did you see the light with your own eyes, or as they're calling it, a sign from God?" Catalyntje asked.

"Yes, I did. My whole family went out to view it for three nights," he reported.

"I watched it, too, and I must admit that it did not fill me with fear, only a strange peacefulness. It was like God was showing me his wonders," Catalyntje said confidently.

"I don't think that is what the Domine is trying to tell us. Please think about his message," Hannah's husband replied, unsettled at her comment. "I will tell Domine that you have received his message."

"Yes, I have. Let's go to the root cellar and get you and your family an apron full of apples. You can eat them before you begin your fast," Catalyntje said, leading him toward the root cellar.

*****

The clear skies didn't last long, and soon, the days were marked by blowing wind and snow. Catalyntje stayed inside and kept herself busy without any visitors. She expected this and had prepared plenty of wood to keep herself warm. The strong winter winds often stole the heat from her house, so she used the trick she'd learned in Amsterdam: she kept large rocks near the fire in the evening and then took them with her to bed, wrapped in a cloth. The stones kept the heat from the fire for a long while, which helped relieve some of the aches she felt during the cold months.

The daily blizzards lasted nearly two weeks, and once they were gone, deep snow remained. Catalyntje couldn't move her door because of the weight of the snow against it; she'd have to use one of the larger windows if she wanted to get outside. Then, one cloudy afternoon, she heard sounds outside near the front of her house.

"Mama, Mama, are you alright? Are you in there?" a voice called.

"Daniel, is that you? Yes, I am here. But I cannot get out," Catalyntje answered with a laugh.

"I can help you," he answered. "Go to the front window so we can talk."

"I think it will take some time to dig you out, but I want to talk to you first," Daniel insisted.

"I am here," Catalyntje said, staring at him as he stooped down to see her through the window.

"Mama, I have bad news to share with you. Annetje, Sarah's daughter, died last week. The cold got to her, and she never recovered. She came down with a fever, and they couldn't help her. I'm sorry to bring the news this way," Daniel replied, his voice cracking.

"Oh, my dear Annetje. She is too young to die, Daniel; she is my oldest grandchild; she is too young to die," Catalyntje repeated in disbelief.

"I know she is," was all he could say.

Catalyntje was silent for a few moments, then she asked, "Is Sarah doing well? I know the heartache of losing a child; it never leaves."

"It has broken her," Daniel reported. "Annetje left behind two small children, and her husband, Dirck, isn't dealing with this very well."

"Daniel, can you get me out of here? I must help Sarah and her children. Can you take me in your wagon?" she asked anxiously.

"I can bring you, Mama. But first, let's get the snow cleared from your door. While I do that, you can start gathering what you need to take with you. You might be staying a few weeks," he suggested. "I will stock up the feed for the animals."

"I will get things ready to go. Thank you for coming to help and bringing me the news," Catalyntje said as she quickly gathered items to bring to Sarah's house.

Sarah needed Catalyntje's presence to help her through this trial. Daniel promised to return for Catalyntje in a few weeks, but she stayed for nearly a month, helping her daughter heal from the crushing sadness that had taken over her life.

Giving Comfort

1681: 75 years old

Catalyntje kept in touch with her children, grandchildren, and great-grandchildren. Sometimes, she took her wagon to their home, and often they visited her. She recognized their pretended errands to come and check on her but always enjoyed their company. Life at her house was relatively quiet, so she was never too tired to visit with her family. Even though they had all left to make their own lives, she was always concerned about them and their well-being.

Early one morning, Catalyntje's son, Daniel, rode to her home to report that Jannetje's husband, Rem, wasn't doing well. Catalyntje knew a fever had kept plaguing her son-in-law, and he couldn't shake it. When Jannetje and her children had visited Catalyntje a few weeks before, she mentioned that Rem seemed to weaken each time the fever brought him down. As Daniel helped Catalyntje onto the wagon, she knew she could do nothing to help Rem, but she also knew Jannetje would need comfort when he was gone.

Once Daniel and Catalyntje arrived at Jannetje's home, her husband, Rem, didn't last long. He had lived for over 60 years, but Jannetje still needed him, and Catalyntje understood that pain. When she'd left her home a few days before, she had planned to stay with her daughter for at least a month to give her the comfort she would need during this time of unbearable loss.

The Only Witness

1685: 79 years old

The winter days kept the ground cold, so Catalyntje always wore extra socks with her boots when she went outside. She also wore wool mittens, an old blue scarf, and her favorite bonnet. As she stepped outside, the scarf danced in the crisp wind, and the smokey smell of the fire inside floated through the air. Even though it was cold, Catalyntje knew it would be a perfect day to bring wood inside. She could tell a storm was coming, which might last longer than a few days. She didn't trust herself to be outside tramping through a blizzard at her age.

Catalyntje trudged to the barn and pulled on the heavy side door where Daniel and his family had stacked the cut wood in piles. He knew this chore had become difficult for her and had taken care of it for her. Daniel's rows of wood were long and not very tall, making it easy for Catalyntje to remove pieces from the stack. Before she got started, she walked to the back of the barn, where she kept a small sled. She had pulled her children around on it when they were young, but now it was her wood sled. It was sturdy enough for the task yet light enough to glide on the crusted snow.

Catalyntje carefully placed seven split logs onto her sled and pulled on the rope to guide it back to her house, where she unloaded it inside and then went back to the barn for more. She planned to do three loads that day and would do more the next day if the weather held out. Each trip seemed to take longer and require more effort, but Catalyntje kept going. As she headed back to the barn for her last load, her eye caught the glint of the cold sun bouncing off a small ship. She could tell it had just landed nearby in Wallabout Bay.

The movement and hard work warmed Catalyntje, and she loosened her scarf as she brought the sled back into the barn. There, she took time to feed her horse and the goats. Then she sat on a bale of straw and called out, "Kip, kip, kip," as she threw small handfuls of feed to the chickens. She enjoyed watching them scurry about as they tried to be the first to get to the food. Feeding chickens was a restful chore and a comfortable way to end a cold day. After Catalyntje felt rested and the chickens lost interest, she gathered nine fresh eggs and carefully put them in her pockets. There were fewer eggs during the winter, but there were enough.

Once inside, Catalyntje removed the layers of clothing she'd worn while working and hung them on the peg shelf to dry. Then she swept the small pieces of wood she'd tracked inside and tossed them into the fire, where they crackled cheerfully. Next, she added more wood, filled the large water kettle with snow to melt, and carefully poured goat's milk into the smaller kettle. Then, she removed her wet socks and placed them on the fireplace mantle. She could feel herself getting colder since she'd gone back inside, so she warmed some milk and added anise seed and a drop of honey. Finally, she pulled her chair next to the fire, and while sipping the warmed milk, she thought about what project she would work on while there was still light.

As Catalyntje gazed into the fire, she heard footsteps outside. Then, someone knocked at her door. When she opened it, she expected it to be her children or grandchildren. It was not. Instead, two well-dressed men stood on her stoop. Catalyntje was surprised and paused before letting them in.

"Good afternoon. I am Governor Thomas Dongan, and this is my assistant, William," one of the gentlemen said, gesturing to the younger man beside him. "We come from New York, hoping to talk to you," he announced officially.

"What would a governor want with me? Especially on such a cold afternoon," Catalyntje asked, welcoming them to sit near the glowing fire.

"We are gathering information for our records about New York before the English ruled here. We would like to know about New Amsterdam, as it used to be called," the governor replied.

"Well, there were plenty of people who lived in New Amsterdam. I am sure many of them have a better memory than I do," Catalyntje said with a smile.

"You are right, there were many others, and we have talked to several of them," the governor agreed. "But none of them were in the colony when it started."

Catalyntje thought for a moment, "I suppose you are right," she replied. "I remember years ago hearing of friends from the ship that crossed the waters with us who have already died. Even my Joris is gone."

"We have questioned many folks and have always come to the same conclusion," the governor said. "You are the only person we know who has lived here since people began settling in this area from the Old World. You were on the first ship that arrived when this place was only a small colony,

312

and you are still alive and have not left. You are the only one who has seen everything that has happened in this place."

"Well, that makes me rather remarkable," Catalyntje said teasingly. "You came in the cold because you thought I might not make it through the winter?" she asked, making the two men squirm nervously. "I just hauled three loads of wood from the barn to my home," she announced, pointing to the stack of firewood along the wall. "I will be around for a while and would be happy to answer your questions."

"We thank you," Dongan answered nervously, still trying to figure out how to take Catalyntje's teasing nature.

"I was settling in to warm myself with some anise milk. May I get some for you two, and then we can visit? You can choose how much honey you'd like in it," Catalyntje offered.

"That would be very kind of you," Dongan answered, relaxing a bit. It didn't take long before Catalyntje brought the two visitors a cup of the sweet-smelling drink. Then she leaned comfortably back in her chair.

"So, you came on the first ship of colonists to arrive here?" Dongan inquired, glancing at his assistant to ensure he was recording Catalyntje's words. She nodded and smiled. "When did you arrive?" Dongan asked.

"Oh, it seems so very long ago," Catalyntje began. "I have been here more than sixty years now; we came in the spring of 1624, Joris and I. He has been gone for over twenty years now, but I have managed. We were newlyweds then and ready to start our lives here. We had nothing to lose leaving Amsterdam, so we married and came straightaway," Catalyntje smiled, staring into the fire. "We came long before any Englishmen were here. The two of us, Joris and I, built a home here in this place. Ahh, I was so much younger then and so full of hope," she paused, gazing out the window at the falling snow. "And this has been a good place. We have worked the land, and it has given us food and trees and kept our family well," Catalyntje said slowly.

"What was your journey like coming here?" the governor asked.

"The waves gave me a time; they certainly did. I could not even stand up for the first part of the trip; I was so sick. But I still love watching the ships enter New Amsterdam harbor. They remind me of our journey across the ocean," Catalyntje said.

"You mean our harbor in New York?" Dongan corrected her.

"You call it that, but I will always call it New Amsterdam. I spent much of my life there, and it was a good place," Catalyntje said firmly.

"Ah, yes, and back to the journey here. Can you tell us more about that?" Dongan asked.

"Once we had sailed for a few weeks, I got to feeling better, so Joris and I went about the ship to meet the others that sailed with us. As I think back about the people on that ship, I realize you are right; none of them are still here. I am the only one," Catalyntje said thoughtfully. "We made some unforgettable friends on that journey. My dear friend, Jannetje, landed here but was gone within a few years from the fever. It broke my heart. She and three other women took on courting while we were on the ship. It ended up that they were all married on board. When we finally all landed at New Amsterdam..."

"In New York," Dongan interrupted.

"As I was saying when we landed in New Amsterdam," Catalyntje emphasized the city's former name, "we all stayed there for a few weeks before the Company separated us. Jannetje and I planned to live near each other and build our homes close to each other, but the Company had other ideas. Joris and I were the only ones from that group assigned to go up north, all the way up the river to Fort Orange. That was a sad day for all of us," Catalyntje said as she quit talking and sipped her drink.

"The Company wanted us up north so we could trade furs with the Mahicans and the Mohawks, which we did," Catalyntje said proudly. "They never gave us trouble, although I must say, I was a little frightened at first. I soon learned, though, that it was not necessary to be fearful. That was long ago, but I have stayed; not everyone has. Some died, and others missed the Old World too much, so they sailed back, but I did not; I have made this place my home, and my children, grandchildren, and even great-grandchildren have prospered here. We have not been without troubles but have done well for ourselves," Catalyntje added.

Dongan could sense that Catalyntje had finished speaking, so he nodded and thanked her for her time. As he and his assistant bundled up to return home, Catalyntje got them a partial loaf of bread to bring with them. They thanked her again before returning to the snowy landscape.

Once they had left, Catalyntje put two more pieces of wood on the fire and took out her mending basket. She pulled the little table near a chair by the fireplace and lit a second candle for additional light. As she stitched on an apron, her mind wove itself in and out of places she'd lived. She recalled all she had learned, loved, and lost at each place. Then, soon, her thoughts turned to dreams, and she shifted into a peaceful sleep, sitting by her snug fire.

*****

The winter was slow to leave. It had been colder than usual, and Catalyntje often found herself asleep in her chair by the fire in the middle of the night. She was usually too tired to get up and put more wood on for the evening, so eventually, the cold woke her up. Then she'd stiffly stand up, reach for her cane, and gently blow the glowing coals until they turned to flames. After spending time reviving the fire, Catalyntje eventually found her way into bed, drawing the curtains around her and pulling the blankets tightly around her chin. Eventually, the crispness of the air changed to warmth, and she'd drift back to sleep.

After nights like these, the morning came all too soon. Catalyntje would lie under the covers and look at the light through the windows, waiting for it to get brighter and possibly a bit warmer.

Sarah

As the days gradually grew warmer, Catalyntje knew she could venture out and visit her family. She enjoyed seeing their gardens and animals and usually brought something with her to share. One early March morning, Catalyntje looked in her pantry. There were no loaves of bread or cheese, so she went to the cellar, carefully watching each step. There, she spotted a basket filled with nine small green squash. These were her favorite because of their hardiness during the long, cold winters. She selected three and put them in the basket she held on her arm. After returning up the stairs and closing the cellar door, she went to the barn, where she got her wagon and horse ready, loaded her supplies, and rode to Sarah's home to spend some time. As Catalyntje approached the house, she saw Sarah sitting on her front stoop, her eyes closed, and her face tilted towards the sun.

"How are you today, my daughter?" Catalyntje called out to Sarah. She walked over to the bench and sat beside her, the sun soothing her cold hands.

"I am well enough but so tired even though the day is young," Sarah answered wearily. "The past few mornings, it has been a struggle to even get started. I haven't been sleeping well and have had a horrible cough that shakes me every night."

Catalyntje leaned over and put her arm around Sarah, "I am sorry to hear that, Dear. The cold has gotten into my bones as well. I came over to spend the day with you and your family. Maybe I can help with some things you have not been able to get done," Catalyntje offered. "I may not be fast, but I can still work."

"That would be wonderful," Sarah smiled with relief. I need to clean the cellar today since spring will be here soon, and it will be time to plant again."

"Yes, it will," Catalyntje nodded. "Can we go in and get some warm milk to start with? I will need to warm my bones before spending time in the cellar," she replied. They both slowly stood up and walked into the house. Sarah put a kettle on to warm milk over the fire while Catalyntje got two cups. Ignoring Sarah's constant coughing as she prepared the milk was impossible.

"Take your time, Dear," Catalyntje said, hoping a slower pace would allow Sarah to breathe instead of cough, but it didn't make a difference.

Catalyntje spent the day with Sarah and did most of the work cleaning the cellar. She tried to include Sarah by asking her how she wanted things organized, but Sarah couldn't focus due to her lack of sleep. Each time she came down to help, the damp air pulled the cough from her, and she had to go back up into the sun. Her husband, Teunis, fixed the evening meal, and Catalyntje tried to keep up with the grandchildren as they fed the animals before it was dark outside. After dinner, Catalyntje let Teunis and the older children clean up after the meal while she got the younger children ready for bed.

"Do you mind if I stay here for the evening, Sarah?" Catalyntje asked.

"Of course not, Mama. I don't want you traveling in the dark. Besides, I think I've worked you too hard today. You are probably ready for some rest," she said with a faint smile.

"You go and lay down; I will bring you a heated stone to keep you warm," Catalyntje offered, walking towards the fireplace to get the smooth rock she had placed there earlier.

"Let me get you some quilts first, Mama," Sarah said, rising from the stool.

"Oh no, dear, you set yourself back down. I know where the stuffed mattress is, and you have a pile of quilts. I can get them just fine," Catalyntje insisted.

"Thank you, Mama," Sarah said weakly, walking to her bed. Catalyntje followed her with the warmed stone wrapped in cloth. Then she returned to the fire and talked to her grandchildren as Teunis brought more wood into the house. Her grandson got the stuffed mattress without being asked while Catalyntje sang a song to the little ones.

Slaap, kindje, slaap

Daar buiten loopt een schaap
Een schaap met witte voetjes
Die drinkt zijn melk zo zoetjes
Melkje van de bonte koe
Kindje, doe je oogjes toe.

"Oma, where did you learn that song?" her granddaughter asked. "You always sing it to us; it is my favorite."

"I learned that song when I lived far across the ocean," Catalyntje answered. "That was a long time ago, but songs stay with you, and you do not easily forget them," she said knowingly, "I am glad you like it."

"I do," her granddaughter said with a broad smile, hugging Catalyntje tightly around the neck. "I am glad you are staying here with us tonight. I will let you sing to me again tomorrow, too," she said excitedly.

"I look forward to that," Catalyntje said. "Now, off to bed."

"Thank you for the mattress," Catalyntje called across the room to her grandson. "That was very thoughtful of you." He smiled and stood a little taller.

The heat from the fireplace warmed Catalyntje. The mattress wasn't as soft as she would've liked, but she was exhausted from her travel and work that day and soon fell asleep. But as she slept, her dreams were unsettling, and her thoughts were about Sarah.

The next day, Catalyntje helped the children with their chores, baked some bread, and brought food from the root cellar to start dinner. She had some things to do at home but felt she would need to return soon to help Sarah.

She left early that afternoon, and on her way home, Catalyntje took a slight detour to visit Daniel. He was glad to see her, and as they worked in his garden, she told him that Sarah wasn't doing well. Catalyntje planned to be there to help and asked Daniel if he would check on her home more often since she would most likely be away helping Sarah. She also requested that he visit his other sisters to inform them of Sarah's illness.

After visiting Daniel, Catalyntje finally arrived home around mid-evening. She was just in time to do her chores before dark. She was exhausted and only did the most important ones before going inside for the evening. Once she got a fire started, Catalyntje was too tired to fix a proper meal, so she took an apple from the basket and a piece of dried bread from the shelf. Then she prepared a cup of hot tea and sat in her chair by the fire with her quilt on her lap. As she ate, her thoughts returned to Sarah. The fire blazed warm, and Catalyntje didn't feel like getting up to work on her mending; instead, she fell asleep in her chair near the warm fire.

Within a day, Catalyntje had her home in order enough to return to Sarah's house. She loaded a basket with food, an extra quilt, and some knitting. She planned on staying for as long as Sarah needed her. She tucked in a few cookies, some tiny dolls she'd made, and an extra ring for rolling in the dirt. She knew her grandchildren would appreciate something new to play with. The sun was up that day as shadows danced beneath the trees, and birds swooped near her as her old horse pulled the wagon along the bumpy road. It was as if they were trying to distract her from the anxious feeling that weighed on her heart.

When Catalyntje arrived at Sarah's house, she was surrounded by the grandchildren, even before she could get out of the wagon. First, they helped her get down, then excitedly looked at the items she'd brought. Next, her oldest grandson led the horse to the barn and fed it fresh hay. As they busied themselves to please Catalyntje, Teunis walked outside and took Catalyntje's arm.

"She is not well, Mama," he said with sadness.

"I have felt it in my heart, Teunis. I am here to stay with you and your family for as long as you need me," Catalyntje offered as tears filled Teunis' eyes.

"Thank you for knowing that we needed you," he answered, keeping his voice firm. "Jannetje and Judith came by yesterday. They spend the day taking turns talking to Sarah and doing work around the house. They were a great help in lifting Sarah's spirits. I suspect you must have spread the word about Sarah's condition," Teunis said with a grateful smile.

"That I did," Catalyntje answered, squeezing Teunis' hand. "Now, you let me help. I am not very quick on my feet, but I am still able, so do not pamper me," Catalyntje said with a wink.

"Thank you again, Mama," Teunis said gratefully.

The days went by quickly for Catalyntje, filled with grandchildren, cooking and working the garden soil. She was correct; she wasn't quick on her feet, but her grandchildren didn't mind. They enjoyed being with Catalyntje; she only needed to give them direction, and they did most of the work.

After only four days, Sarah had become considerably weaker. Her cough continued and now racked her entire body day and night. The doctor had come and given her some medicine but offered little hope. Each of Sarah's children spent time with her throughout the day. They talked to her quietly and worked to keep smiles on their faces. That evening, Catalyntje walked outside with the children to do the evening chores before dark and left Teunis to be with Sarah. Catalyntje kept the children busy for as long as possible so the couple could have time together, possibly for the final time. Catalyntje emptied the turnips from her apron onto the table near the fire when she returned inside. She saw Teunis standing on the other side of the room, tears streaming down his face.

"I have said goodbye to my love," he said, staring at the table.

"Oh, Teunis, I worried that this would happen. Is she in pain? Can we fetch her anything to make her more comfortable?" Catalyntje asked, her eyes also filling with tears.

"I don't think so. She isn't talking anymore, and I suspect she'll be gone by morning," Teunis said solemnly.

"I will sit with her. You get some rest," Catalyntje said, hugging Teunis tightly.

"Thank you for being here, Mama," he said as he sat on a stool by the fire, his face in his hands, sobbing uncontrollably. Catalyntje went into Sarah's room and sat quietly beside her.

"How are you, my sweet Sarah?" she asked. There was no response whatsoever, not even a stirring. Finally, Catalyntje reached for Sarah's cold hand and began to talk to her as if she were listening.

"You know, I remember when you were born at Fort Orange. You were the first baby to come to the colony, and you caused quite a stir. I only had two women to help me, and neither one had ever given birth. You came into the world in a far-away place and filled the air with your small cries. I held you and wept. I was so happy to see your perfect little face. Your papa came in and held you and would hardly give you back to me. He was so proud of you. You were my only child born up the Noort River, between the Indians, snowstorms, and tall trees. It was like no other place on this earth that I've ever been, and you were there too. That is something to be proud of, my dear Sarah."

Catalyntje held Sarah's hand and began to quietly sing to her, "Slaap, kindje, slaap, daar buiten loopt een schaap . . .". It was the old melody she had sung to Sarah when she was a tiny baby in the middle of the wilderness many years before. As this gentle song floated through the house, it comforted all who heard it, but it couldn't stop the tears that dampened their pillows that night.

The hours went by slowly, and then, sometime in the dark of the night, Catalyntje awoke as Sarah suddenly gasped, and then she was gone with no pain or struggle. Now Sarah was with Jacob and Joris in a place where Catalyntje could not be. She stared at the worn face of her daughter, who had just passed her sixtieth year. Sarah had sacrificed so much for her family; she was widowed and bore fifteen children, but she'd always found a way to keep going. The challenges of settling this land and raising such a large family had taken their toll on her. Catalyntje would have done anything to trade places with her to give her daughter more life, but that was not her fate. Instead, she was still here, in this place, far from where she had begun.

The Only One

1688: 82 years old

For the past three years, Catalyntje had noticed changes in herself. First, Sarah's death had fallen heavily on her soul, but life had taught her she would never get over the grief of losing someone she loved. Catalyntje also noticed she'd grown more weary. Her feet shuffled at a slower pace, and it took nearly all her effort to accomplish tasks that used to be easy. In addition, each night, her body ached, and she went to bed earlier now. But with all these difficulties, Catalyntje was determined to continue to do all she could for herself.

She still saved seeds on her shelf and loved the days she spent in her garden. She enjoyed creating things even though her hands were wrinkled and stiff. She often had difficulty making her fingers move as they had when she was younger. It was harder to grip a needle or gracefully control her knitting needles, but the more she used her hands, the more the stiffness left them. Sometimes, Catalyntje spent almost all day sitting near the fireplace sewing aprons or knitting socks and scarves.

Catalyntje never knew when someone would stop by to visit or help her work for the day. She had many relatives and friends who looked out for her and liked helping because they enjoyed being with her. She always had a smile to give and a story to tell. Everyone who visited her went home with something in their hands, which is why she spent time creating things, gardening, and baking. She always baked two loaves of bread at a time, one to eat during the week and the other to give to someone who came to see her. She also kept a pie or cookies on her shelf to share. It was a challenge that kept her moving and doing.

As Catalyntje sat in her chair each day and did handwork, she also had time to reflect on her life and remember the marvelous things she had experienced. Her mind often drifted to the difficult moments, but she worked to keep her thoughts steered toward untroubled times. She enjoyed thinking back on the journey she and Margriet had taken across the Old World and, sometimes, couldn't believe she'd had the courage and strength to do it. Catalyntje always smiled while thinking about her travels across the ocean with Joris. That was a brave time for her, and it was something none of her children had ever done. Catalyntje liked to tell these stories to her family. She described the countryside she'd grown up in and the thriving city of Amsterdam. She wanted her family to know about these places that were important to her. She also wanted them to learn about the people she loved who had lived there.

Catalyntje didn't make it to New Amsterdam anymore since riding back and forth on the ferry was too tiring for her. She remembered the last time she visited and how different it was from when she and Joris had lived there. It was much busier, and she hadn't recognized many faces she saw on the streets. Besides, now she was content to sit on her front stoop at the Wallabout and watch the clouds change shapes as the wind blew through the trees. Although her children warned her against it, she still took trips with her wagon and old horse along the trail to the river's edge. Sometimes, she would sit there all afternoon, watching the waves, the ships, and the birds as the water lapped at the edges of the shore.

Catalyntje had fewer visitors when winter came, but she enjoyed sitting by the warm fire alone, watching the snow and leafless tree branches move in the cold wind. One stormy October day, as she gazed out her window, two men on horseback approached her home. She didn't recognize them and watched as the official-looking pair dismounted and walked toward her door.

Catalyntje waited for their knock, then strolled to the door to see why they had come. The first man introduced himself as William Morris and said he was a justice of the peace in New York. Catalyntje welcomed them in and put another log on the fire to offset the chill she'd let in when she had opened the door.

"Thank you for inviting us in today. We wanted to record events from your life here in New York," Morris replied. "As we've met with others, we've found that you are the only person from the Old World who has lived here through the entire existence of the colony when the Dutch ruled. We heard of an old Mohawk man who might have been here that long, but we can't find him."

"A few years ago, the governor, I think it was, came and asked me about living here, too. I do not know that this old woman has much more to add to her story," Catalyntje teased.

"The records we've read list you as one of the colonists who arrived on the first ship that landed here when it was only a small colony. Of all the people on the list, you are the only person still here. You are the only one who has seen everything that has happened in New Netherland," Morris replied. "No one remembers the first few years at Fort Orange. We think you are now the only one left who experienced what it was like there in the beginning."

"I have been around for a long time. It was 83 years ago that I was born in Pris, which is in the Old World. And you are correct; I did come here with the first colonists. I often think about that trip, especially lately. I think our ship was called the Unity. The Company sent Joris and me up to Fort Orange; they called it that, but it was not much of a fort. They were still building it when we arrived. We all worked hard that summer; I think harder than I have ever worked in my entire life. We did not have much of a home that first winter. Just huts covered with bark to keep us dry," Catalyntje said, looking gratefully at the fire as she spoke.

"The Company wanted us up north so we could trade furs with the Natives, which we did," she said proudly.

"We lived there nearly three years, and the 'Indians were all as quiet as lambs and traded with all ye freedom imaginable.' They never gave us trouble, although I must say, I was a little frightened at first."

"Why did you move then if things were going well up north?" Morris asked.

"Well, there were troubles between the Mohawk and the Mahican tribes; the Company thought it best for us to move closer to where we could be protected. So, we moved to New Amsterdam," Catalyntje added.

Their conversations continued as Catalyntje shared stories of past friends and experiences. As they continued to talk, the justice and his record keeper enjoyed Catalyntje's humor, experiences, and advice. She even talked them into going to the barn with her to feed the chickens and load the wood sled, which they brought back and stacked in her house.

"I hope we have not taken too much of your time today," the justice finally said, glancing towards the window at the darkening sky.

"Oh, that is not a worry. I don't get visitors every day. It was a delight to talk with you," Catalyntje answered.

"We thank you for sharing with us. We have enjoyed your lively stories. May we help you with anything else before we leave?" Morris asked sincerely.

"You could fill that bucket with snow for me to melt. Then you could take some cookies for your return trip," Catalyntje smiled, pointing to the bucket.

After they left, Catalyntje put more wood on the fire and went to bed early, happy to have had visitors.

Memories

1689: 83 years old

Another spring had come to Breukelen, and Catalyntje began working in her garden as she had done every year. She still had the larger garden further from the house, filled with squash, corn, and other crops that loved the long summer day. But today, during one of the first pleasant spring days, Catalyntje planned to stay in the smaller garden near her house. Since she was alone, she only needed the food her family brought her, but she took pride in caring for herself.

Catalyntje still kept seeds tucked at the back of the lower shelf, with each kind wrapped in a separate cloth. On that warm morning, she took some seeds from the shelf, put them in her left apron pocket, and stepped outside into the bright morning sun. She kept her walking stick in her right hand as she carefully walked across the uneven soil. Once she was sure of her footing, Catalyntje stood as tall as she could, took a deep breath of the fresh air, and tilted her head back to face the sun. The heat made her skin tingle, and she stood there momentarily, enjoying the sensation.

On that sunny spring afternoon, Catalyntje completed the first planting of spring crops - lettuce, beets, peas, carrots, and onions. She used her walking stick to dig small trenches where she placed the seeds. She was frustrated that she couldn't crouch beside the rows anymore, so instead, she leaned over each one and tried to drop the seeds into the rows of uneven ground. Unfortunately, they often bounced out onto the top of the soil and sometimes were entirely lost—this flustered Catalyntje since she had been so careful about saving each seed.

As she finished planting, Catalyntje didn't want to go inside quite yet, so she eased herself onto the little stool she kept in her garden. She carefully took her walking stick in both hands and put it in front of her. Then she placed one hand on top of the other over the end of the cane and rested her chin on her overlapping hands. It was enough to allow her to relax, and as she closed her eyes, soon she was only aware of the sounds of the birds in the trees and the touch of the light breeze on her face.

Suddenly, she felt a slight tap, tap, tap on her nose and heard a little giggle.

"Oma, are you sleeping in your garden?" the little voice asked. Catalyntje awoke suddenly to see one of her youngest grandsons looking right into her eyes.

"Oh, I think I was! It is such a lovely day to be outside. Can you guess what Oma planted today?" Catalyntje asked.

"A pumpkin! I know you planted me a pumpkin!" he said excitedly, jumping up and down.

"Oh, not yet, Dear. The sun has to be much warmer for that. How about peas? Do you like peas?" she asked, reaching into her left pocket.

"Yes, I do, Oma! I can take them out of the pods and eat them all," he replied. Catalyntje removed the cloth that held the pea seeds in her hand for him to see.

"Look at these seeds. I just put them into the ground, and they will grow some pea plants," Catalyntje said.

"Can I eat one now?" the young boy asked excitedly.

"Not yet," Catalyntje laughed. "When we see each other again, we can talk about when these peas will be ready, and you can come over and pick all you would like."

"I'll come tomorrow if they are ready then, Oma," he offered.

"Well, it will probably be a few more days than that, but keep coming over to check on them," she hugged him tightly. Her daughter Annetje had been standing in the garden, enjoying the interaction between her son and Mama. As she watched Catalyntje, Annetje was aware of the slowness of her mama's steps but was impressed with her patience with small children.

*****

September had been unseasonably warm, for which Catalyntje was grateful. For as long as she could remember, she'd worked to gather food for the winter, and since it had become more difficult for her to move in the cold and snow, she decided to store all of it inside her house this year. She had enjoyed visitors from nearly everyone in her family that week. They knew she was preparing for winter and had each come to help with this task. Several of her grandsons promised to return the next week to help stack the rest of her wood. Because of her family's help, Catalyntje's only job that day was to gather the remaining apples, and she could do this alone.

The autumn air was crisp that morning, which reminded Catalyntje that the snow would soon be coming. She brought a medium-sized basket outside with her and gathered the last apples from the tree's lower branches outside her window. Once she'd filled it, she realized it was heavier than expected, but she was still able to get it inside and tucked away under her table. Apples were one of her favorites during the cold months, and she could almost smell them cooking over the fire with a light touch of cinnamon.

After getting the apples in, Catalyntje wanted to sit outside for a while. She wrapped her thin cloak from the peg shelf around her narrow shoulders as she sat on her front stoop. She enjoyed the birds calling to one another as she rested and felt the fresh breeze on her face.

Darkness came earlier each night since fall had arrived, and as the sun hid behind the trees, Catalyntje went inside to prepare her evening meal and do some handwork by the fire. But, after eating a simple meal of bread, cheese, and a freshly picked apple, Catalyntje was ready to sleep for the night. She had worked hard that day and felt she had earned an early rest. Before bed, she piled extra logs onto the fire to keep the chill away throughout the night, even though, the week before, she had added extra quilts to her bed since she slept with the nearby window open; the fresh air always helped her sleep better.

Catalyntje took the candle from the table to light her way to bed but paused as her eyes rested on the mortar and pestle her dear friend, Jannetje, had given her long ago. As Catalyntje got into bed and snuggled beneath the quilts, she kept thinking about Jannetje. She remembered them laughing together on the ship's deck a lifetime ago, blissfully unaware of what awaited them in the New World.

With these thoughts in her mind, Catalyntje drifted peacefully to sleep until suddenly, she woke up and realized she had said Jannetje's name out loud, which had awakened her. As she lay there, confused by what had just happened, she heard a gust of wind outside that softly rustled the apple tree leaves by the window. This sound brought memories of her sweet Jacob; he had always enjoyed being outside. He had been so young and excited about life before death had taken him from her, but still, they had shared many delightful times. Catalyntje had to push her mind far back to remember his tiny face and tight hug—such a good boy. Sarah had also left Catalyntje early, but her life had been longer than Jacob's. Sarah had given Catalyntje grandchildren and had always been there to help. And then there was Trijn, dear Trijn. Catalyntje had learned so much from this kind, patient woman and still kept Trijn's journal tucked away on the middle shelf of her kast.

As Catalyntje's mind circled these memories, she drifted in and out of light sleep, remembering all that had happened in her life. She recalled the back-breaking work, the courage, and the happiness that had been part of Joris' life and hers as they had created a home together in New Netherland. She smiled as she reflected on the first day, she met Joris, that afternoon long ago at Dam Square buying fabric. Every detail was still vivid in her mind, as if it had only happened yesterday.

Catalyntje was now fully awake. "Oh, Joris, how I have missed you," she said aloud. "It has been so very long." As tears filled her eyes, she let out a soft sigh and rolled over, her thoughts still on Joris. As she pulled the quilt close to her cheek, a cool breeze blew gently into the room and helped settle her thoughts. She opened her eyes and watched the leaves waving through the window, lit only by the light of the thin moon.

The wind grew colder as the moon slipped behind a cloud, darkening the night. Then, without any notice, Catalyntje's quiet breathing turned silent, and the only sound was the gentle rustle of the leaves outside the window.

Epilogue

Present Day, New York

"Mom, I'm home!" a voice shouted from the front door.

"I'm in the kitchen, Addy!" her mother called out. "Maisie and I just finished frosting a cake. Do you want to try a piece with us before dinner?" she asked, grabbing three plates from the shelf.

"Yes!" Addy replied, throwing her backpack to the floor and joining her mother and little sister at the table.

"We are picking up Dad from work and watching Lincoln's game tonight. Do you have any homework to do before then?" her mother asked.

"I do. We are learning about the history of this area, and I get to choose one person to do a project about," Addy explained with excitement.

"So, do you have any ideas yet?" her mother asked.

"Well, I think I will learn more about a woman our teacher mentioned today named Catalina Trico and her husband, Joris. Mr. Eugene said they were called the 'Adam and Eve of New Netherland.' So, it seems like they would be important. We can only learn about one person, so I'm choosing Catalina," Addy announced confidently.

"It sounds like you're off to a great start. Tell me if you need any help," her mother offered. Addy continued to talk more than she ate, telling how Catalina was on the ship with the first group of colonists going to New Netherland and explaining that the streets of lower Manhattan still follow the same patterns from when the colony started.

*****

Over the next few days, Addy gathered more details about Catalina's life and started to think about what it would have been like back then. She discovered that Catalina had lived to be about eighty-three years old, which seemed very old, especially in the 1600s when there were no hospitals. She also found that Catalina had eleven kids; Addy's family only had three kids, and she wondered how eleven kids would even fit into one house.

Addy then spent the next few days putting together a poster about Catalina for her presentation. She printed maps, typed out facts with bullet points, drew pictures of forts, and colored Dutch flags. She had worked on projects like this before and was good at it since she liked to draw. One evening, as Addy's father tucked her into bed, she asked, "Do you know if there is a statue of Catalina somewhere? She did a lot, so I'm sure she is famous enough that they would have made one. I want to take a picture of it to add to my poster; then it will be finished."

"You know, Addy, I don't think there are any statues of Catalina. But maybe we could find where she is buried and take a picture of her headstone; that is a type of monument," Addy's father suggested. "We could go on Saturday."

The next day, Addy's father helped her do some research. They found that Catalina was buried at the Flatbush Reformed Dutch Church Cemetery in Brooklyn. They planned to visit there that weekend. So, on Saturday morning, they found the bus line to take them to the cemetery to get the last picture for Addy's project.

The bus let them off in an older part of town; the streets were dirty, and the businesses looked run down. Addy stayed close to her father as she always did in crowded places. Her eyes searched for the street name she'd written on the slip of paper in her pocket. They walked four or five blocks before Addy's father spotted the street they were looking for and realized they were standing near the church.

As they looked at the front of the church, they noticed it was under construction and covered with scaffolding. This framework now served as a covering for houseless people. Some sat resting against the side of the church, singing to an unknown audience, while others lay motionless under blankets. Addy and her father passed the front doors and headed to the cemetery gate on the left side of the church. There was a curved metal sign over the entrance, and printed on it were the words: Reformed Protestant Dutch Church of Flatbush, Founded 1654 under the direction of Peter Stuyvesant. Addy's excitement grew as she read the sign; she had found the right place. Her father reached to open the gate, but it didn't move; a lock held it tightly closed.

"So ,we can't go inside?" Addy asked, disappointment heavy in her voice.

"No, it looks like it's locked for construction. Let's walk to the other side of the graveyard, though. Maybe we can get a closer look from there," her father suggested, pointing to the other side of the cemetery. As they walked in silence, Addy didn't pay attention to the crowds of people walking beside her. Instead, she wondered how she would find Catalina's headstone without getting inside the fence. When they finally reached the other side, there were no busy shoppers, just an older couple looking over the cemetery and speaking quietly to each other.

The crooked headstones behind the iron fence were unreadable since the weather had long since worn away their carved letters. As Addy looked at them, they reminded her of smaller versions of the buildings that lined the streets of Manhattan. Interspersed with the headstones were tall oak trees covered with leaves, making a playground for squirrels to go in and out of the gated fence. Addy and her father stood there quietly for a few minutes, hoping this place would somehow share its secrets.

"Dad," Addy said softly, "I think this is where she is."

"I think you're right," her father replied, reaching down to hold his daughter's hand. As Addy looked through the fence, she saw two acorns that had fallen from the tall tree arching over where they stood. She let go of her father's hand and reached her small arm between the iron rails to get them, but her arms weren't long enough.

"Here," her father said, picking up a stick on the sidewalk. "Let's use this," he replied, reaching the stick between the iron posts and pulling the acorns closer. Addy quickly put her hand between the rails and grabbed the two acorns.

"I hope they don't mind if I keep these," she said with a slight smile, placing them inside her sweater pocket.

"I don't think they will mind at all," her father answered, pulling his phone from his pocket to take pictures of the cemetery.

The older couple they'd seen earlier watched the father and daughter as they continued talking to each other. "You don't suppose they are looking for Catalyntje, do you?" the husband asked.

"I was just wondering the same thing. Let's go and ask them," his wife answered, holding her husband's hand. As they approached Addy and her father, the older woman spoke up.

"Good afternoon. I noticed you were looking at this part of the cemetery. Who are you searching for?" she asked, looking at the young girl.

"We are looking for Catalina Trico," Addy answered. "Do you know about her?"

"Yes, I do. She lived about 400 years ago, but I feel like I know her quite well; she's even become sort of a friend to me," the woman replied.

"How can you be her friend if she lived so long ago?" the young girl asked.

"I have spent much of my time reading about where Catalyntje lived and discovering what her life was like. I also learned about her family and the difficult things she went through while she was alive; I've even written about her. So, with learning so many things, I feel like I know her," the woman said with a confident smile.

"My daughter is doing a report about Catalina in school and has been learning about her," Addy's father replied.

"There is a little outdoor cafe on the next block," the husband said. "Would the two of you be interested in joining us for lunch? My wife can tell you all about Catalyntje."

"Dad, can we?" Addy asked excitedly. "I have my little notebook with me."

"This seems like an offer we can't pass up," her father replied. "Thank you," he said, nodding to the older woman.

After a delightful lunch and discussions about Catalina, Addy had several more pages of notes to add to her project. Long after they had finished their meal, Addy's father looked at his watch, "I think we had better get back to the bus. Did you get what you needed for your project?" he asked with a questioning smile.

"I got more than I needed!" Addy answered, clutching her notebook.

"Thank you for helping me," she said, smiling at the woman.

"Of course, it was delightful. I always enjoy telling people about Catalyntje, and I was happy to have someone so interested," the woman replied.

"Can we walk by the cemetery again before we go?" Addy begged her father.

"I suppose we have time for that," he answered, getting up from the table. They thanked the older couple once more and walked toward the cemetery.

"Thanks for bringing me here today, Dad. We found so much more than I thought we would," Addy said.

"You're welcome. It was a wonderful afternoon. On our way home, you'll have to tell me everything you know about this woman, Catalina," her father said.

Addy put her hand in her sweater pocket to be sure the acorns were still there. As she gripped them tightly, she began telling her father everything she had learned about the extraordinary life of Catalyntje Trico.

Acknowledgments

In no particular order, I want to thank those who helped and supported me while writing this book.

Mark, my husband, sat on the steps of a Pearl Street skyscraper and listened to me talk about Catalyntje's life. He always understood my need to spend my days in the 17th century.

My youngest son, Eugene, gave suggestions, discussed ideas, and understood every nuance of this book.

My dad, Wenden Waite, always told me stories from the past when I was young, this led to my love of history. His constant encouragement inspired me to keep writing.

My mom, Laura Waite, read the first draft and shared her thoughts and feelings about Catalyntje as she each chapter.

My brother, John Waite, encouraged me to step outside of my comfort zone and begin writing.

My colleague, Bailey Bronson, read my manuscript and asked questions from the perspective of someone unfamiliar with New Netherland.

Sandra Freels and David van Wie joined the New Netherland Writers group with me. I appreciated their feedback and discussions.

Elisabeth Funk helped me with editing; working with her was a privilege. Her knowledge of the Dutch on both sides of the ocean was invaluable, as was her flawless understanding of the English language. I thoroughly enjoyed our Zoom calls, which were always filled with delightful conversions and stories.

Marilyn Douglas, president of the New Netherland Institute, took a chance on me, a woman from Oregon whom she had never met.

Author and historian Russell Shorto discussed ideas, asked questions, and read portions of my manuscript.

Charley Gehring, Director of the New Netherland Research Center, corresponded with me and showed interest in this book. He is also responsible for translating the Dutch records of New Netherland; without them, there would be no story.

The late R. J. Jippe Hiemstra sat with me at a table in a small cafe in Albany, New York, and discussed the possibility of me writing a book about Catalyntje. He also shared invaluable research from the late Dr. Willem Frijhoff, a professor at Erasmus University in Rotterdam.

The Provincial Secretaries who kept the records of New Netherland on 12,000 rag paper pages so I could access them today.

The Labadist missionary from the 1600s, Jasper Danckaerts, met Catalyntje and wrote a short paragraph about her in his journal. I have read his description of her at least two hundred times; his words have shaped my ideas and feelings about Catalyntje.

Finally, to Catalyntje, whose blood runs through my veins and who would not leave my thoughts. She often looked over my shoulder, curious about my writing and why I wanted her to be remembered.

Lana Waite Holden lives in the Pacific Northwest and works as an educator, teaching history and English to junior high students. Over the past decade, she has begun writing and already has plans for another book. During her free time, Lana likes to wander through the forests of the Cascade Mountains with her husband, read books and old journals, tend to her garden, visit cemeteries, and discover historical facts wherever she can find them.

historicalslant.com

historicalslant1624@gmail.com